Though Gabby had never been a big fan of Westerns, she was mesmerized by the vision of a broad-shouldered, long-legged, masculine cowboy in a black hat and denim jacket.

Beyond gorgeous, he was iconic and, at the same time, utterly original. He dismounted near the place where she'd gotten tangled up last night and he sauntered to the fence with a cool, loose-limbed stride. When he pushed his hat back on his forehead and looked toward the house, she stepped behind the curtain so he wouldn't see her staring.

Their meeting last night hadn't been under the best of circumstances, and he certainly hadn't done anything since then to make her think he was glad to see her. But she'd sensed chemistry between them. Maybe she and Zach would never have a relationship, but she could easily imagine some kissing in their future. She wouldn't mind sticking around at the Roost long enough to see where things with Zach might go.

ABOUT THE AUTHOR

Though born in Chicago and raised in L.A., *USA TODAY* bestselling author Cassie Miles has lived in Colorado long enough to be considered a semi-native. The first home she owned was a log cabin in the mountains overlooking Elk Creek, with a thirty-mile commute to her work at the *Denver Post*.

After raising two daughters and cooking tons of macaroni and cheese for her family, Cassie is trying to be more adventurous in her culinary efforts. Ceviche, anyone? She's discovered that almost anything tastes better with wine. When she's not plotting Harlequin Intrigue books, Cassie likes to hang out at the Denver Botanical Gardens near her high-rise home.

Books by Cassie Miles

MOUNTAIN HEIRESS

&

MOUNTAIN MIDWIFE

USA TODAY Bestselling Author

CASSIE MILES

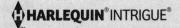

ISBN-13: 978-0-373-69721-2

MOUNTAIN HEIRESS
Copyright © 2013 by Harlequin Books S.A.

The publisher acknowledges the copyright holder of the individual works as follows:

MOUNTAIN HEIRESS
Copyright © 2013 by Kay Bergstrom

MOUNTAIN MIDWIFE
Copyright © 2011 by Kay Bergstrom

Recycling programs for this product may not exist in your area.

Printed in U.S.A.

www.Harlequin.com

CONTENTS

MOUNTAIN HEIRESS

CAST OF CHARACTERS

Gabby (Gabriella) Rousseau—Born and raised in Brooklyn, she's a city girl whose dreams of becoming a fashion designer are put on hold when she inherits a house in the Colorado mountains.

Zach Sheffield—A former rodeo star and all-around cowboy, he owns a horse ranch and is renowned as a trainer/horse whisperer.

Daniel Rousseau—Gabby's ne'er-do-well brother has a gambling problem and is always out to make a quick buck.

Michelle Rousseau—Gabby's deceased great-aunt was a successful artist who left her Colorado home to Gabby and Daniel.

Rene Rousseau—Gabby's other deceased great-aunt and the sister of Michelle. She stayed in Brooklyn and raised Gabby and her brother after their parents died.

Louis Rousseau—The ancestor who established the Rousseau dynasty in Colorado in the 1860s.

Charlotte Potter—A plain Jane teenager who cared for Michelle before she died and blossoms after a glittery makeover.

Rhoda Phillips—Zach's housekeeper has a talent for organizing his business and for bookkeeping.

Jason Fox—The Aspen-based attorney acts as the executor of Michelle's will.

Kevin Fox—The red-haired nephew of the attorney wants to become a professional snowboarder.

Harrison Osborne—The art dealer handling Michelle's work has his hands full with cataloging all the paintings.

Ed Striker—The local handyman works for Osborne.

Sarah Bentley—Her nonprofit organization, Forest Preservation Society, is heavily endowed by Michelle Rousseau.

To Jerry Kreiter and, as always, to Rick.

Chapter One

The night was never this dark in Brooklyn. If she'd been back in her home borough, Gabby Rousseau could have counted on a streetlamp or the glow from a sidewalk window or the never-dimmed glare of Manhattan across the river. But here? In the Colorado mountains? She couldn't see ten feet in front of her, even with her headlights on high beam. Heavy clouds blocked the starlight as sheets of rain pummeled the roof of her poor, tired, little Ford hatchback.

She considered pulling over until the storm let up but she didn't dare. What if her tires sank into the mud at the edge of this skinny road that was more pothole than pavement? Then where would she be? Stuck. In the rain. Without a yellow cab for hundreds of miles.

Dis-as-ter! Her cell phone was out of juice, and the charger didn't work. She had no GPS. For the past hundred miles, the car had been making a clunk that got louder and louder. The heater didn't work, which meant the defroster was defunct and she had to crack a window, which let in the rain. She was wet and cold and, just when she thought it couldn't get any worse, the lightning started.

Zigzag bolts of raw electricity slashed the darkness. In the flash, she saw a stark vision. The clawing branches of a thick forest seemed to grab at her car. Jagged rocks appeared at the edge of the road like evil, ancient sentinels. She glimpsed movement. Something was out there. Probably zombies.

She'd been driving four days—four long, miserable days—across the country. Finally, she was close to her destination. She couldn't give up.

Thunder rumbled like a barrage of cannons. Her fingers tensed on the steering wheel. This morning when she'd started out, the June weather had been hot enough that she'd put on a pair of high-waisted chino shorts and platform sandals—an unfortunate choice of outfit because she was freezing cold. Her legs rippled with goose bumps. Her toes were numb.

Another bolt of lightning cut through the sky. The thunder roared and rumbled.

"Enough." She couldn't take much more. "Come on, Universe. Give me a break."

If it stopped raining, she'd never criticize the weather again. Was the Universe open to a deal like that? "If I find my way, I'll give up anything. No more chocolate. No more overdrafts in the checking account."

She needed something bigger to deal with, something more important, something life-changing. She needed the barely worn, red-soled Christian Louboutin heels she'd picked up secondhand before she left civilization. "That's right, the Louboutins. Go ahead, Universe. Take my shoes. Just let me find the place I'm looking for."

A flash of lightning showed a carved wood sign: Rousseau's Roost. An arrow pointed left. *This is it!*

As the thunder rattled around her, she made the turn. She had asked, and the Universe had answered. She was on her way, nearly there. Survival was within her grasp. Did she really have to give up the shoes?

The final stretch of road to Rousseau's Roost was marked by deep ruts. On the plus side, she was moving away from the scary trees, heading across an open space with a barbed wire fence to her left. Things were looking better, much better. The rain seemed to be letting up.

In another crackle-boom of lightning, she saw the outline of a two-story house with a wraparound porch. In photographs, Rousseau's Roost had a rustic charm that appealed to Gabby. She couldn't believe she owned half of this property. She'd been on her own since she was eighteen, and her living space in Brooklyn had been a series of one-room apartments. Now she was a home owner with a house and a barn and acreage.

Her great-aunt Michelle—who Gabby had met exactly five times in her whole life—had left the property to Gabby and her older brother, Daniel, whom she hadn't heard from since her twenty-third birthday party three years ago. Every attempt she'd made to find him and tell him about this strange windfall had fallen flat, which made her sad. With Aunt Michelle dead, her jerk of a brother was her only living relative. She wouldn't really mind splitting the inheritance with him if they could be a family again.

When she parked in front of the house, the rain had slowed to a drizzle. She turned off the engine. It was entirely possible that the car wouldn't start up again in the morning, but she'd deal with that problem when it happened.

The lawyer who'd contacted her had sent the key to the front door, which she had already attached to the key ring that held her car keys, a couple of keys to friends' apartments that she really ought to mail back to them, a lipstick-sized container of pepper spray and one very special set of rhinestone-embellished keys that she had hoped would unlock her fondest dreams. She remembered the day when she and her three friends had used these keys to open the door to the storefront shop on Myrtle Street. For almost two years, they ran a little boutique where—in addition to seamstress work and fittings—Gabby got to show off her original designs. Then the money ran out.

She pulled her pink hoodie over her damp brown hair and shoved open the car door. All of her earthly belongings were jammed into her compact car, but her primary necessities were in a red polka-dot carry-on she'd kept on the passenger seat beside her. Wrestling that suitcase past the steering wheel, she started toward the front door. Mud splashed on her black platform sandals. No big tragedy, these shoes were past their prime.

The mountain sounds bore no resemblance to the hum of people and cars and electricity in Brooklyn. Out here, she could hear the splat of the raindrops, the rustle of wind through the branches of a leafy tree at the side of the house and—as she stepped onto the porch—a heavy thud like a door slamming. Had that sound come from inside the house?

She stood very still and listened with her ear against the door. She heard a creak and a shuffle as though someone was walking on tiptoe, trying not to be heard. But that couldn't be right. Nobody was supposed to be here. The lawyer had told her that the house wasn't occupied. Did she have an intruder? A squatter?

Her phone was dead so she couldn't call 911 for help. She'd have to face this threat by herself. *Okay, fine. I'm from the big city. I know how to handle muggers.* First rule, don't get too close. Second, make a loud yell to startle them. Rule number three, run like hell.

But where could she run? Turning around on the porch,

she squinted through the misty rain until she saw the lights of another house in the distance. All she had to do was drive to the neighbor's place.

Listening again, she didn't hear another sound. Maybe she'd imagined the slamming door and the squeaky floor-boards. If there wasn't really an intruder, she'd feel like a dope, running away from an invisible boogeyman.

She cleared her throat and pitched her voice to a low, authoritative level. "Hello? Is anybody here?"

Nothing.

Setting her suitcase to one side, she turned the key in the front door until it clicked. When she eased the door open, the hinges whined. An old house like this was bound to make creaks and thumps and rustles. Stepping across the threshold, she reached for the place beside the door where a light switch ought to be. Her fingers glided down the wall. No switch.

The faint light from a couple of stars peeking around the edge of the clouds shone on the carpeted floor in the entryway. The curtains were drawn inside the house, making the interior even darker than outside. She stumbled into a large room, walking like a blind woman with her arms out in front of her until she bumped into a table with a lamp. Groping along the base, she found the switch and turned it on.

A pale glow lit up the parlor. Her great-aunt Michelle had been an artist and was fairly successful, even had some showings in Manhattan. Her taste showed in the eclectic furnishings, which were a crazy combo of claw-foot tables, sleek-lined sofas and jewel-toned pillows.

"Nice," Gabby said. In spite of the desolation, she could get used to living in a place like this.

From the corner of her eye, she saw movement and

whirled around. Standing on the carved, wood staircase in the entryway was the figure of a brown-haired woman in a long, white gown. Not a zombie. Maybe a ghost? Gabby blinked. Was Great-Aunt Michelle haunting the place?

"Who are you?" the ghost demanded.

"Me? Who are you?" Gabby shot back.

"Get out!"

"This is my house." Gabby's fingers tightened on the pepper spray. Ghost or not, this person was skinny and the voice was female. If this came down to a physical confrontation, Gabby liked her odds.

In a rush, the ghost descended the staircase. Her long, stringy hair fell past her shoulders almost to her waist. On the landing that was three steps up from the wooden newel post carved in the shape of a gargoyle, the ghost reached down. When she stood, she was holding a rifle.

"Now," the ghost said. "Tell me who you are."

The odds had shifted. Gabby had the good sense to be scared. She raised her hands beside her head and moved toward the staircase. If she could get past the ghost to the open door, she could run to her car and drive to the neighboring house, like she should have done when she first arrived.

"Take it easy," Gabby said. "My name is Gabriella Rousseau. Michelle was my great-aunt."

"You better have some identification."

"No problem." She was almost to the entryway. "My wallet is in my car."

"Don't take another step."

This girl in the long nightgown couldn't have been more than sixteen or seventeen, and she looked upset. Her eyes were red-rimmed as though she'd been crying. Maybe all she needed was a friend. Gabby tried a smile as she inched her way forward. "How about you put down the gun?"

"I told you not to move."

"Okay, sure." She kept her eye on the bore of the rifle. "You've got nothing to worry about. Look at me. Do I look dangerous?"

"You look stupid in those shorts."

"They were a lot cuter when I put them on this morning." Now wasn't the time for a fashion critique. "Come on, put down the rifle."

"No way. They might have sent you. They might be trying to trick me."

"They? Who are they?"

"Just walk to the door, real slow. I'll be right behind you. One false move and I'll blow a hole in your back."

No way was Gabby going to step into the line of fire. This girl was crazy, and she was trembling so hard that she might accidentally pull the trigger. Gabby needed to take control. As soon as she was even with the rifle, she made a quick pivot and dodged to one side. With her opposite hand, she fired a blast of pepper spray. She grabbed the long barrel of the rifle.

With surprising strength, the thin girl yanked the gun away from her. A gunshot exploded. The girl spewed a string of profanities that would have made a Brooklyn Teamster blush.

Gabby made another attempt to get the gun, but the girl wouldn't let go. They wrestled for the weapon. Gabby yanked hard. Her hands slipped, and she fell backward onto her butt. She dropped her keys and pepper spray. The girl waved the rifle blindly and blasted the head off the wood gargoyle at the foot of the staircase.

It was time for rule number three: run like hell.

Scrambling to her feet, Gabby charged through the open door and dived down the steps leading to the porch. Her car was right there, but it didn't matter because she'd lost the keys. Hunching her shoulders to make herself a smaller target, she ran as fast as she could in the platform sandals, putting distance between herself and the house.

"Get back here," the girl yelled.

Not on your life. Gabby ducked behind a clump of some kind of mountain prickly bush and stared at the house. The figure in white stomped back and forth on the porch with the rifle in her hands, treating the place as though it was her property and she was sworn to protect it. What the hell was going on here?

Gabby decided not to stick around and find out. The crazy girl in the nightgown might decide to get dressed and come after her. The best move would be to run through the drizzle toward the neighbor's lights in the hope of finding reasonable people.

She waited until Crazy Girl went into the house and then made a dash for the road. Leaping across the two narrow lanes, she came to the barbed wire fence on the opposite side. Until now, she hadn't noticed cows or any other wildlife, but it was a good bet that the barbed wire had been erected to keep something penned in. Growing up in Brooklyn, Gabby had zero experience with cattle, but she knew they weren't violent. Cows ate grass, not people.

Carefully, she poked one bare leg between the strands of barbed wires. She lowered her shoulders to squeeze through, and she almost made it. The back of her hoodie snagged. She pulled. The fabric stretched but didn't release. After another pull, she was hooked in two other places. The sweatshirt had to come off. She unzipped the front and wriggled her arms free. Balancing on one foot, she climbed through.

The lights from the neighbor's house were still a long way from where she was standing, and she was freezing cold. The dribbles of rain were already soaking through her long-sleeved cotton T-shirt, which was one of her favorite items of clothing. Her best friend, Hannah, had painted a romantic sketch of the Eiffel Tower on the front.

Gabby needed the hoodie for warmth. She peered at Great-Aunt Michelle's house and saw no sign of Crazy Girl. It shouldn't take more than a couple of seconds to untangle the sweatshirt. She gently maneuvered the fabric, detaching it from one of the barbs, then another. She almost had it free when she snagged the sleeve of her T-shirt. Damn, she didn't want to ruin this shirt that Hannah had worked so hard to make. Quickly, she peeled it off over her head.

Unsnagging the material took a careful touch, but Gabby was accustomed to working with fabric. She manipulated the threads and gently pulled. Both shirts were free and still no Crazy Girl. But someone was approaching. Gabby could hear them getting closer. She turned to face the new threat, clutching her hoodie and her shirt to her breasts to cover her leopard-patterned bra.

A cowboy on a dark horse rode toward her. He wasn't like anything she'd ever seen before. Frankly, she would have been less startled by a zombie attack.

Lightning flashed behind him, outlining his broad shoulders and long legs. When she glimpsed a chiseled profile under the brim of his hat, her heart did a weird little tango. He looked angry. But he was also gorgeous.

Chapter Two

Zach Sheffield dismounted and approached the woman who stood at the edge of his property wearing a pair of shorts, a leopard bra and nothing else. He'd never seen anything like her before. She stared with eyes as big as saucers. Her arms and legs gleamed white against the darkness. She was shivering and talking so fast that he couldn't separate her words into anything coherent.

Whatever she was babbling about didn't matter. All he wanted to do was get her dried off and warmed up so she could go back to Michelle's place where she belonged. Without speaking, he took off his denim jacket and draped it over her shoulders.

"Thank you," she said, "thank you, thank you."

The rain dripped down her forehead, streaks of eye makeup marked her cheeks and her lips quivered. She looked as pathetic as a wet cat, but he didn't waste any sympathy on her. There was a spark of energy in those dark brown eyes that told him she wasn't a helpless damsel in distress.

"You can come with me," he said.

"Where are we going?"

"My place. After you get dried off, I'll take you back to your home."

"Home? I really hope you aren't talking about Rousseau's Roost. I can't go there." She jabbed an accusing finger at the house across the road. "There's a crazy girl in there. She shot at me."

He'd heard the gunfire, but that wasn't why he'd responded. "The crazy girl is Charlotte Potter. She called my house to tell me what happened. After you ran off, she checked your ID and decided you weren't lying about being Michelle's niece."

"Why would anybody lie about being me?"

He shrugged.

She clasped his hand in an attempted handshake. Her fingers were like ice. "I'm Gabriella Rousseau. Everybody calls me Gabby."

The name suited her. "Zach Sheffield," he said.

"I wish we were meeting in different circumstances. I mean, here we are in the middle of the night. In the middle of nowhere." She winced. "Sorry, I'm not putting down this, um, countryside. I'm sure that in daylight, it's lovely, and—"

He tapped the stirrup. "Put your foot in here, and I'll hoist you up."

"Oh, no, that's not going to happen." She took a backward step. "I don't know how to ride."

He wasn't asking her to perform in a barrel race. "You don't have to do anything. Just sit on the horse."

"Why are you people trying to kill me?" She stormed around in a tight little circle. "First, the crazy girl shoots at me. Then, you want me to deal with a gigantic animal. That thing must weigh two tons."

"About eleven hundred pounds," he said.

"What if it steps on me? It's not safe."

Zach had neither the time nor the inclination to stand

in the rain, listening to a tirade from a woman who didn't have the sense to realize that he was helping her. He stuck his foot into the stirrup and swung back into the saddle. "Suit yourself."

"What's that supposed to mean?"

"You can walk. It's about a mile to the house. The ground in this field is kind of uneven, so watch your step. And mind the rattlesnakes."

"Snakes?" She staggered toward him with both arms raised. "I think I'll take that ride, after all."

He reached down, wrapped his arm around her and yanked her off her feet. It took all his strength to lift her onto the horse, especially when her long legs got tangled the wrong way around. When his horse snorted, she yelped and flailed as though she was atop a bucking bronco. He wrestled her around until she was settled into the saddle in front of him.

Exhaling a sigh, she leaned against him. The back of his jacket was wet against his flannel shirt, but when he slipped his arm around her slender body, he liked the way they fit together. It had been a while since he'd been this close to a woman. As his hand molded against her bare midriff, her stomach muscles quivered. A vision of her leopard-patterned bra popped into his head as he urged his horse into a walk toward his ranch house.

"Slow down," she said.

"I don't think that's possible."

"We're really high up. If I fall from here, I could break an ankle."

"It's hard to believe you've never been on a horse before."

"I'm from Brooklyn," she said as though that statement should clarify everything. "I'm not into animals."

"Except for leopards," he murmured.

"I guess I owe you an explanation for why I was half-naked when you found me. It's simple, okay? My clothes got caught on your nasty fence and I didn't want to rip them to shreds."

Her body jostled against him. In spite of the cold rain, a pleasant feeling of warmth radiated from his chest to the rest of his body. When he leaned forward in the saddle, he could smell the strawberry scent of her shampoo.

"I bet you've got other questions for me," she said.

"No, ma'am."

"Ma'am?" She wriggled around in front of him. "Did you just *ma'am* me?"

"Seems appropriate for a lady such as yourself who's never rode a horse."

"And that makes you wonder, doesn't it? What's a city girl like me doing here?"

Zach already knew the short answer. Gabby was here to claim her inheritance—Rousseau's Roost. That information was enough for him. He wasn't the kind of person who needed to rake through other people's business. "I'm sure you've got your reasons."

"Colorado isn't where I'd choose to live," she said. "I'm into fashion and I specialize in original designs, not haute couture gowns but upscale ready-to-wear. You know what I mean?"

"Yep." Zach didn't have a clue and couldn't care less.

"Anyway," she continued, "my work means I need to be in New York or L.A. or some other major fashion mecca. When the lawyer called and told me about Rousseau's Roost, he said it was near Aspen. Is that true?"

"Yep."

"Aspen means glitz and glamor. I thought that movie

stars and European royalty would be my next-door neighbors. Do you know a lot of famous people?"

"Nope."

They were coming closer to his long, low, ranch house. On the porch, he saw his housekeeper with a striped Indian blanket in her hands. As soon as they got there, he'd turn Gabby over to the care of Rhoda Phillips, who would give her something warm to drink and something dry to wear. That was the neighborly thing to do. Though he enjoyed the way this woman from Brooklyn felt in his arms, they had nothing in common. He wasn't looking to start up any kind of friendship.

"Did you know my great-aunt?" she asked.

"Yep."

She waited for five seconds, and then twisted her neck around. "What can you tell me about her?"

"I liked her."

Michelle Rousseau was a good neighbor, sociable when she needed to be and not a pest. She'd traveled a lot and was well-read. Zach had spent many pleasant evenings drinking coffee on her front porch and listening to her stories about faraway places and unusual ideas. He'd been glad when Charlotte moved into the Roost a few years ago to help out with the chores when the work got to be too much for Michelle to handle on her own.

"What else?" Gabby asked. "Did she ever talk about family? Did she mention me?"

"Yep."

He was saved from further conversation when they reached the covered porch where Rhoda stood with her blanket. He swung his leg over the rump of his horse and dismounted. Then he held his arms up to help her.

After the clumsy way she'd gotten on the horse, he expected a struggle, but she surprised him by getting both legs on the same side of the saddle. As she slipped down into his arms, her long, lean body slid against his, descending slowly, until her feet touched the ground. The warm sensations he'd been feeling translated into a sensual heat that didn't bode well for keeping things neighborly and distant.

"Do you want your jacket?" she asked.

The last thing he needed right now was another view of her leopard brassiere. "Keep it."

He turned Gabby by the shoulders and pointed her toward the porch. "This is Rhoda Phillips. She'll look after you."

Zach took the reins of his horse and walked toward the barn. With each step, he told himself not to get attached to Gabby Rousseau. This woman was nothing but trouble.

ON THE PORCH, Gabby gratefully accepted the warm, dry blanket that was being held toward her by a round-faced little woman with her gray hair sticking out from her head like a cap of feathers. On short legs, she bustled like a pigeon, and her long plaid bathrobe was belted beneath her full breasts.

"Come inside," Rhoda said. "We'll have some nice, hot, chamomile tea."

"That sounds great." She glanced toward Zach as he and his horse disappeared around the end of the house. "I think I might have made him angry."

"Don't worry about Zach. He's not a big talker."

"I noticed," Gabby said.

"But he's a good man." Rhoda ushered her through the door into the log house. "When I first came to work for him, I had two teenage boys and no skills. Zach gave me a chance. He was patient and kind. I like to think that he trained me just like he trains his horses."

Gabby wasn't sure if horse whisperer methods were suitable for humans. "Trained you to do what?"

"I basically run the place." She proudly stuck out her breasts. "I do the bookkeeping, the ordering and the billing. Zach isn't much good with computers, so I handle all the online parts of the business so he can concentrate on his work."

"This is a ranch, right? Do you have cows?"

"What? We're not a cattle ranch. Zach breeds, raises and trains horses. My goodness, Gabby, you don't know a thing about us, do you?"

"I guess not."

"Ten years ago, Zach was a star on the rodeo circuit. He got injured, and then started up this horse ranch. He's one of the most sought-after trainers in the West."

Though Gabby wasn't sure what a horse trainer did or what happened on the rodeo circuit, she was suitably impressed. "So, he was a star, huh?"

"But don't mention it. He doesn't like to talk about the old days."

In the pine-paneled living room, Rhoda led her toward the fireplace and indicated that she should sit in a padded rocking chair in front of the brick hearth. The heat from the flickering orange flames in the fireplace was heavenly.

"Take off those silly shoes," Rhoda said, "and warm up your toes. I'll fetch the tea."

Gabby hadn't realized how chilled she was until she began to thaw. Bit by bit, her body relaxed. She unclenched her fists. The tension eased from the muscles in her shoulders. Her long road trip was over. She'd reached her destination, and the overall picture wasn't too bad. Though her first moments at Roost hadn't gone well, Crazy Girl seemed to have a reason for her gun-toting behavior. At least, Zach accepted Charlotte as a rational human being.

Could she believe his opinion? Her first impression of his gorgeousness remained intact. If all she'd wanted was to sit and stare at him, she would have been perfectly content, but she wasn't sure that she could trust the former rodeo star. Rhoda was a lot more forthcoming.

The housekeeper bustled into the room carrying a tray, which she placed on a coffee table beside Gabby's rocker.

"Herbal tea," she said. "And oatmeal cookies. I did some baking this afternoon when it started clouding over. I just love the way it makes the house smell."

The last time Gabby ate was hours ago—a greasy taco and a milk shake. She pounced on the cookies, which tasted healthy in comparison to her diet for the past several days on the road. The lightly sweetened chamomile tea soothed her throat.

"Oh, Rhoda." She licked her lips. "This is fantastic. Can I live with you?"

"Don't be silly, dear. You've got a wonderful adventure waiting." Rhoda sat in the overstuffed chair beside her and tucked her short legs underneath her. "I'm guessing the Roost is going to be a different life than you're used to."

"I don't fit in," Gabby said. "Is it that obvious?"

"The leopard bra and fancy sandals are kind of a clue." Rhoda grinned. "Your great-aunt told me that you'd spent your whole life in the city. She said she didn't know you very well, but she thought you had inherited some of her artistic talent."

"Me?" Gabby took another bite of oatmeal cookie. "I wonder why she said that."

"You're a designer, aren't you? That's art."

Claiming to be an artist seemed pretentious when her most lucrative source of income was alterations like taking up hems and letting out waists. Still, she was flattered. "I guess my work could be called creative."

"Wait until you see the inside of the Roost. There's a studio that you could change into a workroom for sewing and an office and a tremendous view."

"And Charlotte Potter," Gabby said. "What's her story?"

"Her parents—a couple of mean, nasty people—threw her out, and Michelle offered her a place to live in exchange for doing some light chores. Charlotte was devoted to your great-aunt."

Which didn't necessarily mean that she wasn't loony tunes. "She seemed to think that somebody was threatening her, and that they sent me to do their dirty work."

"Treasure hunters."

Gabby almost choked on her cookie. "Say what?"

"It's your family history. Haven't you ever heard of the Frenchman's Treasure?"

Holding the mug of tea to her lips, she leaned forward. "Tell me about it."

"A long time ago," Rhoda said, "way back in the 1870s, your ancestor moved to Colorado to prospect for gold. His name was Louis Rousseau. He always wore a gold hoop earring like a pirate, and he was supposed to be a dashing, handsome man."

Gabby had a vague recollection of a formal photograph in a family album. "He had a wife and two children. And they came from Wisconsin. Was he a trapper?"

"A trapper or a trader. Nobody knows for sure, but he had enough money to buy a huge parcel of land, build the first structure that was called Rousseau's Roost and start a cattle ranch."

If Gabby had known that her ancestor had a treasure, she would have taken more interest in her heritage. It seemed unimportant after her parents were killed in a car accident when she was thirteen. Family, what family? She and her brother were left to be raised by the elderly great-aunt who was Michelle's sister. Aunt Rene had done her best, even though she was in her eighties when she got stuck with a couple of angry teenagers. She was the one who taught Gabby to sew. She'd passed away when Gabby was twenty-one.

"Louis's wife," said Rhoda, "might have been a Sioux Indian, but nobody knew for sure."

"I might be part Native American?"

"A very small part."

"Still," Gabby said, "that's cool. At Thanksgiving in elementary school, the kids who had a Native American background always got to play special parts."

"Back in the 1800s, it wasn't considered cool."

"Tell me about the treasure."

"As it turned out, Louis's wife was very good at raising cattle and children. She had five more while her handsome husband was off on prospecting trips, combing the hills for gold or silver. Though he never filed a claim, he always had cash, which led people to believe that he had a secret stash. The legend grew. People followed him on his trips, but no one learned the secret of the Frenchman's Treasure."

Gabby was captivated by the story of her long-ago past. One of the Rousseau children must have moved back East and established themselves in Brooklyn. But which one? Did she have other relations? Aunt Rene had never mentioned anyone other than Michelle. "How does all this relate to Charlotte?"

"Supposedly, the key to finding the treasure is hidden in the house. And Charlotte thinks it's her duty to protect it."

While Gabby mulled over the idea of a treasure map tucked away behind a brick in the old house, she heard Zach come into the room. In the light from the fireplace, he was even more handsome. His deep-set eyes were a piercing blue. His shaggy brown hair curled over the collar of his plaid shirt. When she looked at him, she couldn't help grinning.

He didn't smile back.

"Now you've heard the legend," he said. "I suggest you forget all about it."

Chapter Three

The last thing Zach needed was Rhoda filling Gabby's head with wild stories about the Frenchman's Treasure. This strange woman from Brooklyn might start tearing down the Roost in the hope of getting rich quick. He took a sip from his steaming mug of herbal tea and gazed into the fire on the hearth, trying his best not to notice how Gabby was clutching the striped blanket over her half-naked body. Didn't this woman ever wear clothes?

"Why should I forget the treasure?" she asked.

Rhoda answered for him. "Zach thinks that if the treasure or a treasure map ever existed, they would have been found by now. And I guess that makes sense. People have been searching for over a hundred and fifty years."

"When it comes to secrets," Gabby said, "time doesn't matter."

What the hell was she talking about? He knew that asking for an explanation would open a can of worms, but he couldn't let her statement stand unchallenged. "Tell me more."

"Think about the archaeologists in Egypt. They're still finding artifacts in the sand, and those things have been hidden for thousands of years."

He hadn't expected her to talk about archaeology.

"I went to a King Tut exhibit in Manhattan," she said. When she gestured, her blanket slipped, giving him another glimpse of the leopard bra. "You wouldn't believe all the gold. And those thousands of years didn't matter. Finding things is just a matter of knowing where to look."

"This is different," he said.

"Think about the last time you lost something and couldn't find it," she said. "You search and you search and you just can't locate it. A couple of days later, you remember that you were in the kitchen when you lost it. You go to the drawer by the door and…ta da! There it is."

Her logic made a certain amount of sense, but Zach wasn't going to concede. He was right about the treasure map. "Michelle used to travel a lot. She'd leave the house vacant for days at a time. We tried to keep an eye on things, but anybody who wanted to search could have gotten in."

"Zach's right," Rhoda said. "Treasure hunters have had plenty of chances to poke around at the Roost."

"Why is Charlotte so worried about it?" Gabby asked.

Rhoda made a tsk-tsk sound. "On the day of Michelle's memorial service, her house was broken into and some of her things were tossed around. They took the typical stuff like computers, a television and electronics. Sheriff Burton thought it was just a burglary."

"But he investigated," Gabby said. "At least, I hope he investigated. That's his job."

"The sheriff did all he could." He didn't appreciate her implication that law enforcement in this area was less stringent than it would be in a city.

"Did he find fingerprints?"

"The thieves wore gloves," he said. "Even out here in the middle of nowhere, criminals know how to avoid being caught."

He'd been with the sheriff when his deputies studied

the crime scene. They'd all come to the same conclusion. Michelle was a wealthy woman, and the thieves had hoped to find something of value while everyone was out of the house at the memorial service. The only person who thought of the Frenchman's Treasure was Charlotte.

"Maybe Michelle's death triggered some kind of clue," Gabby said. "Was there anything in her will?"

"That's a thought," Rhoda said. "We should check with the lawyer."

Zach shot her a glare. He couldn't believe Rhoda was considering Gabby's nonsense. "Michelle's will isn't public information. The thieves wouldn't know about it."

Gabby wasn't deterred. "Bad guys could have broken into the lawyer's office and—"

"Forget about the treasure." He paused to sip his tea. "If I believed there was a real danger from treasure hunters, I wouldn't leave Charlotte alone in the house."

"Is that so?" Gabby arched an eyebrow. In spite of being a drenched mess with her hair hanging in limp strands and makeup smearing her cheeks, she managed to look sophisticated. "And I suppose you're never wrong."

"Seldom," he said.

For a long moment, she held his gaze. He recognized the defiance in her dark brown eyes. She wasn't the sort of woman who was going to take orders and back down. Everything he said, he would have to prove. For the first time, he saw the family resemblance. Gabby was a lot like her great-aunt.

Rhoda stood. "Why don't you come with me, Gabby? I'll get you some dry clothes. Then Zach can take you back to the Roost."

Without looking away from him, she said, "Not on horseback."

"He'll take the truck," Rhoda promised.

Zach watched as the two women went down the hall toward the bedrooms. Gabby was going to be a handful, no doubt about it. He'd been prepared not to like her. During those last difficult months when Michelle's health was failing, Gabby couldn't be bothered to visit. And yet, when she heard of her inheritance, she hightailed it across the country to stake her claim.

Before he met her, he was ready to dismiss her as an ungrateful, greedy relation who only wanted to take advantage of her great-aunt's inheritance. But now, he wasn't so sure. She had an innocence that seemed real. She wasn't a great beauty but she carried herself with confidence, even while wearing those sandals.

Dealing with her was going to be complicated. He looked down into his mug of herbal tea and wished it was whiskey. One day at a time, he had to take Gabby one day at a time.

GABBY FELT ALMOST human after washing her face, dragging a comb through her chin-length hair and changing into dry clothes. On the bottom, she wore a pair of Rhoda's faded red sweatpants that were Capri-length on her long legs. The zip-up sweatshirt fit just fine on top. Shoes were a problem. Gabby's feet were at least two sizes larger than Rhoda's and much too small to fit into a pair of sneakers belonging to Zach. For now, her sandals would have to do.

When she climbed into the passenger seat of Zach's big, old truck, she was hit by the smell of dirt and wet dog. "Do you have a dog?"

"Three."

"I'm guessing they aren't pocket poodles that fit nicely in a Gucci bag."

"Two hounds for hunting and a border collie named Daphne." He looked over his shoulder. "I'm surprised

Daphne didn't run up to meet you when you crossed onto my property."

"Is she a guard dog?"

"She's a border collie," he said in a tone that you'd use with a slow learner. "The breed is known for their intelligence."

"So Daphne probably took one look at me and decided I wasn't a threat."

"Yep."

When he cranked the engine, the radio came on. Of course, it was tuned to a country and western station. She had dozens of more questions, but talking to Zach had thus far proved futile. The man seemed determined to either ignore her or snap her head off every time she opened her mouth. Still, it didn't hurt to keep asking. "How old is Charlotte?"

"Don't know," he said.

"Could we call a truce? I've had enough of the strong, silent treatment."

He shrugged.

"I know you're lying about not knowing anything about Charlotte," she said.

"How do you know?"

"Because you care about what happens to the kid. When you said that you'd protect her from treasure hunters, your voice was forceful." She'd liked his protective, masculine tone. "And your jaw was as hard as steel. You're not going to let anything bad happen to her."

"Damn right, I won't."

"So, how old is she?"

"Eighteen or nineteen. She stopped going to high school last year. I'm not sure if she graduated."

The road between the two houses was filled with ruts. The rain had stopped but the tires splashed through puddles as they drove. "Has Charlotte talked to you about her future plans?"

"Nope."

"Rhoda said her parents were out of the picture. I'm guessing the girl doesn't have a place to live. Do you think she'd be willing to stay with me for a while?"

"Do you want her to stay?"

"Of course, I do." Gabby hadn't expected to find anyone at the Roost, but she was glad to have bumped into a possible cohort, even Crazy Girl. "For one thing, I need all the help I can get."

"That's for damn sure," he muttered.

"For another, I don't want to kick Charlotte out before she's ready to go. I appreciate what she did for Michelle." If Gabby had been closer to her great-aunt, she might have known when her health was failing. "I nursed my other great-aunt Rene in the last years of her life, and I know that caring for the elderly isn't easy, even when they're cool like Michelle. I wish I'd been here."

The first time she heard of Michelle's death was a phone call from her lawyer, Jason Fox. He'd faxed a copy of the will and Michelle's last wishes to be cremated and have her ashes spread. Gabby really hadn't known her great-aunt well enough to grieve, but she'd felt empty, like a part of her was gone. It hadn't seemed like there was anything left for her to do.

Zach cleared his throat. "Rhoda asked Charlotte if she wanted to stay with us, but she refused."

"Because of the treasure hunters."

"She and Michelle were real close," he said. "It's going to be hard for her to let go."

Empathy and understanding from Zach? That was a surprise. "Does Charlotte have other friends? Somebody her own age?"

"She likes working with the horses."

"Like you."

She knew almost nothing about him but suspected there were interesting stories about how the former rodeo star became the owner of a successful horse ranch. Now wasn't the time to push for details, but she was curious.

When they pulled up in front of the house, she saw that Charlotte had been busy in her absence. She'd moved the suitcases and boxes from the back of Gabby's car to the front porch of the house, and she'd gotten dressed. In her jeans and puffy vest with her long hair tied back and a navy blue Denver Broncos baseball cap on her head, she looked like a teenager—a teenage boy. When it came to clothing, Charlotte was definitely the "before" version— sorely in need of a makeover.

She tromped through the mud to Gabby's side of the truck and yanked the door open. "I'm sorry."

Gabby noticed the red splotch on the side of her face where she'd hit her with the pepper spray. "I'm sorry, too."

When she climbed down from the cab of the truck, Gabby couldn't help but notice Charlotte's discomfort. The thin girl shifted her weight back and forth. Her eyes were downcast. Her arms folded around her middle, and her shoulders hunched as though she was expecting to be beaten. This behavior wasn't the way to make friends. Gabby's second lesson—after she showed Charlotte the wonders of moisturizing—would be on how to meet people without curling into a ball of nervousness.

"Come here." Gabby pulled her close and gave her a hug. "I truly, deeply appreciate everything you did for my great-aunt."

"You got it backward," Charlotte said. "Michelle took me in and gave me a place to live."

"And you cared for her. All I know from the lawyer was that she died from heart failure. Was she in the hospital?"

"Only once."

Charlotte tried to pull away, but Gabby held her. "Can you tell me about it? What did the doctors say?"

"They put in a stent." Her voice was a little shaky. "They found other medical problems. With her lungs and her liver. The doctors said she didn't have long to live. They wanted her to stay at the hospital and rest, but…" Her voice trailed off into silence.

"I didn't know my aunt well," Gabby said, "but I know she made her own choices and lived her life the way she wanted. I expect she chose the way she wanted to die."

"At home." A sob trembled through Charlotte's narrow shoulders. "As soon as she could walk, she got out of that hospital bed and hired a nurse to come back to the Roost with us and take care of her medication."

"You did everything you could to help."

"It wasn't enough."

Charlotte collapsed against her. Though her body was wrenched with powerful emotion, she didn't make a sound. Her silent tears touched Gabby's heart. This poor girl had no support system whatsoever. There had been times in Gabby's life when she'd felt alone and bereft of family, but her experience was nothing compared to Charlotte's abject loneliness.

Gently, Gabby stroked her back. The girl was so thin that her ribs stuck out. She felt as delicate as a baby bird. Looking past Charlotte's shoulder, Gabby saw Zach watching them from the porch. His expression was oddly gentle, and he almost seemed to be smiling.

"It's okay," Gabby murmured. "We're going to take care of each other. Do you think you can stay here with me?"

"Yes," Charlotte said quickly. She broke away from the

hug, sniffled and looked Gabby in the eye. "I'm really glad I didn't shoot you."

It went without saying that Gabby was also happy about that outcome. "We need to talk about that gun."

With her sleeve, Charlotte wiped the moisture from her cheeks in a gesture that couldn't have been less feminine. "I need the rifle. There are these guys who are trying to break into the house. Treasure hunters."

"But I'm here now," Gabby said. "Nobody will try to break in with both of us here."

"What if they do?"

"We call the police."

"It'll take them at least a half hour to get here."

She hadn't thought of the timing. Living at the end of a rutted road without street signs was different than being in Brooklyn. "I don't like guns."

"Because you don't know how to use them," Zach said. "If you're going to live here, you need to learn how to defend yourself and your property."

"Zach can show you," Charlotte said. "He's a really good teacher. Maybe tomorrow you can have a lesson."

"Great," she muttered. "Until then, can we at least put the gun away somewhere? Leaving it on the stair landing seems dangerous."

"Yes, it does." Zach gave Charlotte a puzzled look. "Have you got an explanation?"

"I couldn't sleep, and I was going upstairs and then back downstairs. If I was all the way down in the kitchen, my rifle wasn't going to do me much good if it was up in my bedroom closet. So I left it in the middle."

"You know better," he said. "You don't leave a loaded weapon out where anybody could pick it up and use it."

She scowled. "I know."

"Gabby could have stumbled over the rifle and caused an accident."

"I get it." Charlotte rolled her eyes. "It's lucky that both Gabby and me are going to be staying here. If you put the two of us together, you have one smart person."

Before Gabby could object to being labeled as Tweedle-Dee to Charlotte's Tweedle-Dum, she heard a confirming *woof.* On the porch, sitting beside her pile of belongings, was a black-and-white dog with pointed ears. One eye was blue and the other brown. The dog seemed to be grinning at them. "Daphne?"

"What's she doing here?" Zach asked.

Charlotte went to the dog and scratched behind her ears. "Right after Gabby took off, Daphne showed up and started following me. She hasn't let me out of her sight. It feels like she's herding me."

"Keeping you safe." Zach looked over his shoulder, scanning the darkness that surrounded the house. "Daphne senses things we don't see."

A psychic collie? Gabby would have laughed if she hadn't felt a prickling on the back of her neck. She didn't want to think about the coyotes and other possible dangers that Daphne might be seeing with her two-colored eyes.

ABOUT A MILE from the front porch of the Roost, a man in black crouched beside a fence post and peered through the night vision scope mounted on his rifle. He wanted a better look at the new girl. In spite of the three times magnification, he couldn't make out details at this distance. She was taller than average and kind of clumsy in the way she walked. And she was a hugger. When she'd wrapped her arms around Charlotte, a flicker of envy had gone through him. He'd been keeping an eye on sweet little Charlotte for the past month and had developed an interest in her, even though the girl was as plain as a female sage grouse.

Having another person at the Roost would make his search more complicated, and time was running out. He needed a new tactic, needed to be smarter. The more he thought about it, the more he suspected that Michelle had hidden what he was looking for. At this point, he didn't care as much about the money as he did about the potential prison time. He wouldn't let himself be locked away. Sweat trickled between his shoulder blades. His knit cap was itchy on his ears. He wasn't going to let anyone take away the expensive goodies he'd been buying for himself. He'd taken the risk and deserved those things.

Had that old bitch Michelle told Charlotte where she'd hidden her secrets? Had she left instructions for the new girl?

He shifted his scope and focused on Zach Sheffield. If the neighbor decided to get involved with these women, it was going to be trouble. Zach liked to pretend that he was upright and honest—a rodeo hero and a role model. But there was a time, not so very long ago, when he'd been desperate and angry, prone to lashing out first and asking questions later.

As the man in black watched, his finger twitched on the trigger. Life would be easier if he eliminated these obstacles. *Pop, pop, pop.* Three shots. Three dead bodies. Sheriff Burton would never figure out who did it.

Chapter Four

The next morning when Gabby awoke, sunshine was pouring through the two bedroom windows, assaulting her with blinding force. With a groan, she curled into a fetal position and covered her face with one of the down pillows on her queen-size bed. What was the deal with the light in Colorado? Either it was pitch-dark or glaring like a laser.

"Nature," she grumbled into her pillow.

These annoying variances in the weather were natural phenomena—something you had to live with when you were in the mountains. In the city, the temperature wasn't consistent, but you didn't have to deal with the ups and downs. Life could be arranged to minimize your time outdoors. You could stay inside for days and survive by ordering pizza and Chinese, two options that probably weren't available at the Roost. No Chinese? It took a moment for that loss to sink into her early morning consciousness. No crispy egg rolls. No General Tso's chicken.

Another groan harmonized with a growl from her stomach. Eating nothing but her own cooking was a miserable thought. Could she live with that? Did she want to? Gabby needed to make a decision about whether she wanted to stay in Colorado or go back to the place she still considered home.

Peeling back the corner of the pillow, she checked her wristwatch. Already after nine o'clock? No, wait, her watch was still set on Eastern Time. In Brooklyn, it was nine and the corner bakery would already be running low on her favorite almond muffins and the kids would be dashing down the sidewalks to school and the commuters would be waiting to catch the D train.

Here, in the middle of nowhere, the time was fifteen minutes past seven, and it was unbelievably quiet. Nobody was rushing anywhere. Cell phones weren't ringing. The only tweeting came from the birds outside the window.

She'd heard somewhere that country people were early risers but hoped that Charlotte didn't follow that code. They hadn't gotten to bed until nearly midnight after dragging her suitcases and boxes into this upstairs bedroom at the top of the stairs. Charlotte had called this one of the guest rooms, but the space was large enough for a master suite. In addition to the queen-size brass bed, there was a dresser and a standing wardrobe, both of which were painted a deep coral and decorated with faux antiquing. The hand-stitched quilt on the bed used some of the coral mixed with greens and yellows in a zigzag pattern. The walls were a clean, crisp white with a stucco finish. It was a pleasant room, homey but not cluttered.

Opposite her bed, above the dresser was a large canvas that she suspected had been done by her great-aunt. The painting showed a bedroom where a bare-legged girl with her hair falling forward to cover her face sat reading a book. She was reflected in a standing mirror that made her smaller and that mirror was reflected in another and another until the girl vanished.

The style was fascinating, realistic but also surreal. Gabby knew quite a bit about fabric and textile, but she wasn't an art expert. Her great-aunt's work made her think of what might happen if Norman Rockwell hooked up with Salvador Dali. The subject matter of this picture was more interesting to her. It could be an allegory of going deeper and deeper inside yourself until you completely disappear. Or maybe the other way around, starting from nothing and getting bigger and bigger. Either way, the painting gave a sense of secrecy as though there was more than met the eye.

In the somewhat sketchy history of the Rousseau family, Great-Aunt Michelle was a woman of mystery. There must have been an important reason why she left Brooklyn and moved West, but Gabby didn't know what it was. When she had asked her other great-aunt—Michelle's sister—the response was always evasive. If she stayed at the Roost, Gabby wanted to uncover those family secrets. If she stayed…

She tossed the quilt aside, got out of bed and went to the window that looked down on the bumpy driveway leading to the house. A flash of sunlight glinted off the roof of her little car, and she offered up a quick prayer to the Universe that it would start up with no problem this morning. Last night, there had been a lot of sputtering and clunking, and she really needed to take the car in for servicing.

Beyond the road that bisected Michelle's property and Zach's ranch, she saw the evil barbed wire fence that attacked her last night. His cozy house was in the distance, but he was already out and about, riding across the field on a black horse with a coat that glistened as though it had been polished with lacquer.

Though Gabby had never been a big fan of Westerns, she was mesmerized by the vision of a broad-shouldered, long-legged, masculine cowboy in a black hat and denim jacket. Beyond gorgeous, he was iconic and, at the same time, utterly original. He dismounted near the place where she'd gotten tangled up last night and sauntered to the fence with a cool, loose-limbed stride. When he pushed his hat back on his forehead and looked toward the house, she stepped back behind the curtain so he wouldn't see her staring.

Their meeting last night hadn't been under the best of circumstances, and he certainly hadn't done anything since then to make her think he was glad to see her. But she'd sensed chemistry between them. Maybe she and Zach would never have a relationship, but she could easily imagine some kissing in their future. Peeking around the edge of the curtain, she watched him walk back toward his horse. At this distance, she couldn't really judge the way he looked from behind, but she'd noticed last night and he was fine. She wouldn't mind sticking around at the Roost long enough to see where things with Zach might go.

There was a tap on her bedroom door. Charlotte poked her head inside. "Glad you're up. I was thinking about breakfast."

"Usually I just have coffee."

She came all the way into the room. "That's a real pretty nightgown."

"I love fancy lingerie." Gabby ran her fingers along the flowing lines of her lavender satin chemise with the ivory yoke. "A woman should feel glamorous at least once a day, even if she's alone in bed. And nightwear is one of the easiest things to make."

"You made that?"

"I had some scraps left over from a prom dress I did for one of the girls in the neighborhood. I stitched it together and voila!" She came toward Charlotte whose long hair was fastened in two tight braids that made her look twelve years old. "I could make something for you."

"It's not practical. That silky material isn't warm."

"Which is why you have a robe." From the rail at the end of the bed, she picked up a long black satin kimono that she'd embroidered with silver roses and slipped it over her chemise. "I saw your nightgown last night—very *Little House on the Prairie.* You might like to try something different, just for a change."

Charlotte couldn't resist stroking the smooth fabric of the kimono, but her forehead pinched in a scowl. "I've got no need to dress up."

"Fashion isn't about need. It's about desire and dreams." Gabby needed to be careful not to push this odd, shy girl too far. Charlotte needed a friend more than a makeover. "Let's go downstairs. I think I changed my mind about breakfast."

She slipped into a pair of sparkly ballet flats that were going to be totally useless at the Roost, except for using as slippers and followed Charlotte out the door. If she decided to stay, a shopping trip for footwear would be absolutely necessary.

ZACH GLANCED AT Daphne, who was sitting in the passenger seat of his truck. The black-and-white dog raised an eyebrow and shook her head as though she was worried about the current situation. So was he.

Earlier this morning, he'd been riding the fence line along his property to make sure Gabby hadn't torn the barbed wire apart, and he'd discovered a footprint. The grass beside a fence post was tamped down, and he could see the clear outline of a boot heel. Someone had been standing at this spot—about a mile from the front porch of the Roost—for long enough to make an impression. Though Charlotte's theory about treasure hunters still seemed as far-fetched as a pirate ship sailing over Mount Sopris, the footprint indicated that someone had been watching the house, spying on them. Combined with the break-in during Michelle's memorial, Zach had reason to be concerned.

Gabby's arrival made the situation worse. While Charlotte was a nervous little thing who might get herself into trouble with her misplaced handling of her rifle, Gabby was a loose cannon. The first time he'd seen her, she was wearing a leopard bra and not much else. How the hell could he predict what she'd say or do?

As they approached the house, Daphne's ears pricked up and she made a grumbling noise deep in her throat.

"You're right, girl. This could be trouble."

Though Zach knew he couldn't really talk to his dogs or his horses, he'd always felt like he could communicate with animals. He respected their intelligence and their instincts, which were a hundred times sharper than his own. When Daphne sensed danger, he paid attention.

Reaching over, he scratched behind her ears. "Don't worry. We'll keep an eye on them. Michelle would have wanted it."

Daphne's mouth dropped open in what looked like a grin. The dog had liked being around Michelle and spent a lot of time curled up at the base of her easel while she painted. Zach couldn't help wondering if Daphne understood that Michelle was gone and not coming back. More likely, the dog would always approach the Roost with the expectation of greeting the former owner. And who was Zach to say Daphne's instincts were wrong? Michelle Rousseau might still be here in spirit.

He parked his truck and went to the front door, which stood wide-open in a blatant invitation to intruders. The smell of smoke hung in the air. He stepped inside. "What's going on?"

Gabby rushed down the hall from the kitchen. In a pair of tight red jeans and a loose jacket striped with neon colors, she looked like an urban butterfly. "I was baking."

Clearly, that wasn't the whole story. "And?"

"Charlotte made breakfast this morning, and it was really good. Scrambled eggs and Canadian bacon. So, I thought I'd help out, and I remembered those yummy cookies Rhoda gave me last night. I was cooking. Everything was going fine. And then this dish towel caught fire."

"Uh-huh."

"All under control," she said with a confident smile.

"Uh-huh."

Today, she had on makeup—a bit of lining around her dark eyes and pink lipstick that emphasized the fullness of her mouth. With her dark hair framing her face, she was striking, almost beautiful. He had an urge to tell her, to caress the delicate lines of her face and to taste those pretty lips.

"Zach, can I ask you a favor?" Before he could respond, she continued, "I made an appointment to see my great-aunt's lawyer at two o'clock this afternoon. His office is in Aspen, and I need to take my car in for a checkup. It would help if you came with me, in case I have to leave my car overnight."

"Sure." He had already cleared his appointments for today, anticipating problems at the Roost.

"I appreciate it."

When she reached over and casually patted his arm, a current of electricity shot up to his shoulder and spread across his chest. He enjoyed the effect she had on him but hated feeling out of control. The time had come to get a grip. "There's something important we need to discuss."

"Anything, you can talk to me about anything."

From the top of the staircase, he heard Charlotte's voice. "Here I come," she shouted, "ready or not."

The feminine creature that descended the stairs had Charlotte's long hair and her nervous blue eyes. Otherwise, she was unrecognizable. The makeup she was wearing didn't cover the hot red blush on her cheeks. Her legs were encased in fishnet stockings, and she wore a short, tight skirt. Her blouse was long-sleeved, lacy and showed curves he never knew Charlotte had.

At the bottom of the stairs, she spun in a clumsy circle, clearly having trouble maneuvering in her high heels. With a huge smile, she looked up at him. "What do you think?"

"You're real sparkly."

"Glitter makeup," Gabby said.

"Me and Gabby wear the same size. She's a couple of inches taller, but we're pretty much the same. I don't know about these shoes, though. They're kind of big."

"Get used to it," Gabby said. "Those shoes are Louboutins. They're really expensive, and they're yours now, Charlotte. The Universe told me they should belong to you." She nudged Zach's arm. "Doesn't she look great?"

"It's a change." He didn't particularly like the transformation, but he was glad to see Charlotte happy. "You look real pretty."

She actually giggled. Zach was certain that he'd never seen this young woman do anything so girlie, and he was damn sure that this fluffy attitude wasn't the best for discussing security needs. Still, he had to try. "I need for you both to listen to me."

"Give me a second." Charlotte stumbled into the front parlor and sank into a white leather chair. "The shoes aren't working. Trade with me, Gabby. The ones you're wearing have straps."

"If you insist."

They swapped shoes. When Gabby stood, the extra couple of inches from her expensive heels made her almost as tall as he was. She strutted a few paces and grinned down at her shoes. "They fit me, but they belong to you, Charlotte."

"Whatever."

"Ladies," he said, "we need to talk about security. This house isn't a fortress, but you need to do what you can to discourage unwanted intruders. You can start by keeping the doors closed and locked."

"You're right." Gabby strode to the door, pulled it shut and flipped the latch. "Better?"

He gave a terse nod. "The same goes for the windows. I want you to check and make sure they're all locked."

"I'm pretty sure they are," Charlotte said as she stomped around in the shoes with straps. "Oh, yeah, these are good."

Gabby hitched her arm through Charlotte's and asked, "Want a cookie?"

"Only if I make some lemonade."

"Not milk?"

"I like to drink something sour when I eat something sweet."

They were ignoring him. Zach cleared his throat to get their attention. "Ladies, we need to—"

"Come on, Zach. Have a cookie."

"I don't want a damn cookie."

"Well, I do." Gabby pulled out a long strand of Charlotte's hair and asked, "Have you ever thought of coloring your hair? Maybe going blond?"

Charlotte giggled again. "I couldn't."

Zach was ready to bang their heads together. Last night, Charlotte had been scared and brandishing a rifle. Today, she cheerfully sashayed down the hallway, leaving a faint trail of glitter makeup. She'd been suckered in by Gabby's bad influence. Even Daphne had turned traitor. The dog trotted along after the two women, wagging her tail.

Earlier, when he'd seen the boot print and realized the danger might be real, his first thought was to take Charlotte and Gabby to his house and leave the Roost for whoever wanted to tear the damn place apart. Unfortunately, he doubted that either of these women would agree to that solution unless they were hog-tied, bound and gagged. He had to come up with something else. And he needed for them to pay attention.

In the kitchen, they were nibbling at the cookies. In the sink were the burned remains of two dish towels. Gabby waved to him. "You've got to try these, chocolate chip and yummy."

Clearly, she was the leader. If he convinced Gabby that there was danger, Charlotte would do whatever she said. Keeping his voice low so he wouldn't yell, he said, "I want to talk to you. Alone."

"Something wrong?"

"Now."

"Sure." She patted Charlotte on the arm. "Why don't you make some of that lemonade?"

In her high heels, Gabby strolled past him, went down the hallway, stopped beside the staircase with the shattered gargoyle on the newel post and faced him. "You look mad."

Initially, he hadn't intended to tell her about the boot

print because he didn't want to frighten her. He'd changed his mind. A healthy dose of fear might be just what she needed. "I found a footprint down the road along the fence line. It's evidence that someone was spying on the house last night."

"Spying?" Her eyes opened wide, and then she looked down as though she was unable to face the truth. Her thick black lashes formed crescents on her smooth cheeks. "Are you sure?"

"Evidence." He repeated the word. "I saw footprints."

"Do you think it was a treasure hunter?"

"I don't know. Last night, there was a watcher. During the memorial service, there was a break-in. It's enough to make me think that you and Charlotte aren't safe here."

When she looked up at him, her dark eyes shone with the most appealing light he'd ever seen. The kick-ass city girl was gone, replaced by a woman who was softer, gentler and a little bit scared. "I shouldn't have come here."

"This isn't your fault."

"I don't know how to deal with this kind of threat. I can't call 911. It doesn't do much good to run because there's no place to hide in all this open land. I can't use a gun. Last night, I was barely able to escape from Charlotte."

"If you listen to me, I can show you what to do."

"Remember me? The girl who's afraid of horses?" Her full lips lifted into a half smile. "I can't do it. This isn't my world."

He should have been glad that she realized she didn't belong in the mountains. It would save him a truckload of grief if he said goodbye and sent her on her way. But he didn't want her to leave, not like this. "I didn't think you were a quitter."

"I'm not." She straightened her shoulders. "I drove four long miserable days to get here. You think that was easy?"

"Nope."

"The smart thing would be to talk to the lawyer, get the estate settled and back to Brooklyn. In the meantime, I could stay at a motel."

"You could," he said.

"But I came here to find out more about myself, my family and Michelle. I want to know who she was and why she stayed here. My brother and I are the last of the Rousseaus. How can I turn my back on my heritage?"

"So you're not quitting."

She tossed her head and stuck out her chin. Her vulnerability transformed into rock-hard stubbornness. "I didn't say that."

"Then you're staying."

"I didn't say that, either." With her index finger, she jabbed at his chest. "You should stop jumping to conclusions."

He caught hold of her wrist. "It's not my fault, either."

When she tried to yank her hand back, he held on. On her heels, she stumbled toward him. Her face was inches away from his. And then she kissed him.

The brush of her lips against his was so unexpected that he didn't quite believe it had happened. At the same time, her kiss had a profound effect. It changed everything.

Chapter Five

It had only been a chaste little kiss. Not really a kiss at all; Gabby had only touched his mouth with hers. The last time she'd kissed a guy like that was when she was seven years old and Jimmy Franzini had dared her to do a flip off the monkey bars in the school playground. She did it. Then she kissed him.

When she was seven, she'd felt triumphant. *So there, Jimmy Franzini.* Right now, as she leaned against the wall in the entryway of the Roost, her heart was dancing a tango, and she couldn't swallow. Zach Sheffield was most definitely not a seven-year-old boy. He was one of the most virile men she'd ever met, and he wasn't going to let her skip away into the playground without consequences. Should she apologize? No way, she wasn't sorry. The best thing was to act like it never happened.

But when she took a step toward the kitchen, he slipped his arm around her waist and pulled her snug against his chest. There was no point in struggling; he was too strong, all muscle. More importantly, she didn't want to break away. The heat from his body sparked a fire that raced through her blood. Her chin tilted up, and she gazed into his blue eyes. He kissed her hard enough to take her breath away. When his tongue penetrated her mouth, she actually felt a little bit woozy as though she was melting.

He ended the kiss and stepped back. "Are you ready to listen to me now?"

"Uh-huh."

She looked up at him and blinked. Though she was never at a loss for words, all she could do was stare with a stupefied gaze. A kiss like that deserved a comment. She had to say something. "Zach?"

"What?"

"Next time, take off your hat."

As she followed him back to the kitchen where Charlotte was peering into the side of the stainless steel toaster, trying to see her reflection, Gabby struggled to make sense of what had just happened. His kiss was incredible. In her experience, which wasn't all that extensive, she had to rank it in the top ten, maybe the top three or even number one. But did it mean anything? There was physical chemistry between them; she'd felt it from the start. But the differences between them were too vast to calculate.

Even though she'd implied that she wasn't a quitter and would stay at the Roost, that decision wasn't firm. It was just as likely that she'd get her car serviced and head back to Brooklyn, where she belonged. How could she stay here with the threat of imminent danger and bad guys watching the house? For the moment, she knew only one thing for sure: Zach was in charge. She was willing to let him take the lead. For now.

"Here's what we're going to do," he said. "We need to go through the whole house to check on overall security. Then we'll talk about procedures in case of a break-in."

"Okay," Charlotte said. "Want some lemonade?"

Something cold to douse the flames raging inside her? "Perfect."

Gabby chugged half the tall glass of lemonade while Zach went to a door at the rear of the large kitchen. He twisted the key in the lock. "We'll start here."

"You're going to be surprised," Charlotte said to her. "The house is bigger than it looks in photographs and from the road. The first Roost was built by the Frenchman and his wife in the 1800s."

Gabby's common sense had returned enough for her to comment. "But this kitchen looks completely modern."

"It's new," Charlotte said. "The front part of the house was built in the 1950s. Michelle had it renovated a couple of times, including a recent update of the kitchen. It's basically a two-story with five bedrooms upstairs."

"Michelle didn't move out here until the sixties," Gabby said, recalling a bit of family history. "Who owned the Roost before that?"

"I think the property has always belonged to the Rousseau family, but it was vacant for a long time and fell into disrepair."

"Why did they move back?"

Zach explained, "After World War II, Aspen began to develop a world-wide reputation as a ski resort, and the property values skyrocketed. The Roost is especially attractive because you've got a good well and your family owns the water rights. One of your relatives sensed a good deal and hired a contractor to build the two-story. I think the first plan was to sell, but they moved back in."

He pushed the door from the kitchen open. "This center area isn't the oldest part of the house. It was added on when the family got bigger. At one time, this area was a kitchen, living room and bedrooms. Michelle had it gutted, leaving only the essential support beams and outer walls. She turned it into a studio."

She followed him onto a small landing and down three stairs to Michelle's art studio—an open space that was nearly as wide as the two-story house it was attached to. If it was possible to fall in love with a room, Gabby was smitten. The ceiling peaked in the center. There were so many skylights and windows that it was unnecessary to turn on the overhead lights. In one corner was a potter's wheel. One entire wall was waist-high storage cabinets. A double-wide garage door had been installed, probably to allow large projects to be easily moved in and out.

Nearest the house were the remnants of a former kitchen—a fridge, double sink and plenty of counter space. Though the art supplies had been cleaned up and put away, paint spatters outlined the work areas.

Two freestanding gas fireplaces provided heat, but neither was turned on, leaving a chill in the air and a sense of vacancy. Gabby felt a pang of regret that she'd never really known her great-aunt. This had been the place where Michelle did her creative work. Now the easel in the center of the room stood empty.

Daphne trotted across the tiled floor to the easel, sniffed around and settled down beside the stool. Charlotte squatted down beside the dog and scratched behind her ears. "I miss her, too."

"Daphne used to come over all the time," Zach said. "She'd sit in that very spot and watch as Michelle worked."

"She remembers her friend." Gabby was touched. "You told me that border collies were smart."

"With great instincts. I always have the feeling that she sees and hears things that I don't."

She was surprised to hear Zach talking about feelings.

Maybe their kiss had loosened him up. She opened one of the cabinets and found several blank canvases. "What happened to Michelle's paintings?"

"She'd been clearing things out for a while," Charlotte said. "Her agent picked up the last few after she died."

Gabby had heard that the work of a deceased artist went up in value. "Her agent?"

"Harrison Osborne. He owns an art gallery in Aspen and handled most of Michelle's inventory and sales."

Gabby made a mental note to contact Mr. Osborne. Those last paintings might be worth a lot. She closed the storage cabinet, moved back toward the center of the studio and slowly rotated in a full circle. "This is an amazing space. The natural light is wonderful, and there's so much room to spread out. I'm beginning to understand why my great-aunt loved it here."

"It's kind of a shame," Charlotte said, "that the studio won't be used by another artist."

"It would work just as well for a fashion designer."

Gabby could easily visualize work areas for her two sewing machines and cutting table. If she added a couple of racks, there would be plenty of room to hang her designs. Her dressmaker dummies hadn't been able to fit in the car, and she'd sold them to another designer in Brooklyn. No problem. She could buy new ones. In the meantime, she'd recruit Charlotte as a model. The studio was big enough that she could use part of the space as a runway to see how her designs moved.

Ideas burst inside her head like popcorn in the microwave. She hadn't been this excited in a long time. Ever since she and her friends had lost the lease to their boutique, her inspiration had been lagging. Sure, she had business—there was always work for a good seamstress who could do alterations, but she hadn't felt like creating anything new. The world of fashion had kicked her butt. The scene was too competitive, and she was tired of being rejected.

Working in this studio, she might tap into the energy that had made her great-aunt into a successful artist. Gabby didn't aspire to the heights of haute couture, but she wanted to make a living doing something she loved.

"Too many windows," Zach said as he prowled the perimeter. "Plus four separate exits, including the garage door. The studio offers too many access points for an intruder. Until we're certain there's no threat, the door to this studio remains locked. Do both of you understand?"

"I don't get it," Charlotte said. "Yesterday, you didn't think there was danger."

"Changed my mind," he said. "Let's keep going."

Gabby pulled herself away from her dreams. "There's more?"

He crossed the room to another door beside the garage door. This one wasn't locked. "If we had a bird's-eye view of the floor plan, you'd see the two-story front house attached to the studio, which hooks up to the old house through this door. When the Roost was operating as a cattle ranch, they used this space as a bunkhouse for the ranch hands."

"Was this the original structure?"

He nodded. "Some of it was built in the 1870s."

"I almost never went back there." Charlotte joined him. She was walking with an almost normal gait, getting used to her new strappy shoes. "Sometimes, I'd find Michelle in the old house, just sitting there."

"Did she say why she'd go there?" Gabby asked.

"Something about being closer to her family." Her voice lowered. "I think she was talking to ghosts."

Gabby wondered if she'd hear the same ghostly whispers from her long-ago ancestors. This had been the home of Louis Rousseau, the Frenchman, with his gold hoop earring and his Sioux wife.

"Nobody has lived here in years," Zach said. "I told Michelle that the upkeep on this part of the house wasn't worth the effort, but she was attached to it. She kept the place in decent shape, replacing broken windows and shoring up the walls that were battered by years of snowstorms and high winds."

Gabby stepped through the door and into another century. Her ancestors had built these walls. They had peered through these windows and slept beneath this ceiling.

She shivered. The studio had been chilly. The old house was downright cold, even though the sun was shining and the temperature on this June morning was in the seventies. When Zach flipped a light switch, nothing happened.

"The electricity must be disconnected," he said.

Ghosts preferred darkness. Long shadows stretched across the floor and onto the old, dusty furniture. On one wall was a huge rock fireplace. A stale odor hung in the air, and Gabby rubbed her nose to get rid of the nasty smell. She wasn't sure that she liked this part of the house. While the studio had been bright and filled with positive energy, the original Roost was creepy. She could almost believe that mysterious secrets were hidden back here.

When her eyes became accustomed to the dim light, she followed Zach into another room. Though the Roost had been maintained, it was obvious that nobody lived here. In one room, several cardboard boxes were scattered on the floor. They seemed to be full of rags and old clothes.

The kitchen was disgusting. Major appliances had been removed, leaving filthy spots on the ancient linoleum. Drawers hung open. The shelves were mostly bare except for a thick coat of dust. Years of cooking smoke and grease had permeated wallpaper that had once been beige with orange lilies.

Gabby pulled her arms close to her side. She didn't want to touch anything. This was one of the worst messes she'd ever seen, and that included a former boyfriend's one-room basement apartment inhabited by cockroaches as big as your fist. "I'm with you, Zach. I think this part of the Roost should be torn down."

"What about the treasure map?" Charlotte asked. "If it's hidden anywhere, it should be in here."

"Did the burglars come through this part of the house when they broke in? Did they search in here?"

"No," Charlotte reluctantly admitted. "And they took electronic stuff that they could resell."

That crime sounded like a common theft, just a couple of criminals taking advantage of a vacant house. She was beginning to think they had nothing to worry about from treasure hunters.

"In here," Zach called out.

In a small bedroom, he stood beside a torn curtain and broken window. The lower pane of glass had been shattered near the latch, which had been unfastened. The casement window was open. Though she couldn't actually see footprints, it was obvious that the coating of dust on the floor had been disturbed

An intruder had entered here. The shards of glass below the window frame were tangible evidence, which meant Zach was right. There was a threat.

"Charlotte, can you tell if anything is missing?"

She shook her head. "I don't even know what's back here. We need to get flashlights and come back to investigate."

"Or," Gabby said, "we could call the police."

"Why bother?" Charlotte frowned. "The last time the sheriff was here, he didn't find anything."

"No fingerprints? No trace evidence?"

"Trace evidence," Zach said, "like the fibers and microscopic specks they find in the television shows."

She realized it was unlikely. "Doesn't hurt to look."

He took his cell phone from his pocket. "I'm putting in a call to the sheriff, but I doubt he's going to find anything to put under a microscope."

Pitkin County wasn't the world Gabby was accustomed to. Break-ins like this happened all the time in Brooklyn, but there were also investigations and cops and forensic teams. She was beginning to realize that out here in the back country, they were pretty much on their own.

Chapter Six

Three hours later, Gabby dropped off her car with a me-chanic Zach said she could trust. Though she didn't have the money to spend on servicing, the car needed help. It took a jump to get started and the clunking noise had turned into a metallic-sounding whine—a real fingernails-on-blackboard sound—whenever she turned left. Waving goodbye to her unhappy hatchback, she climbed into the passenger seat of Zach's truck and fastened her seat belt.

This was the first time they'd been alone since their kiss. She wouldn't mind talking about that moment, but there wasn't much to say. She couldn't explain her first impulse to plant one on him, and she was still recover-ing from the heart-stopping hotness when he'd kissed her back. Gabby opted for a less-difficult topic. "Do you think Charlotte is going to be okay at the house?"

"She's not by herself," he reminded her. "Rhoda and Daphne are with her. And Sheriff Burton is on the way."

Over three hours had passed since they discovered the break-in. The sheriff wasn't exactly rushing to the scene of the crime, but she didn't complain. Things worked on a different schedule here.

Last night when she'd been driving near this area, the rain had kept her from noticing the rugged hills, snow-capped peaks and clear blue sky. Every view was worthy of a picture postcard. The natural beauty almost made up for the inconvenience of living here. Almost. It had taken nearly forty-five minutes to drive to the mechanic on the outskirts of Basalt. "How far are we from Aspen?"

"About half an hour," he said. "From here, it's mostly uphill. There's a two-thousand-foot difference in elevation between Basalt and Aspen."

"How high are we?"

"Aspen is about eight thousand feet. If we stay on this road, we'll go higher, hitting Independence Pass and the Continental Divide."

"A divide?" She tried to visualize a map of the United States. "Shouldn't a continental divide be in the middle of the continent?"

"It's an invisible line that divides the watershed. On the western side of the mountains, water flows to the Pacific. On the east, it goes toward the Gulf of Mexico."

As a person who'd spent most of her life at sea level in Brooklyn, she'd never given a single thought to watershed. "I've never been this high."

"The air is thinner. If you're feeling tired, you might blame it on the altitude."

There hadn't been time to feel tired. Since her arrival in Colorado, she'd been shot at, ridden a horse, been kissed by a gorgeous cowboy and discovered a break-in. Now she was on her way to conduct serious business in Aspen with Jason Fox, her great-aunt's attorney. She'd changed into a sedate business suit in black linen, which seemed appropriate for discussing her great-aunt's will.

She hoped there wouldn't be problems at this meeting. Mr. Fox had assured her that she and her brother were Michelle's primary beneficiaries as long as they fulfilled a few simple terms. But he hadn't seen fit to outline those terms, and that worried her. If there was a financial component or she had to hire a lawyer of her own, she couldn't handle it. Her credit cards were maxed, and her life savings were mini. And what would happen if she decided to sell the Roost?

No point in worrying. Until she knew what was up, she'd just have to trust the Universe. As the truck climbed higher, she turned toward Zach. He was a puzzle she might be able to solve. His conversation had expanded beyond the one syllable responses, but he wasn't an open book when it came to talking about himself. Hoping to pry out a few details, she asked, "How did you get to be a rodeo star?"

"I'm pretty good at roping. And I can stay on board a horse that's trying to pitch me off his back."

"A bucking bronco." She'd seen the movies. Finally, this was something she knew about. "And you have to stay on for eight seconds. I'd like to see that."

"You're in luck. There's going to be a small rodeo in Snowmass next week."

"Are you going to ride?"

"I'll be a judge." He didn't sound happy about that job. "I'll be shaking hands, smiling and handing out prizes."

"Why did you quit?"

"It was time."

"Do you miss the competition?"

"Nope."

Oh, swell, they were back to the one-word responses. She guessed there was more to the story of his rodeo career. He must have had fans and fame and all the other perks that went with being a popular athlete. "You'll probably see a lot of people you know."

"I'm a judge. That's all."

"Well, judging should be good promotion for your ranch."

"That's what Rhoda says when she signs me up for these things."

Maybe the way to get Zach talking was to focus on other people, like his housekeeper. "How did you meet Rhoda?"

"Through a friend of a friend."

"She told me that you showed her what to do."

"Not really."

She felt him shutting down, retreating into himself. "She said that you trained her the way you train your horses. Since you probably don't use a bridle and reins, how did you do it? And why? You could have hired someone who had experience."

His jaw tightened as though he was physically holding back. "It's complicated."

"I want to know," she said, "in case you're planning to use the same training techniques on me."

"Have you ever heard of a mustang?"

"The car?"

"The horse," he said. "Mustangs are wild horses that used to range free across the open prairies. According to legend, they might be harnessed but would never truly be tamed. I think of you as a mustang."

"A horse?"

"That can't be tamed."

"I'm going to take that as a compliment."

She eyed him suspiciously. Had he kissed her as part of a program to control her? To show her who was boss? Zach played the role of the strong, silent type, but he wasn't naive or innocent. *Complicated* was a good word to describe him.

When they drove into Aspen, she was disappointed;

the village wasn't as glamorous as she'd been led to expect. The streets were clean, the landscaping nicely tended and the modern hotels and condos blended very well with stone and brick buildings that were much older. But this place looked like dozens of other ski towns. "What makes Aspen such a big deal?"

Zach pushed his cowboy hat back on his forehead. "Did you happen to notice the view?"

The town nestled in the Roaring Fork Valley and was surrounded by forested hills and ski runs. In the distance were peaks that towered higher than ten Empire State Buildings. "Okay, this is spectacular scenery, but I was interested in something other than trees and rocks. I thought this was one of the most expensive places in the country and everybody who lived here was a billionaire."

"If you're in the market for a ten-million-dollar chalet, I could take you on a tour of Starwood." There was a glimmer of irritation in his sexy blue eyes. "Why do you care?"

"Marketing." Her research before she left Brooklyn told her that Aspen had its share of high-end designers like Gucci and Prada. Ralph Lauren even had a home here. But there were other shops that didn't sound so exclusive. If she could get her designs into a couple of places on consignment, she might be able to make a living. "I need to find a place where I can sell my clothes."

"And you want to figure out how much you can charge."

"It's called capitalism." She wasn't a natural businesswoman, and she really had to think about how to make a profit. "Don't worry. I'm not planning to cheat anybody."

"I didn't say you were."

"You gave me that look."

"What look?"

"Disapproving," she said. "As if you think I'm a big

city person who wants to take advantage of the locals. Not true. Sure, I've sold original wedding gowns with tons of lace and embroidery for over a thousand dollars because the handwork was intensive and it took me weeks to get it right. But I've also peddled silk-screened T-shirts from a sidewalk stand for ten bucks apiece. So don't accuse me of trying to scam my customers."

"Fine."

She paused to take a breath. She hadn't intended to go off on a tirade, but she couldn't stop herself. Where did he get off by judging her? "If anything, I don't set my price point high enough. I'm worth more."

"I get it."

"Do you? From the first moment we met, you've been looking down on me and disapproving. Do you think I'm trying to run a con game?"

He pulled up to the curb outside a three-story building in weathered brick and turned off the engine. "Can I talk now?"

"Please do."

"You're right, Gabby. I didn't have high expectations for you." His voice was calm and measured. When he focused his attention entirely on her, the rest of the world seemed to fade away. "Family was important to Michelle, and you never bothered to visit, not even when she was ailing. Then you find out you're an heiress, and you come running. But I think there's more to you."

"More what?" she demanded.

He reached over and rested his hand on top of hers. Like his voice, his touch soothed her. "When you gave that little speech, I could almost hear Michelle's voice. You've got her fire and her grit. I don't think you're a bad person or a con woman."

"Well, I certainly hope not because—"

"I'm not done talking yet. There's one more thing I want to say." He squeezed her hand. "In my opinion, you're worth a whole lot more than you even realize."

His thoughtful compliment floored her. The man didn't say much but when he spoke, it was good. Once again, he had rendered her speechless.

"Hop out," he said, bringing both hands back to the steering wheel. "This isn't a legal parking space. I'll drop you off and catch up with you in the lawyer's office."

She climbed out of the truck, grabbed her imitation Birkin bag in fake crocodile and walked up the sidewalk to the building's entrance. Her apprehension about meeting with Fox had been replaced by a sense of well-being, and this positive feeling was entirely due to Zach. He thought she was like Michelle. Though gritty and fiery didn't make for a description she would have chosen, she appreciated being compared to a strong, successful artist who was *worth more than she realized.*

On the second floor, she entered an office with a brass plaque beside the door that said: Wesley, Warren and Fox, Attorneys at Law. The wainscoted reception area was furnished with expensive leather furniture and dark wood coffee tables, which were probably supposed to make clients feel that Wesley, Warren and Fox were solid, old-fashioned and prosperous. The young man behind the front desk didn't look like he belonged here. His attire—a camel jacket and untucked shirt—were too casual. As soon as she entered, he bounded out from behind his desk and offered his hand. "I'm Kevin. You must be Gabriella Rousseau."

She nodded. "I am."

"Sorry for your loss. I liked Michelle."

"Thank you."

"So, I guess you'll be living at the Roost."

"I haven't made that decision yet."

Kevin pushed his long red hair off his forehead and flashed a whitened smile. "My uncle said to show you right in. Can I get you something to drink? Coffee or tea, maybe something a little stronger?"

Why would she want a strong drink? Was there something he wasn't telling her? "Coffee, black."

He ushered her through an office area where a couple of people were working with computers. The door to Jason Fox's office stood ajar. Kevin showed her inside a large room with an array of legal texts on one wall and a large west-facing window. The afternoon sunlight poured across a carved oak desk and onto the blue-and-beige patterned Aubusson carpet.

The elder Fox was also a redhead. Unlike his nephew, his thinning hair was combed back from his forehead. He was dressed in a classy three-piece suit, and the cuffs of his cream-colored shirt were monogrammed. His pale blue eyes assessed her as he shook her hand and offered the standard condolences.

He directed her to a brown leather sofa and took a seat in the matching armchair. The window light shining behind him made it difficult for her to read his expression, and she suspected that the positioning was purposeful. He could see her more clearly than she could see him.

After they exchanged pleasantries about her trip across the country and Kevin delivered her coffee with a wink and a smirk, Gabby's apprehensions returned. She took a sip of the delicious French Roast. The time had come to cut to the chase. "When we talked about Michelle's will, you mentioned a few simple terms that I would have to fulfill."

"You and your brother, Daniel. Unfortunately, I still

haven't been able to locate him. In my position as executor of Michelle's will, I had wanted to talk with both of you."

"That's not going to happen." She angled her head in an attempt to see him better. "What are these terms?"

"Before we get into specifics," he said as he rose from his chair and went to the desk, "I'd like for you to review the holdings of Michelle's estate."

He placed a thick folder and a bound portfolio on the coffee table in front of her. It would take hours to go through these pages. Gabby thought of her own meager belongings; she could write down everything she owned on the back of an envelope. "All this?"

"In the folder are legal papers, including deeds, insurance policies, agreements and tax documents as well as a checkbook showing the final payments I've made as her executor. The portfolio deals with her artwork, and I'm sorry to say that it's not complete. I'm still waiting for her agent, Harrison Osborne, to report on other paintings that are out on consignment."

Nervously, she opened the portfolio. The first several pages provided an accounting tally of paintings and sales. Farther back in the book were photographs of artwork and indications of what was happening to them. "I noticed other paintings in the house. Should those be included in this inventory?"

Fox leaned back in his chair and steepled his fingers. "Some of the art in the house has already been cataloged. There was one oil painting that she wanted you to own. It's called *Girl with Book and Mirror.*"

She remembered the painting in her bedroom. "I think I know which one it is."

"Congratulations, it's yours. Osborne will provide you with the authentication. If you decide to sell, I suggest you go through him since he is the foremost expert on Michelle Rousseau."

If Michelle had wanted her to have that particular painting, there must be a reason. "I'd never sell a keepsake like that."

"I wasn't aware that you and your great-aunt were so close."

His condescending tone bordered on a sneer, and she figured that Fox was another person who didn't approve of the way she had treated her great-aunt. His judgment was unfair. After all, Michelle had been the adult and Gabby the child during most of their relationship. And Michelle was the one who had abandoned Brooklyn. Definitely unfair, but Gabby wouldn't defend herself. She wished things had been different between Michelle and herself, and she didn't owe the attorney an explanation of her family dynamic.

When Kevin showed Zach into the office, she almost cheered. At least, she had one person on her side in what was beginning to feel like a war between her and Fox. Zach made an impressive ally. Not only was he a big guy but he was cool enough to be intimidating. In his white, Western-style shirt with pearl buttons and his navy blue sport jacket, he was the very picture of cowboy chic. Instead of sitting beside her on the sofa, Zach took a position beside the desk that kept him from facing the glare from the window.

"I'd rather stand," he said. "I've been sitting in the truck all the way over here."

"Very well." Fox scowled as he returned to his chair and turned to her. "Shall we start with the insurance policies?"

"It's going to take a while to go through all this paperwork. I'd like to hear about the terms I'll be required to fulfill."

"Of course."

Curious, she asked, "Why didn't you explain these terms when we first spoke on the phone?"

"I was bound by the will. Your great-aunt forbade the mention of her requirements until you were here in Colorado."

"Why?"

"Let's just say that she had some unusual ideas." Though she couldn't clearly see Fox, she heard a smug tone in his voice, and she sensed that the ax was about to fall.

Bracing herself, she said, "I want to know."

"Your great-aunt had a strong sense of her heritage, and she wanted the Roost to remain in the hands of a Rousseau. She arranged for a monthly stipend to be paid from her estate for the care of the property. I can't give you an accurate statement of the amount because we haven't determined the final figures."

"How about a ballpark number?" Gabby asked.

"It would be sufficient to pay monthly bills and provide for basic living expenses."

So far, so good. Even if she didn't stay at the Roost, a caretaker would need that stipend. "What else?"

"In order for you to inherit the estate, Michelle stipulated that you and/or your brother, if we can ever locate him, must agree to live at the Roost for the period of three years. You cannot be absent for more than two months per year."

She'd never heard of anything like this. "Can she do that? Tell me where to live? When I can come and go?"

"The will is very specific. Of course, you can fight it.

These terms are odd, somewhat Draconian. But a legal dispute would take years to work through the court system."

Confused, she looked toward Zach for some kind of reassurance. He shook his head. No help from that direction. "What if I refuse?"

"If you choose not to live there, you forfeit your claim on the estate. It will be sold, and the proceeds will go to Sarah Bentley's Forest Preservation Society."

"Who?"

"Ms. Bentley runs a nonprofit organization dedicated to protecting and managing the local flora and fauna."

And why should she receive the bulk of the estate? What was going on here? "I don't understand."

Fox rose from his chair and joined her on the leather sofa. When he took her hand and held it between both of his, she felt trapped and threatened at the same time. Maybe she should walk away before it was too late. Rule number three when confronting a mugger: run like hell.

"It's all right," Fox assured her. Like his nephew, his teeth were exceptionally white; she imagined those fangs sinking into her neck and sucking her blood. "I'll do all that I can to help you."

"Can you rewrite the will?"

"I'm afraid not. I promise that you won't walk away empty-handed. However, in order to participate financially in the bulk of your great-aunt's legacy, you must live at the Roost."

She didn't like it. But she didn't have much choice.

Chapter Seven

On the street outside the attorney's office, Zach sucked down a breath of fresh air. He'd been stifling while he watched Fox use his wiles to manipulate Gabby into a corner. The lawyer was like a rattlesnake that had cornered a baby rabbit and was playing with his prey. "I don't trust that guy. He's up to something."

"Like dictating the terms of my life," Gabby said. Her arms were filled with the fat legal file and the portfolio with the inventory of artwork. "Is it possible that Fox invented those crazy terms? It doesn't seem like something Michelle would do."

He wasn't so sure. "She was really interested in the Rousseau family heritage. I know she did research online to trace your ancestors. Did you know there was a famous artist named Rousseau?"

"Henri Rousseau," she said, shifting her burden from one arm to the other. "He was a Postimpressionist. And there was also a famous philosopher. Those are the names that pop up when you do a search for Rousseau, but our family isn't related to either of them. I guess that Rousseau is a fairly common name in France, like Russell."

Taking the hefty file and portfolio from her, he directed her to the right. "Let's get something to eat."

"Kevin offered me a strong drink as soon as I came into the office. I wish I'd taken it."

Getting drunk wasn't a solution, as he well knew. But he understood her desire to escape from the complications that had been literally laid at the doorstep of the Roost. "I don't blame you for being overwhelmed."

"Here's the crazy part. I was seriously considering moving here. Michelle's old studio at the Roost would make a perfect workroom for my designs and sewing. And there really isn't any reason to go back to Brooklyn. No boyfriend. No job worth keeping. And I gave my share of the apartment I was renting to my roommate, whose fiancé moved in with her."

"This might be the time for you to change location."

"That's exactly what I was thinking, but not anymore." She dug into her purse and took out a pair of sunglasses. "When Fox said living at the Roost was mandated by the will, I wanted to run, to be anywhere but here. I hate being told what I have to do."

"Why am I not surprised?"

Midway down the next block, they entered a casual restaurant that featured thirty-two varieties of burger, ranging from tofu to steak tartare. At half past three in the afternoon, there were only a few other patrons, and Zach chose a table for four where there was room enough to open the file folder and take a peek inside. His suspicions of Fox made him wonder how the attorney might benefit financially based on Gabby's decisions.

After they'd ordered—a portobello mushroom sandwich and draft beer for her and a cheeseburger and soda for him—he flipped through the papers until he found a copy of the actual will. The document was over twenty-five pages, single-spaced and written in lawyer language that made it difficult to skim. He noticed that Michelle's initials were on every page.

Gabby took off her sunglasses and leaned across the table toward him. "What are you looking for?"

"An indication of what Fox hopes to gain."

"If he sells the place, there's probably some kind of commission." She tilted her head as though she could read the fine print upside down. "He might have made some kind of side deal with the Forest Preservation lady."

"Sarah Bentley? Not likely." He'd met Sarah on a committee that planned local rodeo events. Her concerns matched his own: making sure the animals were treated humanely. "She's not the kind of person who would get involved with shady business."

"What was her connection with Michelle?"

"I don't know."

"Did Michelle ever talk to you about this plan to make me live at the Roost?"

"Not in so many words." He remembered many evenings when he and Michelle sat on her porch and watched the sunset. The subject of family seldom arose. Zach had cut all ties with his parents back in Wyoming, didn't know if they were dead or alive and didn't really give a damn. Michelle had confided a secret he wasn't ready to share with Gabby.

"Did she ever say why she settled here?" she asked.

He pieced together other bits of conversation into a narrative that didn't reveal too much. "She used to talk about being a rebel—an artist who lived to express herself. Then she'd laugh and say, 'We all did crazy things in the sixties.'"

"I don't think Michelle ever stopped doing crazy things, and I guess that served her well as an artist." Gabby sipped her beer and licked her lips. "But it doesn't explain why she set up these conditions for me to live at the Roost."

He saw hints of Michelle in the way she cocked her chin and the intensity in her dark eyes. But Gabby wasn't a rebel who would take off across the country on a whim. "Maybe she wanted to give you a chance to follow your dream."

"Then she should have consulted with me first. My dreams start with getting more schooling. Then I'd take an internship in Paris or Milan."

"Exotic places."

"The fashion capitals of the world," she said, "but I can't complain about not being exposed to the latest trends. I lived so close to Manhattan, twenty minutes away on the subway. During Fashion Week, I sneaked into more events than most people see in a lifetime."

"Did you ever think about being a model?"

"Not possible," she said. "I'm a few inches too short and definitely not a size zero."

"You're pretty enough."

A huge smile spread across her face. "So are you. You'd make a terrific model."

Parading around in dress-up clothes sounded like the worst kind of punishment. "I'm just a cowboy."

"That's why you'd be great. Women love cowboys."

He was saved from further speculation when their food arrived. As he dug into his burger, he watched her. You could learn a lot about a woman from how she ate. Gabby had ordered a feminine choice with the mushroom sandwich, but she wasn't afraid to pile on the pickles and tomatoes, pick up the whole thing and open her mouth wide to take a chomp. She attacked her food with the kind of gusto he'd seen in her before. She definitely wasn't shy. As she chewed, she moaned with pleasure. It was an animal sound that he associated more with the bedroom than the lunch table. Not particularly ladylike. She swabbed her French fries through a glob of ketchup and popped them into her mouth. Not ladylike at all.

"You're staring," she said.

"I like to see a woman who enjoys her food."

"My manners aren't the greatest. Back in Brooklyn, I usually grab something from a corner bodega or a fruit stand and eat on the run."

"Do you cook?"

"Not without setting fire to the dish towels." She washed down the fries with a swig of her beer. "That's one of the great things about living in a big city. You're never far from a place that serves something yummy. And there's so much variety—Italian, Asian, Mexican, Greek. I love all the different tastes. How about you?"

He looked down at his cheeseburger. "I'm a meat-and-potatoes guy. On occasion, I'll try something different."

"And I like nothing better than a big juicy steak."

He could tell she was fibbing, trying to fit in with her new surroundings. He doubted she could change that much. She came from a different world. At her core, Gabby was a city woman who dreamed of visiting Paris and ate sushi with chopsticks.

Despite their differences, he wasn't willing to step aside and let her get railroaded. If anything, she needed his protection more than a cowgirl who was born and bred in the mountains. Glancing over at the file folder, he said, "Don't worry. We'll figure out what Fox is after."

She wiped the corner of her mouth with her napkin. "I barely had a chance to check out the numbers, but I noticed in the art portfolio that Michelle's work was selling for big bucks. The real wealth in her estate might not be the property. It could be her paintings."

"You're right." He hadn't considered the artwork. Living so close to Michelle and watching her work, he'd come to take her art for granted. "While we're in town, we should pay a visit to her agent."

Their meeting with Fox couldn't have been much worse. He hoped Osborne would be more helpful.

THE OSBORNE GALLERY wasn't easy to find. Instead of being located among the high-rent retail boutiques, the gallery was on the outer edge of town. If there hadn't been a sign by the edge of the road, Zach would have thought this place was a private residence with an overabundance of weird lawn sculptures. He parked the truck in a small gravel lot where there were two other vehicles.

Gabby unsnapped her seat belt and peered through the windshield at a huge gray-ish statue that must have been ten feet tall. "What do you think that's supposed to be?"

"Looks like a tree with wings."

"Four sets of wings," she said. "Maybe it's supposed to represent motion, like a tree springing into the air."

Either way, the thing was damn ugly. He shoved open his door. "Let's get this over with. Bring the portfolio."

"Don't forget to lock the doors to the truck. Fox made me promise that I wouldn't lose the legal papers, even if these are only copies."

Under his breath, he muttered, "And we wouldn't want to disappoint Fox."

He'd never been good at dealing with people in authority, especially those who enjoyed lording it over everybody else. More than once, he'd turned down a client who had plenty of money but a nasty attitude. People like them didn't deserve to own horses.

He followed her along the flagstone pathway that wound through several other odd statues to a wide deck outside a good-sized house with a shake-shingle roof. In this area, a property like this would be worth millions. Selling other people's art must be profitable. Rather than walking right in, he pressed the doorbell.

The double doors swung open, framing a tall, thin man with a gray ponytail and a fringed vest that hung down to his knees. He wore shapeless pants that draped over the tops of his sandals. The front of his loose-fitting shirt was open to the waist, showing off a necklace that reminded Zach of a dream catcher.

When Gabby introduced herself, he wrapped his arms around her. "My dear, I've been expecting you."

"Did Mr. Fox tell you I might visit?"

"In my morning meditation, my spirit guide said I would connect with Michelle. I'm Harrison Osborne. Welcome."

"Nice to meet you," she said as she detached herself from his embrace. "And this is Zach Sheffield."

He stuck out his hand to avoid getting hugged. Osborne's eyes were too bright, his palms were sweaty and he kept licking his lips—all symptoms of drug use. Zach had to wonder if the art dealer might have an addiction problem.

Osborne led the way into his gallery, which was bright, well lit and divided with partitions allowing more wall space for hanging paintings. The artwork ranged from detailed landscapes to bold splashes of color. Osborne regarded each with a genuine fondness as though seeing it for the first time. He grabbed Zach's arm and dragged him over to a large canvas filled with zigzag lines. "Do you feel it? The ocean?"

Zach shut him down before he could launch into a sales pitch. "I'm not in the market, and I'm pretty sure I couldn't afford any of these paintings."

Osborne dropped his arm and turned to Gabby. "I don't have any of your great-aunt's work on display because I'm prohibited from selling it until the inventory is complete."

"That's why we're here." Gabby went to a seating area beside a window and placed the portfolio on the coffee table. "What can you tell me about paintings that haven't been listed?"

"No time to talk," Osborne said with an extravagant wave of his hands. "I'm dreadfully busy."

As far as Zach could tell, there was no one else in the gallery and no sign of pressing business. Osborne's claim to be busy was a ruse. He wasn't going to let this guy hustle them out the door without answers. "You probably know that Gabby is Michelle Rousseau's heir. If you want to continue handling her artwork, you might want to make time for us."

"Where are my manners? Would you care for tea?"

Gabby nodded. "That would be lovely."

When Osborne darted through the partitions and disappeared into another part of the house, she whispered, "Did Michelle ever mention him to you?"

"Never."

She flipped open the neatly inventoried portfolio. "It's hard to believe anybody so scattered could put together these tidy lists. He must have an accountant or something."

And they weren't going to learn anything by sitting politely and waiting for Osborne to make another flamboyant appearance. Zach knew better than to let an addict take control of the situation. "Let's see what he's doing."

They picked their way through the artwork to a door in the rear wall that opened into a room with a dining table and chairs. Unlike the bright, clean display area, this was a place where someone lived. On the opposite side of the room, there appeared to be a kitchen. Hearing voices, Zach paused to eavesdrop.

Osborne was talking to another man. His words were rushed. "Why did they come here? I don't need this kind of pressure. It's too much for me."

"Deal with it," the other man said.

"It's so easy for you. If I lose my reputation, I lose everything."

"Then get rid of them."

Chapter Eight

If Gabby had been alone, she would have been terrified. *Get rid of them?* Those words sounded nasty and much too lethal for her to deal with. Luckily, Zach was here. She grabbed his jacket and tugged. In her opinion, it was time to bolt.

But he had a different idea. He shuffled his feet to make the sounds of footsteps on the hardwood floor. Loudly, he said to her, "I think he came back this way."

"What are you doing?" she whispered.

"Making them think we didn't overhear."

When he strode across the dining room, she followed, making sure to keep his large, muscular body between her and the threat. In the kitchen, Osborne stood behind a marble-topped island. The man leaning against the countertop had the thick neck and heavy shoulders of a bodybuilder. His dark hair was cut military style. This was the guy who said that he wanted to get rid of them, but Zach stepped right up to him, introduced himself and asked, "Is that your truck out in front?"

"That's right."

She remembered the clean red truck with a logo stenciled on the door, and a name she didn't recall.

Zach's memory was better. "Ed Striker."

"Right, again."

"We've met before."

"About four years ago," Striker said. "I delivered a couple of horses to your ranch for Adele Berryman."

"I remember." Zach grinned. "Mrs. Berryman had some strange ideas."

Striker didn't grin back, but he nodded. "Yeah, she did."

"Well?" Osborne opened the refrigerator and grabbed a bottle of water and took a long drink from it. "Aren't you gentlemen going to tell us what these strange ideas were?"

"She had a pair of remarkable horses," Zach said, "thoroughbred Arabians, a male and female. Mrs. Berryman called them Angelina and Brad. By all rights, they should have been producing pretty little colts and fillies, but they didn't have an interest in each other. I told Mrs. Berryman that there were a number of places she could go for an insemination procedure, but she had it in her head that there needed to be a natural attraction. And she thought I could help."

Gabby couldn't believe it. "You did sex therapy for a horse couple?"

"I'm not taking credit," Zach said, "but Brad and Angelina have produced two sets of twins in the past four years."

"I'll be damned," Osborne said.

Zach confronted the other man. "What are you doing here, Striker?"

"He does handyman work for me." Osborne took another sip of water and held the bottle to his forehead. Though it wasn't hot, he was perspiring. "Packing and shipping these artworks, especially the sculptures, is difficult, and Striker has a knack for it."

With a body like Striker's, heavy lifting was a given, and she wondered what other skills he might have. She was still having trouble reconciling the neatly organized portfolio with Osborne's flighty personality. "Is Ed also an accountant?"

"Why would you think that?" Osborne asked.

"The catalog of my great-aunt's work is so precise. I expected you to have someone who handled those details."

"I handle all the records myself." Osborne stuck out his skinny chest and preened. "I'm an MBA and trained accountant, which is why my clients stick with me. I make them money."

She revised her first impression of him. The baggy clothes and sandals were a costume he wore to make people think he was artsy-fartsy. Osborne was, in fact, a raging capitalist. "So it's not all about the art?"

"Aren't you a sweet, naive, little thing." He reached over and patted her cheek. "I appreciate the talent, but this is a business."

"Is that what your spirit guide told you?"

"Ouch." He yanked his hand back and looked toward Zach. "She bites."

"Yes, she does."

Actually, she was more comfortable with the MBA version of Harrison Osborne, even if he did want to get rid of her. "Let's skip the tea and go back in the other room. I have some questions."

Striker was already heading for the door. Before he left, he glanced back over his shoulder at Zach, who was still watching him. For a moment, they stared at each other, communicating on a primal male level as though they were a couple of chimps warning each other off. She wanted to believe that Zach won that confrontation, but she wouldn't forget Striker's hostility. The handyman seemed like the most obvious person to stage a break-in at the Roost.

In the display room with the portfolio in front of her on the coffee table, Gabby sat on the sofa. "Mr. Fox said the inventory wasn't complete. Why is that?"

"Give me a break," Osborne said. "It's only been a few weeks, and it's time-consuming to track these things down. Some of the paintings are on display in museums or at schools. Others are in other galleries and haven't sold."

She watched Zach saunter through the gallery and take a position beside one of the front windows. From there, he could see the parking lot and make sure that Striker got into his red truck and drove away. Having Zach on her side gave her the confidence to believe that she might just find her way through this mess and come out the other side in one piece.

She opened the portfolio to the front pages that listed paintings that had been sold and their sale price. "This goes back twenty-five years. There are hundreds of listings."

"That's not an inventory I threw together overnight," Osborne said. "Sales figures need to be updated every year for accounting and for taxes. Michelle had copies."

Gabby made a mental note to search Michelle's office for these records. "How do you keep track of it all?"

Osborne sat cross-legged on the rug opposite her. "When Michelle completes a painting, I fill out a single-page Certificate of Authenticity, signed by her and by me. After the work is purchased, I send the certificate to the new owner and keep a copy for my files as a record."

She flipped through the portfolio to the pages for unsold artworks. Each painting had a photograph and a brief description, including details such as size, title, date and asking price. "Is this the certificate?"

"It's the same information. The original signed certificates for unsold paintings are valuable, and I have them locked away in my safe."

Zach left the window and sat beside her. "You're supposed to turn all that stuff over to the lawyer, right?"

"When I have everything completed, yes."

Leaving the portfolio open on the coffee table, she thumbed through page after page, amazed by her great-aunt's output. "There's a lot in here."

"Michelle was prolific."

Gabby stopped on a page that had information about the painting but no photograph. "Why isn't there a picture?"

Osborne toyed with his necklace and licked his lips. "Michelle told me about these paintings, but I never saw them."

Zach asked, "How do you know they exist?"

"Read the descriptions," he said. "They're very specific, and she wanted a record."

When she leaned forward to read, Zach did the same, moving closer so he could see the page. His thigh brushed against hers. The rough fabric of his jeans rubbed against her skirt and the bare skin above her knee.

With an effort, she concentrated on the written description. Her voice was only a little bit breathless when she said, "This painting is titled *Tarot Arcana VI*. It's only three inches by five—a little bit larger than a playing card."

"I never saw these last five Tarot paintings, numbered VI to X." Osborne scowled at the book. "It's a shame. She did others in the series, and they've acquired a reputation. I know at least three collectors who would bid on these paintings."

"But you haven't seen them," Zach said.

"If I had, I would have insisted on bringing them here. I have a secure storage area, temperature controlled with no windows. That's where I'm holding the rest of Michelle's paintings."

"The ones you took from her studio," Gabby said. "That was probably a good idea."

"It was necessary. You've already had a break-in at the Roost. I shudder to think what might have been stolen." He untangled his legs and got to his feet. "Are we done here?"

"For now, we are." Gabby dug in to her fake Birkin and took out her cell phone. "I have to call to see if my car's ready."

When she turned the phone on, she saw that she had four messages, which she checked, figuring that the car mechanic might have already called. The last name on the message list surprised her. It was Daniel Rousseau. Her brother had finally gotten in touch with her.

DRIVING BACK TOWARD home, Zach kept his eyes trained straight ahead through the windshield, staring at the beginning of sunset and trying not to listen to Gabby's phone conversation with her brother. She was hard to ignore. In the space of five minutes, she'd gone from squeals of laughter to a furious tirade.

He didn't want to be distracted by her family issues when they had more pressing problems, mainly the break-ins at the Roost. That threat was tangible but didn't worry him as much as the unspoken danger he'd felt when they talked to Fox or at their meeting with Osborne. It was clear to Zach that Michelle's estate represented a significant amount of money, and these men wanted to stake their claim.

First, he had to deal with the break-ins. The best way to make sure Gabby and Charlotte were safe was for him to stay overnight at the Roost as a bodyguard. But that solution had dangers of its own; sleeping down the hall from Gabby put him in a precarious position. He couldn't deny that he was attracted to her. Just the thought of her stretched out in her bed started his imagination rolling. What if she heard a sound and called for him, and he responded by running into her bedroom, and she threw her arms around his neck, and he kissed away her fears?

He shouldn't even think about making love to her. They were different people from different worlds, opposite ends of the spectrum. Even if she ended up spending three years at the Roost to fulfill the terms of the will, she'd still be a city girl who hated horses. The idea of them having a relationship was like thinking a coyote might cozy up to a jackrabbit without anybody getting hurt.

"No way, Daniel." She held the phone in front of her face and yelled at it. "I'm not giving you my credit card number. You need to be here. Figure out how to do it by yourself."

When she ended the call, she let go with a curse, one of the few he'd heard from her. Her cheeks flamed bright red as she glanced over at him. "I didn't mean that the way it sounded. I love my brother."

"I can tell."

"Here's the part that really makes me mad. He didn't call me because of the ten million messages I've left for him with people who might have been able to find him. He knew I was looking for him, but did he care? No way."

"Why did he call?"

"He had a message from Fox that said the magic word—*inheritance*. Daniel called me because he thought he could get something for nothing."

"Did Fox tell him the terms?"

"Daniel doesn't care. He told me to take care of the details. Can you believe it? 'Deal with it, Gabby.' And then I should send him his money. Does that sound fair to you?"

"Nope."

She continued, "I don't know why I should expect him to be different. Family means nothing to him. He wasn't there when Aunt Rene died, and he doesn't even remember Michelle's name. All he wants is to grab the money and run."

That description sounded much like Zach's first opinion about Gabby, but he'd come to understand there was more to her. Instead of being solely motivated by greed, she was curious about Michelle and had regrets that they hadn't known each other better. "Is your brother coming here?"

"I hope so." Her gaze dropped to the phone in her lap. "I haven't seen him in years."

"Why's that?"

"He took off with some girl. Then he was in Alaska. Then something else, there was always something else."

Zach was familiar with the pattern. When he first left home, he'd done his share of aimless drifting until he discovered rodeo. For a long time, his family had been the other bronc busters and bull riders.

"We used to be so close," she said. "After my parents died, he sat at the foot of my bed every night until I fell asleep. If he hadn't been there with me, I might never have stopped crying. It was silly, really. I was thirteen and shouldn't have been such a baby."

"It's not childish to miss the people you love."

"I still miss them, especially my mom." She lifted her head. Though she smiled, her dark eyes reflected a deep sadness. "Today has been tough."

"Yep." He knew she hated his one-word responses, but

he didn't have anything to add. Leaving his parents was one of the smartest things he'd ever done.

"But it's not all doom and gloom." She forced a smile. "The mechanic said the repairs to my car won't be expensive. He has to send to Denver for a part and will keep the car for a couple of days, but it's fixable and cheap."

He liked the way she always found a way to focus on the positive. With what he'd seen today, she was going to need that attitude. "We should talk about Osborne."

"He's a strange one. Under the weird clothes and ponytail, he seems to be a sharp businessman. I guess we shouldn't be surprised. After all, Michelle was no fool, and she stuck with Osborne for over twenty years."

"Those missing Tarot paintings worry me," Zach said.

"Me, too. According to Osborne, there are buyers lined up for those pictures. They're valuable. And they're small enough to hide in the Roost. Those Tarot paintings could be the *real* hidden treasure and the *real* reason for the break-ins."

"That means the threat is *real*." Hidden artwork made more sense than the mythical Frenchman's Treasure, but Michelle's little paintings weren't something that could be easily turned into cash. "There aren't many people who'd know what to do with the art, even if they found it."

"Osborne would," she said. "He even knows the buyers. Maybe, after all these years, he's gotten tired of making only a commission on Michelle's work. Maybe he wants the whole enchilada for himself. And he could send his friend Striker to do the dirty business of breaking in and stealing."

"Striker is number one on my list of suspicious persons."

"Here's the part I don't understand," she said. "If Osborne planned to steal the paintings, why did he tell us about them? Why did he record them along with all of Michelle's other work? He could have kept those paintings a secret and sold them on his own. I'd probably never find out about it."

"Michelle might have left a record, maybe a sketch or a note. If we discovered the discrepancy, it would have been hard for him to explain." He had another concern. "Besides, we can't expect rational behavior from Osborne. He's on drugs."

He watched for her reaction. Some people were shocked and appalled by addiction, but Gabby hadn't led a sheltered life. She merely shrugged. "I noticed the sweating and twitching and licking of lips, but there might be another cause."

"Such as?"

"He might be ill. Or he might be having a reaction to some kind of prescription meds."

That was how it started. Zach knew from personal experience how those little pills made you feel better and then became more important and then took over your life. "Why are you defending him?"

"He organized all those listings. That's the opposite of erratic behavior."

A high-functioning addict developed skills for hiding their terrible secrets. Again, experience was Zach's guide. "Think about it this way. A drug habit isn't cheap. Osborne might be desperate for money, desperate enough to take risks in handling Michelle's estate."

When she turned toward him, he could feel her scrutiny. She was studying him, assessing him. "Is there something you're not telling me?"

"Nope."

His addiction to painkillers and to alcohol wasn't a story he was willing to share with anyone outside his twelve-step program. Lucky for him, Rhoda had once been part of that group. If he really needed to spill his guts, she'd listen. And he'd do the same for her.

Gabby didn't need to know. He didn't want to see the disgust in her eyes or, even worse, the sympathy. Nine years ago, he'd hit rock bottom. Since then, he'd been sober. End of story.

"Tomorrow," she said, "we'll need to start searching the house. Now that we know what we're looking for, it might be easier. And I should go through the paperwork in Michelle's office."

"For tonight, you and Charlotte need protection. I'll stay at the Roost."

It was the only way he could be sure that they were safe.

Chapter Nine

At half past nine o'clock, Gabby crawled between the sheets of her queen-size bed at the Roost. She never went to sleep this early, but she was exhausted, maybe the result of the altitude thing Zach had told her about. Being too high made your energy low.

During dinner, she'd barely been able to keep her eyes open while Zach lectured her and Charlotte about being careful and not wandering off to investigate by yourself. He was in his element, taking charge and giving orders. He'd made up a schedule for bodyguard duty. He'd patrol the house until one o'clock. Then Toby Hatch, one of his most trusted employees, would take the next shift.

When he'd introduced Toby, Gabby had managed a weak hello, but the young man barely noticed her. His attention had been riveted on Charlotte, who'd kept up her new look with a fresh coat of glitter makeup and a form-hugging purple dress from Gabby's wardrobe. Charlotte's look would have been far more sophisticated if she hadn't insisted on wearing her dusty cowboy boots. Maybe tomorrow, they'd talk about footwear.

Snuggled under the quilt and blankets, Gabby tried to embrace the quiet of the rural country outside her windows, but she missed the hum of the city. So much was changing. So much had happened today.

She felt like she was standing at the brink of a major life shift and didn't know if the people pushing her toward the edge—people like Fox and Osborne—were friends or enemies. Apart from Rhoda and Charlotte, the only person she trusted was Zach. And she was a long way away from figuring him out. He hadn't really opened up to her. Most of the time, he treated her like an annoyance. The only constant between them seemed to be their mutual physical attraction, which just might be enough. Thinking about him, she smiled and drifted closer to sleep.

It seemed like only a few minutes later when she remembered that she hadn't closed the shades. She groaned. The bed was too comfortable to leave, but she didn't want to be wakened in the morning by sunrise.

She pried one eyelid open. The red digital numbers on the bedside clock showed that it was eleven-thirty. She'd already been asleep for two hours. *Get up and pull the shades.* Moonlight poured through the uncurtained windows. In a few short hours, that soft glow would become a thousand-watt glare.

Forcing herself to move, she leveraged into a sitting position on the bed. Then she saw him. Zach stood by the window, watching her. What?

"Yesterday," he said, "you kissed me."

Her brain struggled to make sense of his appearance. Should she be freaked out that he was in here? Did they need to have a little chat about boundaries? "Technically," she said, "you're wrong. It's not midnight, which means it's still today, technically."

"Fine." He reached for the bedside lamp and turned it on. "This morning, you kissed me."

She threw up her hand to ward off the light. "You kissed me back."

"I'm glad you're awake. I was reading through the legal documents, and I think I know what Fox is up to. We need to talk."

"Now?" She realized that she wasn't wearing much. Her lingerie for tonight was a pale blue satin slip that draped low on her chest. With a yank, she pulled the quilt up to her chin. "You can't just come waltzing into my room."

"But I did."

For once, he wasn't wearing his hat, and his brown hair fell across his forehead. When he grinned, the fine lines at the corners of his eyes deepened. In the glow from the bedside lamp, he seemed more approachable than usual. He looked open, friendly and, of course, gorgeous.

To be honest, she didn't mind that he'd invaded her personal space. In fact, she wanted him to come closer. "Were you spying on me?"

"I knew you were awake."

"That's a little weird, Zach."

"Should I go?"

"Stay." She flung out her arm and caught hold of the sleeve of his soft flannel shirt. When she tugged, he sat on the edge of the bed. "You're here now. We might as well talk."

The front of his brown plaid shirt was unbuttoned and hung open. Underneath, a white V-neck T-shirt gleamed in the lamplight. She wondered if he was still wearing his boots. Did cowboys make love with their boots on?

"The way I figure," he said, "there are two ways Fox can make money from Michelle's estate. The standard procedure is for him to charge his billable hours as executor. But he also gets a commission if you decide not to stay at the

Roost for three years and he handles the sale of the properties with proceeds going to the Forest Preservation Society. By the way, money from the sale of paintings is considered part of the estate and also goes to Sarah Bentley."

Though she was trying to listen, she couldn't make sense of what he was saying. His words jumbled in her mind. As he listed dollar amounts and percentages and other facts that he'd gleaned from the folder of legal papers, she focused on his lips and remembered their first kiss.

He stopped talking. The quiet in her bedroom wrapped around them like a soft, warm blanket.

"Gabby, did you hear me?"

"Give me a quick summary."

"If Fox can get you to move out, he'll make several hundred thousand bucks. Do you understand what that means?"

"I should get my own lawyer?"

"You could, but Fox isn't a fool. I'm sure all his paperwork is in order. That's what worries me."

"Why?" She'd been paying attention well enough to understand what he was saying, but she still didn't follow. "If he's following the law, there's nothing I can do."

"Fox might be behind the break-ins." The smile was gone from Zach's handsome face. His blue eyes had a serious cast. "He might be trying to scare you off."

Her fingers tightened reflexively, and she clutched the blankets against her breasts. "Oh, good, another threat."

"I didn't mean to frighten you."

"Could have fooled me," she said. "You creep into my bedroom in the middle of the night, wake me out of a deep sleep and tell me that my lawyer is plotting against me."

"It's just a theory."

"I don't want to talk about it." There had been enough threats for one day. "Why did you mention our kiss?"

"I'm not sure." He looked away from her. "I might have been half-asleep."

"You were thinking about it. I guess I've been thinking the same thing." She had been wondering if it would happen again, wondering how she'd react if he took her in his arms, again. And she'd been hoping.

"I don't want to hurt you, Gabby. You and me, we're from different worlds."

"Different planets," she said. "We're light-years apart."

"It's crazy to think the two of us could be together, not in any long-term kind of way."

"That doesn't mean we can't be…" She had intended to say friends, but that wasn't how she felt about him. Friends didn't kiss each other the way they had. "We can still be close."

"Close, huh?"

She wondered if he was familiar with the idea of friends with benefits. In usual circumstances, she wasn't the type of woman who had casual flings, but there was nothing usual about this trip to Colorado. From the first time she saw Zach, she was attracted to him. To be sure, a committed relationship would never work between two people who were so different. But there were other possibilities.

"I like you, Zach. And I appreciate everything you're doing to help me. It goes far beyond the scope of being a good neighbor."

"Like I told you, I cared for Michelle." He turned his head, and his gaze met hers. "She'd want me to protect you."

"What do you want?"

"You."

Reaching across the bed, he gently caressed the line of her cheek. His touch drew her like a magnet. She leaned toward him. Sitting back against the pillows didn't work anymore. She curled her legs under her and rose up on her knees. The quilt she'd been holding fell from her grasp, exposing her blue satin gown.

Zach dropped his hand from her face and sat back, taking his time to study her. A wolfish smile curved his mouth. "Come closer."

"How close?"

"Like this." His hand circled her waist, and he pulled her into his lap. He kissed her gently, tasting her lips and nuzzling against her cheek, nibbling on her earlobe. His breath was hot and moist.

She wrapped her arms around his neck and pressed against him. When her satin lingerie slid against him and rode up on her legs, he ran his hand along her bare thigh. A shiver went through her, not because she was cold.

His touch set off a chain reaction of pure heat. As his kisses became gradually more demanding, the intensity threatened to overwhelm her. If she didn't stop him now, she wouldn't be able to hold back.

He maneuvered her around, lifting her as though she weighed no more than a gossamer scarf. She found herself stretched out on the bed, lying on her side with Zach beside her. His leg was across hers, pinning her in place.

Breathing hard, he looked down at her. "I like what you're wearing."

"I made it myself." Why did she tell him that? She didn't care if he was impressed by her sewing skills.

"You're talented."

"I want you to think I'm hot."

"Don't worry." He kissed the tip of her nose. "I do."

When she gazed into his eyes, she was mesmerized by the color, the facets of blue. He was such a gorgeous man, so strong, so powerful. Closing her eyes, she arched against him, molding her body into his.

And yet, a sliver of doubt cut through her. Was this the right timing? A tiny voice in her head reminded her that she'd only just met Zach and there were so many other things going on that she might not be thinking clearly. She didn't want to make a mistake with him.

In spite of her raging desire, she hesitated.

Immediately, he sensed the change in her mood. "Something wrong?"

She pulled slightly away from him. When she laid the palm of her hand against his chest, she felt his heart beating. "Zach, I—"

"Too soon." He rolled off her. "I was afraid it might be."

A moment ago, she feared that making love would mess up their relationship or friendship or whatever this was between them. Now she was afraid that she'd been too quick to say no. "There'll be another time."

"I know."

In one smooth move, he got off the bed and started toward the door. His hand was on the doorknob when regret slammed into her. She called after him. "Wait."

He pivoted to face her. From across the room, she couldn't read his expression. "What is it, Gabby?"

"You've been going through all those legal papers. And you think Fox might want to scare me so I'd leave the Roost."

"Yep."

"What if I decide to stay?"

"It's all about fulfilling the terms of the will. There are three possible scenarios. The first option is if you, or your brother, live at the Roost for three years. Then the entire estate passes to you. Second option—you leave, Sarah Bentley inherits from the sale of the property and Fox earns a fat commission."

"And the third?"

"This third possibility is outlined in the legal documents. It's something Fox is aware of." His jaw tensed. "If you and your brother die, you can't fulfill the terms of the will. Sarah inherits. Fox wins."

She wished she hadn't asked.

Chapter Ten

Zach had planned to be at the Roost by ten o'clock in the morning. Toby Hatch was still at the house, and that young cowboy had all the makings of a capable bodyguard. But Zach wanted to be there, setting up security and making sure that Gabby and Charlotte were safe.

He'd had one foot out the door when Rhoda reined him in and reminded him of an unavoidable meeting with a committee from the Pitkin County Rodeo, who were already on their way to his ranch. Though he'd tried to avoid getting involved, he was the local expert when it came to rodeo, and the event actually was a good opportunity to promote his ranch. Business always picked up after he was introduced as a two-time World Champion rodeo cowboy.

By the time he finished with the three-person committee, it was almost noon. Rhoda called him into the kitchen, where she was packing a tamale casserole into a cardboard box along with a container of fresh fruit, homemade bread and cookies. "Take this with you."

"Don't you think Charlotte and Gabby can cook for themselves?"

"Skinny girls like them hardly know how to turn on an oven. Besides, they've got other things on their minds.

They don't have time to get into town and do grocery shopping."

"They can manage. Gabby's car is going to be at the shop until tomorrow, but Charlotte has the truck."

"I want to help them." Rhoda planted her fists on her round hips and confronted him. "You spent half the night over there protecting the girls. Let me feed them."

"Yes, ma'am." He knew better than to argue. "But if you don't want to be feeding those baby birds for the rest of your life, you should schedule a trip to the market and some cooking lessons."

"And what are you going to be doing this afternoon?"

"Teaching Gabby how to shoot."

She chuckled. "Are you sure you want to do that?"

"She needs to know how to take care of herself." He knew there were risks when it came to arming her. Gabby seemed to be scared of anything resembling wildlife, and he didn't want her blasting away at tree squirrels and crickets. "I'll be sure to emphasize gun safety."

"You don't want her going off half-cocked. Pun intended." Rhoda grinned. "Gabby kind of reminds me of Michelle. I like her."

"So do I."

He didn't make that statement lightly. Gabby wasn't the type of woman he was usually attracted to, but he couldn't push her out of his mind. She demanded attention. Her constant chatter should have driven him up the wall, but she amused him and provoked him in a good way, making him think. And there was that unexpected chemistry that robbed him of common sense and made him act like a lunatic.

He still couldn't believe he'd gone into her bedroom last night. No doubt, he should have waited until morning. But when he'd realized that Fox had a motive to stage the break-ins and would benefit from getting Gabby permanently out of the way, Zach had to warn her. When he'd first slipped into her room and saw her sleeping, she looked so sweet and delicate. It ticked him off that people like Fox and Osborne were trying to hurt her.

She was practically defenseless—didn't have the money to stage a legal battle and didn't have the skill to handle a physical confrontation. This sure as hell wasn't a fair fight. Zach had to step in, and he had always taken the side of the underdog. Watching her sleep, he'd wanted to protect her. And then his thoughts went in a less-noble direction, which was when she woke up and he mentioned their kiss.

It was probably for the best that they hadn't made love last night. He scooped up the box and carried it out to the truck. Before he got behind the steering wheel, he looked around for Daphne. The border collie was nowhere in sight.

When he pulled up in front of the Roost, his dog was on the porch, keeping watch with her two-colored eyes. She bounded off the porch and greeted him, wagging her tail and giving him a doggy grin.

He scratched behind her ears. "Are you moving in over here?"

Daphne cocked her head and barked.

"I know it's not because the food's better," he said as he unloaded the cardboard box. "Must be the company."

Two woofs.

"I'm warning you, puppy. I'll be real disappointed if you start wearing glitter and bows."

Gabby opened the front door and stepped onto the porch. When she saw him, her face lit up with a smile. "I thought Daphne's bark sounded happy."

"Because I'm bringing food."

She rushed toward him. "Can I help?"

As usual, she wasn't dressed for the outdoors. Her shorts were too short. Her top had sparkles around the neck. And her shoes were shiny ballet slippers. She looked real pretty, but he didn't tell her. It was better not to talk about anything personal.

He carried the box inside, through the house and into the kitchen. As soon as he set it down on the counter, Gabby pounced. She dug through the bags until she found the fruit. "Did Rhoda put this together?"

"She seems to think it's her job to feed you and Charlotte or else you'll starve to death."

"Not true." She grabbed an apple. "I'm eating more now than I usually do because Charlotte insists on breakfast. And she makes fabulous scrambled eggs and bacon. Two days in a row. I'm beginning to think that's all she makes."

"And you? What do you cook?"

"You'd think I'd have great culinary skills, wouldn't you? After all, I'm French. I ought to know my way around a quiche or a crepe or a cassoulet. But my great-aunt Rene concentrated on teaching me how to sew." She took a bite of apple. "Yum."

Last night, she'd bragged about how she'd made her sexy blue nightie herself. He didn't want to dwell on those dangerous thoughts and changed the subject. "What have you been doing this morning?"

"I told Charlotte about the missing Tarot paintings, and we've started our own treasure hunt. I left her and Toby to search in the studio. He's kind of adorable with that shy smile and the buzz cut. I think Charlotte likes him. Anyway, I thought they deserved some time alone. I've been digging through Michelle's office."

"Have you found anything?"

"Tons of paperwork and correspondence," she said as she nibbled at the apple. "There's a folder for Sarah Bentley. I thought there might be something significant inside, but it was just a couple of thank-you notes for contributions Michelle made to Sarah's Forest Preservation Society and a few candid family photos from the headquarters of the Society. It sounded like Michelle had visited a few times."

She'd never mentioned to Zach that she and Sarah were friends. There was a lot about Michelle that he didn't know. "What else did you find?"

"It's mostly from ten years ago. I'm guessing that after Michelle got a computer, she did more of her work online. And we'll never know what was on her computers. The desktop and the laptop were both stolen in the robbery that happened during the memorial service."

He hadn't given much thought to the missing computers. Any kind of electronics seemed like an obvious target of burglars, but there might have been a more sinister reason for the theft. "What about backup copies? Maybe a thumb drive."

"Finding something that small in the chaos of her office is going to take some heavy-duty searching." She finished off her apple. "Is there something else we need to do today?"

He nodded. "Do you have jeans?"

"Of course, I do. Designer jeans."

"Put them on. We're going for a hike."

Her eyes narrowed suspiciously. "Why?"

"You're too big of a coward to go anywhere on horseback, and we need to get to a place where you can't do much damage."

"I'm not a coward, but you're right about the horseback riding. Why would I damage anything?"

"I'm going to teach you how to shoot."

She didn't look happy about his plan, but she didn't refuse. "Do you really think it's necessary?"

"You need to be able to defend yourself in case of a break-in…or something worse."

He hadn't forgotten their worst-case scenario discussion last night. In order to get his paws on the commission, Fox needed her to be gone or to be dead.

THE WATCHER STAYED in his vehicle, confident that it was well hidden, not visible from the Roost or from Zach's horse ranch. He couldn't see them, either. But that was okay. He had a better method of surveillance.

Yesterday, in the dark before dawn, he'd picked the lock on the back door of the Roost and gone inside. His objective had not been to search but to infiltrate. He'd planted a listening device in the kitchen. Given more time, he could have bugged the whole house, but it was better to be cautious. He'd slipped out the door before anyone was the wiser.

And now, he sat in a quiet aspen grove, about a half mile from the house, and listened through a headset while they made their plans. When Gabby and Zach talked about the missing computers, he'd talked back to their voices through the microphone. "How dumb are you people?"

No self-respecting burglar would bother stealing an old desktop computer. Outdated electronics weren't worth the gas it took to drive to a pawn shop. Their stupidity was a plus for him. If they ever figured out what was really going on, he'd be in serious trouble, the kind of trouble that sent people to prison. The stakes were high. That was for damn sure.

He wasn't going to let some little bitch from Brooklyn get in his way. She didn't deserve the inheritance and wasn't smart enough to hang on to it.

The real problem was Zach Sheffield. Not only was he capable of defending Gabby but he was savvy and tough as boot leather. He needed to be dealt with. The rodeo was coming up. Maybe an unfortunate accident could be arranged.

GABBY DASHED INTO her bedroom to change clothes. Playing with guns wasn't her idea of a good time, but she couldn't help being happy about spending time with Zach. After what happened last night, she'd worried that things might be awkward between them. Happily, that wasn't the case.

Left to herself, she might overanalyze their attraction, might consider it to be fate or a sign from the Universe that they were meant to be together. But Zach had a knack. No matter what kind of emotional turmoil might be roiling behind his steely blue eyes, he could ignore it. He kept everything buried.

Changing from shorts to her vintage, boot-cut, black Ralph Lauren jeans took only a minute. Since Zach said they'd be walking, she slipped into her running shoes, reminding herself that she really needed to pick up some hiking boots. Charlotte had several pairs of shoes that were appropriate for everyday wear, but her feet were a size smaller than Gabby's.

When she checked her reflection in the mirror, she noticed the painting opposite her bed—*Girl with Book and Mirror.* Michelle had specifically selected this picture for her. Why? What was special about this piece?

She opened the door to her bedroom, went to the stairwell and called out, "Zach, would you come up here?"

He appeared at the foot of the staircase. "What is it?"

"Just come."

In her bedroom, she stood a few feet away from the painting and stared, searching for a hidden message. The girl who was reading the book had brownish hair and her features were completely obscured. She could be anyone. Her casual clothes—shorts and a button-up pink shirt—made her look like she'd been playing outdoors and had just come inside.

Zach poked his head into the room. With one hand clinging to the doorjamb, he seemed hesitant to enter. "Well?"

"You knew Michelle better than I did. Why would she give me this painting? Is there something here that might be a clue?"

"Like what?"

"A piece of furniture," she suggested. "Do you recognize the standing mirror? Or the window frame?"

"The window looks like the ones in the old part of the Roost." He came a bit closer to study the picture but kept his distance from her as though he didn't want to touch her. "The braided rug on the floor reminds me of one that used to be in the old house."

"Is there anything else that looks like the old house?"

He squinted at the bookshelves in the painting. Though none of the titles on the spines were readable, they appeared to be leather-bound. "There are books over there—old, yellowed books about to crumble."

"Has this painting always been in this room?"

"I don't know. Why do you ask?"

"Do you see the way the girl in the painting is holding her hand? It's almost like she's pointing across the room at the closet."

And a closet would be a terrific place to hide the Tarot

paintings. Gabby opened the closet door and peered inside. Her blouses and dresses hung from the rack, and her shoes were neatly lined up on the floor, but it had been completely empty when she moved into this bedroom. The walls and ceiling appeared to be solid with no evidence of a secret cubbyhole. The floor was finished with the tongue-and-groove hardwood that covered most of the upstairs.

She got down on her hands and knees. "There could be a loose baseboard and a hiding place behind it."

While she felt along the boards, completely ruining the last of her manicure, Zach stood watching with his arms folded across his chest. "I think you're just trying to avoid your shooting lessons."

"It's important to find those missing paintings."

"And what if you do?" he asked. "You turn them over to Osborne, he sells them and life goes on."

"A life without break-ins," she said. "When the paintings are gone, there's nothing of value hidden in the house. And the burglars give up."

"Unless finding the paintings wasn't the ultimate goal."

She knew he favored the theory that Fox was trying to intimidate her, but she wasn't so sure. Until she was, she and Charlotte would keep searching.

After she'd gone all the way around the closet, she lovingly put her shoes back in order and crawled out. Zach stood by the window looking out. His position was similar to when she first saw him last night, and a shiver went down her spine. It might be time for them to get out of the bedroom and put some distance between themselves and the bed.

"I give up," she said.

"I had another idea for why Michelle might have left you this painting. It's kind of obvious."

Then why hadn't it occurred to her? "Okay, what?"

"It could be a literal message." He crossed the room and went to the painting. Reaching up, he lifted the two-by-four-foot picture off the hook on the wall. "A couple of years ago, I had a stallion that I loved. When he died, Michelle gave me a painting of him. On the back of the canvas, she wrote his name and signed it."

He flipped the painting around, and she saw the words, painted in a soft blue. She read aloud, "Family is the greatest treasure. All my love, Michelle."

Gabby's eyes misted over. She might not have found a hundred-thousand-dollar cache of Tarot paintings, but this discovery was priceless.

Chapter Eleven

"I don't see why we have to go so far," Gabby complained as she trudged behind Zach. "Why can't you teach me to shoot closer to the house?"

"Safety," he said.

"I'd be careful."

"What makes you think I'm talking about your safety? I'm thinking of the innocent bystanders."

She put her head down and kept walking. The vacant land behind the Roost went from a flat area with tumble-down fence posts and no barbed wire to an incline lead-ing into pine trees and rugged boulders. She was pleased that hiking uphill didn't strain her leg muscles. Living in Brooklyn, she hardly ever used her car. The only reason she owned the little hatchback was because she took it in trade for an elaborate bridal gown from a girlfriend who worked at a body shop. In New York, everybody walked everywhere, and Gabby was in good shape. But she was winded, probably due to that high altitude thing.

Pausing to catch her breath, she turned and looked back at the Roost. From this perspective, she saw how the original part of the house attached to the studio. The old structure showed signs of wear where it had been patched, shored up and rebuilt. Much of the paint had worn away, leaving weathered wood, and the roof sagged. It was remarkable that the place was still standing, given that it had been constructed in the 1870s. Michelle must have dedicated a lot of time, effort and money to maintaining the original Roost.

Gabby remembered what Charlotte had said about Michelle sitting in the old house and communicating with the ghosts of their ancestors. The Rousseau family—living or dead—was hugely important to her. As the message on the back of the painting suggested, family was to be treasured. And yet, her great-aunt hadn't made any particular overtures to Gabby when she was growing up. Their connection was tenuous, not loving. Sure, Gabby was sad when she'd learned of Michelle's death, but she wasn't devastated. Not like when Rene died four years ago.

Zach called to her. "Are you coming?"

Instead of climbing higher, she continued to stare at the house. "I remember when Michelle came to Brooklyn for Rene's funeral."

"I can't hear you."

She turned and looked up the hill toward him. "If family was so important to her, why didn't Michelle make more of an effort to know me?"

He shrugged. "She talked about you."

"You said that before." She started climbing, energized by anger and frustration. "She thought I might have a smidgen of her talent. Well, big whoop. Why didn't she tell me? Do you see any photos of me around the house? No, you don't. Supposedly, she treasured me and the rest of the family, but when she came to Brooklyn for her sister's funeral, she only stayed for one day."

She powered up the last few paces, joining him in a flat

clearing surrounded by forest. "If Michelle cared about me so much, why did she set up these crazy terms in her will?"

"I don't know." He drew an automatic gun from a hip holster and ran his hand along the barrel.

"She could have invited me for a visit." She caught her breath. "She could have talked to me and gotten to know me instead of hiding out in her mountain sanctuary like a modern day Georgia O'Keeffe."

"That door swings both ways."

Of course, he was right. "I didn't know much about her beyond the fact that she was a successful artist."

"A wealthy artist," he said.

In the back of her mind, Gabby had been aware of her great-aunt's wealth, but she'd never approached Michelle for a loan, not even when she could no longer afford to keep her boutique open. "I never expected an inheritance."

"Some people might say you've come out ahead on this deal."

"It's not about the money. I would have rather spent time with Michelle, watching her paint and talking about her life. For me, it's never been about money." The realization hit her like a splash of cold water. The terms of the will, though unreasonable, didn't anger her as much as the missed opportunity. Michelle was a complex, mysterious, interesting woman, surrounded by an artist's mystique. "There's still plenty to learn about Michelle, about this heritage that I barely know anything about. I've made my decision. I'm going to follow the terms of the will and stay at the Roost."

"But not for the money."

"I won't lie. Having enough money so I don't have to worry about paying the rent would be great, but that's not the biggest reason."

"Then, why?"

"Living here worked for Michelle. Maybe it'll be lucky for me. The Universe is teaching me a lesson. In a weird way, I'm staying because of family."

"As good a reason as any," he said as he sauntered across the flat clearing and made a stack of three smaller rocks on top of a flat boulder. "It's hard to understand families."

"That sounds like the voice of experience."

"Maybe," he said as he made another stack of rocks.

His every move seemed precise and calculated, from his gait to the way he pushed his hat back on his forehead. He wasn't the kind of man who second-guessed himself or wandered aimlessly. As she watched him, she wondered—for the ten-millionth time—why he'd come into her bedroom last night. There must have been a reason. He'd said he wanted to talk about Fox, but that discussion could have waited until morning. And why had Zach mentioned their kiss?

Since she'd decided to stick it out at the Roost, she needed to define her relationship with him. Diving into a wild, passionate fling with her next-door neighbor seemed like a very bad idea. If they made love and things went wrong, she couldn't avoid seeing him.

But could she settle for just being friends? Every time she looked at his gorgeous face and sexy body, she started drooling like one of Pavlov's dogs desperate for a treat. That response definitely had to stop. She'd be wiser to think of Zach as a new friend, to learn something about his life and his past. "Seems like all we've done is talk about me and my crazy family. Tell me about you. What are your parents like?"

"I left home when I was seventeen and never went back."

She waited for him to continue, but he said nothing more. She asked, "Where did you grow up?"

"Wyoming."

"Did you live in a city or on a ranch?"

"Ranch."

"Come on, Zach. You've got to give me more than one-word answers. How am I going to get to know you?"

"I'll talk after our shooting lesson."

"Do you promise?"

"Yeah, sure. If you cooperate, I'll tell you something— one thing—about my past."

"You're on, cowboy."

He came toward her, holding the gun at his side. "Here's your first safety lesson. Never point a gun, whether or not it's loaded, at anything you don't want to shoot."

"What if I don't want to shoot anything?"

"This is for your protection, Gabby. Pay attention."

Though she would have preferred not playing with dangerous weapons, she feigned cooperation by nodding. "Why didn't you bring Charlotte's rifle?"

"Learning how to use a rifle is harder than a handgun. And it's not necessary for you to master long-range marksmanship. You're not going hunting."

"So true," she mumbled. "Tell me again why I need to know how to handle a gun?"

"When you're face-to-face with a bad guy and there's no way to escape and no one to help you, a gun might come in handy." He stood beside her, picked up her right hand and placed the weapon in it. "Hold the grip. Get the feel of it."

The dark metal felt cold and was heavier than she'd expected. "What kind of gun is this?"

"A Glock 21, it's a .45 caliber automatic," he said. "Don't put your finger on the trigger until you're ready to shoot."

While he explained about various mechanisms, she balanced the weight in her hand. She had to admit that holding something so lethal was kind of exciting. She wanted to be as cool as an action heroine in a movie, but she couldn't envision herself in that role.

She lowered the weapon. "This isn't for me. I'm not a shooter. Guns are made for killing."

"That's why I'm teaching you." His voice was low and patient. "Handling a weapon is a great responsibility. You need to know what you're doing."

"I don't think I could ever shoot another human being."

"Sometimes, it's enough to pull the trigger. The noise will scare them off."

"Show me." She held the weapon toward him.

He took the gun from her, held it in a two-handed grip, pivoted and fired.

The blast was so loud that she covered her ears, but she didn't take her eyes off him. He looked natural and poised. A quick glance showed her that he'd hit his target. The first stack of rocks had tumbled. He fired again and the second target was gone.

"I want you to notice my stance," he said.

"Uh-huh." You bet, she noticed. He looked like a real-life action hero who could take down twenty bad guys without breaking a sweat.

"I'm square to the target. My knees are loose and relaxed. My arms are straight, but I don't have my elbows locked because there's some recoil when I fire. You try it."

As she mimicked the way he was standing, he gave calm instructions about softening her knees and loosening her shoulders. "This doesn't feel like target practice," she said.

"Concentrate on what you're doing, Gabby. Don't forget to breathe."

"Like Yoga."

"Whatever works for you." He placed the Glock in her right hand and lifted her arm so she was holding it straight out in front of her. "Your left hand comes up here to steady your grip. You don't want to be shaky."

A tremble rippled through her, but that shaking had little to do with the gun in her hand. His touch aroused her. Even though he was acting like a dispassionate instructor, he was still Zach, still sexy. "What next?"

"Look down the barrel and line up the sights. Use your right eye. If you want, you can close the left."

It took an effort to focus, but she understood what he meant. "Should I aim at anything?"

"What do you see?"

"A tree," she said. "I'll shoot that."

"Okay, get ready. Don't pull the trigger, just give it a squeeze. When you slip your index finger into the trigger space, be careful. The safety is off."

She did as he said. "Now?"

"Keep your eye on the sight, elbows relaxed, squeeze."

The blast rattled her eardrums. The recoil jolted her backward against his chest. A rush of adrenaline went through her. "That wasn't so bad."

"Do it again." Holding her shoulders, he leaned close to her ear and whispered, "This time, don't stumble."

The noise was still startling, but she was ready for the recoil this time when she squeezed the trigger. Firing the weapon felt easier. "Better?"

"You're doing great," he said. "Keep shooting until the bullets are gone."

"How many is that?"

"It holds thirteen rounds, and we've fired four times. Nine more shots."

"Should I aim at anything?"

"Sure, but don't worry about accuracy. Your goal is to get comfortable with your weapon."

By the time she'd gone through nine more shots, she felt like a pro. Though she still objected to guns on principle, she accepted the need for knowing how to use one. While living at the Roost, 911 wasn't a real effective option.

He took the gun from her. "Do you want me to show you how to load it?"

"It's something I need to know."

She watched and listened as he illustrated how to remove the used clip and insert another. When she did it herself, she felt more in control of her weapon. *Her Glock?* Her boutique-loving friends in Brooklyn would never believe this.

"You're ready for more," he said. "Let's work on accuracy."

He set up more stacks of rocks, and she blasted away. Though she aligned the sights, she wasn't hitting anything. Zach murmured encouragement, adjusted her stance and moved her closer to the rocks. Finally, with her tenth shot, she hit the target and let out a cheer. Without thinking of the consequences, she hugged him with her free arm.

As soon as she pressed against him, a surge of sensual awareness raced through her body. Her chin nestled in the crook of his neck. In spite of the gun, which she kept pointed at the ground, this felt so very right.

"Gabby, do you still have your finger on the trigger?"

"I do."

"Take it off slowly so you don't accidentally shoot me in the foot."

An embrace while holding a Glock was tricky. Carelessness was how people got hurt…in more ways than one. When she was around Zach, she had to be wise.

After releasing the trigger, she stepped back. "Sorry."

"Finish off the clip," he said.

Though her last three shots weren't precise, she managed another hit. "One out of three isn't bad."

"You're feeling confident. That's good. Now you can reload, and we'll get back to the Roost."

Remembering his instructions, she ejected the used clip and replaced it. "I'm glad you made me do this. Learning how to shoot is part of living here, and I'm going to have to make adjustments."

"Maybe tomorrow, I can teach you how to ride."

The idea of climbing up on a huge animal still freaked her out. "Aren't we supposed to pick up my car tomorrow?"

"And I promised to stop by the arena where they're holding the rodeo."

A rodeo meant more horses and other livestock. Not her favorite thing, but she was determined to get comfortable with this new lifestyle. "Can I come with you to the rodeo?"

"Yep."

Though still experiencing residual tingles from their embrace, this conversation seemed more like two friends. She remembered their deal. "You promised to tell me something about your past."

"Fair enough." He took the Glock from her and slipped it into the holster clipped to his belt. "Since you're going to be my neighbor, there are a couple of things you should know about me."

"I'm ready."

When she looked up at him, he held her gaze. Unflinching, he said, "I'm a drug addict and alcoholic."

She gritted her teeth, not wanting to appear shocked or surprised. Disapproval was the furthest thing from her mind. A few years ago, a good friend had made a similar declaration to Gabby. She knew a few things about addiction. "When did it start?"

"From the time I was a kid, I'd always done my fair share of drinking. I never really saw it as a problem, not even when I was having a shot or a couple of beers every day."

His expression was as still as a mask. He did nothing to betray his emotions, but she knew that talking about something so personal was hard for him, and she was glad that he trusted her enough to talk to her.

He continued, "About ten years ago, I got injured real bad in a rodeo accident, busted my ankle and my arm and cracked three ribs. It hurt to move and to breathe, hurt like hell. Even worse, I knew my career was over."

"Why?"

"I was a World Champion cowboy, and I knew I'd never get back to that level. To make a long, miserable story short, I got addicted to painkillers with a booze chaser and ended up in the hospital. When I bottomed out, I started going to a twelve-step program, which I still attend every year on my anniversary. I've been sober for nine years."

"Congratulations." She didn't know what to say next and had to be careful not to destroy the fragile bond that had grown between them. He had opened up and made himself vulnerable. In this moment, she was more attracted to him than their physical chemistry dictated. They had become more than friends, more than a wild fling. She was falling in love with him.

She took his hand. "Let's go home."

Chapter Twelve

As he walked beside her down the hill, Zach felt almost light-headed. Talking about his addictions wasn't something he did, but he'd told Gabby. And she hadn't jumped all over his story, pushing for more details and offering sympathy. Instead, she'd quietly absorbed his words and offered no judgment. It amazed him that a woman who talked a mile a minute was capable of such perfect stillness.

When they reached the path that circled the original house, she looked at the window that was still broken. "I should get that fixed. Michelle would want the place to be kept up."

"There's a handyman she used to call," he said. "Charlotte probably has his phone number."

"Not Ed Striker, I hope. He's scary. Do you remember what he said? That he wanted to get rid of us?"

He hadn't forgotten Striker but had concentrated so much on Fox that he hadn't paid as much attention to Osborne as a suspect. "I'm glad you reminded me."

They came around to the front of the new house just as a shiny black SUV parked beside Zach's truck. Kevin Fox hopped out of the driver's seat and waved. What the hell did he want?

The passenger door swung open, and another man

stepped out. He was as tall as Zach with dark brown hair and eyes. His gaze lit on Gabby. As soon as he smiled, Zach saw the family resemblance.

"Daniel," Gabby shouted, "is it really you?"

"In the flesh."

She dashed toward him, flung herself into his arms and hung on tight. In spite of her complaints about her big brother, she obviously adored him. When she ended the hug, she patted his arms and shoulders as if to reassure herself that he was standing there in front of her. "I didn't expect you so soon. How did you get here?"

"I talked to the lawyer, and he bought me a plane ticket to Aspen. It seemed like I needed to be here and figure out all this stuff with Great-Aunt Michelle's will."

"But you said that I should handle it."

"Changed my mind," he said as he walked toward the porch. "This is the place, huh? How much land comes with it?"

"Daniel, I want you to meet Zach Sheffield. He's our neighbor to the south."

When they shook hands, Zach noticed the unhealthy pallor in his skin tone and a scar near his left eye. Whatever Daniel had been doing in the years he'd been out of touch with his sister, it didn't involve being outdoors. Zach's first guess was that Daniel had spent some time in prison. For Gabby's sake, he hoped he was wrong.

She grabbed her brother's arm and dragged him up the stairs to the porch. "I've missed you so much. What's going on in your life? Do you have a girlfriend? Well, of course, you do. You always had the girls lining up."

The front door was locked, per Zach's instructions for minimal security, and Gabby dug into her pocket to find her key. "We'll need to get more keys made so you can come and go whenever you want."

"I'm not moving in," he said.

"Yeah, we'll have to talk about that." She glanced over her shoulder. "Zach and Kevin, are you coming?"

"Sorry," Kevin said, "I need to get back to work."

"Me, too," Zach said. He didn't really have to leave. In fact, he'd called in two other men who occasionally worked for him to take up the slack while he was busy with Gabby. But he wanted a little time alone with Kevin Fox. This might be an opportunity to find out what his uncle was really up to. The younger Fox wouldn't be as guarded as the wily, old lawyer.

As soon as Gabby and Daniel closed the door, Zach said, "Nice gesture from your uncle, buying a plane ticket for Daniel to come out here."

"Uncle Jason never does anything just to be nice. You can bet he'll charge the expense to the Rousseau account."

Zach expected as much, and it didn't bode well for Daniel's integrity that he accepted help from Fox, putting himself in the attorney's debt. "I suppose that's fair."

Kevin leaned against the fender of the SUV and looked up at the two-story house as though seeing it for the first time. "So this is the famous Roost—the new part, right?"

"The original house is attached at the back. You can't see it from this angle."

"It's a decent property, should sell for a good price."

"If Gabby decides to sell," Zach reminded him.

"No way will she want to stay." He swept his long red hair off his forehead. "She's a city girl who's into fashion. What's she going to do out here? Make little outfits for the jackrabbits?"

His wide grin and freckles made him look like a kid,

but Zach sensed a threat. "How long have you worked for your uncle?"

"This is just a summer job while I'm off school." He pointed to the logo on the black-and-gold hoodie he wore over his button-down office shirt. "I'm at University of Colorado in Boulder."

"Working at the law office must be an easy job. All you have to do is answer the phone."

"I wish," he said. "My uncle talks to me about everything. He's trying to show me that being a lawyer is cool, and I should go to law school."

"But that's not what you want."

"I want to be a professional snowboarder, like Shaun White, the famous redhead." Kevin's smug grin hinted that he put himself in the same category as White who had won countless events in the Winter X Games and two Olympic gold medals. "You know what I mean. You were an athlete, a two-time World Champion rodeo star."

"I like to win. I bet you're the same way."

"Maybe I should give rodeo a try. There's that thing coming up in a couple of days."

Zach wasn't above using his past. "I can get you a pass to go behind the chutes. It's a good place to meet cowgirls."

"You're on." He checked his wristwatch—a gold Rolex. "I've done a little riding. Maybe I could compete."

"Yeah, sure." The kid had an ego, and Zach played to it. "Have you and your uncle talked about Michelle's will? I'd like to hear your opinion."

"From what Uncle Jason says, the Rousseau family has always been eccentric, like that whole thing with the Frenchman's Treasure. Do you think it exists?"

"Do you?"

"You know what I think? If they tear down the original

house, they'll find a secret cave underneath it. The only reason Michelle kept that old dump standing was to keep the treasure hidden. I mean, she rebuilt almost an entire wall and patched up other sections."

How did Kevin know what kind of work had been done on the old house? Earlier he'd given the impression that he'd never been here before. The aspiring snowboard champion wasn't to be trusted. "You had a chance to talk to Daniel on the drive from the airport. What does he think about the will?"

"The dude doesn't know beans about his great-aunt, except that she had money. And he wants his share." Kevin shrugged. "I don't blame him. He's strapped for cash."

"How so?"

"He's a dealer in an Atlantic City casino, and he's working double shifts to pay off some debts."

The job accounted for Daniel's pale complexion, which was better than a stint in prison but not by much. Zach suspected that when Daniel wasn't dealing, he had a seat at the poker tables. "Gambling debts."

"He didn't say how deep in the hole he was, but I'm guessing it's bad."

Apparently, Kevin had never heard of attorney-client privilege and had no problem revealing personal details. Zach pursued his advantage. "According to the will, Daniel has to wait three years before he gets the big bucks."

"He'll settle for less," Kevin said. "He needs money now."

That statement answered the question of why Fox bought a plane ticket to bring Daniel here. If Daniel was convinced to take the money now, he could influence his sister. Then Fox would be free to sell the property and make his commission. "Did your uncle offer Daniel a pay-off to sell?"

Kevin scowled. It must have dawned on him that he'd said too much. "I don't know."

"That's what I'd do," Zach lied, trying to get back on the kid's chatty side. "I'd give Daniel and Gabby some cash and send them on their way."

"That's the smart decision." Kevin opened the door to the SUV. "See you at the rodeo."

As Zach watched him drive away, he wondered about the extent of Kevin's responsibilities at his uncle's law firm. The kid might enjoy getting out of the office and staging fake break-ins to scare Gabby away from the Roost.

SEEING HER BROTHER brought back a surge of happy memories for Gabby. From their childhood when they were a family with a mother and father to the difficult teenage years with Great-Aunt Rene, Daniel had always been a presence in her life. He was the big brother who protected her from bullies and teased her about her clothes and held her when she wept.

Somewhere along the line, that relationship had changed, and now she was the one who worried about him. Like her, he'd always been skinny, but he didn't look healthy. She hated that he was working in a casino. Not that she had anything against those establishments, but Daniel had always been a gambler. He didn't need to be that close to temptation.

Seated at the kitchen table with Charlotte, Daniel entertained them with fancy card handling and tricks. He'd always been a charmer. Charlotte hung on his every word, and Daphne sat by his feet. After he dealt four hands for stud poker, he flipped his cards over to show four aces.

Charlotte was impressed.

Gabby was irritated. "You cheated."

"That's right. But did you see how I did it?"

"I don't want to know," she snapped as she swept the cards from his hands. "Nothing good comes from cheating."

"You sound just like Great-Aunt Rene."

"A wise woman."

When he reached down to scratch behind Daphne's ears, the dog looked up at him with adoring two-colored eyes. He flashed a smile at Charlotte. "Gabby was always the good girl who got home on time for curfew, made good grades and did her chores."

Loyally, Charlotte said, "There's nothing wrong with that."

Charlotte still glittered. She was wearing one of Gabby's short skirts and a blue tunic blouse that brought out the color in her eyes. Her long, straight hair was pulled into a side ponytail that hung past her shoulder.

"Saint Gabriella," Daniel said with disdain. "And where did it get you? You're sitting here, just like me, waiting for an inheritance."

"How much did Fox tell you about the will?"

"Enough," he said. "We should let him sell the place. He told me he'd give us a payoff from his commission, a good chunk of change. I say we do it. Take his offer."

Daphne gave a woof of agreement.

"What about the Frenchman's Treasure?" Charlotte asked. "You don't want to give that up."

Immediately, Daniel perked up. "Tell me more about this treasure."

While Charlotte rambled on about the Rousseau family myth, Gabby watched her brother's dark eyes grow bright as he leaned forward and listened, captivated. When had he become so greedy? As a kid, he'd always shared with her, sometimes giving her the last jelly bean instead of keeping it for himself. Now he was the picture of avarice, licking his lips in anticipation of finding a buried treasure.

If she could convince him to stay at the Roost with her for three years, the change might be good for him. His basic needs would be covered, and he could take the time to look more deeply into himself and figure out what he really wanted to do. The idea appealed to her, as well. They'd be a real family.

"Fox didn't tell you everything," she said. "Michelle's unsold artwork is worth a great deal of money. I have the paperwork upstairs from her art dealer."

"Do we inherit these paintings?"

"Not unless we stay here for three years. One of us has to be in residence at all times." She looked him straight in the eye. "I've already decided that I want to stay."

Charlotte bounced out of her chair and gave Gabby a quick hug. "I'm so glad. It's okay if I live here, isn't it?"

"Absolutely," Gabby said. "Michelle would have wanted it that way."

Her idea of a family was taking a more solid form. Charlotte would be the little sister she never had. Daniel would be himself. With Daphne staying over here all the time, they even had a dog. And she had hopes for a serious relationship with Zach, a mate who would make her family truly complete.

Daniel leaned back in his chair with his long legs stretched in front of him. "I need money now."

"I kind of guessed that." She bit her tongue to keep from lecturing him. "At least, you need to take a look at the numbers before we make a decision."

"It'll have to wait until later." He stood and picked up his small carry-on bag. "I'm tired. Can you show me where I should sleep?"

"Upstairs."

She and Charlotte directed him to the fourth bedroom, which wasn't as spacious or as nicely furnished as hers but was closer to the bathroom. Daniel dropped his bag on the floor and turned to her. "I've missed you, Gabby."

"Promise me that we won't go so long without seeing each other." She hugged him again. "I have a million regrets about not spending more time with Michelle, and I don't want the same thing to happen to us. Family needs to stick together."

"I'm willing to try."

In her bedroom, Gabby changed into a less-clunky pair of shoes while Charlotte sat on her bed and flipped through a fashion magazine. She held up a photograph of a very blonde model. "Do you think I should dye my hair?"

"It's so long and silky that I'd hate to mess with it."

"But it's dull, old brown."

"Tomorrow, I'm going to pick up my car. I could look for a rinse to brighten the color."

"Yes," Charlotte said. "Are you going to the place where they're having the rodeo?"

"I think so."

"Maybe I should go with you." She frowned. "But if Toby stays here to watch the house, I want to be with him."

Gabby sensed a little romance brewing between these two. "He's a cute guy. Is he going to compete in the rodeo?"

"He still hasn't decided, but he'll do trick riding with some of the other guys who work for Zach. They always put on a show before the rodeo gets started."

"I didn't realize this was such a big event."

"It's not like Cheyenne Frontier Days, but it's kind of a big deal around here. Let me show you what I'm wearing."

She jumped off the bed and ran to her bedroom with Daphne at her heels. When they returned, Charlotte was holding a faded, red, long-sleeved, Western-style shirt with a pair of boots embroidered on the yoke. "I guess I have to wear jeans with it."

"Or a denim skirt."

"Do you have one?"

"If we get my sewing machine set up in the studio, I can make you one in a couple of hours." Gabby took the shirt and held it up. Though it wasn't bad, the snaps were loose and the fabric had seen better days. "Do you love this shirt?"

"I did when I first got it. But that was three years ago. It's a little tight across the bust."

"I can make a new one with some fancy embroidery, maybe something like roses or hummingbirds."

"You can do that?" Charlotte gaped.

"Embroidery was one of my great-aunt Rene's favorite things. It's not hard. The machine does all the work. I just point it in the right direction. What color do you like?"

"Blue, please. With black embroidery and maybe some sparkles."

"When is the rodeo?"

"Saturday. Three days from now."

"Plenty of time," Gabby said. "You'll be the prettiest cowgirl there. Toby will be impressed."

Charlotte knelt down beside the dog. "Did you hear that, Daphne? I'm going to be pretty."

The dog gave her a big sloppy lick on the cheek and pulled back with glitter on her tongue.

Charlotte pointed to the painting that rested against the dresser. "What happened? Did it fall off the wall?"

"Zach and I took it down." Gabby flipped the picture to show the back side. "Look what we found."

Charlotte read the message about family being the greatest treasure. "Treasure," Charlotte said. "Why would she use that word?"

Gabby shrugged. "In her will, Michelle left this specific painting to me. Did she ever talk to you about this picture?"

"It was one of her favorites. I remember the day, about six months ago, when we moved it to this bedroom. And she said something about books being the key to your imagination. She was always giving me things to read."

"Where was the painting hanging before?"

"In the old house," Charlotte said. "One of the reasons we moved it was because the roof was leaking and the insulation is bad. She wanted all the artwork moved before it snowed last winter. This painting always hung in a place of honor on the wall to the left of the old fireplace."

Gabby remembered the pointing finger of the girl in the painting that led her to search the closet. What if that finger was pointing to something in the old house?

Chapter Thirteen

After dinner, Gabby went to the studio where she'd spent the afternoon arranging her sewing equipment. This was her first time in this room after dark, and when she turned on the lights, using four different switches by the door, she was pleased. Bright illumination flooded the entire space in the large room. Though not as pure as sunlight, the overhead system provided the kind of clarity an artist like her great-aunt would need to work at night.

Carrying an armload of fabric, she descended the stairs and crossed the room. Michelle's easel still stood in place. Moving it didn't seem right.

She added the fabric that Rhoda had given her to a pile of clutter on one of the large worktables. Later, she'd figure out a storage system for material, thread, zippers and accessories. For right now, her attention needed to be on the new shirt for Charlotte.

The whole gang had eaten dinner at Zach's house, taking advantage of Rhoda's wonderful cooking, and the formerly timid Charlotte couldn't stop talking about the clothes that were being made especially for her. She was like a cowgirl Cinderella getting ready for the ball, smiling and shyly flirting with Toby.

Gabby was content to play the role of fairy godmother.

Her new life in the mountains seemed to be shaping up beautifully. She was reunited with her brother, surrounded by people who liked her and ready to embark on a relationship with Zach. Throughout the incredible meal of fried chicken, potato salad and asparagus spears, they had been exchanging glances that got warmer and warmer as the dinner wore on. By the time they got to the chocolate cake dessert, she was afraid to look at him. One more glimpse and she just might burst into flames.

She couldn't help wondering about what would happen later tonight. Since Zach had the first shift patrolling the house after the others had gone to bed, it wouldn't be difficult for her to get him alone. Luring him into her bedroom shouldn't be a problem. But what happened next? To seduce him or not to seduce him, that was the question.

Her first instinct was to accept the magnetism that she'd felt from the first moment she saw him and make love. But she had doubts. As her brother had so annoyingly pointed out, Saint Gabriella was a good girl who obeyed the rules and didn't throw caution to the winds. She didn't want to mess up a possible future with Zach by moving too fast. But why should she wait? How could she tell him that she liked him too much to make love to him?

As if summoned by her thoughts, Zach entered and stood in the doorway, looking down at the studio. "You've changed things around."

"Welcome to my sewing room." She gestured grandly. "This big mess is supplies that I still need to sort. Over here is an area where I can do sketches for my designs. There's a long table for cutting fabric. There are two sewing stations."

"Looks good to me," he said as he came down the stairs. "I'm glad you're using the studio. Michelle would approve."

Daphne trotted along behind him. After she got her pat on the noggin from Gabby, the border collie sniffed her way around the perimeter, checking her surroundings.

"Well, Daphne?" Gabby spread out a few yards of a turquoise twill fabric on the cutting table. "Do you approve?"

The dog sat beside her and cocked an eyebrow as though she was withholding judgment until she saw what Gabby could do with her brand-new studio. If Daphne was expecting million-dollar art, she'd have a long wait.

Zach perched on the stool beside her table. "What are you working on?"

"I promised Charlotte that I'd make her a fancy new Western-style shirt for the rodeo. She wants to look pretty for Toby, and I can use the practice. Charlotte's idea is a rose pattern for the embroidery and lots of sparkles. How much bedazzling is too much?"

"Some of these shirts are real ornate, but that's usually for evening or for performers."

"Speaking of performing," she said, "I heard that you do some trick riding at the start of the rodeo."

"Not me." He grinned. "I'm way too dignified and out of practice to flip in and out of the saddle. Some of the guys who work for me put on a show."

"I've thought of you in many different ways," she said as she moved closer. "*Dignified* isn't one of them."

He rested his hand on her shoulder and gave a gentle squeeze. "How would you describe me?"

She wanted to say sexy, but that probably wasn't the best place to start. "Patient."

"That sounds pretty damn boring."

"You already know that you're good-looking—some might say gorgeous—and smart. Patience is a special quality. You're not quick to judge. You're kind and thoughtful. You're a grown-up without making rules or demands."

He stroked her hair and tucked it back behind her ear. "My word for you is *spontaneous*. You're full of surprises. There's never a dull moment with you."

Before their compliments led to kisses, she backed off. Most definitely, she didn't want to make love in her studio with the rest of her little patchwork family wandering around in the house. "I need to get started on my sketches for Charlotte's shirt."

"Are you testing my patience?"

"Maybe."

"It's okay. You're worth the wait." He drew the gun from his hip. "Before I get distracted, I want to give you the Glock. Our lesson doesn't mean much if you aren't armed."

She looked down at the dark metal of the weapon. "What should I do with it?"

"Put it away somewhere safe. But keep it handy in case you need to use it."

She went to the nearest cabinet, a place where Michelle stored her paints, and placed the gun on an eye-level shelf. "I'd almost forgotten the danger."

"Don't worry. I'll keep you safe."

She watched him as he left the studio. It went without saying that his long legs and tight butt looked great in jeans, and it took some serious willpower to keep her from running after him, tackling him and dragging him up to her bedroom.

With her sketch pad open on the table in front of her, she started drawing pictures of ideas for the embroidery design. Sewing the shirt itself would be easy, especially since she had Charlotte's old shirt to use for a rough pattern.

Zach had left the door to the kitchen open, and she heard

the others talking and laughing. She smiled to herself as she started a sketch. Everything was going so well.

THE LISTENING DEVICE he'd planted in the kitchen of the Roost picked up two conversations going on at the same time. Toby and another cowboy talked about trick riding. The others were telling jokes. Listening hard, he heard the voices of Zach, Daniel, Charlotte and Toby. Everybody was in the kitchen except Gabby.

From a distance, he saw light shining through the windows in the studio. That told him where she was. Are you alone, city girl?

She was a problem. Standing in the center of the situation she blocked him from making a move. He had to get past her, to show her that she didn't belong here. If he eliminated her, he accomplished his goal. And he'd be free, wouldn't have to take orders. He could do anything and go anywhere.

He had to take charge before he lost control. Zach and his men had gotten smart about security and installed new dead bolts that couldn't be opened with a lock pick. The only way in was to break a window.

He climbed out of his vehicle and closed the door softly. There was no telling how long Gabby would be alone. He'd have to move fast so she wouldn't have a chance to scream.

GABBY WAS HALFWAY through the second sketch, which was mostly butterflies, when she remembered *Girl with Book and Mirror.* Charlotte had told her that the painting had formerly hung in the old house, on the wall left of the fireplace. From that position, the reading girl might be pointing to a clue.

Checking out her hunch would only take a minute. She

looked toward the corner door leading to the old house. Should she get someone to accompany her? Zach would say yes. He was adamant about security.

When she turned toward the open door to the kitchen, she heard laughter and the rumble of her brother's voice. He was enjoying himself, as was everyone else. Gabby didn't want to interrupt.

She glanced over at Daphne. "You'll come with me, won't you?"

The dog thumped her tail against the floor.

"Problem solved," Gabby said. "Just in case, I'll take the Glock. That should be enough security."

She unlocked the door to the old house, and then picked up a flashlight and her gun. The light spilling in from the studio was swallowed by the darkness on the other side of the door. The atmosphere felt chilly and intimidating. There might be ghosts living here, and they might not take kindly to her intrusion.

She looked down at Daphne. Animals were supposed to be able to sense unearthly presences. If the dog took off running, Gabby vowed to follow. "Do you see anything, Daphne?"

The dog moved a little closer to her leg. Either Daphne was trying to protect her or hiding behind her. Gabby suspected the latter.

Together, they entered the old house. The floorboards creaked with every step. If Gabby recalled the layout correctly, the fireplace was in a room to the left. Her flashlight beam slid across an old, busted sofa and a coffee table that hadn't been dusted in months, maybe not in years. Michelle had taken the trouble to keep the walls standing but hadn't been concerned about cleanliness. Why was this place so important to her? What memories was it hiding?

The flashlight beam played across the bookshelves and hit the rock fireplace that looked like it had been built by hand, maybe by the first people who lived here, Louis Rousseau and his Sioux wife. They were like characters from a history book.

A breeze stirred the air, and a thin, lace curtain rippled. Not ghosts but the broken window. Tomorrow, Gabby needed to get that fixed.

A door slammed.

The light gust of wind wasn't anywhere near strong enough to move a heavy door. She heard a footstep. Someone else was in here.

Gabby turned off her flashlight and scooted back against the wall. Ducking into an alcove, she squatted and pulled Daphne close against her. Was her timing so bad that she'd just happened to stumble in here in the middle of a break-in? Or had he been waiting for her?

Daphne gave a low whine, and Gabby held her tighter. *Don't bark, please don't bark.* If she charged the intruder, Daphne might be hurt. In Gabby's mind, that was worse than if she herself was injured. The need to keep the dog safe gave her the courage to raise the gun and slip her finger into the trigger hold. The safety was off. If she squeezed, the Glock would fire.

Holding her breath, she crouched in the dark. Moonlight through the filthy windows made it possible to see outlines of the furniture, but she couldn't tell if anybody was in the room with them.

She glimpsed movement near the front door and tried to brace the gun two-handed the way Zach had showed her. She couldn't manage it, not while holding the dog. She'd have to shoot one-handed. *I don't want to shoot.*

If she killed anyone, even an intruder, she couldn't live with the guilt.

Footsteps creaked across the floor. He was coming closer. She had no choice. Aiming in the general direction of the door, she squeezed the trigger. The blast of the gun shocked her. It sounded louder in the enclosed space. The smell of gunpowder was intense.

Daphne wriggled to get free, but Gabby held her tightly. "No, Daphne. Stay."

She fired again and again. Three shots, she still had ten left. Again, she fired.

She heard one word. *"Bitch."*

Four more shots rang out. Gabby knew they'd come from her weapon, but she wasn't aware of squeezing the trigger. Operating on panic and adrenaline, she reacted without knowing what she was doing.

Daphne broke free and leaped toward the door. Gabby raced after her, pausing once to take a stance and shoot blindly into the darkness that surrounded and smothered her.

The next voice she heard was Zach's. "Are you all right?"

"Where's Daphne?" Gabby shouted.

"It's okay. She's right here."

Gabby ran toward the light from the studio, dashed through the door and slammed it behind her. Charlotte and Daniel and Toby and the other cowboy were gathered around, staring at her. She wanted to tell them she was okay, but she couldn't talk, couldn't breathe.

"Finger off the trigger," Zach said.

Her hand was frozen. "I can't move."

Gently, he peeled the gun from her hand. "Did you see someone?"

"I heard him."

Zach nodded to the men who worked for him. "Check it out."

Both men drew their weapons. Toby took the flashlight from her, and they plunged into the darkness. Daphne— the furry little traitor—stood at the door and barked. If the dog had sounded the alarm before, Gabby might not have gone into the old house.

She could see the anger in Zach's eyes, but he didn't yell at her. Scolding her was unnecessary. She knew that she'd taken a risk. The thought of what might have happened hit her all at once, and she felt dizzy. "I need to sit down."

Bracing her shoulders, he guided her to a stool. "You've got to breathe. Take long, slow breaths."

With her throat constricted, she could barely manage a shallow gasp. Struggling, she forced herself to inhale and exhale until her panic subsided. Closing her eyes, she leaned against his chest. "I'm sorry."

Charlotte held her hand. "I'm glad you're okay."

"What were you doing?" Daniel asked.

When she opened her eyes, they were all staring wide-eyed, and she felt terrible for worrying them. "I wanted to follow up on a clue. The painting of the girl with the book used to hang in the old house, and I thought her hand might be pointing to something important."

"Hold on." Daniel held up his hand like a traffic cop. "You lost me, sis."

While Charlotte filled him in with enough details so he'd understand, Zach leaned close and whispered, "Never scare me like that again."

"I didn't mean to—"

"I know." His calm voice soothed her. "I'm not letting you out of my sight for the rest of the night."

Daniel interrupted, "I'm up to speed. Actually, it sounds like Gabby had a fairly good idea."

Toby and the other cowboy returned to the room. Toby reported, "Whoever was in there is gone. Should we go outside and look for him?"

"Check the perimeter of the house," Zach said. "Stick together."

Toby gave a quick nod. Charlotte's young beau was acting like a regular hero. "We'll take care of it."

"Then I want you to board over that broken window," Zach said. "The rest of us are going to follow up on Gabby's clue."

After rummaging around to find enough flashlights, their makeshift search party went into the dark old house. Gabby imagined that she could still smell the gunpowder. When she looked at the alcove where she and Daphne tried to hide, she shuddered.

Tail wagging, the dog looked up at her with a goofy expression. Her mouth was open, and her pink tongue lolled out on one side.

Gabby looked to Zach. "I know you think Daphne is really smart, but I'm not so sure."

"Says the woman who went into the haunted house all by herself."

"Woof."

Charlotte led the way to the fireplace and aimed her flashlight beam at an empty hook on the wall. "The painting was right there."

"Which means," Zach said, "the girl in the picture was pointing in the direction of the bookcase."

Charlotte shook her head. "I doubt there's much of a clue in those books. If I was a treasure hunter, that's the first place I'd look for a map."

"This isn't about treasure," Gabby reminded her. "It's about family."

The beams from their flashlights illuminated the spine of the old dusty books. Many were leather-bound classics, like *The Three Musketeers* and *Wuthering Heights,* but several were of a more modern vintage, including several thrillers. One title jumped out at her: *Confessions* by Jean-Jacques Rousseau.

When she took the thick book from the shelf, Daniel asked, "Is he a distant relative?"

"Not as far as I know."

He reached for a copy of *Treasure Island.*

The pages were yellowed but not crumbling. She doubted that this volume had been around since the 1800s, but it certainly wasn't new. Carefully, she looked through the book. In the middle, she found a small piece of folded paper pressed between the pages. When she removed the stained scrap, she felt the brittle texture.

"What have you got?" Zach asked.

"Looks like a letter." Written in French, it started with *"Mon Cheri"* and ended with *"Je t'adore, Louis."* If there were ghosts in the house, this was their calling card. "It's a love letter."

Chapter Fourteen

In the kitchen, Zach sat at the table and watched as Gabby and Charlotte went through the old book with painstaking care. They removed four old scraps of paper and two others that had been written by Michelle. The task required a delicate touch, and they were using tweezers from Gabby's makeup bag to keep from handling the paper.

He'd meant what he'd said about not letting her out of his sight. Her knack for being spontaneous was a good thing, and he liked the way she hopped from one topic to another, always keeping him guessing. But he didn't want another surprise like the one she'd just given him. Her spontaneous search in the old house could have gotten her hurt.

It couldn't be a coincidence that she'd run into the intruder. He must have been watching her through a window, biding his time, waiting until she was alone and vulnerable to attack.

Aware of the need for more security outside the house, Zach had called in his whole crew to keep watch. And he intended to take Gabby with him tonight when his shift ended. Tonight, she'd stay at his house where he knew she was safe.

With the tweezers, Gabby unfolded one of the older papers and placed it on a piece of plastic on the countertop. She pulled her hands back. "This paper is so fragile, over a hundred and fifty years old. I should take these love letters to an expert to make sure they don't fall apart."

"It would be a shame to lose them," Charlotte said.

Daniel sauntered into the kitchen. "And we need to find a translator."

"I can figure out most of the words."

"You?" Her brother scoffed. "How do you know French?"

"If you'd ever paid attention, you would know that Great-Aunt Rene spoke the language, and she had a friend from Paris." Gabby leaned over the counter to study the note and read a few sentences in musical French. "He says that he misses her hair, which is as black as midnight, and the stars in her eyes. It's very romantic."

"And cheesy," Daniel said. "You'd think a French guy could come with something more original."

"Like you could do better," she teased.

Daniel ignored her comment. "The reason we need a translator is that there might be a clue about the location of the treasure hidden in the letters. We've got to look at every word to see if there are secret meanings."

"I hate to burst your bubble," Zach said as he rose from the table, "but the Frenchman's Treasure is a myth. Like El Dorado or the Lost Dutchman Mine."

"How can you be so sure?"

"People around here have been looking for a long time. Somebody would have found it."

"But we're got new information," Daniel said. "Michelle specifically gave this painting to Gabby. And the painting was arranged to point out a clue. Why would she go to all that trouble if there wasn't something important to find?"

"You might have already found it," Zach said. "She

might have been directing you toward the love letters. It's your family's heritage."

Gabby whirled around to face them. "Hair spray," she said.

"What about it?" Daniel asked.

"Hair spray holds things together. I've used it as a fixative to preserve my sketches, and it might work on this old paper." She frowned. "Or I might ruin everything."

Charlotte dug into the makeup bag she'd brought downstairs so they could find tweezers. She pulled out a pink aerosol container. "You could try the spray with one of the notes from Michelle. I want to know what those say."

Gabby unfolded the note from Michelle and placed it on the counter. With a long sweep of her arm, she sprayed the note. A powdery scent floated through the kitchen. She squinted as she studied her handiwork. "It didn't smear the writing. That's a good sign."

"But this note is probably only a couple of years old," Charlotte reminded her. "Can you make out the handwriting?"

Gabby read aloud:

"To my family, I have lived a full and eventful life. Though I left you long ago, you have never been faraway in my thoughts. I would not change my life decisions. Perhaps, I would add to my experience by spending more time with you, especially with you, Rene, my stubborn sister. I have come to believe that we can never escape our DNA and must embrace our legacy."

Zach recognized the tone and the lack of sentiment. Michelle had never been one to cry over the past. She never offered excuses or apologies. "That sounds like her."

"It does," Charlotte agreed.

He and Charlotte and Michelle had a lot in common. They had all three been young when they left their parents' house and made their way in the world. None of them had been orphaned, like Gabby and her brother, but they'd made the choice to leave. Charlotte had been the luckiest; she had Michelle to catch her when she fell.

"There's a sketch," Gabby said. "It's a young version of Rene with a high-collar shirt and a long, thick braid hanging over her shoulder."

Charlotte moved close to study the small sketch. "She looks more like Daniel than you."

Zach took a look at the picture. He agreed with Charlotte. There wasn't a physical similarity between Gabby and her great-aunt from Brooklyn. He saw hints of Michelle in the almond shape of her eyes, but they weren't alike, either. Gabby was unique.

"Here's the other note from Michelle," Gabby said. "It's mostly a pencil drawing of a landscape with mountains and a river. It says, 'Open eyes, open heart, wide horizon.' Sounds like poetry."

Zach studied the picture. "This looks familiar."

"The scene is probably from nearby."

"Not the landscape itself but the picture. I think she did a painting of this view. I might have seen it in the portfolio of her art that Osborne put together."

"The portfolio is upstairs in my bedroom," Gabby said. "Let me get this all put away and we'll take a look."

While she carefully stacked the old papers between sheets of plastic, her brother and Charlotte both headed up to bed. For a few more minutes, Gabby puttered around in the kitchen, putting mugs into the dishwasher and wiping down the countertops. As she rattled off a list of errands they needed to run tomorrow, he had the distinct impression that she was avoiding a more serious discussion.

Finally, they went upstairs to her bedroom and closed the door. They sat on opposite sides of her bed with the art portfolio open between them. He flipped through page after page, occasionally pausing to admire Michelle's artwork. It didn't take him long to find the picture he'd remembered.

When he showed it to Gabby, she said, "You're right. That's the same picture. The one she hid in the pages of that book looks like a preliminary sketch for this one."

He read the title of the painting. *"Welcome Home."*

"Do you know this location?" she asked.

"Not that I can recall." He grinned. "You might have noticed that there's a lot of land outside the front door."

She smiled back. "Can I ask you an important question?"

He nodded.

"When I bumped into that intruder, was it nothing more than bad timing? A horrible coincidence?"

"I don't think so." He wished he could give her a better answer. "I think the creep was watching you through a window, waiting for a chance to get you alone."

"That's a relief." She sprawled back against the pillows. "If it had been a coincidence, I'd have to conclude that the Universe had it in for me."

"And that's better?" He would never understand this woman. "You don't mind that some psycho is stalking you?"

"Of course I do. But psychos can be dealt with. Bad luck follows you everywhere you go."

"And you're going with me tonight," he said. "You'll

stay at my place. That's safer for everybody else who's living here, and I want to keep an eye on you."

A sexy smile curved her lips. "You convinced me."

A FEW HOURS later, Gabby was settled in a pleasant bedroom at Zach's house. There was only one thing wrong with it: this wasn't *his* bedroom.

Before she and Zach had left the Roost, leaving a patrol of cowboys behind to keep watch, she'd told Charlotte that she'd be spending the night at Zach's. As she explained the security reasons for her decision, the logic sounded purely transparent. Even someone as unsophisticated as Charlotte had noticed the attraction between Gabby and Zach. She'd given a wink and a nod, assuming they'd be going to bed together.

Her brother's reaction had been much the same. He had even told her that he approved of Zach, as though she was asking for his blessing after all these years they'd spent apart.

Though she wasn't one to worry too much about other people's opinions, she was fairly sure that everybody else would think she and Zach were having sex. The only person who hadn't gotten the message was...Zach. Did he expect her to make the first move? She knew his bedroom was next door to this one because he'd pointed it out when he'd dropped off her overnight bag and stowed her Glock in the top drawer of the nightstand beside her bed.

Unable to decide what to do, she paced in a tight circle between the dresser and the windows. Should she go to his room? If she approached him, she knew he'd welcome her and they'd make wild, passionate, amazing love. What would that do to their relationship? He'd begun to trust her. He'd shared a piece of his soul when he told her about his addiction.

Did they need more time? Should she wait until she knew everything about him? With the way he dribbled out information one word at a time, learning all about him might take decades, and she didn't want to waste another minute.

The obvious solution was to talk to him. She cinched her black kimono more tightly around her waist and tiptoed into the hallway. The door to his bedroom was ajar and the lights were on. Summoning up her courage, she entered.

"Zach, I want to…" Her sentence faded away. He wasn't in the room. That was when she heard the splashing from the shower in the adjoining bathroom.

This might not be the best time to approach him, but she was primed for this talk. She opened the bathroom door. "Zach?"

When he pulled aside the plaid shower curtain and poked his head out, steam from the hot water swirled around him. "What's wrong? Did you hear something?"

"There's no danger." She stared at the rivulets of water dripping down his forehead. His wet hair was spiky and sleek at the same time. She could see enough of his chest to remind her that behind that curtain he was naked. She stammered, "I j-j-j-just wanted to talk. Is that okay?"

"Yep."

"You don't mind?"

"Nope."

He ducked back into the shower in a bathtub, leaving her in the steam to talk to a curtain. Having come this far, she wasn't going to back down or change her mind. "When I decided that I'd follow the terms of the will and stay at the ranch, it changed the way I thought about you. Can you hear me?"

"I hear just fine."

She pulled down the fuzzy lid on the toilet and sat. "We have this crazy physical chemistry going on. Every time I look at you, I get buzzed. And I know you feel it, too."

"What was that about a bus?"

"Buzzed," she said more loudly. It was exactly the way she was feeling right now. "Buzzed as in getting all hot and tingly and turned on. At first, I thought we should just have a fling. After a few nights of wild passion, we could both go our separate ways, which are so very different, worlds apart. Do you know what I mean?"

"I'm a man, Gabby. I was born knowing the meaning of casual sex."

"Then you might not like what I'm going to say next." She unfastened the sash on her kimono. It was getting hot in here. "I want more than casual sex."

He didn't respond. Not a "yep" or a "nope" or anything else. She listened to the thrumming of the shower, hoping she hadn't taken a wrong turn.

Swallowing her embarrassment, she continued, "I want to be friends and also to be lovers. Even though it might be hard and I might get hurt, I want a relationship with you."

Her statement hung in the steamy air like a dark, ugly storm cloud. This conversation wasn't going the way she'd hoped, and she was beginning to feel foolish. She should have just gone to bed in her separate room, pulled the cover over her head and pretended that she didn't care.

He leaned halfway out of the shower and extended his hand. "Join me."

"In the shower?"

"I'm not sure how we'll handle a relationship. Hell, I'm

not even sure what that means for you and me. But at least we'll be clean."

That was good enough for her. She stood and slipped out of the kimono. Her lingerie for tonight was a simple peach tricot with cap sleeves and a scoop neck. She could have played coy and fished for compliments about how pretty she looked, but an incredible naked man was reaching for her. In seconds, she peeled off the gown, shed her bikini panties and took his hand.

As she stepped over the porcelain wall of the bathtub and entered his shower, her gaze slid from the top of his head to his toes in a quick and remarkably thorough survey, considering that he didn't give her time to look twice. He pulled her against him. His skin was slick and smooth, covering his hard-muscled chest. The water from his body moistened her, and she reveled in an explosion of sensation that took her breath away. She was being pulled into a rushing current and abandoned herself to the moment. Whether or not they were meant to have a relationship, this felt so right.

As he kissed her, his left hand splayed across her back, holding her close while the right hand cupped her buttocks and fitted her against his groin. A wildfire raced through her, and she imagined the water sizzling when the droplets hit her superheated flesh.

A groan rumbled in his throat, and the sound was exciting because it meant he wanted her as much as she did him. Her doubts vanished. This was meant to be.

He turned her around so the spray from the shower sluiced down her back. As she arched her neck to get her hair wet, his hands roamed her body. He cupped the fullness of her breast and flicked the nipple with his thumb, sending another surge of pleasure through her.

He gazed into her eyes. "Should I wash you?"

"Am I dirty?" Though gasping and in the throes of amazing passion, she still managed to be a smart aleck. "Am I a dirty, dirty girl?"

He swatted her naked butt. "Maybe we can talk about that later. Right now, I'm afraid we'll run out of hot water."

"I don't want a cold shower."

"Then we should take this to the bedroom."

Stepping out of the shower, they took their time toweling each other dry, and she had a chance to admire his lean physique. The word *gorgeous* wasn't enough to describe his sinewy arms and torso. He was perfect.

"You could be a male model," she said.

"Shoot me now."

"I know lots of women who would buy anything you were wearing. They'd dress up their boyfriends, but none of the other men would look as good as you do."

"Whoa, Gabby, I'm supposed to do the sweet-talking."

She combed her wet hair straight back from her forehead. "Is that how this works?"

"Your ancestor—Louis the Frenchman—knew how to tell his wife that she was beautiful. That's why he wrote those letters. I'm not as good with words."

"I prefer a man of action."

In his bedroom, she pulled back the comforter while he closed the door. Earlier, he'd told her that he'd leave his bedroom door open so he could hear if an intruder approached.

She asked, "Shouldn't you leave that open?"

"Why?"

"Security," she said. "With the door open, you can hear if the bad guys come sneaking up on us."

"That was when I thought you'd be sleeping next door,

and I might need to rescue you. That's not necessary." He leaned against the door for emphasis. "Everything that's precious to me is right here in this room."

"Me?"

"You," he said.

He was a man of few words, but they were all the right ones. She opened the sheets and slid between them. Tonight she would share his world. Tonight they would make love. Tonight they would truly start their relationship.

Chapter Fifteen

The next morning, Gabby was wide-awake a few minutes before seven, even though Zach's bedroom curtains kept the room nice and dark. Being careful not to wake him, she snuggled against his shoulder in a position that had become familiar. The more she learned about him, the more she wanted to know. And every intimate detail felt like a revelation. She knew he was ticklish just below his rib cage. His left arm and leg bore the scars from the rodeo injury that ended his career. Last night, they'd made love again and again. She'd expected to be tired but was energized instead. Maybe the cure for altitude sickness was spending the night in the arms of a cowboy.

After dropping a little kiss on his chin, she reluctantly left the bed and tiptoed into the bathroom where her kimono hung on a wall hook. Though she would have preferred to spend the whole day naked in bed, they had a million things to do, ranging from the mundane to the exceptional, from picking up her car to tracking down an expert who could preserve the hundred-fifty-year-old love letters.

In the mirror over the sink, she saw her hair sticking out in all directions. Her blow-dryer was in the other bedroom, along with her clothes and makeup, but she didn't want to run and get them. For now, she'd just dampen her hair and comb it back. The arid Colorado climate made her straight hair even straighter, which was actually a plus. If she kept her bangs trimmed, styling would be unnecessary.

When she returned to the bedroom, Zach was yanking open the curtains. He hadn't bothered to get dressed, and she admired the view. Coming up behind him, she slid her arms around his middle. "Good morning."

"Great morning." He swiveled and gave her a lazy kiss. "I'd like to take you back to bed."

"I'd like that, too."

"But I'm already running late. I need to get out to the stables and give the men their instructions for what needs to get done today."

"So early?"

"The day starts when the sun comes up." He gave her another quick kiss. "Get dressed and meet me in the kitchen for breakfast."

She didn't want to be apart from him. "Do you mind if I look in your closet?"

"Why?" His blue eyes narrowed. "What are you up to?"

"I'm thinking about the shirt I'm designing for Charlotte, and I thought you might have some fancy embroidery that would inspire me." She sauntered over to his closet door. "May I?"

"Suit yourself."

While he was in the bathroom, she flipped through the shirts and jackets hanging on the rack. In the back, she found several Western-style shirts. Almost all of them were snap front and long-sleeved with piping on the breast pockets. Most of the fabrics were plaid or a neutral color, but a couple of these shirts were worthy of a Western-wear peacock with metallic fringe draped across the chest and multicolored, curlicue embroidery covering the yoke. If a low-key guy like Zach was willing to get so fancy, she had to wonder what a more flamboyant cowboy would wear.

While she got dressed, an idea began to form in her mind. If she started selling custom embroidered shirts, she could live at the Roost and still have a fashion career. This might be a viable possibility.

In the kitchen, Rhoda greeted her warmly, but Gabby sensed an undercurrent of tension from the busy little woman who zipped around the large kitchen, putting together breakfast burritos with green chili. Gabby was certain that Rhoda knew she'd spent the night in Zach's bed, and she didn't want things to be difficult between them.

Rhoda dashed into the dining room to freshen the coffee of two ranch hands who were eating their breakfasts. When she returned, she said, "Help yourself to the burritos warming on the stove. Use as much chili as you want, but be careful, it's hot."

"I'll just have coffee for now," Gabby said as she poured herself a cup. "Can we talk?"

Rhoda halted beside the sink, tucked her hands into the pockets of her pin-striped chef's apron and leaned against the counter. "What's on your mind?"

"I want you to know that I care about Zach."

She nodded. "Go on."

"We've only known each other a couple of days, but it feels like I've been waiting to meet him all my life." Gabby sipped her strong black coffee. "This isn't a casual fling. It's…"

"You don't have to explain."

"But I do. Ever since I got here, I've been hearing about the Rousseau family, heritage and legacy. The way I see it, you're the closest thing to family that Zach has. If I have a relationship with him, you're part of it."

"There's only one thing I'd like to know about your relationship." She cocked her head to one side, a movement that was oddly similar to Daphne. "Are you going to go running back to Brooklyn and break his heart?"

Gabby considered for a moment before answering. She didn't want to make a promise she couldn't keep. "That's not my intention. I'm planning to live at the Roost for three years."

"That's not what your brother says."

"I make my own decisions," Gabby said. "Daniel doesn't tell me what to do."

Rhoda opened her arms and gave her a hug. "I wish Michelle had brought you out here sooner."

"So do I."

Gabby stepped back. "Did Zach tell you what we found in the old house?"

"He told me that you almost got nabbed by the intruder."

Gabby had almost forgotten the danger. So much else had happened. "In the old house, tucked inside a leather-bound volume, we found love letters written in French by Louis Rousseau."

"What did they say?"

"My French isn't great, but there was some beautiful language about her hair as black as midnight. It's a shame that people don't write love letters anymore. They're so romantic. I can imagine his wife reading them over and over."

"It's different now," Rhoda said. "The romantic notion of a love letter is nice, but I'll take the convenience of technology any day of the week. I finally convinced Michelle to do her correspondence on the internet."

"I would have thought she'd like computers as another means of artistic expression."

"That was the problem. Michelle and I would sit down to work on her accounts, and she'd get distracted by some new way to mash photographs together." Rhoda crossed the kitchen and started filling a paper plate with a burrito and fruit. "I love my computer. If it wasn't for email and texting, I'd never know what my sons were doing."

"Do they live around here?"

"One of them is in college in Denver. The other works at a winery near Grand Junction."

As soon as she finished putting together the plate, Zach appeared in the kitchen doorway. Rhoda handed him the burrito and a travel mug of coffee.

"You're running late," she said. "You've got three or four men waiting out in the stables, and there are two more in here finishing breakfast."

"When those guys are done eating, send them out to the corral. We've got a full day."

"If you're going into town, I have a list of things I need from the market."

"No problem." Turning away from Rhoda, he strode across the kitchen toward Gabby, set his coffee mug on the counter and rested his hand at her waist. His lips grazed her cheek for a quick kiss, and he lowered his voice to a sexy whisper. "You smell good."

"So do you."

"Be ready to go by half past nine," he said as he headed for the door.

Zach gave orders like a man who was accustomed to being in charge, but she wasn't that obedient. "Where should I meet you? I need to go back over to the Roost and change clothes."

"You'll figure it out. Nine-thirty." He left the kitchen.

She turned to Rhoda. "You and Zach operate like clockwork. How did you know when to dish out his food?"

"From down the hall, I heard the door to his room close." She grinned. "This is our morning pattern. He's always sleeping late, and I'm always pushing food at him."

Gabby went to the kitchen window and looked out at the corral where Toby was riding in a circle on a dappled horse with a black mane. Zach stood at the fence, eating his burrito with his hands and talking to two other men in cowboy hats. Then he signaled to Toby. The scene was incredibly Western.

Gabby had a sinking feeling in the pit of her stomach. If she was ever going to have a deep relationship with Zach, she needed to learn something about horses and riding.

ZACH WAS MILDLY surprised when he drove his truck to the Roost to pick up Gabby and found that she was ready to go. The bigger shock came when she ran through a very organized list of errands they needed to accomplish, starting with the rodeo site in Snowmass.

"The last thing we should do on our way home," she said, "is go to the mechanic and pick up my car."

"You've got it all figured out." He allowed himself to relax, leaning back in his seat and gazing through the windshield at the fresh spring day. The grasses were green and the mountain fields were dotted with bright red and blue wildflowers.

"When I want, I can be efficient," she said. "I ran a boutique in Brooklyn for almost two years, and I wasn't lucky enough to have a brilliant assistant like Rhoda, who would do my accounting and keep my orders current."

"Rhoda is amazing," he said. "I don't think I would have survived without her."

"She mentioned something about doing computer work for Michelle. And I wondered if Michelle might have used Rhoda's computer for correspondence and note-taking."

"It's possible." He remembered the two women having tea in the afternoon and chatting at the dining room table with the laptop computer open beside them. "Why would that be important?"

"Michelle's other computers were stolen. She might have left backup data with Rhoda."

Every clue was worth checking out. While his men were keeping the security patrols at the Roost, Zach was confident that there would be no more break-ins. But he didn't want this to be a permanent situation. They needed to find the intruder and figure out who he was working for. Either Fox or Osborne, it had to be one of them. Nobody else was connected with Michelle, and Zach refused to believe in random attacks from treasure hunters.

Beside him, Gabby was on her cell phone, talking to the librarian in Aspen and asking about someone who might know how to preserve old paper. After three more phone calls, she'd located a man who had a rare book collection. "He'll be home all morning and we can just drop by. His address is in Snowmass. Does that sound good?"

"Yep."

Gabby reached over and stroked the sleeve of his tan shirt. Her touch made him feel good and reminded him of last night's lovemaking. He had never been with a woman who was so comfortable with her nudity. When she left the bed, she walked tall and proud, not hiding her body or playing self-conscious games. Being naked was natural to her, which was ironic considering that her career was about getting dressed up.

He was eager for tonight and tomorrow and the night after that. To tell the truth, he wouldn't mind skipping all these errands and taking her to one of the fine hotels in Aspen where they could spend the day making love and eating steak from room service.

Again, she pulled at his sleeve, and he realized that her gesture wasn't meant to be seductive. The only thing getting fondled was the fabric.

"Nice material," she said. "Would you consider this shirt to be everyday wear or something special?"

"I wouldn't wear it to muck out the horse's stalls. But it's not fancy."

"Not like that metallic fringe shirt I found in your closet." She beamed a wide grin. "I'd like to see you in that. It's very Elvis."

"What's the deal with you and the shirts?"

"I think this is going to be my new business," she said, "custom, embroidered Western shirts. I'm sure I could get some of the local shops to carry them on consignment. And I could also sell them online."

He had to admit that it wasn't a bad idea. Cowboys were willing to pay a high price for a custom shirt. "You might be onto something."

"You inspire me."

This time, when she leaned close and slid her hand along his inner thigh, he had no trouble reading her message. He really wished this long day of errands would be over.

The rodeo arena in Snowmass was a venue also used for other sports, like baseball and soccer, but they did a good job of preparing for the various events. Since this was close to Aspen, no expense was spared, and there was a greater than usual concern about potential animal cruelty. A lot of wealthy environmentalists lived in this area. At one time, Aspen had tried to pass a law banning fur coats.

He parked his truck in the lot, and they went toward the bleachers to look for the guy who was running this show and the people who were giving him a hard time.

"Why are we here?" Gabby asked.

"To reassure the animal rights people that everything is on the up-and-up. For some reason, they want to talk to me, even though this event has been sanctioned by the PRCA and everybody has agreed to abide by all their rules."

"What's a PRCA?"

"Professional Rodeo Cowboys Association," he said.

During his competitive years, Zach had been to rodeos that were badly run. The bulls and horses were mistreated, crammed into tiny chutes and shocked with prods to make them buck. Whenever he encountered cruelty, he withdrew from the competition, reported them and made a ruckus. He wasn't a crusader or political in any way, but he'd gotten a reputation.

In the center of the ring, the man-in-charge was talking with two people Zach recognized. One was a reputable stock contractor who supplied the animals for rough riding. The other was a woman that Gabby would want to meet.

"That's Sarah Bentley," he said.

"The Forest Preservation Society lady?"

"Yep."

When Zach introduced them, Sarah focused intently on Gabby as she shook her hand. "I've been thinking that I should pay you a visit."

"I'm glad to meet you. I understand that you were friends with my great-aunt Michelle."

"And I understand that you're standing between the FPS and a huge amount of income."

The battle lines had been drawn. Sarah's attitude seemed too mercenary for a tree hugger, but Michelle's estate was a significant contribution, one worth fighting for.

Zach revised his earlier list of two suspects. Sarah Bentley had more to gain than anyone else if Gabby and Daniel decided to sell the Roost.

Chapter Sixteen

Gabby had reason to dislike this woman, but decided to give her the benefit of the doubt. Michelle must have seen something good in Sarah Bentley. And Gabby would try her hardest to look for the positive, in spite of Sarah's pea-green peasant shirt, which did absolutely nothing for her long strawberry-blond hair. Her sandals were those heavy, ugly, easy-to-walk-in things that looked like Dutch clogs with a couple of pieces cut out. Gabby had always thought that if you wanted your feet to look that big, you might as well go for clown shoes. The platform sandals she was wearing were a thousand times more attractive.

"When you've finished your business here," Gabby said, "I'd like to talk."

"I'm done," Sarah said quickly as she shook hands with the men. "I've already checked the references for the stock contractor, and he appears to be satisfactory. Besides, Zach says he's reputable, and I trust Zach's opinion."

As he shook her hand, Zach said, "I didn't know my recommendation carried so much weight."

"It's because of Michelle," she said. "She told me that you bought several horses that had been abused in rodeos."

"Yep."

"I appreciate a man who takes action."

Was she flirting with Zach? Gabby's fingers drew into a fist. Sarah was making herself more unlikable by the minute. With a toss of her head, she pivoted and headed toward the bleachers circling the ring. "Are you coming, Gabby?"

Through tight lips, she responded, "Why not?"

As they walked side by side, Gabby took her measure. In a physical sense, they were evenly matched. Gabby stood a couple of inches taller in her platform heels, but Sarah was probably in better shape from hiking and doing mountain exercise things. Not that Gabby was planning to get into a fight with this woman.

"Zach is really good-looking," Sarah said.

You should see him naked. "We're dating."

"That's quick work. You only got here a few days ago. You're from Brooklyn, right?"

"You seem to know a lot about me, but I know nothing about you, other than you formed a bond with my great-aunt."

"Michelle and I shared a passion for taking care of the forests. With the oil companies moving in, it's important to safeguard this beautiful land. When I have the money from the sale of the Roost, I can pay for the legal battles that are surely coming."

Gabby climbed onto the bleachers and sat. "Did Michelle visit you at the Preservation Society?"

"When we first met, she wasn't aware of the FPS. She'd booked a room at the bed-and-breakfast I run. There was only one other guest, and we had time to chat. I watched her while she painted outdoors."

"Was she doing landscapes?"

Sarah nodded. "She saw things differently. She told me that she always looked through open eyes."

Gabby remembered the notation on the bottom of the

landscape sketch they'd found last night. Watching Sarah's reaction, she repeated those words. "'Open eyes, open heart, wide horizon.'"

"Is that a poem?" Sarah didn't sit beside her in the grandstand. Instead, she paced back and forth in her clumsy sandals as though she had somewhere else to be.

"It's something Michelle thought was important." *Too important to share with you.*

"What is it, Gabby? Is there something you want to say to me?"

"I hate to disappoint you, but I'm not planning to sell the Roost. I'm going to live there."

"That's not what Mr. Fox told me."

"It's not his decision," Gabby said. "I think there's a smaller stipend earmarked for the FPS."

"Thanks for telling me where I stand." She turned on her heel and walked away. "See you at the rodeo."

Gabby waved at her retreating form. "Nice to meet you."

It would have been even nicer to never see Sarah Bentley again, but Gabby didn't kid herself. The terms of the will tied them together. Until it was settled, they'd have to deal with each other.

She rejoined Zach in the arena as he was finishing his business with the other two men. With Sarah out of the picture, her mood immediately brightened. She couldn't help noticing that both of the other men were wearing Western shirts.

"Gentlemen, do you mind if I ask you a fashion question?"

They exchanged a glance and shrugged.

"Would you be interested in a custom embroidered Western shirt? You could choose your own design or even make up something totally original."

"Like a tattoo," said the stock contractor, a man who was burly enough to handle bulls. "My nickname is Rooster. I believe I would appreciate a shirt with chickens running across the back."

The other man nodded. "I'd look at custom embroidery."

She smiled at them both. "Thanks for your opinions."

Back in the truck, Zach rolled his eyes. "There's no stopping you now."

"I'm on my way to being an embroidery mogul." She mentally reviewed her list of things to do. "Our next stop should either be the rare books collector or a place where I can buy boots."

He didn't want to get roped into a shopping expedition. "What kind of boots?"

"Don't worry. This isn't about style. It's purely practical. If I'm going to spend my days running round at the ranch, I might as well have the appropriate footwear."

"Good way to avoid a broken leg."

"Your opinion is duly noted."

During their first stop at the insanely cluttered house of the rare books collector, Zach heard more than he ever wanted to know about the wonders of preserving old paper. As it turned out, Gabby had been on the right track with her hair spray. The collector sold them a specially formulated spray and advised sealing each sheet in a plastic baggie. The process sounded boring as hell to Zach, but he wasn't the one who was going to be spraying and sealing.

Their next stop was problematic. Zach explained, "To get to the market and shoe stores, we'll be going past the mechanic's place where we left your car. Should I drop you off to get your car and meet up with you at home?"

"How far out of the way is it?"

"Not far," he said, "eight or nine miles."

She widened her eyes, pleading with him. "I'd really like for you to come with me. You can show me which market is the best, and which shoe store."

"If you're looking to me for shopping advice, you're in serious trouble." His job was to take the detailed list of supplies that Rhoda gave him and fill the order. He didn't go from place to place looking for bargains. "One stop at one market, that's my rule."

Gabby wasn't listening. With a graceful flip of her wrist that was both charming and annoying, she suggested, "Maybe we could get lunch."

He drove to the intersection for Highway 82 and took a left. "What did you and Sarah talk about?"

"She thinks you're hot. I told her that if she ever mentioned your hotness again I'd rip her face off. Not really, but I thought about it."

"Good restraint."

"Fox told her that I was definitely moving out, and she was already figuring out how to spend money she doesn't have. I don't know why Michelle liked this woman. She's a grumpy, environmental witch."

"Who thinks I'm hot," he reminded her. "Did she seem threatening?"

"Really? Threatening, as in staging break-ins to convince me to move?"

"That's what I'm asking."

She thought for a moment and then shook her head. "I don't know. She seems to be absolutely politically correct, but if she thought it would serve the greater good to get me out of the way, who knows what she might do."

By the time they'd completed their errands and had lunch, it was almost three o'clock. He was itching to get back to the ranch. In addition to the regular work and rid-

ing lessons, he needed to work with his team on their trick
riding exhibition before the rodeo.

After she picked up her car from the mechanic and
paid with a credit card, he asked, "Do you want to follow
me home?"

"You don't have to show the way. I have my GPS rout-
ing. I'll probably get there before you do."

"I'll stop at the Roost first and drop off your groceries."

Her goodbye kiss lasted long enough to spark memories of last night. If he had gone through all this running
around with anyone else, Zach would have been snarling.
Gabby made the errands seem like an adventure. As he
watched her sashay over to her car, he regretted that she
wouldn't be wearing her platform sandals as much. The
boots she'd purchased were practical. But the ridiculous
shoes suited her.

GABBY HAD BEEN joking about beating Zach back to the
Roost, but that was what happened. Her little hatchback
had regained its pep after the tune-up and zipped along
the mountain roads. She parked in front and went to open
the door. She'd be ready for Zach when he showed up with
the groceries.

Standing on the porch, she took the key from her pocket
and aimed it toward the lock, but the door was already
open. She pushed the opening wider and peeked inside.
"Charlotte? Are you here? Daniel?"

No need to panic. There could be a simple explanation,
like they'd gone to Zach's or had accidentally left the door
open. She didn't want to be scared, but the adrenaline was
already flooding her system. If anything had happened to
Charlotte or her brother, she couldn't stand it. *Please, let
them be all right.* The Universe wouldn't be so cruel. If

they were hurt, it would take more than a pair of Louboutins to make it better.

Daphne raced around the edge of the house. Her loud, frantic bark was a clear warning. Something was wrong, terribly wrong.

Should she go inside? She hadn't brought the Glock with her while they were doing errands, hadn't thought she needed her own protection while Zach was with her. All she had was her tiny canister of pepper spray that had proved to be ineffective with Charlotte, who was basically harmless. Against an intruder, the pepper spray was a bad joke.

Daphne continued to bark, and Gabby went down the steps toward her. If only the dog could talk and tell her what happened.

When she saw Zach's truck coming down the road, she started waving her arms over her head as though signaling an airplane to land. "Hurry, Zach. I need you."

He must have gotten the message because the truck sped up. When he pulled up to the house, a plume of dust followed in his wake. He leaped from the truck.

As soon as his boots hit the ground, she was in his face, talking fast. "I came home and found the door open. When I yelled for Charlotte or Daniel, nobody answered."

Beside her, Daphne continued to bark.

If they'd been in the city, this is when they would have called 911, and a police car would pull up with sirens blaring. That wasn't going to happen here.

Zach got back into his truck, dug into the glove compartment and took out a handgun. "I want you to get in your car, take Daphne and drive to my place. Send Toby and the other men over here."

"I'm not leaving."

"There's no time to argue."

"Agreed," she said as firmly as she could without being able to breathe. "I'm coming inside with you. That's final."

"Then stay back. Don't get in the way."

He ran onto the porch, holding the gun in both hands. She followed Zach inside, staying as close as a shadow. Daphne went as far as the door, but then dropped out. Her barks came less frequently.

Zach checked out the front room and dining room. He went into the kitchen. "Damn it."

She peeked around his arm and saw Daniel lying on his belly near the sink. His head was bloody. He wasn't moving.

Gabby rushed to his side and knelt beside him. Her heart felt like it was jumping out of her chest, but she had to be calm and help her brother. Her fingers pressed against his throat, and she easily found the carotid artery. The rhythm of his pulse was strong and steady.

His dark hair was matted around the wound on the back of his skull, but there wasn't much blood.

"Daniel," she said, "Daniel, wake up. We're here now. You're going to be all right."

Zach had left her to check out the rest of the house. He returned with his gun still in his hand. "There's a window broken at the front of the house. That's how he got in."

"He has a pulse, but he's not moving." She bent down close to his ear. "Daniel, can you hear me?"

He groaned. It was the most beautiful sound she'd ever heard. Then his arm moved and he rolled onto his side. "What the hell happened?"

When she hugged him, he winced, but she was glad for any sign of life. Her brother was going to live. All was right in the Universe.

Chapter Seventeen

At the urgent care clinic, Daniel was being his usual rebellious self. The doctor had told him that he had a concussion and should go to the hospital in Aspen or Glenwood to stay overnight for observation. Daniel wouldn't cooperate. With his head wound bandaged, he sat on the examination table, fully clothed and refusing to change into a gown.

Gabby stood beside him, fuming.

"I'm ready to go home," Daniel said. "I'm fine."

"Is that your studied medical opinion?"

"This is nothing but a whack on the head. They took X-rays. My skull isn't cracked. I don't have amnesia."

The story he'd told them on the frantic drive to the clinic had been simple. He'd been in his bedroom taking a nap when he'd heard a noise from downstairs that sounded like a window breaking. He'd gone to investigate, and someone had hit him from behind. He hadn't seen the person who attacked him.

"If we were in the city where medical care is easily available," Gabby said, "I might be more inclined to take you home and watch you myself tonight. But we're isolated out here. I don't know how to take care of you if something goes really wrong."

"Like what?"

"Like you could have a seizure or go into a coma." The very nice doctor had explained all this. "A concussion means the wiring in your brain is messed up. Anything could happen."

"And if it does, you bring me back here."

"It took us half an hour driving like maniacs to bring you to this urgent care facility. It's another half hour to get to a fully staffed hospital where you can check in overnight. And that's where you need to be."

"I can't pay for it, Gabby. I don't have insurance."

She was well aware of his uninsured status. When she checked him in, they required payment, and she'd drained the last few bucks left from her credit card to pay for his X-rays and the bandages. "We'll find a way to cover the cost."

"Fine," he said petulantly. "If you get the money, I'll go to the hospital."

Why was his health care her responsibility? She had insurance for herself, even though it was expensive and she would have preferred spending her hard-earned cash on something more important, like shoes. But she'd done the necessary thing and gotten herself signed up. Daniel should have done the same.

She left him in the tiny examination room and went out to the waiting area. Zach wasn't sitting where she'd left him twenty minutes ago after she'd reported that Daniel was doing well. She looked through the window and saw him pacing back and forth on the sidewalk with his cell phone to his ear.

She could ask Zach to loan her the money, but it wasn't right for him to shoulder that burden. She didn't want him to think she was using him. They'd barely started their relationship. How could she ask him for money? She couldn't. Daniel was her problem, not his.

Since she wasn't employed, she couldn't arrange for an advance on her salary. But there was the promise of income in her future. Fox had said that she'd receive a stipend for staying at the Roost. She could call the lawyer. After all, he'd paid for Daniel's plane ticket, which showed he was willing to invest in the estate.

But Zach hated Fox and suspected him of being behind the break-ins. Asking him for a loan was like making a deal with the Devil. She'd have to be careful and smart. *Smarter than a sly attorney?*

As soon as she stepped outside, Zach ended his phone call and came toward her. "Is he okay?"

"He's peachy. He thinks he should go home."

"And you don't agree."

"Whoever said 'he ain't heavy, he's my brother' didn't know Daniel." She slipped her arm through his, needing to draw on his strength to get through this. "Holding a family together is really hard work."

"Which is one of the reasons I don't have one," he said. "What did the doctor say?"

"A concussion can lead to all kinds of other problems— seizures, strokes, comas, aneurisms or all of the above. The doc advised that Daniel check into a hospital for overnight observation."

"But Daniel doesn't think that's necessary."

"We're going to do this my way." Her brother might be a gambler, but she wasn't. Risking his life based on nothing more than a hope that he'd be okay wasn't an option. She had to call Fox. There wasn't a choice.

"That means the hospital," he said. "Right?"

"Right. I wish I had my car," she said. "There's no reason for you to drive all the way to Aspen and wait with me at the hospital."

"Already taken care of," he said. "Charlotte and Toby are driving here in your car as we speak."

"You're a genius."

"A hot genius," he reminded her.

"I need to make a few phone calls, to arrange the hospital."

Her cell phone weighed heavy in her hand. Contacting Fox would be one of the most difficult steps she'd ever taken, perhaps one of the most foolish. Seeking privacy for her desperate act, she returned to the clinic and punched in the lawyer's phone number.

MAKING A DEAL with the devil had its rewards. After Gabby explained the situation to Fox, he promised to take care of everything, and he did. The hospital admission process was smooth sailing. Instead of being dismissed as an uninsured indigent creep, Daniel was met by a nurse with a wheelchair and taken to a private room where two different doctors paid him a visit.

His attitude had taken a dramatic shift. No longer uncooperative, he reveled in the attention. Sitting up in his bed and wearing his hospital gown, he held out his hand to her. When she grasped it, he pulled her onto the edge of his bed. "Thanks, Gabby. I forgot what it was like to have somebody care about me."

His sentiment touched her. When they were kids, she and Daniel had been close. "I think this is what families are supposed to do."

"I care about you, too."

His X-rays had been taken again, and he was scheduled for a CT brain scan. As the hospital staff ran a series of other tests, Gabby could almost hear a cash register in the background, ringing up one charge after another.

Her brother was worth it.

Later that evening, one of the doctors came to his room to talk with them. "The good news is that we aren't expecting a negative outcome from the brain trauma. We'll know more tomorrow."

"What's the bad news?" Daniel asked.

"You're suffering from an upper respiratory infection and exhaustion. The primary treatment for all these conditions is rest. We have you checked in for tonight, but I'd suggest at least one more night in the hospital."

Gabby felt the blood drain from her face as though she was being suctioned by a vampire vacuum. Her brother's stay in the hospital was going to cost a small fortune. Somehow, she'd have to find a way to pay Fox back that didn't mean losing the Roost.

Leaving Daniel to get the rest he needed, she went downstairs to the cafeteria for coffee. The steaming mug sat in front of her on the table, but she couldn't summon the energy to lift it to her lips. Only a few short hours ago, her future had been rosy. So quickly, everything had changed. The little family she'd been putting together had fallen apart. She'd found her brother on the floor in the kitchen, half-dead. And his life-threatening injury revealed an illness he hadn't even been aware of. Nothing felt set and orderly. She'd lost control and had willingly given Fox an opportunity to take advantage of her.

Most of all, she worried about Zach. He'd be furious that she'd made contact with Fox and had accepted his help. If he found out that she'd taken a loan from Fox, he'd be angry. From the moment he met the attorney, Zach had been convinced that Fox was bad news. It might be better not to tell him, to keep this loan a secret.

She wasn't actually lying to Zach. She just wasn't telling him everything. That rationalization would have to stand. There hadn't been a choice.

TOO TIRED TO drive home from the hospital, she'd spent the night sleeping in uncomfortable chairs in waiting rooms. One of the staff doctors would be seeing Daniel at ten in the morning when he'd give her the word about whether or not he could be released. She left the elevator and strolled down the pale blue corridor leading to her brother's private room. At the door, she saw Daniel propped up in bed talking to a red-haired man in a suit—Fox. She stepped back and eavesdropped on their conversation. The constant hum of hospital noise made it difficult to hear clearly, but she caught the gist of what they were saying. Fox subtly advised Daniel to sell the Roost, and her brother agreed. They both thought her attitude was an obstacle to an otherwise smooth transaction. She heard Fox say, "Gabby means well." And Daniel kicked in with, "She doesn't really understand business."

She clenched her jaw. She hated being patronized and told to step aside. If it was the last thing she ever did, she would show these two jerks that she understood exactly what she was doing.

After loudly clearing her throat, she walked into the room and went directly to Fox. "Thank you for stopping by."

"I think of you both as family."

Did foxes eat their young? "How kind you are."

"Michelle was very special to me," he said. "I want the best outcome for both of you."

"And for yourself," she said.

For a moment, the veneer of civility peeled back to show what he was really thinking. Fox radiated a powerful avarice. He'd do just about anything for money. Gabby despised him.

They smiled pleasantly at each other as the doctor came into the room and warmly shook hands with Fox, who was obviously a big deal at this facility. It came as no surprise when the doctor consulted his charts and advised that Daniel stay for another day so they could continue to monitor his brain activity.

Gabby bit her lower lip to keep from blurting out a comment about how Daniel's brain hadn't been active in years.

After the doctor left, she leaned across the bed to kiss her brother's forehead. "I need to get back to the Roost. I'll check in from time to time. Give me a call when you're ready to be released."

She was halfway down the corridor when Fox caught up to her. The first time she'd met him, she hadn't noticed that he was a few inches shorter than she was in her platform sandals. She stretched her neck to make herself even taller.

There was something she needed to say, even though she didn't want to. Her words came through gritted teeth. "Thank you for helping us out with a loan. You made it possible for Daniel to get the very best care."

"You're a polite young woman, well brought up."

"And I'm as stubborn as Michelle. I should tell you that I intend to fulfill the terms of the will and live at the Roost for three years."

His blue eyes were almost colorless. "I'm sure we can come to a different understanding, and I will forgive your loan."

"I'll find a way to pay you back."

She lengthened her stride and walked away from him, aware that she was only avoiding trouble, not escaping it.

HE WAS DONE with watching the Roost. Gabby's idiot brother had almost caught him planting another bugging device in the living room. It was a close call, too close.

When he'd knocked the brother out, he'd hit him too hard. For a couple of minutes, he'd thought the guy was dead. Law enforcement didn't pay much attention to break-ins, but homicide was something else.

He was glad to leave the Roost in his rearview mirror. Keeping watch had gotten too complicated. All night long, the cowboy security guards were on patrol. Too many people were running in and out during the daylight hours. It was like breaking into Grand Central Station.

He'd have to find another way to deal with Gabby.

Chapter Eighteen

Zach hadn't known Gabby was back at the Roost until he gazed across the grassy land that separated their houses and saw her car parked in front of the porch. He wondered why she hadn't called him. Having her brother in the hospital had really knocked her sideways. She'd been shattered when they entered the kitchen and found Daniel lying there. As she'd told him many times, her brother was all she had left of her real family.

He'd missed her in bed last night. To be sure, a sick brother took precedence, but she hadn't called. It was like she'd been avoiding him, which was not an encouraging start for what she insisted on calling a relationship. They might have been too quick to label this attraction.

At the front door to the Roost, he used his key to enter. Upstairs, Charlotte was singing a pop ballad about being crazy in love. He couldn't remember ever hearing her sing before. That young woman was changing faster than a kaleidoscope, finally allowing herself to shine. He called to her, "Hey, Charlotte."

She appeared at the top of the staircase with a towel wrapped around her head. "I'm dying my hair. Do you think Toby will like me as a blonde?"

"He'd like you if your hair was green." The shy, young

cowboy who had worked at the ranch for two years needed to be with somebody like Charlotte—a girl who wouldn't overwhelm him. "I saw Gabby's car. Where is she?"

"In the studio, working on my new shirt. I told her that she didn't have to finish it for the rodeo tomorrow. With her brother in the hospital, she doesn't have time. But she insisted. She wants people to notice her custom embroidery."

Diving headfirst into her new shirt-making business, that sounded more like the Gabby he knew. He went through the kitchen to the entrance for the studio. Though he hadn't spent much time in this room with Michelle, he'd always liked the wide, open space and the many windows. And he liked the way Gabby had changed it, draping colorful materials across portions of the walls and turning the tables into work areas. The sewing machine whirred, and Gabby bent over her work, concentrating hard.

He descended the stairs quietly, not wanting to startle her and cause her to make a mistake. When she looked up and lifted her hands from the fabric, he spoke. "Busy?"

Hearing his voice, she bolted from her chair and raced toward him, not stopping until she'd flung both arms around his neck and kissed him. Right away, he noticed a difference in her kiss. A feeling of desperation?

"I missed you," she said.

Her dark eyes were more serious. The carefree smart aleck seemed to be hiding behind a heavy curtain. "Are you all right?"

"I'm worried. Like I told you on the phone, Daniel has more wrong with him than the concussion. He's suffering from exhaustion. He told me that for the past couple of months, he's been working double shifts to make extra money."

"To pay off gambling debts," he guessed.

"He didn't admit it, but I know that's the problem. He buried himself under too many IOUs and now he can't see daylight."

"You know that gambling is an addiction."

"You bet. No joke intended." But she smiled anyway, and he was glad to see her lighten up. "My dad had a similar problem. On the night when he and my mom were killed in a car accident, they were driving back from Atlantic City. He'd just won big, and then he was gone."

"I'm sorry." He was beginning to understand why luck played such a big role in her philosophy of life.

She took his hand and dragged him across the studio. "Come take a look at Charlotte's shirt. It's butterflies and roses."

The yoke of the turquoise shirt was embroidered in shining black thread in a flowing design. "Did you draw this picture?"

"I made it especially ornate to contrast the simple lines of the shirt. I'm thinking of adding some silver clothing studs that would look like dewdrops on the roses."

"Michelle was right. You've got talent."

"I'm a scribbler. She was an artist."

In the few minutes they'd been talking, she'd lost some of her grim melancholy. He wanted to encourage her and tease her until she was back to full Gabby. "Let's get out of here and relax."

"Can't take the time," she said. "I want to finish this shirt. The rodeo is tomorrow, and I want people to see the shirt and want to buy one or two."

"How are they going to do that?"

"I already have a site on the internet where you can order my designs, and business cards that direct you there.

But I need to change my photo gallery to highlight Western wear."

"Charlotte will let you take some pictures of her."

"Yes, but most of the sales in Western shirts go to men." She was eyeing him like a slab of steak. "You'd look good in a black shirt with a white design. Of course, the embroidery has to be horses."

"You want me to be your model."

"Like Sarah Bentley said, you're hot."

He didn't love this idea, didn't even like it much. But he didn't want to turn her down when she was so excited about her project. "Will I see you tonight?"

"Can you come over here? With Daniel in the hospital, Charlotte is all alone, and I want to keep her company."

"Works for me," he said. "I'll be getting up extra early to load the trick ponies into the big trailer and transport them over to the arena."

She fidgeted and looked back at her sewing machine. "I should get back to work."

After a peck on the cheek, he left her in the studio. Her mood was off-kilter, and he wanted to find out why. After seeing her brother hurt, she might have changed her mind about living at the Roost. If that was true, why was she gung ho about her Western shirts? She might be worried about money. Daniel's care at the hospital wouldn't be cheap. He had to face the possibility that she was having regrets about last night.

Had he done something to cause her unhappiness? They'd spent the day together yesterday, and she hadn't been upset. Gabby wasn't the type of woman to take offense and hold a grudge. If something was wrong, she'd blurt it right out. Or would she?

By the time evening rolled around, he was still clueless.

He put together a portion of Rhoda's baked ham and a loaf of fresh-baked bread for Gabby and Charlotte. It came as no surprise when Toby offered to drive over to the Roost to take his turn as a bodyguard.

Zach warned, "Charlotte did something to her hair, so be sure you notice that it's different. No matter what it looks like, tell her it's pretty."

"I wouldn't be lying," he said. "She always looks pretty."

"How come it took you so long to notice?"

"Before Gabby got here, Charlotte dressed like a boy. I couldn't see her shape under those sweatshirts."

"And now she wears glitter and miniskirts. That's what they call feminine wiles."

When they arrived at the Roost, Charlotte was on the porch waiting for them. Her hair was slightly blonder in color, but Zach was glad he'd given Toby a heads-up so the young man could say the right things. In simple situations, Zach was confident in his relationship abilities, but he wasn't feeling that way when he entered the kitchen with his food supplies and confronted Gabby, who sat at the kitchen table with her shoulders slumped and her head drooping. She looked like a graphic illustration of depression.

He couldn't really compare her emotional turmoil to that of a wild mustang, but some of the same principles applied. First, he assessed her physical situation: terrible posture, dark circles under the eyes and shallow breathing.

"You're tired," he said.

"I spent last night sleeping on chairs in the hospital waiting room."

"When was the last time you ate?"

"I'm not hungry."

That was the depression talking. He could see that her

body needed nourishment and hydration. In the refrigerator, he found a bottle of water that he placed on the table in front of her. "Drink this."

There was a bowl of fruit on the table and he pulled it toward her. "Try the banana."

She looked at him with suspicious eyes. "What are you doing?"

From working with horses, he knew better than to let her see that he was manipulating her. He tossed out a distraction. "I'm making a ham sandwich." He went to the counter, found a knife and began slicing. Another distraction. "Did you finish Charlotte's shirt?"

"I did and it's really nice." She peeled the banana and took a bite. "And I'm almost done with yours."

Now was not the time to tell her that he wasn't going to play male model. "How do you know my size?"

"I measured one of your shirts to use as a pattern. It's something Rene taught me to do. When we went clothes shopping, we hardly ever bought anything. We'd check out the styles and the fabrics, go home and make the clothes ourselves."

"Apart from the savings, what did you like about making your own outfits?"

"It's satisfying to start out on a project and see it through to the end. With clothing, I produce a tangible product that's also useful."

He placed the sandwich in front of her and sat at the table. If she'd been a mustang, this would have been the point when he tossed a blanket on her back to get her accustomed to the feel of a saddle.

She took a bite, chewed slowly and swallowed. "This is good. Maybe I was hungry, after all."

Satisfying her need for sleep meant he probably

wouldn't find out what was bothering her tonight. He'd have to wait, to be patient.

They'd gone up to her bedroom early, and he'd selected her most modest nightgown. "Put this on."

"Why? You're just going to take it off."

"I want to make love," he said honestly. Thinking about having her in his arms occupied most of his waking thoughts. "But you need to rest. I can wait."

"You're a very unusual man."

Or a complete idiot. "Good things are worth waiting for. You've had a rough couple of days."

He stripped down to his boxers and slipped under the sheets beside her. Though his intention was simply to cuddle, he was fully aroused and ready for a lot more. *Later,* he told himself. They had plenty of time for earth-stopping passion, later.

Within minutes, she was asleep, breathing steadily, curled up in his arms. Holding her gently, he kissed her forehead and succumbed to a sense of warm contentment as he sank into a pleasant sleep.

Hours later, he was wakened by her kiss. He kept his eyes closed as his hands stroked the silky skin of her bare back, gliding over the curve of her slender waist until he cupped the fullness of her buttocks. Their clothes were gone. He didn't remember taking anything off, but he was naked. And that was good. He guided her position so she was on top of him with her legs splayed on either side of his hips.

He opened his eyes. She hadn't turned on a lamp, and the room was dark, but he could see the outline of her delicate profile. Her lips were parted, and she was breathing deeply as she slid down his body. Moving slowly, she dropped kisses along the way as she descended from his neck to his chest to his hips and lower. Her tongue laved his flesh. Her hands gripped and kneaded.

Unable to hold himself in check for one more second, he reversed their positions so he was on top. He'd thought far enough ahead to bring condoms, which he stashed in her bedside table beside the Glock. When he was ready, he lowered himself onto her body, feeling every inch of her body pressed against him.

He returned her kisses and doubled them until she was arching against him, demanding release. He parted her thighs and entered her, claiming her, accepting the driving tension that could only be satisfied by making love. She matched his thrusts, driving him to go harder and faster until he couldn't hold back.

His body shuddered in release, and he collapsed onto the bed beside her, breathing hard.

She whispered, "Was it worth waiting for?"

"It was Christmas, New Year's and my birthday rolled into one."

"You're going to look great in the Western shirt I'm making for you."

"Can't wait."

Though he'd been taking care of her, wrangling her like a wild mustang, Zach felt like he was the one being tamed.

Chapter Nineteen

The plan was for Gabby, Charlotte and Rhoda to leave for the rodeo at ten o'clock, skipping the morning events, which were mostly for families and kids. The 4-H clubs would show off the livestock they'd raised themselves, and there would be contests for kids, all of which sounded weird to Gabby. Mutton busting involved a child hanging onto a sheep for as long as they could. There was a contest based on pulling the ribbon off the tail of a calf or a goat.

Not being a fan of smelly animals, Gabby didn't think they'd be missing much if they didn't watch the Little Britches events. She wondered what these ranch kids would think of playing stickball in the street in Brooklyn or cracking open a fire hydrant to cool off in the spray.

The trick riding was at one, before the main events. That was what she really wanted to see. The difficult part of her scheduling was figuring out when she needed to be at the hospital to pick up Daniel. Taking him to the rodeo instead of home to bed would probably be against the doctor's advice, and she told Gabby and Rhoda that they should take two cars in case she needed to leave early.

When she got Daniel on the phone at the hospital, he sounded great. "Apart from a minor headache, I'm fine."

"Did the doctors tell you what you're supposed to do when we get home?"

"The typical, healthy stuff," he said, "like drinking plenty of water and getting a full eight hours of sleep. And exercise. I should get started on an exercise regimen."

That simple advice came at a high cost, but she was glad that Daniel was well. "When will you be released?"

"Here's the thing, Gabby. You don't have to pick me up."

An alarm bell rang inside her head. She had a bad feeling about this. "Why not?"

"Fox arranged for me to stay at a place where I can concentrate on recuperating. And, here's the best part, it's free."

The alarm clanged louder. Anything involving Fox was bound to be trouble. "Where is this magical free place?"

"It's a bed-and-breakfast. The owner is Sarah Bentley, the woman who runs the Forest Preservation—"

"I know who she is," Gabby snapped. *Clang! Clang! Clang!* How could her brother be so blind? Didn't he see that he was being manipulated? "You're not going there. I'll pick you up."

"Sorry, sis, the reservations are already set. I met Sarah yesterday, and she seems like a reasonable person. Working with her shouldn't be a problem."

"Of course, she's being nice to you. If she convinces you to sell the Roost, her save-the-trees club gets tons of money."

"Is that such a bad thing?"

"Since when are you an environmentalist." She wanted to jump through the phone and strangle him. "Let me put it in terms you understand. If she gets the money, you don't. We don't just lose the house. We also lose all the money from Michelle's art."

"My mind is made up," he said. "I'll call you tomorrow."

When she ended the call, she couldn't have been more furious. When she'd contacted Fox, she thought she'd be on the hook for an outrageous loan but had never suspected that he'd convince Daniel to turn against her.

GABBY AND CHARLOTTE rode together in her car, and Rhoda drove her own truck because she needed to bring some gear from the ranch that the guys forgot this morning. Zach had left Gabby's bed before sunrise to supervise the loading of the trick horses for their event.

When she parked in the lot beside the arena, Gabby felt the excitement vibrating off Charlotte. Her blonder hair suited her, and her turquoise shirt with the custom embroidery looked terrific. She had to be one of the prettiest cowgirls in Pitkin County. As they walked toward the arena, she waved to a couple of teenage girls who did double takes and then motioned for her to join them.

"Do you mind if I go with them?" Charlotte asked.

"Have fun." Gabby patted her back. "Be sure to tell everybody where you got your shirt."

On her own, she wandered among several booths that had been arranged in a small fairground. The woman who ran a quilt store chatted with her about the patchwork, elbow-length jacket she was wearing. Gabby had styled herself for the rodeo in skinny black jeans, platform shoes, the jacket and a couple of chunky bracelets. Fashion made her feel put together, and she needed all the reassurance she could get, especially after her brother's defection to Sarah Bentley.

There were a few other craft booths that featured home-sewed items, and Gabby left her card with each. She was kind of surprised to find so many people who sewed and worried that there might be others doing fancy Western shirts.

When she saw Zach striding through the crowd toward her, the first thing she noticed was his saucer-sized, gold-and-silver All-Around Champion Cowboy belt buckle.

He gave her a kiss on the cheek. "You look pretty, kind of urban, but pretty."

She tapped the buckle. "This is a subtle accessory."

"I thought you'd like it. How's your brother?"

This would be difficult to explain without mentioning her loan from Fox, but she didn't want to risk getting into an argument with Zach. "Daniel is leaving the hospital and staying at Sarah Bentley's bed-and-breakfast."

"How did he meet her?"

"Fox."

Zach's attitude switched from easygoing to angry in the blink of an eyelash. "Why?"

"Fox is trying to turn my brother against me and force me to sell. And Daniel is falling for it."

"He doesn't control you, doesn't own you. He can't force your hand, Gabby. I won't let him."

"That's what I need to hear." It wasn't exactly true, but she needed the confidence boost. With Zach's support, she felt unstoppable even though Fox had her barricaded behind huge obstacles.

He took her hand. "Almost time for the trick riding. Let's go."

As they made their way through the stands, every other person greeted Zach. Until now, she hadn't realized what it meant to be a local celebrity, and she liked being with him. On a purely practical level, an endorsement from Zach on her shirts meant something in the rodeo world.

In the announcer's booth, Zach took his place beside

the man with the microphone. Looking down at the arena, she saw Toby and three other cowboys who worked for Zach behind the gates. Toby waved to signal that they were ready.

After the announcer welcomed the crowd, he introduced Zach. "Two time All-Around World Champion Cowboy and owner of Sheffield Ranch, Zach Sheffield."

Zach waited a moment for the applause to die down, then he spoke into the microphone. "Before we get started, I want to take just a minute to remember a very special lady that many of you knew and loved, a longtime resident of this area, an artist. Join with me in a salute to the memory of Michelle Rousseau."

His impromptu eulogy gave her chills. Looking out at the crowd, she noticed several people bowing their heads. Her great-aunt had made an impact on the people around her. Gabby hoped she could do the same.

"Let's get started," he said. "These trick riders work at my ranch and practice when they should be mucking out the stalls in the stable."

The four men burst into the arena. Gabby still wasn't a fan of horses, but these were beautiful animals, especially when they reared back on their hind legs and held that pose. The cowboys rode together in formation, then peeled off and circled around in precision maneuvers that brought them within inches of collisions.

By himself, Toby maintained a full gallop across the ring while dismounting on one side and jumping over to the other side and back again. The others followed, doing the same dangerous trick. The most impressive part, in her mind, was the speed of the galloping horse. "How do they do that?"

"The real skill comes in training the horse," Zach said.

"If the mount doesn't have a steady gait, the rider can't balance."

The tricks involved hanging off the saddle, flipping around to ride backward and standing. For their finale, all four cowboys stood on their horses and circled the ring.

"Thanks," Zach said into the microphone. "If you want to learn how to do those things, give us a call at Sheffield Ranch, and we'll try our best to talk you out of it."

As she followed Zach away from the booth, Gabby inhaled the pungent air. Before today, the closest she'd come to a rodeo was a petting zoo, which hadn't been a lovely experience. In the ring, a couple of guys in clown outfits were setting up barrels. "What are those for?"

"Barrel racing. The riders weave in and out of the barrels without bumping into them. The winner has the fastest time."

"I never dreamed I'd say this, but I'd like to watch."

Because Zach was a rock star in the world of rodeo cowboys, they had access to anywhere in the five tiers of seats. He found them a space at the ground level fence that circled the ring.

At the far end of the ring were the chutes that held the bucking broncos and the bulls. She recognized Rooster, the stock contractor, climbing over the chutes and checking the gates. She saw a flash of red hair. "Over by the chutes," she said, "is that Kevin Fox?"

Zach squinted. "He shouldn't be there."

"Maybe he's competing."

"He's not signed up. I checked." He leaned closer to her. "I spotted somebody else you know. He's behind us, at the end of the stands."

She looked over her shoulder. Though Ed Striker wore a cowboy hat and a denim shirt, his overly muscular body made him stand out in a crowd. His neck was as big as her waist.

"All the suspects are here," she muttered, "except for Sarah and Fox, who are busy brainwashing Daniel."

"Let's go see what the younger Fox is up to," Zach muttered. "I feel like giving somebody a hard time."

The area behind the chutes was a different atmosphere. She sensed the competitive tension, and the animal smell was overwhelming. Looking down at her feet, Gabby wished she'd worn the practical boots she bought yesterday. The dirt path where they were walking was enclosed by metal rails on both sides. "What happens here?"

"The stock is kept in enclosures in back. The horses and bulls run through this alley and get herded into their chutes." He paused to greet some of the cowboys who stood in a row on a tall, wooden, benchlike platform that lined the alley. Behind her back, she heard the clank of metal. A moment later, there was a shout. "He's loose. Get out of the alley."

Before Gabby could figure out what he was talking about, a black bull came around the corner at the far end of the alley. The animal was huge, as big as a minivan, and he looked angry to see her standing in his way.

Kicking off her shoes, she made a dive for the metal rails and climbed them as fast as she could. As she reached the top, Zach was beside her. He braced her arm, holding her so she wouldn't fall while other cowboys herded the escaped bull back to the enclosure.

"It's okay," he assured her. "They've got it under control."

"Did you see that thing?" Her voice quavered. "He was huge."

"I'm glad you got out of the way."

She hadn't planned her escape. Everything had happened too fast for her to think, much less be scared. She was just beginning to understand that if she'd stayed where she was, frozen in place, the bull would have trampled her. That was *not* the way she wanted to die. Her tombstone would *not* say "Squashed by a Bull."

Zach helped her down from the rail, and her bare feet sank into the dirt. "Rodeos are messy."

"Things like that hardly ever happen," he said darkly. "I have a suspicion that it wasn't an accident. Somebody turned that Brahma loose."

And they'd seen Kevin Fox near the chutes. She stuck her feet back into her platform shoes and followed Zach to the area where the animals were penned. Inside the metal enclosure, she saw the bull that had come after her. He didn't look so vicious when he was shuffling around with his big ugly friends.

She stayed within reaching distance of Zach while he asked questions and found out that the pen had been opened but nobody had seen who did it.

He turned to her. "Not an accident."

Someone was trying to kill her. Step by step, the threats had been escalating. First, there was a burglary while no one was in the house. Then there was the broken window, followed by the person who stalked her in the old house and finally the assault on Daniel.

Zach looked past her shoulder. "Striker is standing right over there."

"Earlier, he was on the other side of the arena." She turned her head to look. Striker was talking to Osborne, who looked particularly out of place with his long ponytail and dashiki shirt. "Do you think they followed us?"

"I'm going to find out."

Zach stalked toward the man with the bodybuilder physique. Striker looked dangerous, but she had absolute confidence in Zach, especially since he was within shouting distance of dozens of guys who'd be happy to come to his aid.

Neither Striker nor Osborne backed down. The art dealer stepped toward them. "I thought we'd find you at the rodeo. There's something I need to say."

"I don't want to hear it," Zach said, "unless it's the truth."

"How clever you are." Osborne drew himself up to his full height. "I want to confess."

Chapter Twenty

"I assure you," Osborne said, "that I acted alone. No one else should be blamed for any of the unfortunate acts I'm about to tell you about."

Zach didn't believe him. Osborne wasn't the type of person who broke windows and committed assault. He was protecting Striker. "Go on."

"And I wish to apologize, especially to you, Gabriella. I should have been straightforward with you from the start, and we could have avoided—"

"Oh, please," Gabby said. "There's no way I'll forgive you. You almost killed my brother."

"What?"

"Daniel was in the hospital for two days with a concussion after you hit him on the head."

Osborne turned and looked toward Striker, who gave a nearly imperceptible shake of his head. Either they were really good actors or they didn't know Daniel had been attacked.

"I would never assault someone." Osborne took a hankie from his pocket and swabbed the sweat from his forehead. "Never.

"Save us some time," Zach said. "Tell us what you did."

"On the day of Michelle's memorial service, I took advantage of the fact that you would all be absent, and I broke into the Roost to steal the computers."

"That's a pretty neat trick, because you were at the service. I saw you."

"My alibi," he said. "I timed my departure to give me just enough time to commit the burglary."

"And then what?" Gabby prompted. "What else did you do?"

"Isn't burglary enough?"

Burglary left too many incidents unexplained. From the start, Zach had thought that Fox was using the break-ins as a way to scare Gabby away. He might have been inspired by Osborne's clumsy attempt. "Why did you do it?"

"As it so happens, my efforts were fruitless. Over the years, I've sold paintings of Michelle's that I hadn't reported to her. I needed to steal her records to make sure they matched mine." He licked his lips. "She didn't keep her records on those computers."

"Rhoda has them," Gabby said. "Zach's housekeeper did record keeping for Michelle."

"I robbed the wrong house."

Zach nodded. "You haven't done anything right. Not even this so-called confession. You're not a burglar. Your pal, Striker, did the dirty work."

"That allegation can't be proved," he said archly.

Proof when it came to the original burglary was nonexistent. The sheriff had investigated, looked for fingerprints and written the crime off as vandalism. Why was Osborne so anxious to take credit?

He'd committed fraud with the paintings, but that was a white collar crime that would likely result in nothing more than a slap on the wrist and a fine. Something had compelled him to step forward. Zach took a guess. "Is Fox your attorney?"

"Jason Fox?" Nervously, Osborne glanced left and right. "Actually, I have used Mr. Fox on occasion. Why?"

"He went through the records and found the fraud, didn't he? Fox told you to confess and promised that you'd get off easy."

"Attorney-client privilege," Osborne said.

Zach knew he was right. "We're not going to be making any deals with you. Let's find the sheriff."

After Osborne had been locked up for a few days, he might be more prone to tell the truth.

GABBY LOVED DANCING, and felt like celebrating after Osborne had been taken into custody by Sheriff Burton. A country and western band was performing that night after the rodeo, and she would have liked to try a Texas two-step or a square dance. But when Zach told his men that he'd load up the six-horse trailer and take their trick ponies back to the ranch, she readily volunteered to go with him and left her car keys with Charlotte.

While Zach and Toby loaded the performing horses into the huge van attached to the back of Zach's heavy-duty truck, sunset painted the sky in shades of magenta and gold streaked with purple. Zach caught her staring and commented, "You don't have skies like that in Brooklyn."

"What do you mean? We have sunsets in New York."

"Not like this, with the mountains rising up to touch the clouds and the wind in your hair and the soft whinny of horses in the background."

"And the smells," she reminded him.

"Does Brooklyn smell like perfume?"

"Touché."

During the drive back to the ranch in the huge truck, she made him a deal. "I finished your shirt this morning. If you pose in it for me, I'll do something for you."

"What kind of something?"

"Name it," she challenged.

He thought for a few seconds. "You'll learn how to ride."

That was a big promise. When she first arrived, riding was unthinkable. She'd gotten to the point where she didn't mind touching the horses, but she hadn't actually gotten up in a saddle. If she stayed at the Roost, knowing how to ride would be a good skill to have. "It's a deal."

Since everybody else was at the rodeo, the stable behind his house felt empty and deserted. She wasn't much help when it came to the actual unloading of the horses that had to be led one by one from the trailer to their stalls, but she followed his instructions for watering and feeding the animals. Daphne bounded up beside her and gave a cheery woof.

"Are there dog sports?" she asked.

"Hunting dogs have a lot of skills. Not Daphne. Her talent for herding is innate. If I drop her in a meadow full of sheep, she'll race around until they're all herded. It's like she can't help herself."

"Is that right?" She ran her hands through Daphne's thick, black-and-white fur. "Are you an obsessive-compulsive herder?"

Vigorous tail-wagging was her answer.

When they were done at the stables, she stared across the field toward the Roost. None of the lights were on, and the house had taken on a dark, ominous aspect. "I want to take those photos of you tonight. Is it safe to go to the Roost?"

"Tonight, we don't have our cowboy bodyguards," he said. "But I think I can take care of you."

She'd be the last person to doubt his protective abilities, but there was a valid reason to worry. "Somebody tried to kill me today."

"Osborne is spending the night in jail."

"But his buddy, Striker, is still walking around. And he's the kind of thug who might carry a grudge."

He went to the office at the front of the stable, unlocked the door and went inside. When he returned, he carried two handguns and a rifle. "Does this make you feel safe?"

"Why do you have so many weapons in here?"

"The horses are the most valuable commodity on the ranch. If anyone threatens them, I need to be able to fight back." He tucked one of the pistols behind his belt and handed the other one to her. "I don't think we should walk from here to there. The moon is almost full tonight, and we'd make an easy target."

"Unhitching the trailer looks like a big job."

"We'll take my other car."

She followed him from the stable to a two-car garage attached to the house. Throughout the time she'd been here, she'd never seen him drive anything but the truck, which made sense because he was almost always hauling something.

He opened the garage. Inside was a cherry-red Corvette.

She gave a low whistle. "I thought the horses were the most valuable thing around here."

"Sometimes, you've just got to put the top down and go real fast."

The fancy sports car was evidence that he had more money than she'd thought. Making her a loan to pay for

Daniel's hospital stay wouldn't have been a huge burden on him. She should have asked. Why didn't she ask?

She slipped into the smooth leather passenger seat and listened while he revved the powerful engine. She wasn't really into cars but couldn't help appreciating the luxury. The short drive to the Roost seemed like a waste for a high-performance vehicle that could do so much more, but she was anxious to take the photos of him in the custom embroidered shirt and get her internet sales going. She hadn't handed out many of her business cards, but Charlotte told her that she'd given away more than twenty-five.

In the studio, she showed him the shirt. The fabric was heavy black twill, and gleaming white embroidery showed a herd of wild horses with wildly curling manes racing across the yoke. A smaller version of the pattern decorated the cuffs.

He took it from her. "This is so beautiful it's a shame to put it on. Seriously, Gabby, should I take a shower?"

"I like the way you look right now. All rugged and masculine. Go ahead, put it on."

In the workstation set up for sketching, she found her digital camera. The lighting in the studio was excellent, even at night, but she didn't want him to be standing next to a sewing machine or a pile of fabric. The most rugged part of the room was the wood staircase that attached to the kitchen. The old wall behind it could have been outdoors.

When he sauntered toward her in the shirt, she congratulated herself on having a good eye. Zach looked better than the male models she'd seen and worked with because he was real. He hadn't gotten that lean muscular physique by working out in a gym. His body came from real work.

She posed him on the staircase with his thumb hitched

in his pocket. Before he had a chance to put on a fake smile, she snapped a photo. Not bad, but she could do better.

"Take off your hat."

"I want you to know that I feel like a damn fool doing this."

"Don't lose the hat, just hold it in your hand."

"You've done this before," he said.

"Taking pictures of models is part of being a designer. You've got to have a way to display your work."

She studied him for a moment, trying to be dispassionate and looking for flaws. There really wasn't much to criticize. His blue eyes were to die for. His features were symmetrical. Still, she sensed that she needed a different angle to bring out a truly sellable picture. What was it about him that was so irresistible?

The answer flashed as brightly as the neon signs in Times Square. "Untuck the shirt and unfasten the snaps."

He gave her a slow, sexy grin. "Are we going to do porn?"

"You wish." And so did she, to be honest. "Just open the shirt about two inches."

Though he did as she asked, the pose seemed stilted. Gabby went to him and arranged the shirt to show off the embroidery. She opened the front to expose his lean midsection. Most of the male models she'd worked with shaved their chests. Zach was so much more natural, so much more attractive.

She should have moved back to her position for taking the picture, but photography wasn't uppermost in her mind. Grasping the front of his shirt, she pulled him closer for a kiss. His lips were warm.

Though she fought to stay detached, sensual heat oozed

through her, replacing her rational thoughts with remembered images of their naked bodies entwined.

He whispered, "Are we done?"

"No."

Determined, she jumped backward and prepared to shoot. The camera trembled in her hands. It took all her willpower to keep her hands still and take three rapid shots one after the other. She couldn't wait anymore. "That's a wrap."

He strode across the studio and swept her up in his arms, easily lifting her. Holding on to his neck, she asked, "What are you going to do with me?"

"It's a long way up to the bedroom."

"Too long."

He carried her to the cutting table and stretched her out amid the bright swatches of fabric. Slowly and deliberately, he undressed her, kissing each new expanse of skin as he freed her from her garments.

He took off his jeans, and then she stopped him. "Leave the shirt."

She would always remember him this way, making love to her wearing a design she had created especially for him.

THE NEXT MORNING, Zach and Gabby were up and about before Charlotte had dragged herself out of bed. Gabby had heard her come home last night a little after midnight, which was the perfect time for the cowgirl Cinderella to come home from the ball.

Yesterday's events had begun to sink in. After a simple breakfast, they sat at the kitchen table and discussed their plans over coffee. The first thing Gabby wanted to do was rescue her brother from the clutches of Sarah Bentley. Zach focused more on contacting the sheriff and finding out if Osborne had implicated Fox.

"And we still don't know who released the bull from the chute," she said. "Who's trying to kill me?"

"I wouldn't put it past Striker. It's something he might do out of sheer meanness."

She agreed. "But Osborne was there with him, and he wouldn't let his trained gorilla get out of hand."

"That leaves Kevin Fox."

She really didn't know what to make of that young man. He seemed utterly normal. But he certainly had an out-size ego. From the first time she met him, she'd thought he knew more than he was letting on.

"There's one more piece of investigating I need to do," she said. "Yesterday, I preserved Louis Rousseau's love letters, following the procedure the book collector told me about. Then, I got them translated."

"How? Do you know somebody who's fluent in French?"

"I used a service on the internet. I scanned in the French document, and they're going to get back to me with the English version."

"If this is about treasure hunting," Zach said, "we should forget it. That's nothing but a waste of time."

"We might as well check it out. There could be a turn of phrase that would entice Daniel to leave that woman."

In the studio, she eyed the cutting table where they'd made love last night. It was her new favorite place in the house. Then she opened her laptop, retrieved the translated document and started reading from the screen.

"The one with the reference to midnight hair seems to be more of the same. She's so beautiful and he misses her so much, blah, blah."

"Is that any way for a romantic to talk?"

"I'm a tired romantic."

The second letter started much the same as the first, and then it took an unexpected turn. "This is an apology. He's telling her that he's sorry and he'd rather chop off his arm than to hurt her. He begs her to keep her eyes open and her heart open so they can find a wide horizon."

"Open eyes, open heart, wide horizon," Zach said, leaning over her shoulder to see the computer screen. "Like the note on Michelle's landscape sketch."

They were onto an important discovery. She could almost hear the puzzle pieces falling into place. "Michelle wanted us to connect the sketch with this letter." She read more of the translated document. "There was another woman. Louis was having an affair."

"Not exactly an unusual story." He stood and walked away from her workstation. "Men have affairs all the time. Even in the 1870s."

"But it means something. Michelle went to a lot of trouble, leaving this trail of clues. I wonder why she didn't just tell me."

"There must have been a reason."

Gabby would have enjoyed a story about Louis Rousseau, the Frenchman who married a Native American woman and wore a gold earring like a pirate. His affair would have been one more colorful chapter. "Michelle liked her secrets. I never knew why she turned her back on her family in Brooklyn."

"I know why," he said.

His simple statement surprised her so much that she rose from her seat. "She told you?"

"We talked several times a week. Before Charlotte came, she was alone, maybe lonely."

She approached him. "I want to know."

"I'm not going to tell you right now. I want you to think about it," he said. "Once I expose Michelle's secret, I can't take it back. I can't unring that bell. Her story becomes a permanent part of your family legacy."

He was warning her, and she'd be wise to pay attention. Zach wasn't the kind of man who was easily alarmed.

Chapter Twenty-One

What kind of terrible thing could have driven Michelle from Brooklyn? A little later, Gabby sat at the kitchen table and called Daniel on his cell. He sounded even more cheerful than yesterday. Her mood was in sharp contrast to his. Tersely, she said, "I'm coming to pick you up. Be ready by ten o'clock."

"It's all good," he responded. She could almost hear the smile in his voice. "Excellent."

"What's going on?"

"Sarah and I have the whole inheritance thing figured out. It's the perfect solution, and we all come out winners."

"Winners? This isn't a poker game, Daniel."

"Hell, no, this is a sure bet."

She hated that he was using gambling phrases to talk about their inheritance and the terms of the will. In the past few days, they'd gone through so much, and none of it was good. Had he already forgotten that he'd been assaulted and almost died? "I'm leaving soon. Be ready."

Zach came up behind her and gently massaged her back. When he rolled her head from side to side, she heard a series of pops from the tense muscles at the base of her neck. "Feels good."

"Relax." He glided his skillful hands down her arms. "Think about your breathing and relax."

"I'm so glad I met you. You're the best thing that's ever happened to me."

"Better than inheriting a house? Better than starting a business?"

"Absolutely."

"Better than finding your brother and making new friends like Rhoda and Toby and Charlotte?"

"I can't believe she's still asleep. I should wake her up before we leave to pick up Daniel. It's best if she stays with Rhoda while we're gone. I don't want a repeat performance of the attack on Daniel."

He leaned down and kissed her behind the ear. "You go wake her. I'm going to put my pretty Corvette away."

"I wish we could drive it to the bed-and-breakfast. But it's a two-seater, and I'm bringing Daniel back if I have to drag him, kicking and screaming."

Upstairs, she tapped on Charlotte's door and peeked inside. "Are you awake?"

"I was just lying here, thinking. Those girls I hung out with at the rodeo would hardly talk to me in high school. And I have a boyfriend. And I'm…blonde. How did this happen?"

"It was time for you to come out of your shell. When you did, you saw the world was a pretty decent place."

When she sat up in the bed, Charlotte accidentally exposed the real reason she'd been hiding out in her bedroom. She had a big red hickey on the left side of her throat. "I love my life."

"You need to get out of bed. Zach and I are going to be gone, and I don't want you staying here alone. You'll have to go over to Rhoda's."

"Okay."

"And you might want to wear a turtleneck."

Charlotte giggled as Gabby closed the door.

In her bedroom, she changed into her new, practical boots. They weren't pretty but definitely comfortable. The rest of her outfit was simple—a long shirt, vest and jeans. The only nod to fashion was the leopard-patterned scarf around her neck.

Zach had hit a bull's-eye when he reminded her of all the positive things that had happened—the house, the business, the new friends. She was basically an optimist. Her mother had been the same way, but none of the other women in her family were naturally cheerful. Rene always expected rain, even on sunny days. And Michelle was a complicated bag of neuroses. Her troubled, secretive life might have been part of her artistic genius. Whatever the cause, Gabby wanted to know her secret. All the secrets— even her own shameful decision to contact Fox—had to come out.

On their drive to the bed-and-breakfast, Zach was in the passenger seat of Gabby's little hatchback. He didn't like riding shotgun. His fingers itched to get on the steering wheel and his foot kept stomping on an imaginary brake.

Gabby pulled up at a four-way stop at a deserted inter- section in a field and waited while a fat black crow wad- dled across the road. She exhaled a sigh and said, "I'm ready to talk about Michelle's secret."

He'd expected her to ask; her curiosity wouldn't let her close her eyes to the truth. Though Gabby wanted to be- lieve that family was the root of all happiness, she knew better. "It's not a pretty story."

"I'm not going to shoot the messenger," she promised.

"There is something that puzzles me. Of all the people she could have chosen to confide in, why did Michelle pick you?"

"We were kindred spirits," he said. "We both left home when we were young, and that decision changed us."

"Then this is also a story about your past," Gabby said. "Bonus."

"What makes you think I'm going to tell you about my past?"

"Because the truth—no matter how ugly—is better than being haunted by secrets. First, tell me about you."

"My family had a small ranch in Wyoming and not much money. I had a younger brother who died when he was nine from a rare genetic heart disorder."

"I'm sorry."

"Me, too."

Zach had been fourteen when his brother passed away. That might have been the first time he looked for relief in a bottle of his dad's rotgut whiskey. "My parents were afraid to have any other kids."

"Because the illness was inherited," she said.

"They didn't want to take a chance on having another child who died young, so they put their heads down and kept working. My mother was a shy, sad woman. My dad was mean as a snake. To his credit, he never hit my mother or me."

When he looked back on the silent misery of his childhood, Zach saw his father as a coward who wouldn't raise his hand to another human because he feared the consequences. "He was the worst kind of abuser."

He glanced over at Gabby. Though her eyes focused on the road, she was listening intently. He could have ended his story here, and she wouldn't know the difference. There was no rule that said he had to reveal every part of himself, and he'd rather stay a hero in her eyes.

But he trusted her.

"My father hurt things that couldn't fight back. Animals."

The truth was poison. Zach hated to think of his father's blood running through his veins. "Any dog that got in his path got a sharp kick in the ribs. I saw my father skin a rabbit alive. When I tried to stop him, he called me a sissy and told me to keep my mouth shut. I learned to do just that. I could go days without saying a word, shuffling along on a dark path and never looking up."

"You're not your father," she said.

"Do you really want to hear more?"

"I wish there wasn't more to tell. I wish you could have had a happy ending."

"No such luck."

The GPS directions indicated a left turn, and he waited until she was back on route. Going home, he'd insist on driving.

"When I was seventeen," he said, "I came home from high school and I saw my dad beating one of our horses. I told him to stop, but he wouldn't. He wouldn't listen to me until I dragged him away from that poor animal and hit him hard enough to knock him down. Then I hit him again. He cowered in front of me, and I was glad to see his pain. That's when I knew."

"When you knew what?"

"I was like him. He'd taught me how to use my fists to hurt somebody else. He lay there in the dirt with his mouth bleeding, and he told me he was going to press charges and have me locked up in jail. I left and never went back."

"You did the right thing," she said.

"I never doubted that leaving was the right move," he said. "Beating my father was wrong. There's no good reason to lay hands on another person."

"It's not something you've made a habit of doing. You're not the kind of man who solves his problems with his fists."

"I've run into situations when I had to fight."

"Of course," she said, "and you've taken on bucking broncos and Brahma bulls. But you're a patient man."

He trusted her, and she accepted him with all his dark history and all his flaws. He might be in love with this woman.

"And now," she said, "tell me about Michelle."

He knew how important family was to her, and he hated to poison her mind. "Are you sure?"

"I've thought about it. I'm ready."

"Michelle was a victim. She never told me the name of the Brooklyn man who raped her, but it happened more than once to both Michelle and her sister."

"Rene? She was abused?"

"Both girls. They told their mother, and she did nothing to stop the abuse because she didn't want to disrupt the family, which Michelle considered ironic. Neither she nor her sister ever married or had children. The Rousseau family line ends with you and your brother."

"Cold revenge," she said.

"That's why Michelle left and never went back to Brooklyn."

"I wish they'd spoken up, but I understand." Her hand trembled on the steering wheel. "It happened a long time ago, sixty years in the past when abuse wasn't talked about."

"Are you okay?"

"My grandfather was their brother. He's been dead for twenty years. Was it him?"

"We'll never know."

According to the GPS directions, they were less than a mile from Sarah's bed-and-breakfast. The land around them was forested and rugged. At a wide space in the road, Gabby pulled her car onto the shoulder and parked. "I need to take a minute to calm down."

He got out of the car, came around to the driver's side and opened her door. Without speaking, he took her hand and pulled her out of the car. "Let's take a walk. Stretch your legs."

Though there wasn't any traffic, he guided her away from the road into a path through the pine and conifer forest. Leafy green shrubs brushed against their legs as they walked uphill.

"I still want a family," she said. "In spite of the awful past—starting with Louis Rousseau's infidelity—I believe a family can be nurturing."

"The trick is choosing the people you want to be close to."

"Like Rhoda?"

"I'd rather have her for a favorite aunt than anybody else. And Charlotte makes a good little sister."

"What about us?" She didn't pause to look at him but kept hiking. "Where do we fit in a family structure?"

"You're sure as hell not my sister."

They had climbed to the top of a ridge. From this vantage point, they looked down at a sprawling cedar lodge, Bentley's Bed-and-Breakfast. She wrapped her arm around him and rested her head against his chest. Since she wasn't wearing her platform shoes, she was a couple of inches shorter than usual.

A shudder trembled through her. "My God, look at this view."

It was unusual for her to comment on the scenery. While cruising around in the Aspen area, they'd driven through spectacular mountain vistas, and she'd barely taken note. He asked, "What about the view?"

"Don't you recognize it? There are two high mountains, and I can see the beginning of a river."

He saw it. "It's the sketch Michelle drew."

Gabby's great-aunt had led them to this spot, and he had the feeling that even more secrets were about to be revealed.

Chapter Twenty-Two

The door to the bed-and-breakfast swept open as Gabby charged toward it. Her brother welcomed her with open arms as though he was the new owner. "Wait until you hear what Sarah and I figured out."

She held up her hand to stop him. "Is she your new girlfriend?"

"We're business associates."

As long as it wasn't monkey business, they were okay. The way Gabby figured, Michelle had led them along this convoluted trail because of a connection in the distant past—a family connection. The details swirled around in her head like a crazy stew of secrets. It was entirely possible that Daniel and Sarah were related.

Zach stepped onto the porch beside her. "Let's go inside, sit down and find out how much Sarah knows."

"How much do I know about what?" Sarah stood behind them with an armload of firewood.

"The past," Gabby said.

Sarah climbed the two steps to the wide wraparound porch where rugged wood chairs had been arranged for guests. "Don't think you can give me a history lesson, Gabby. My roots are deep, all the way back to the 1800s."

Gabby took Zach's hand for support as they followed

Sarah into a clean, charming living room with rustic decor that was in harmony with the setting. On the wall beside the fireplace hung a grouping of five small paintings of Tarot cards. Gabby pointed to them. "These are unusual."

"A gift from Michelle."

Gabby nodded. It seemed appropriate for the paintings to be here, hiding in plain sight. "I want to talk about your roots. How much do you know about your ancestors?"

"There were a lot of strong women." Sarah arranged her load of firewood in a metal log bin. "The first I know about was Prudence Hanover. She raised a family and single-handedly ran a boardinghouse for miners."

"What about her husband?"

"She was a widow. Her first husband was killed in the Civil War, and she never married again. But there was a man in her life. She had three children with him."

When Sarah stood and faced her, Gabby noticed her coloring. In spite of the strawberry-blond hair, Sarah's eyes were as dark as her own. If she looked deeper, Gabby was sure she'd find other similarities. "Do you have any idea who fathered Prudence's children?"

"I do. Michelle told me." She scowled. "Would you like to guess the name of that original boardinghouse?"

"Wide Horizons," Gabby said. "In a letter to his wife, Louis Rousseau mentioned it."

Daniel circled around them. "Gabby, what the hell are you talking about?"

"I had those letters from Louis translated," she said. "One of them was an apology. He was having an affair, and I'm guessing it was more than a casual fling if he had three children."

"I still don't get it," Daniel said.

"Louis Rousseau was the longtime lover of Prudence Hanover."

Daniel's head swiveled as he focused on Sarah, then on Gabby, then on Sarah again. "We're cousins?"

Sarah strolled across the room and stood at the front window, looking out. "Michelle figured it out. She even had an explanation for the myth of the Frenchman's Treasure. Instead of hitting a gold strike, Louis found two strong businesswomen. Your ancestor was a terrific rancher, who usually made a profit, and mine had a fairly successful boardinghouse. If one of them was running low on cash, he'd borrow from the other and tell her it came from his treasure."

"Louis was a dog," Daniel said.

"I should have told you." Sarah turned to face them. "But Michelle swore me to secrecy."

Gabby nodded. "She did that a lot."

"In any case, I think Daniel and I have come up with an equitable solution for the inheritance. We sell the Roost, the estate passes to me and I make a side agreement with you to divide up the proceeds three ways."

Their plan benefitted Sarah and Daniel with an immediate cash return, but Gabby was deeply unsatisfied. "I don't want to give up ownership of the Roost."

Zach backed her up. "And I don't want Fox to get his commission for the sale."

"If we present him a united front," Sarah said, "we can negotiate him down. He's going to be here in about fifteen minutes."

A shock went through her. The last thing she wanted was to have Fox and Zach in the same room together. She didn't want him hearing about her loan from the lawyer.

After he'd shared the darkest secrets of his life with her, she couldn't repay him with deception.

"I have a better idea," Zach said. "I'll buy the Roost and sell it back to Gabby."

His generous offer stunned her. "It's a lot of money. I can't ask you to do that."

"I can handle it."

She believed him. Zach could handle anything, but she didn't want to start their relationship in his debt. Taking his arm, she pulled him toward the front door. To Sarah and Daniel she said, "Excuse us for a moment."

Outside the bed-and-breakfast, she hurried toward a path leading into the surrounding forest. Their escape came none too soon. As they went into the trees, she glimpsed Kevin Fox's black SUV turning into Sarah's parking lot.

Her timing was all wrong. Earlier, when she and Zach were standing on the ridge overlooking Sarah's place, Gabby had been ready to spill her own secret about Fox. Zach had trusted her and told her everything, and she owed him the same trust. But then, she'd seen the view, and they'd rushed here.

When they were far enough away from the house that they couldn't be seen, she stopped and gazed up at him. His expression was open and caring. She didn't want to lose him. "I've been keeping a secret, and it's driving me crazy."

He took a few paces away from her, leaned his hip against a boulder and folded his arms over his chest. "I meant what I said about buying the Roost. I can afford it."

"I don't want to take money from you. I want us to go into this relationship as equals."

"I don't measure worth in dollars and cents."

"Do you have to be so wise? So understanding?" She

batted at the low-hanging branch of a pine tree. Her decisions seemed petty and foolish. "I did a really dumb thing. At the time, it seemed smart. I was scared that Daniel would die if he didn't get proper medical aid. He doesn't have insurance. And I didn't have enough ready cash to pay for his treatment."

"What did you do?"

"I borrowed the hospital money. From Fox."

She was almost afraid to look at him, but she couldn't hide from what she'd done. She watched the light fade from his blue eyes. His jaw tensed. "You went to Fox."

"I had to take care of my brother."

He pushed away from the boulder he'd been resting against and turned his back as though he intended to walk away from her without another word.

She pleaded, "Say something."

"All your talk about families and relationships doesn't mean a thing if you can't turn to each other when things go wrong. That's why families are different from friends or lovers. When you need help, a family is there for you."

"That's why I did it. For Daniel."

"You'd do anything for him because he's your brother. But not for me." He shot a glare over his shoulder. "You don't trust me."

"Forgive me." Her heart ached. "Don't hate me."

"I don't," he said quickly. "We can be friends, maybe even lovers. But we aren't family, and we sure as hell don't have a relationship."

As he walked away, she sank to the ground and buried her face in her hands. Too devastated to cry, she rocked back and forth. The Universe wasn't going to save her from this sadness. She'd made her own mistake. Somehow, she'd have to find a way to live with it.

She heard a rustling in the trees. Was Zach coming back? Was he going to forgive her? She was afraid to look.

She heard one word. "Bitch."

Her head jerked up. She was staring into the watery blue eyes of Kevin Fox. "It was you, stalking me in the old house."

He gestured with a handgun. "On your feet, Gabby. I'd rather not shoot you, but I will."

"You're the intruder, the person who kept breaking into the house. You almost killed my brother."

"Yeah, yeah, and I let out that bull to trample you. Except for that first burglary, it's been all me. And I'm really sick and tired of driving back and forth to your cruddy side of the mountain." He held the barrel of the gun only an inch away from her nose. "Get on your feet. We're going to take a walk."

"And if I don't?"

With a flick of his wrist, he slapped the gun against the side of her head. Pain exploded inside her skull. She fell but got back up.

"Move it," he said.

She stumbled to her feet. When she touched her temple, her fingers were wet with blood. It would have been better if she'd passed out. She started walking.

The groomed pathways around the bed-and-breakfast were all neatly marked. Sarah probably had maps of them. This one was called the Cascade Trail.

She walked in front, her head throbbing with each movement. When she slowed down, he prodded her with the gun. She asked, "Why did you do it?"

"It was a little scheme my uncle and I cooked up. Taking the money from Michelle's paintings and not entering it into her accounts."

"Fraud," she said. "Osborne was doing the same thing."

"Michelle was old and rich, an easy mark."

"Were you all working together?"

"Osborne is an idiot. He took the computer that turned out to be worthless. He'll take the fall, and my uncle will get him off with a minimum sentence."

"You were looking for the accounting books, the information that Rhoda kept."

"At first," he said, "then we figured that the real problem was you. We needed to get you out of the picture. That way, my uncle could stay in control. With some fancy juggling, he could keep everything covered up. But you wouldn't budge."

She realized that Sarah and Daniel's plan to sell the house would play right into their hands. "Was Sarah involved?"

"She knows Uncle Jason, but she's too high-minded to get her hands dirty."

She heard a rumbling noise. A sign on the trail said: Cascade Falls. After a sharp turn, she saw the waterfall. The trail went up to the ledge behind the gushing water. She guessed the height was about four stories, enough to kill her if she plummeted to the rocks below.

She wiped at the blood on her forehead. "You're not going to get away with this."

"Sure I will. Nobody would believe that Sarah would take a fall like this. But you?" He laughed. "You don't know your way around the mountains. And accidents happen."

She could dig in her heels and refuse to cooperate, but he'd just knock her on the head and carry her unconscious body up the hill. If she was going to die anyway, she wanted people to know she'd been murdered. She had to make him use his gun.

When he prodded, she pivoted. The swift motion sent a renewed burst of pain into her skull. She grabbed for his weapon, but Kevin was fast.

He jumped back. Using the handle on the gun, he whacked her shoulder and knocked her to the ground.

She didn't hear Zach approach, but she saw him leap from the path above and knock Kevin off his feet. Through blurred vision, she saw him disarm Kevin. The redheaded man went down after one punch. The fight was over before it had started.

Zach stood over Kevin with his gun pointed at the other man's midsection.

"I hate bullies," Zach said.

"Don't hurt me."

"I'm a real good shot," Zach said. "I could shoot your ear off. Or put a hole in your kneecap. That would end your snowboarding career."

"I'll cooperate."

"What do you think, Gabby? Should I shoot this bully in the leg just to watch him cry?"

She was immediately aware of two things: she wasn't going to die, and Zach had changed his mind. He hadn't gone into the bed-and-breakfast. "You were coming back to me."

"If you have your cell phone, this would be a handy time to call Sarah and the sheriff. I want to get these Foxes into jail where they belong."

There was only one thing she wanted to know. "Do you forgive me?"

"Gabby? The phone?"

She staggered to her feet, ignoring the pain. "Don't

get me wrong, Zach. I'm truly grateful that you saved me from certain death."

"And I love you."

"I love you, too. Oh, my God, I love you. But I still want to know. Will you, please, forgive me?"

He smiled. "Yep."

JUST BEFORE CHRISTMAS, Gabby sat at the cutting table where she and Zach had made love and signed the final papers to settle the estate of Michelle Rousseau. Their final solution, worked out with Zach's attorney, satisfied everybody. Daniel received a hefty cash settlement, as did Sarah's Forest Preservation Society. Zach had purchased the Roost, which made sense because his ranch bordered the property, and he deeded the house back to Gabby.

She gazed up at him and smiled. "Ownership really doesn't matter, does it?"

"Not really," he said. "After we're married, it's all family property."

"Still, it seems right and proper for a Rousseau to own this place."

Charlotte dashed up to her with a piece of fabric in her hand. "Would you call this color teal or peacock-blue?"

"Teal."

Her custom embroidered shirts were doing well with internet sales, a phenomenon that she entirely attributed to the sexy photo of Zach in the black-and-white shirt. Charlotte worked for her full-time, and they'd hired two other part-time seamstresses.

Zach leaned down and kissed the top of her head. "I want to talk to you about having a Rousseau own the Roost. After we get married, your name is going to change."

"I'll hyphenate."

"Rousseau-Sheffield is a lot to write."

She patted the bump on her abdomen where the next addition to their family was growing. "This kid will be smart enough to figure it out."

* * * * *

MOUNTAIN MIDWIFE

CAST OF CHARACTERS

Rachel Devon—After a devastating career as an EMT and relationships gone wrong, the thirty-one-year-old nurse-midwife moves to the mountains, looking for solitude and serenity.

Cole McClure—An undercover FBI agent from L.A., he hates the mountains. Betrayed by his superiors and pursued by a master criminal, he fights through a blizzard to protect a newborn.

Penny Richards—Nine months pregnant, she's given up every bad habit that would threaten her baby, except for robbing a casino.

Goldie Richards—In the first twenty-four hours of the baby's life, she's been shot at, pursued and threatened.

Ruby Richards—Penny's mother and Goldie's grandmother, she is more deeply involved in crime than she knows.

Jim Loughlin—The Grand County deputy sheriff will do anything to help the midwife who helped deliver his baby.

Frank Loeb—A sadistic thug, he won't let a bullet stop him from finding his share of the loot.

Wayne Prescott—The field agent in charge of the Colorado FBI office does his best to find his undercover agent.

Jenna Cambridge—Penny's best friend, she's a high school economics teacher in Granby with a good head for numbers.

Xavier Romero—A former snitch who owns the Stampede casino in Black Hawk.

Baron—The mysterious criminal mastermind uses gangs of underlings to rob banks and casinos.

Here's to my buddy, Cheryl.

And, as always, to Rick.

Chapter One

Some babies are yanked into the world, kicking and screaming. Others gasp. Others fling open their little arms and grab. Every infant is unique. Every birth, a miracle.

Rachel Devon loved being a midwife.

She smiled down at the newborn swaddled in her arms. The baby girl—only two hours old—stared at the winter sunlight outside the cabin window. What would she be when she grew up? Where would she travel? Would she find love? *Good luck with that, sweet girl. I'm still looking.*

Returning to the brass bed where the mom lay in a state of euphoric exhaustion, Rachel announced, "She's seven pounds, six ounces."

"Totally healthy? Nothing to worry about?"

"A nine-point-five on the Apgar scale. You did good, Sarah."

"We did. You and me and Jim and..." Sarah frowned. "We still haven't decided on the baby's name."

Voices rose from the downstairs of the two-story log house near Shadow Mountain Lake. Moments ago, someone else had arrived, and Rachel hoped the visitor hadn't blocked her van in the circular driveway. After guiding Sarah through five hours of labor, aiding in the actual birth and taking another two hours with cleanup and postpartum instruction, Rachel was anxious to get home. "It's time for me to go. Should I invite whoever is downstairs to come up here?"

"Jim's mother." Sarah pushed her hair—still damp from the shower—off her forehead. "I'd like a bit more time alone. Would you mind introducing the baby to her grandma?"

"My pleasure. If you need anything over the next few days, call the Rocky Mountain Women's Clinic. I'll be on vacation, but somebody can help you. And if you really need to talk to me, I can be reached."

Sarah offered a tired smile. "I apologize in advance for anything Jim's mother might say."

"That sounds ominous."

"Let's just say there was a reason we didn't want Katherine here during labor."

Rachel descended the staircase and handed the baby girl to her grandmother, who had positioned herself in a rocking chair beside the moss rock fireplace. With her bright red hair and sleek figure, Katherine seemed too young to be a granny.

After a moment of nuzzling the baby, she shot Rachel a glare. "I wasn't in favor of this, you know. In my day, this wasn't the way we had babies."

Really? In your day, were babies delivered by stork?

Katherine continued, "Sarah should have been in a hospital. What if there had been complications?"

"Everything was perfect." Jim Loughlin reached down and fondly stroked his baby's rosy cheek. His hands were huge. A big muscular guy, Jim was a deputy with the Grand County sheriff's department. "We wanted a home birth, and Rachel had everything under control."

Skeptically, Katherine looked her up and down. "I'm sorry, dear, but you're so young."

"Thirty-one," Rachel said.

"Oh, my, I would have guessed eight years younger. The pixie hairdo is very flattering with your dark hair."

Her age and her hairstyle had nothing to do with her qualifications, and Rachel was too tired to be tactful. "If there had been complications, I would have been prepared. My training as a certified nurse-midwife is the equivalent of a master's degree in nursing. Plus, I was an EMT and ambulance driver. I'm a real good person to have around in any sort of medical emergency."

Katherine didn't give up. "Have you ever lost a patient?"

"Not as a midwife." A familiar ache tightened her gut. Rescuing accident victims was a whole other story—one she avoided thinking about.

"Leave Rachel alone," Jim said. "We have something else to worry about. The baby's name. Which do you like? Caitlyn, Chloe or Cameron?"

His mother sat up straight. "Katherine is a nice name. Maybe she'll have red hair like me."

Rachel eased her way toward the door. Her work here was done. "I'm going to grab my coat and head out."

Jim rushed over and enveloped her in a bear hug. "We love you, Rachel."

"Back at you."

This had been a satisfying home birth—one she would remember with pleasure. Midwifery was so much happier than emergency medicine. She remembered Katherine's question. *Have you ever lost a patient?* Though she knew that not everyone was meant to survive, her memories of victims she couldn't save haunted her.

As she stepped outside onto the porch, she turned up the fur-lined collar of her subzero parka. Vagrant snowflakes melted as they hit her cheeks. She'd already brushed the snow off the windshield and repacked her equipment in the back of the panel van with the Rocky Mountain Women's Clinic logo on the side. Ready to roll, Rachel got behind the steering wheel and turned on the windshield wipers.

Heavy snow clouds had begun to blot out the sun. The weatherman was predicting a blizzard starting tonight or tomorrow morning. She wanted to hurry home to her condo in Granby, about forty-five minutes away. Skirting around Katherine's SUV, she drove carefully down the steep driveway to a two-lane road that hadn't been plowed since early this morning. There were other tire tracks in the snow, but not many.

After a sharp left, she drove a couple hundred yards to a stop sign and feathered the brakes until she came to a complete stop.

From the back of the van, she heard a noise. Something loose rattling around? She turned to look. A man in a black leather jacket and a ski mask moved forward. He pressed the nose of his gun against her neck.

"Do as I say," he growled, "and you won't be hurt."

"What do you want?"

"You. We need a baby doctor."

A second man, also masked, lurked behind him in her van.

The cold muzzle of the gun pushed against her bare skin. The metallic stink of cordite rose to her nostrils. This weapon had been recently fired.

"Get out of your seat," he ordered. "I'm driving."

Fighting panic, she gripped the steering wheel. "It's my van. I'll drive. Just tell me where we're going."

From the back, she heard a grumble. "We don't have time for this."

The man with the gun reached forward and engaged the emergency brake. "There's a woman in labor who needs you. Are you going to turn your back on her?"

"No," she said hesitantly.

"I don't want you to know where we're going. Understand? That's why you can't drive."

"All right. I'll sit in the back." Her van was stocked with a number of medical supplies that could be used as weapons—scalpels, scissors, a heavy oxygen tank. "I'll do what you say. I don't want any trouble."

"Get in the passenger seat."

Still thinking about escape, she unfastened her seat belt and changed seats. Her purse was on the floor. If she could get her hands on her cell phone, she could call for help.

The man with the gun climbed into the driver's seat. She noticed that his jeans were stained with blood.

His partner took his place between the seats. Roughly, he grabbed her hands and clicked on a set of handcuffs. Using a bandage from her own supplies, he blindfolded her.

The van lurched forward. Only a moment later, they stopped. The rear door opened and slammed shut. She assumed that the second man had left. Now might be her best chance to escape; she was still close enough to the cabin to run back there. Jim was a deputy and would know how to help her.

She twisted in the passenger seat. Before her fingers touched the door handle, the man in the driver's seat pulled her shoulders back and wrapped the seat belt across her chest, neatly and effectively securing her into place.

"Who are you?" she demanded.

He said nothing. The van was in motion again.

She warned, "You won't get away with this. There are people who will come after me."

He remained silent, and her tension grew. She'd been lying about people looking for her. Tomorrow was the first day of a week vacation and she'd already called in with the information about Jim and Sarah's baby. Rachel lived alone; nobody would miss her for a while.

The blindfold made her claustrophobic, but if she looked down her nose, she could see her hands, cuffed in her lap. Helpless. Her only weapon was her voice.

She knew that it was important to humanize herself to her captor. If he saw her as a person, he'd be less likely to hurt her. At least, that was what the police advised for victims of a kidnap. *Am I a victim?* Damn, she hoped not.

An adrenaline rush hyped her heart rate, but she kept her voice calm. "Please tell me your name."

"It's Cole," he said.

"Cole," she repeated. "And your friend?"

"Frank."

Monosyllables didn't exactly count as a conversation, but it was something. "Listen, Cole. These cuffs are hurting my wrists. I'd really appreciate if you could take them off. I promise I won't cause trouble."

"The cuffs stay. And the blindfold."

"Please, Cole. You said you didn't want to hurt me."

Though she couldn't see him, she felt him staring at her.

"There's only one thing you need to know," he said. "There's a pregnant woman who needs you. Without your help, she and her baby will die."

As soon as he spoke, she realized that escape wasn't an option. No matter how much she wanted to run, she couldn't refuse to help. The fight went out of her. Her eyes squeezed shut behind the blindfold. More than being afraid for her own safety, she feared for the unknown woman and her unborn child.

COLE MCCLURE CONCENTRATED on the taillights of Frank Loeb's car. The route to their hideout was unfamiliar to him and complicated by a couple of switchbacks; he didn't want to waste time getting lost.

The decision to track down the midwife had been his. It was obvious that Penny wasn't going to make it without a hell of a lot more medical expertise than he or any of the other three men could provide.

Cole glanced at the blindfolded woman in the passenger seat. Her posture erect, she sat as still as a statue. Her fortitude impressed him. When he held the gun on her, she hadn't burst into tears or pleaded. A sensible woman, he thought. Too bad he couldn't explain to her that he was one of the good guys.

She cleared her throat. "Has the mother been having contractions?"

"Yes."

"How far apart?"

"It's hard to tell. She was shot in the left thigh and has been in pain."

She couldn't see through the blindfold, but her head turned toward him. "Shot?"

"A flesh wound. The bullet went straight through, but she lost blood."

"She needs a hospital, access to a surgeon, transfusions. My God, her body is probably in shock."

Cole couldn't have agreed more. "She won't let us take her to a doctor."

"You could make her go. You said she was weak."

"If she turns herself in at the hospital, she won't be released. Penny doesn't want to raise her baby in jail. Can you understand that, Rachel?"

"How do you know my name?"

In spite of her self-possessed attitude, he heard a note

of alarm in her voice. He didn't want to reveal more information than necessary, but she deserved an explanation.

"When I realized that we needed a midwife, I called the women's clinic and pretended to want a consultation with a midwife. They gave me your name and told me that you were with a woman in labor."

"But they wouldn't tell you the patient's name," Rachel said. "That's a breach of confidentiality."

"Frank hacked their computer." The big thug had a sophisticated skill set that almost made up for his tendency toward sadism. "After that, finding the address was easy."

When they discovered that Rachel had been sent to the home of Sarah and Jim Loughlin, it seemed like luck was finally on Cole's side. The cabin was only ten miles away from their hideout.

Frank Loeb had wanted to charge inside with guns blazing, but Cole convinced him it was better to move with subtlety and caution. Every law enforcement man and woman in the state of Colorado was already on the lookout for them. They didn't need more attention.

"You're the casino robbers," she said.

"I wish you hadn't figured that out."

"I'd be an idiot not to," she said. "It's all over the news. How much did you get away with? A hundred thousand dollars?"

Not even half that amount. "If you're smart, you won't mention the casino again."

He regretted dragging her into this situation. If Rachel could identify them, she was a threat. There was no way the others would release her unharmed.

Chapter Two

Though the blindfold prevented Rachel from seeing where they were going, the drive had taken less than twenty minutes. She knew they were still in the vicinity of Shadow Mountain Lake, still in Grand County. If she could figure out her location, she might somehow get a message to Jim, and he could coordinate her rescue through the sheriff's department.

The van door opened, and Cole took her arm, guiding her as she stumbled up a wood staircase. Looking down under the edge of the blindfold, she saw it had been partially cleared of snow. The porch was several paces across; this had to be a large house or a lodge.

She heard the front door open and felt a gush of warmth from inside. A man ordered, "Get the hell in here. Fast."

"What's the problem?" Cole asked.

"It's Penny. She's got a gun."

Rachel stifled a hysterical urge to laugh. Penny had to be every man's worst nightmare: a woman in labor with a firearm.

Inside the house, Cole held her arm and marched her across the room. He tapped on a door. "Penny? I'm coming in. I brought a midwife to help you."

As Rachel stepped into the bedroom, she was struck

by a miasma of floral perfume, antiseptic and sweat. Cole wasted no time in removing the blindfold and the handcuffs.

From the bed, Penny stared at her with hollow eyes smeared with makeup. Her skinny arm trembled with the effort of holding a revolver that looked as big as a canon. A flimsy nightgown covered her swollen breasts and ripe belly, but her pale legs were bare. The dressing on her thigh wound was bloodstained.

"I don't want drugs," Penny rasped. "This baby is going to be born healthy. Hear me?"

Rachel nodded. "Can I come closer?"

"Why?" Her eyes narrowed suspiciously. "What are you going to do?"

"I'm going to help you have this baby."

"First things first," Cole said. "Give me the gun."

"No way." Penny's breathing became more rapid. Her lips pulled back as she gritted her teeth. Her eyes squeezed shut.

Even wearing the ski mask, Cole looked nervous. "What's wrong?"

"A contraction," Rachel said.

A sob choked through Penny's lips. Still clutching the gun, she threw her head back, fighting the pain with every muscle in her body. She stayed that way for several seconds. Instead of a scream, she exhaled a gasp. "Damn it. This is going to get worse, isn't it?"

"Here's the thing about natural childbirth," Rachel said as she moved closer to the bed. "It's important for you to be comfortable and relaxed. My name is Rachel, by the way. How far apart are the contractions?"

"I'm not sure. Eight or ten minutes."

"First baby?"

"Yes."

Experience told Rachel that Penny wasn't anywhere near the final stages of labor. They probably had several more hours to look forward to. "Can I take a look at that wound on your leg?"

"Whatever."

Rachel sat on the bed beside her and gently pulled the bandage back. In her work as an EMT, she'd dealt with gunshot wounds before. She could tell that the bullet had entered the back of Penny's leg—probably as she was running away—and exited through the front. The torn flesh was clumsily sutured and caked with dried blood. "It doesn't appear to be infected. Can you walk on it?"

Defiantly, Penny said, "Damn right I can."

"I'd like you to walk into the bathroom and take a bath. Treat yourself to a nice, long soak."

"I don't need pampering." Her raccoon eyes were fierce. "I can take the pain."

Rachel looked away from the gun barrel that was only inches from her cheek. She didn't like Penny, didn't like that she was a criminal on the run and definitely didn't like her attitude. But this woman was her patient now, and Rachel's goal was a successful delivery.

"I'm sure you're tough as nails, Penny." Rachel stood and stepped away from the bed. "But this isn't about you. It's about your baby. You need to conserve your strength so you're ready to push when the time comes."

Cole approached the opposite side of the bed. "Listen to her, Penny."

"Fine. I'll take a bath."

Rachel went to the open door to the adjoining bathroom. As she started the water in the tub, she peered through a large casement window, searching for landmarks that would give her a clue to their location. All she saw was rocks and trees with snow-laden boughs.

Penny hobbled into the bathroom, using Cole's arm for support. As he guided her through the doorway, he deftly took the revolver from her hand.

"Hey," she protested.

"If you need it, I'll give it back."

Hoping to distract her, Rachel pointed to the swirling water. "Do you need help getting undressed?"

Penny glared at both of them. "Get out."

Before she left, Rachel instructed, "Leave the door unlocked so we can respond if you need help."

With Penny disarmed and bathing, Rachel turned to Cole. "I need fresh bedding and something comfortable for her to wear. It'd be nice to have some soft music."

"None of these procedures are medical," he said.

She leaned toward him and lowered her voice so Penny couldn't hear from the bathroom. "If I'd come in here and wrenched her knees apart for a vaginal exam, she would've blown my head off."

He blinked. His eyes were the only part of his face visible. "I guess you know what you're doing."

"In the back of my van, there are three cases and an oxygen tank. Bring all the equipment in here." She stripped the sheets off the bed. "And you can start boiling water."

"Hot water? Like in the frontier movies?"

"It's for tea," she said. "Raspberry leaf tea."

Instead of leaving her alone in the bedroom, he opened the door and barked orders. She tried to see beyond him, to figure out how many others were in the house. Not that it mattered. Even if Rachel could escape, she wouldn't leave Penny until she knew mother and baby were safe.

She went to the bathroom and opened the door a crack. "Penny, are you all right?"

Grudgingly, she said, "The water feels good."

"Some women choose to give birth in the tub."

"Naked? Forget it." Her tone had shifted from maniacal to something resembling cooperation. "Is there something else I should do? Some kind of exercise?"

Her change in attitude boded well. A woman in labor needed to be able to trust the people around her. Giving birth wasn't a battle; it was a process.

"Relax," Rachel said. "Take your time. Wash your hair."

In the bedroom, Cole thrust the fresh sheets toward her. "Here you go."

"Would you help me make the bed?"

He went to the opposite side and unfolded the fitted bottom sheet of soft lavender cotton. He'd taken off his jacket and was wearing an untucked flannel shirt over a long-sleeved white thermal undershirt and jeans with splotches of blood on the thigh.

She pulled the sheet toward her side of the bed. "We're probably going to be here for hours. You might as well take off that stupid mask."

He straightened to his full height—a couple of inches over six feet—and stared for a moment before he peeled off the black knit mask and ran his fingers through his shaggy brown hair.

Some women would have considered him handsome with his high cheekbones, firm chin and deep-set eyes of cognac-brown. His jaw was rough with stubble that looked almost fashionable, and his smile was dazzling. "You're staring, Rachel. Memorizing my face?"

"Don't need to," she shot back. "I'm sure there are plenty of pictures of you on Wanted posters."

"I said it before, and I'll say it again. I'm not going to hurt you."

"Apart from kidnapping me?"

"I won't apologize for that. Penny needs you."

Rather than answering her challenge, he had appealed to her better instincts. Cole was smooth, all right. Probably a con man as well as a robber. Unfortunately, she had a bad habit of falling for dangerous men. *Not this time.*

"Don't bother being charming," she said. "I'm going to need your help with Penny, but I don't like you, Cole. I don't trust a single word that comes out of your mouth."

He grinned. "You think I'm charming."

Jerk! As she smoothed the sheets, she asked, "Which one of the men out there is the father of Penny's baby?"

"None of us."

Of course not. That would be too easy. "Can he be reached?"

"We're not on vacation here. This is a hideout. We don't need to invite visitors."

But this was a nice house—not a shack in the woods. Finding this supposed "hideout" that happened to be conveniently vacant was too much of a coincidence. "You must have planned to come here."

"Hell, no. We were supposed to be in Salt Lake City by now. When Penny went into labor, we had to stop. The house belongs to someone she knows."

The fact that Penny had contacts in this area might come in handy. Rachel needed to keep her ears and eyes open, to gather every bit of information that she could. There was no telling what might be useful.

By the time Penny got out of the tub, Rachel had transformed the bedroom into a clean, inviting space using supplies from her van. The bedding was fresh. A healing fragrance of eucalyptus and pine wafted from an herbal scent diffuser. Native American flute music rose from a CD player.

Before Penny got into bed, Rachel replaced the dressings on her leg wound, using an antiseptic salve to ease the pain. In her work as a nurse-midwife, she leavened various herbal and homeopathic methods with standard medical procedure. Basically, she did whatever worked.

Though Penny remained diffident, she looked young and vulnerable with the makeup washed off her face. Mostly, she seemed tired. The stress of labor and the trauma of being shot had taken their toll.

Rachel took her blood pressure, and she wasn't surprised that it was low. Penny's pulse was jumpy and weak.

When her next contraction hit, Rachel talked her through it. "You don't have to tough it out. If you need the release of yelling—"

"No," she snapped. "I'm not giving those bastards the satisfaction of hearing me scream."

Apparently, she was making up for her weakened physical condition with a powerful hostility. Rachel asked, "Should I send Cole out of the room while I do the vaginal exam?"

"Yes."

He was quick to leave. "I'll fetch the tea."

Alone with Penny, Rachel checked the cervix. Dilation was already at seven centimeters. This baby could be coming sooner than she'd thought. "You're doing a good job," she encouraged. "It won't be too much longer."

"Is my baby okay?"

"Let's check it out."

Usually, there was an implied trust between midwife and mom, but this situation was anything but usual. As

Rachel hooked up the fetal monitor, she tried to be conversational. "When is your due date?"

"Two days from now."

"That's good. You carried to full term." At least, there shouldn't be the problems associated with premature birth. "Is there anything I ought to know about? Any special problems during your pregnancy?"

"I got fat."

Rachel did a double take before she realized Penny was joking. "Are you from around here?"

"We lived in Grand Lake for a while. I went to high school in Granby."

"That's where I live," Rachel said. "Is your family still in Grand Lake?"

"It's just me and my mom. My dad left when I was little. I never missed having him around." She touched her necklace and rubbed her thumb over the shiny black pearl. "Mom gave me this. It's her namesake—Pearl. She lives in Denver, but she's house-sitting for a friend in Grand Lake."

They weren't too far from there. Grand Lake was a small village—not much more than a main street of shops and lodging for tourists visiting the scenic lakeside. "Should I try to contact your mother?"

"Oh. My. God." Penny rolled her eyes. "If my mom knew what I was up to, she'd kill me."

Her jaw clenched, and Rachel talked her through the contraction. Penny must have had some Lamaze training because she knew the breathing techniques for dealing with the pain.

When she settled back against the pillows, she said, "If anything happens to me, I want my mom to have my baby."

"Not the father?"

"Mom's better." She chewed her lower lip. "She'll be a good grandma if I'm not around."

Considering a premature death wasn't the best way to go into labor. Rachel preferred to keep the mood upbeat and positive. "You're doing fine. Nothing bad is going to happen."

"Do you believe in premonitions? Like stuff with tarot cards and crystal balls?"

"Not really."

"My friend Jenna did a reading for me. Hey, maybe you know her. She lives in Granby, too. Jenna Cambridge?"

"The name isn't familiar."

"She's kind of quiet. Doesn't go out much," Penny said. "Every time I visit her, I try to fix her up. But she's stuck on some guy who dumped her a long time ago. What a waste! Everybody falls. The trick is to get back on the bicycle."

Though Rachel wasn't prone to taking advice from a pregnant criminal who didn't trust the father of her baby, she had to admit that Penny made a good point. "Doesn't do any good to sit around feeling down on yourself."

"Exactly." She threw up her hands. "Anyway, Jenna read my cards and told me that something bad was going to happen. My old life would be torn asunder. Those were her words. And she drew the death card."

Her friend Jenna sounded like a real peach. Pregnant women were stressed enough without dire warnings. "The death card could mean a change in your life. Like becoming a mom."

"Maybe you're right. I have changed. I took real good care of myself all through the pregnancy. No booze. No cigs. I did everything right."

Except robbing a casino. Rachel finished hooking up

the monitor and read the electronic blips. "Your baby's heartbeat is strong and steady."

When Cole returned with the raspberry tea, Rachel moved into the familiar pattern of labor—a combination of her own expertise and the mother's natural instincts. Needing to move, Penny got out of the bed a couple of times and paced. When she complained of back pain, Cole volunteered to massage. His strong hands provided Penny with relief. He was turning out to be an excellent helper—uncomplaining and quick to follow her instructions.

When the urge to push came, Penny screamed for the first time. And she let go with a string of curses. Though Rachel had pretty much heard it all, she was surprised by the depth and variety of profanity from such a tiny woman.

Cole looked panicked. "Is this normal?"

"The pushing? Or the I-hate-men tirade?"

"Both."

"Very typical. I bet you're glad you took the gun away."

"Hell, yes."

A mere two hours after Rachel had arrived at the house, Penny gave birth to an average-sized baby girl with a healthy set of lungs.

Though Rachel had participated in well over two hundred births, this moment never failed to amaze her. The emergence of new life gave meaning to all existence.

Postpartum was also a time that required special attention on the part of the midwife. Penny was leaking blood onto the rubber sheet they'd spread across the bed. Hemorrhage was always a danger.

Rachel held the newborn toward Cole. "Take the baby. I need to deal with Penny."

Dumbstruck, he held the wriggling infant close to his chest. His gaze met hers. In his eyes, she saw a reflection of her own wonderment, and she appreciated his honest reverence for the miracle of life. For a tough guy, he was sensitive.

Her focus right now was on the mother. Rachel urged, "You need to push again."

"No way." With a sob, Penny covered her eyes with her forearm. "I can't."

She had to expel the afterbirth. As Rachel massaged the uterus, she felt the muscles contract, naturally doing what was necessary. The placenta slipped out. Gradually, the bleeding slowed and stopped.

Cole stood behind her shoulder, watching with concern. "Is she going to be okay?"

"They both are."

Penny forced herself into a sitting position with pillows behind her back. "I want my baby."

With Cole's help, Rachel clipped the cord, washed the infant and cleared her nose of mucus. The rest of the cleanup could wait. She settled the new baby on Penny's breast.

As mother and child cooed to each other, she turned toward Cole in time to see him swipe away a tear. Turning away, he said, "I'll tell the others."

"Whoa, there. You're not leaving me with all the mess to clean up."

"I'll be right back."

Rachel sank into a chair beside the bed and watched the bonding of mother and child. Though Penny hadn't seemed the least bit maternal, her expression was serene and gentle.

"Do you have a name?" Rachel asked.

"Goldie. She's my golden child."

From the other room, she heard the men arguing loudly.

Catching bits of their conversation, Rachel got the idea that they were tired of waiting around. *Bad news for her.*

When the gang was on the run again, they had no further need for a midwife. She was afraid to think of what might happen next.

Chapter Three

In the bedroom, Cole stood at the window and looked out into a deep, dark forest. Fresh snow piled up on the sill. He could hardly believe that he was considering an escape into that freezing darkness. He lived in L.A. where his only contact with snow was the occasional snowboarding trip to Big Bear Lake. He hated the cold.

A month ago, when the FBI office in Denver tapped him for this undercover assignment, he'd tried to wriggle out of it. But they'd needed an agent who was an unfamiliar face in the western states. The operating theory was that someone inside the FBI was connected to the spree of casino and bank robberies.

He stepped away from the window and began repacking Rachel's medical equipment in the cases from her van. Both of the women were in the bathroom, chatting about benefits of breast-feeding and how to use the pump. As he eavesdropped, he marveled at how normal their conversation sounded. For the moment, Penny wasn't a hardened criminal and Rachel wasn't a kidnap victim. They were just two women, talking about babies.

And he was just an average guy—shocked and amazed by the mysteries of childbirth. He didn't have words to describe how he'd felt when Goldie was born. He forgot where he was and why he was there. Watching the new-born take her first breath had amazed him. Her cry was the voice of an angel. Pure and innocent.

In that moment, he wanted to protect Penny instead of taking her into FBI custody.

And then there was Rachel. Slender but muscular, she moved with a natural grace. Her short dark hair made her blue eyes look huge, even though she wasn't wearing any makeup. He felt guilty as hell for dragging her into this mess. Top priority for him was to make sure Rachel escaped unharmed.

From the bathroom, he overheard her say, "Your body needs time to recover, Penny. You should spend time in bed, relaxing."

"Don't worry. I'm not going anywhere."

"Will the men agree to let you sleep tonight?"

"They'll do what I say," Penny said airily. "They can't leave me behind."

"Why not?" Rachel asked.

"Because I'm the only one who knows where the money is hidden."

Cole feared that her confidence might be misplaced. Frank and the other two were anxious to get going. No doubt, they could force Penny to tell them about the stash from five different robberies in three states.

Rachel seemed to be thinking along the same lines. "What if they threaten you?"

"They wouldn't dare. My baby's father is the head honcho. The big boss. If anybody hurts me, they'll answer to him."

Cole held his breath. *Say his name, Penny.* He needed to know the identity of the criminal mastermind who controlled this gang and at least five others. They referred to him as Baron, and he was famous for taking bloody revenge on those who betrayed him. Cole's reason for joining this gang of misfits was to infiltrate the upper levels of the organization and get evidence that could be used against Baron.

Rachel asked, "Does he know about Goldie?"

"Don't you remember? I told you all about Baron, about how we met. Damn, Rachel. You should learn to pay attention."

"Sorry," she murmured.

"He loves me. After this job, he promised to take me home with him, to raise our baby."

"Is that what you want?"

"You bet it is." Penny giggled. "Want to know a secret? A little while ago, I called Baron and told him about Goldie. He's coming here. He ought to be here any minute."

Not good news. Cole might have been able to convince the others in the gang to release Rachel. These guys weren't killers, except for Frank. Baron was a different story; he wouldn't leave a witness alive.

From the bathroom, he heard Rachel ask, "How does he know where you are? Cole said this house wasn't a scheduled stop."

"Simple," Penny replied. "This is Baron's house."

That was all Cole needed to hear. He could find Baron's identity by checking property records. As far as he was concerned, his undercover assignment was over. He reached into his jeans pocket, took out his cell phone.

This wasn't an everyday cell. Though Cole didn't need a lot of fancy apps, he'd used the geniuses at the FBI to modify his phone to suit his specific needs.

The first modification: he could disable the GPS locator. Unless he had it turned on, he couldn't be tracked. His handler—Agent Ted Waxman in L.A.—wasn't thrilled with the need for secrecy, but Cole needed to be sure his cover wouldn't be blown by some federal agent jumping the gun.

Second, his directory of phone numbers couldn't be read without using a five-digit code. His identity was protected in case somebody picked up his phone.

Third and most important, his number was blocked to everyone. Waxman couldn't call him with new orders and information. Cole, alone, made the decision when he would make contact and when he needed help.

Now was that time. He activated the GPS locator to alert Waxman that he was ready for extraction. Response time was usually less than an hour. Cole intended to be away from the house when that time came.

He slid the phone into his pocket and called out, "Hey, ladies, I need some help figuring out how to pack this stuff."

Rachel came out of the bathroom. Right away, he could see the change in her demeanor. No longer the self-assured professional, she had a haunted look in her eyes. Beneath her wispy bangs, her forehead pinched with worry. She whispered, "What's going to happen to me?"

Now would have been a good time to flash a badge and tell her that he was FBI, but he wasn't carrying identification. "I'll get you out of here."

Her gaze assessed him. During the hours of Penny's labor and the aftermath, a bond had grown between them. He hoped it was enough to make her cooperate without the reassurance of his credentials.

She asked, "Why should I trust you?"

"You don't have much choice."

Penny swept into the room and went to the travel bassinette where her baby was sleeping. "Be sure that you put all the baby stuff in the huge backpack so I can take it with me."

"Like what?" Cole asked.

"Diapers," Rachel said. "There's a sling for carrying newborns. And you'll need blankets and formula."

"But I'm breast-feeding. My milk already came in. Does that mean my boobs are going to get small again? Jenna said they would."

"Your friend Jenna doesn't have children. She doesn't know." Rachel's hands trembled as she sorted through the various baby items. "I don't have a car seat I can leave with you. You'll need to buy one as soon as possible."

Cole saw an opportunity to get Rachel alone. He wanted to reassure her that help was on the way. He asked her, "Don't you have a baby seat in your van?"

"I want it." Penny climbed onto the bed and stretched out. Her pink flannel robe contrasted her wan complexion. "Get it for me."

Rachel said, "I need that car seat for emergencies. If I have to transport a child to a hospital or—"

"Don't be stupid, Rachel. You're not going to need that van anymore. You're coming with me. I need you to help me with Goldie."

Rachel recoiled as though she'd been slapped. "I have a job."

"So what? You'll make more money with me than you would as a midwife." Penny propped herself up on one elbow. "Come here and help me get these pillows arranged."

Rachel did as she'd been ordered, then she turned toward Cole. "I'll help you get the car seat out of the van. The straps are complicated, and I don't want you to break it."

From the bed, Penny waved. "Hurry back. I want more tea."

He grabbed Rachel's down parka from the bedroom closet and held it for her. She hadn't said a word, but he knew she'd made a decision to stick with him. Not surprising. Trusting Penny to take care of her would be suicidal.

RACHEL DIDN'T HAVE A PLAN. Trust Cole? Sure, he'd shown sensitivity when the baby was delivered. The whole time he was helping her, he'd been smart and kind, even gentlemanly. But he also had kidnapped her and jammed a gun into her neck.

All she needed from him was her car keys.

When they stepped outside through the side door of the house, he caught hold of her arm and pulled her back, behind the bare branches of a bush and a towering pine. Edging uphill, he whispered, "Duck down and stay quiet. Something isn't right."

The night was still and cold. Snowflakes drifted lazily, and she was glad for the warmth of her parka and hood. Behind them was a steep, thickly forested hillside. Peeking around Cole's shoulder, she saw the side of the house and the edge of the wooden porch that stretched across the front. Since she'd been sequestered in the bedroom with Penny and hadn't seen the rest of the house, she hadn't realized that it was two stories with a slanted roof. To her right was a long, low garage. Was her van parked inside? She couldn't see past the house, didn't know if there was a road in front or other cars.

Through the stillness, she heard the rumble of voices. There were others out here, hiding in the darkness.

She whispered, "Can you see anything?"

"A couple of shadows. No headlights."

Mysterious figures creeping toward the hideout might actually be to her advantage. She prayed that it was the police who had finally tracked down the gang. "Who is it?"

"Can't tell." His voice was as quiet as the falling snow; she had to lean close to hear him. "Could be the cops. Or it could be Penny's boyfriend."

"Baron." He sounded like a real creep—much older than Penny and greedy enough to want his pregnant girlfriend to participate in a robbery. "Penny said this was his house. Why wouldn't he just walk inside?"

"Hush."

For a moment, she considered raising her hands above her head and marching to the front of the cabin to surrender. It was a risk, but anything would be better than being under Penny's thumb.

Gunfire from a semiautomatic weapon shattered the night. She heard breaking glass and shouts from inside the house.

She wasn't a stranger to violence. When she was driving the ambulance, she'd been thrust into a lot of dicey situations, and she prided herself on an ability to stay calm. But the gunfire shocked her.

Shots were returned from inside the house.

There was another burst from the attackers.

She clung to Cole's arm. "Tell me what to do."

"We wait."

The side door they'd come through flung open. Frank charged outside. With guns in both hands, the big man dashed into the open, firing wildly as he ran toward the garage.

He was shot. His arms flew into the air before he fell. His blood splattered in the snow. He didn't attempt to get up, but she saw his arm move. "He's not dead."

"Don't even think about stepping into the open to help him," Cole whispered. "The way I figure, there are only two shooters. Three at the most. They don't have the manpower to surround the cabin, but they have superior weapons."

Though her mind was barely able to comprehend what she was experiencing, she nodded.

He continued, "We'll go up the hill, wait until the shooting is over and circle back around to the garage."

Taking her gloved hand, he pulled her through the ankle-deep snow into the surrounding forest. Behind them, gunfire exploded. Anybody living within a mile of this house had to be aware that something terrible was happening. The police would have to respond.

Crouched behind a snow-covered boulder, Cole paused and looked back. "We're leaving tracks. They won't have any trouble following us. We need to go faster."

Her survival instinct was strong. She wanted to make a getaway, but there was something else at stake. "We can't leave Penny here. Or the baby."

A sliver of moonlight through clouds illuminated his face. In his eyes, she saw a struggle between protecting the innocent and saving his own butt. "Damn it, Rachel. You're right."

Sadly, she said, "I know."

They retraced their steps to the house. Instead of using the door, Cole went to the rear of the house. He stopped outside a window. Inside, she saw the bathroom where she and Penny had been talking only a little while ago.

He dug into his pocket, took out her car keys and handed them to her. "If anything happens to me, get the hell out of here. Hide in the forest until you can get back to the garage."

The car keys literally opened the door to her escape. Her purse was in the van. And her cell phone.

When he shoved the casement window open, she said, "All those windows were latched."

"I opened it hours ago," he said. "I expected to be escaping from the inside out. Not breaking in."

Walking into a shoot-out was insanity. But the alternative was worse. She couldn't leave a helpless newborn to the mercy of these violent men.

Cole slipped through the window, and she got in position to follow.

"No," he said. "Stay here."

There wasn't time to argue. He needed her help in handling Penny and the baby. She hoisted herself up and over the sill.

As soon as she was inside, she heard the baby crying. In the bedroom, Cole knelt beside Penny's body on the floor. She'd been shot in the chest. Her open eyes stared sightlessly at the ceiling.

Rachel reached past Cole to feel Penny's throat for a pulse. Her skin was still warm, but her heart had stopped. There was nothing. Not even a flutter. Penny was gone. After her heroic struggle to bring her baby into the world, she wouldn't live to see her child grow. Fate was cruel. Unfair. *Oh, God, this is so wrong.*

From the front of the house, the gun battle continued, but all she heard was the baby's cries. If it was the last thing she ever did, Rachel would rescue Goldie. Moving with purpose, she took the baby sling from the backpack. When she snuggled Goldie into the carrier, the infant's cries modified to a low whimpering.

Cole grabbed the backpack filled with baby supplies. They went through the bathroom window into the forest.

They were only a few steps into the trees when he signaled for her to stop. He said, "Do you hear that?"

She listened. "It's quiet."

The shooting had ended. The battle was over. Now the attackers would be coming after them.

Chapter Four

Cole went first, leading Rachel up the forested hill and away from the house. The cumbersome backpack hampered his usual gait. He hunched forward, moving as quickly as possible in the snow-covered terrain. Even if there had been a path through these trees, he wouldn't have been able to see it. Not in this darkness. Not with the snow falling.

His leather jacket wasn't the best thing to be wearing in this weather, but he wasn't cold. The opposite, in fact. He was sweating like a pig. Though breathing hard, he couldn't seem to get enough wind in his lungs. After only going a couple of hundred yards, his shoulders ached. His thigh muscles were burning. This high elevation was killing him. He estimated that they were more than eight thousand feet above sea level. What the hell was a California guy like him doing here? His natural habitat was palm trees.

He picked his way through the rugged trunks of pine trees and dodged around boulders. After he climbed over a fallen log, he turned to help Rachel. She had the baby in the sling, tucked inside her parka.

She ignored his outstretched hand and jumped over the log, nimble as a white-tailed deer.

"Careful," he said.

"I'm good."

Her energy annoyed him. Logically, he knew that Rachel lived here full-time and was acclimated to the altitude. But he wanted to be the strong one—the protector who would lead her and the baby to safety.

Hoping to buy a little time to catch his breath, he asked, "How's Goldie?"

Rachel peeked inside her parka. "Sleeping. She's snuggled against my chest and can hear my heartbeat. It probably feels like she's still in the womb."

They needed to find shelter soon. It couldn't be good for a newborn to be exposed to the cold.

"I have a question," she said. "Why are we going uphill?"

"Escape."

"If we go down to the road, we'll be more likely to find a cabin. Or we could flag down a passing car."

He looked down the hill. The lights from the house were barely visible. "We're going this way because we can't risk having the guys who attacked the house find us. They'll be watching the road."

"They'll be looking for us? Why?"

If the gunmen worked for Baron, they wouldn't leave without the boss man's baby. If they were Baron's enemies, the same rationale applied. Goldie was a valuable commodity. "It's not us they're after."

Her arm curled protectively around the infant. "The police ought to be here soon. Somebody must have reported all that gunfire."

It was too soon to expect a response from his GPS signal, but he trusted that the FBI was closing in on this location. "Nothing would please me more than hearing cop sirens."

"You can't mean that." Her earnest gaze confronted him. "You'll be taken into custody."

He'd almost forgotten that she still didn't know his identity. As far as Rachel was concerned, he was the guy who kidnapped her at gunpoint. An armed robber.

"If I got arrested, would you be heartbroken?"

She exhaled a puff of icy vapor. "No."

"Maybe a little sad?"

"Let me put it this way. I wouldn't turn you in."

Her response surprised him. He had her pegged as a strictly law-abiding citizen who'd be delighted to see any criminal behind bars. But she was willing to make an exception for him. Either she liked him or she had a dark side that she kept hidden.

He turned to face the uphill terrain. "We'll keep moving until we know we're safe. Then we can double back to the road."

The brief rest had allowed him to recover his strength. He slogged onward, wanting to put distance between them and the men with guns. In spite of the burn, his legs took on a steady rhythm as he climbed. Coming through a stand of trees, he realized that they'd reached the highest point on the hill. He maneuvered until he was standing on a boulder and waited for Rachel to join him.

"This is a good lookout point. Do you see anything?"

Together, they peered through the curtain of trees. The snowfall was thick. Heavy clouds had blocked out the light from the moon and stars.

"There." She pointed down the hill.

The beams of a couple of flashlights flickered in the darkness. They weren't far away. Maybe eighty yards.

He and Rachel were within range of their semiautomatic weapons.

He ducked. She did the same.

The searchers were too close. His hope for escape vanished in the howling wind that sliced through the tree trunks. He and Rachel had left tracks in the snow that a blind man could follow. Peering over the edge of the boulder, he saw the flashlights moving closer. There was only one way out of this.

He slipped his arms out of the backpack. "Take the baby and run. Get as far away from here as you can."

"What are you going to do?"

"I'll distract them."

Going up against men with superior firepower wasn't as dumb as it sounded. Cole had the advantage of higher ground. If he waited until they got close, he might be able to take out one of them before the other responded.

"There's something you haven't considered," she said.

"What's that?"

"Snow."

While they'd been climbing, the full force of the impending blizzard had gathered. The storm had taken on a fierce intensity.

She grabbed his arm and tugged. "They won't be able to see us in the blizzard. The wind will cover our tracks."

Great. He wouldn't die in a hail of bullets. He'd freeze to death in a blizzard.

"Come on," she urged. "I need you. Goldie needs you."

He shouldered the pack again. Going downhill should have been easier, but his knees jolted with every step. At the foot of the slope, they approached an open area where the true velocity of the storm was apparent. The snow fell in sheets. His visibility was cut to only a few yards, but he figured they could cover more distance if they went straight ahead instead of weaving through the trees.

When he stepped into the open, he sank up to his knees. His jeans were wet. His fingers and toes were numb.

"Stay close to the trees," Rachel said. "It's not as deep."

At the edge of the forest, the snow was over his ankles. He trudged through it, making a path for her to follow. One minute turned into ten. Ten into twenty. Inside his boots, his feet felt like frozen blocks of ice. The snow stung his cheeks. So cold, so damned cold. If he was this miserable what was happening to Goldie? Fear for the motherless newborn kept him moving forward. He had to protect this child, had to find shelter.

But he'd lost all sense of direction in the snow. As far as he could tell, they might be heading back toward the house.

Trying to get his bearings, he looked over his shoulder. He doubted that the bad guys were still in pursuit. Any sane person would have turned back by now.

As Rachel had predicted, the snow was already drifting, neatly erasing their tracks.

He couldn't tell how far they'd gone. It felt like miles, endless miles. Needing a break, he stepped back into the shelter of the forest. His chest ached with the effort of breathing. His eyes were stinging. He squeezed his eyelids shut and opened them again. Squinting, he looked through the trees and saw a solid shape. A cabin. He blinked, hoping that his brain wasn't playing tricks on him. "Rachel, do you see it?"

"A cabin." Her voice trembled on the edge of a sob. "Thank God, it's a cabin."

He helped her up the small embankment, and they approached the rear of the cabin. No lights shone from inside.

The front door was sheltered by a small porch. Cole

hammered against the green painted door with his frozen fist. No answer. Nobody home.

He tried the door handle and found it locked. He was carrying lock picks, but it was too cold to try a delicate manipulation of lock tumblers. He stepped back, prepared to use his body as a battering ram.

"Wait," Rachel said. "Run your hand over the top sill. They might have left a key."

"We need to get inside." He was too damned cold and tired to perform a subtle search. "Why the hell would anybody bother to lock up and then leave a key?"

"This isn't the city," she said. "Some of these little cabins are weekend getaways with different families coming and going. Give it a try."

He peeled off his glove. His fingers were wet and stiff, but he didn't see the whitened skin indicating the first stage of frostbite. When he felt along the ledge above the door, he touched a key. It seemed that their luck had turned.

Shivering, he fitted the key into the lock and pushed open the door. He and Rachel tumbled inside. When he shut the door against the elements, an ominous silence wrapped around them.

RACHEL DISCARDED HER GLOVES and hit the light switch beside the door. The glow from an overhead light fixture spilled down upon them. They had electricity. So far, so good.

She unzipped her parka, glad that when she left the house this morning—an eternity ago—she'd been smart enough to dress for subzero weather. This jacket might have saved her life...and Goldie's, as well. She looked down at the tiny bundle she carried in the sling against her chest. The baby's eyes were closed. She wasn't moving. *Please, God, let her be all right.*

Cole hovered beside her, and she knew he was thinking the same thing.

Rachel slipped out of her jacket. Carefully, she braced the baby in her arms and adjusted the sling. *Please, God.*

Goldie's eyes popped open and she let out a wail.

Rachel had never heard a more beautiful sound. "She's okay. Yes, you are, Goldie. You're all right."

Looking up, she saw a similar relief in Cole's ruddy face. He'd torn off his cap and his hair stood up in spikes. His lips were chapped and swollen. Moisture dripped from his leather jacket. In spite of his obvious discomfort, he smiled.

Grateful tears rose behind her eyelids, but she couldn't let herself fall apart. "Are we safe?"

"I'm not sure," he said. "Tell me what Goldie needs."

The interior of the cabin was one big open room with a couple of sofas and chairs at one end and a large wooden table at the other. The kitchen area formed an *L* shape. A closed door against the back wall probably led into the bedroom. The most important feature, in her mind, was the freestanding propane gas fireplace. "See if you can get that heater going."

She held Goldie against her shoulder, patting her back and soothing her cries. The poor little thing had to be starving. There was powdered formula in the backpack of supplies, but they needed water.

In the kitchen, Rachel turned the faucet in the sink and was rewarded with a steady flow. This simple, little cabin—probably a weekend getaway—had been well-prepared for winter. No doubt the owners had left the electricity on because the water pipes were wrapped in heat tape. The stove was electric.

Cole joined her. "The fireplace is on. What's next?"

He looked like hell. Hiking through the blizzard had been more difficult for him than for her. Not only did he go first, but his jacket and boots also weren't anywhere near as well-insulated as hers. She wanted to tell him to get out of his wet clothes, warm up and take care of himself, but she didn't want to insult his masculine pride by suggesting he wasn't in as good a shape as she was.

"Help me get stuff out of the backpack."

Near the cheery blaze in the propane fireplace, they dug through the baby supplies and put together a nest of blankets for Goldie. When Rachel laid the baby down on the blankets, her cries faded. Goldie wriggled as her diaper was changed.

Cole frowned. "Is she supposed to look like that?"

"Like what?"

"Like a plucked chicken. I thought babies were supposed to have chubby arms and legs."

"Don't listen to him." Rachel stroked Goldie's fine, dark hair. "You're gorgeous."

"Yeah, people always say that. But not all babies are beautiful."

"This is a golden child." She zipped Goldie into a yellow micro-fleece sleep sack. "She's beautiful, strong and brave—not even a day old and she's already escaped a gang of thugs and made it through a blizzard."

The baby's chin tilted, and she seemed to be looking directly at Cole with her lips pursed.

He laughed. "She's a tough little monkey."

"Newborns are surprisingly resilient." She held Goldie against her breast and stood. "I'm going to the kitchen to prepare the formula. Maybe you want to get out of those wet clothes."

"What about you?"

Her jeans were wet and cold against her legs, and her feet were cold in spite of her lined, waterproof boots. "I'd love to take off my boots."

"Sit," he ordered.

Still holding the baby, she sank onto a rocking chair. The heat from the fireplace was making a difference in the room temperature. She couldn't allow herself to get too comfortable or she'd surely fall asleep. This had been the longest day of her life; she'd attended at two birthings, been kidnapped and escaped through a blizzard.

Cole knelt before her and unfastened the laces on her boots. He eased the boot off her right foot, cradled her heel in his hand and massaged through her wool sock. His touch felt so good that she groaned with pleasure.

"Your feet are almost dry," Cole said. "Where do I get boots like this?"

"Any outdoor clothing and equipment store." Anyone who lived in the mountains knew how to shop for snow gear. "You're not from around here."

"L.A.," he said.

This was the first bit of personal information he'd volunteered. She'd entrusted this man with her life even though she knew next to nothing about him. "What's your last name?"

"McClure." He pulled off the other boot. "And I'm not who you think I am."

Chapter Five

Rachel gazed down at the top of Cole's head as he removed her other boot. Much of his behavior didn't fit with what she expected from an armed robber. He was too smart to be a thug but dumb enough to get involved with killers. *Who is he?* In the back of her mind, she'd been waiting for the other shoe to drop. Literally, this was the moment.

He'd said that he wasn't who she thought he was. What did that mean? Did he have superpowers? Was he actually a millionaire? She refused to be seduced by excuses or explanations. Rachel knew his type. He was a tough guy—dangerous, strong and silent…and sexy.

"You know what, Cole? I don't want to hear your life story."

He sat back on his heels. "Trust me. You want to know."

"Trust you?" Not wanting to upset Goldie, she kept her voice level. Inside, she was far from calm. "You don't deserve my trust."

"That's not what you said when I was saving your butt."

"I didn't ask for your help."

"Come on, Rachel. I could have left you in the middle of a shoot-out. I'm not a bad guy."

"If you hadn't hidden in the back of my van and kidnapped me—" she paused for emphasis "—kidnapped me at gunpoint, I wouldn't have been in a shoot-out."

"There were circumstances."

"Don't care." Right now, she was supposed to be on vacation, relaxing in her cozy condo with a fragrant cup of chamomile tea and a good book. "I want this nightmare to be over. And when it is, I never want to see you again."

"Fair enough." He stood and stretched. "Take care of Goldie. I'm going to make sure we're secure."

"Go right ahead."

COLE OPENED THE CABIN DOOR and stepped onto the porch. The brief moment of warmth when he'd been inside the cabin made the cold feel even worse than before. The blizzard still raged, throwing handfuls of snow into his face. The icy temperatures instantly froze his bare hands. In his left, he held his gun. In his right, the cell phone. His intention was to call for help. Shivering, he turned on the phone. His power was almost gone. He had no signal at this remote cabin. Holding the phone like a beacon, he turned in every direction, trying to make a connection. *Nada. Damn it.* He hoped the GPS signal was still transmitting his location to his FBI handlers.

The windblown snow had already begun to erase their tracks. Drifts piled up, nearly two feet deep on one side of the log cabin walls. In this storm, visual surveillance was nearly impossible. He couldn't see past the trees into the forest. All he could do was try to get his bearings.

In front of the house was a turn-around driveway. Less than thirty feet away, he saw the blocky shape of a small outbuilding. A garage? There might be something in there that would aid in their escape.

The wide front door of the garage was blocked by the

drifting snow, but there was a side entrance. He shoved it open and entered. The interior was unlit, but there was some illumination from a window at the rear. The open space in the middle seemed to indicate that this building was used as a garage when the people who owned the cabin were here. Under the window, he found a workbench with tools for home repair. Stacked along the walls was a variety of sporting equipment: cross-country skis, poles and snowshoes.

He'd never tried cross-country skiing before, but Rachel probably knew how to use this stuff. She was a hardy mountain woman. Prepared for the snow. Intrepid. What was her problem, anyway?

He'd been about to tell her that he was a fed and she had no more reason to fear, but she'd shut him down. Her big beautiful blue eyes glared at him with unmistakable anger. She'd said that she didn't give a damn about him.

He didn't believe her. Though she had every reason to be ticked off, she didn't hate him. There was something growing between them. A spark. He saw it in her body language, heard it in her voice, felt it in a dim flicker inside his frozen body. Maybe after they were safe and she knew he was a good guy, he'd pursue that attraction. Or maybe not. He had a hard time imagining Rachel in sunny California, and he sure as hell wasn't going to move to these frigid, airless mountains.

Leaving the garage, he tromped along the driveway to a narrow road that hadn't been cleared of snow. No tire tracks. Nothing had been on this road since the beginning of the storm.

He looked back toward the house. Though the curtains were drawn, he could still see the light from inside. If anyone came looking for them, they wouldn't be hard to find.

CRADLING THE BABY on her shoulder, Rachel padded around in the kitchen in her wool socks. She heard the front door open and saw Cole stumble inside. He locked the door and placed his gun on the coffee table. *And his cell phone.*

"Why didn't you tell me you had a phone?" she asked.

"It's almost dead. And I can't get a signal."

Warily, she approached the table. "Who were you trying to call?"

"Somebody to get us the hell out of here."

"Like who?" She wasn't sure that she wanted to be rescued by any of his friends. *Out of the frying pan into the fire.*

"I'm not trying to trick you." He tossed the phone to her. "Go ahead. See if you can get the damn thing to work."

She juggled the phone and waved it all around while he went through the door to the bedroom. He hadn't been lying about the lack of signal, but that didn't set her mind at ease.

Returning to the kitchen, she focused on preparing the formula—a task she'd performed hundreds of times before. Not only was she the third oldest of eight children, but her responsibilities at the clinic also included more than assisting at births. She also made regular visits to new moms, helping them with baby care, feeding and providing necessary immunizations.

The water she'd put into a saucepan on the stove was just beginning to boil. Since she had no idea about the source of this liquid, she wanted to make sure germs and bacteria had been killed. Ten minutes of boiling should be enough. A cloud of steam swirled around her. From the other room, she heard doors opening and closing. She hoped Cole was changing out of his wet clothes. He looked half-frozen.

His well-being shouldn't matter to her, but she'd be lying if she told herself she wasn't attracted to him. All her life, she'd been drawn to outsiders and renegades. There was something about bad boys that always sucked her in.

Her first serious boyfriend had owned a motorcycle shop and had tattoos up and down both arms. He definitely hadn't been the kind of guy she could bring home to meet her stable, responsible, churchgoing parents, which might have been part of her fascination with him. She'd loved riding on the back of his Harley, loved the way he'd grab her and kiss her in front of his biker friends. He hadn't been able to keep his hands off her. He'd called her "baby doll" and given her a black leather jacket with a skull and a heart on the back.

On the very day she'd intended to move in with him, she'd discovered him in bed with another woman, and she'd heard him tell this leggy blonde stranger that she— the blonde bimbo—was his baby doll.

Even now, ten years later, that memory set Rachel's blood boiling. Before she'd departed from motorcycle man's house, she'd gone into his garage, dumped gasoline on her leather jacket and set it on fire.

After that ride on the wild side, she should have learned. Instead, she'd gone through a series of edgy boyfriends— daredevils, rock musicians, soldiers of fortune. Like an addict, she was drawn to their intensity.

Cole was one of those guys.

True, he had risked his life to rescue her and Goldie. He wasn't evil. But he wasn't somebody she wanted to know better.

Using a dish towel, she wiped around the lid of the container before she opened the powdered formula. There was food for Goldie, but what about them? Searching the kitchen, she found a supply of canned food and an opened box of crackers. There was also flour and sugar and olive oil. If they got snowed in for a day or two, they wouldn't starve to death. *A day or two?* The idea of being trapped with Cole both worried and excited her.

One-handed and still holding the fidgeting baby, she measured and mixed the formula. "Almost done," she murmured to Goldie. "You'll feel better after you eat."

One of the reasons Rachel had moved to the mountains was to get away from sexy bad boys who would ultimately hurt her. As a midwife, she didn't come into contact with many single men and hadn't had a date in months. *Fine with me!* She preferred the calm warmth of celibacy to a fiery affair that would leave her with nothing but a handful of ashes.

Bottle in hand, she returned to the living room just as Cole stepped out of the bathroom, drying his dark blond hair with a towel. He'd changed into a sweatshirt and gray sweatpants that were too short, leaving his ankles exposed. On his feet, he wore wool socks.

"Did you take a shower?" she asked.

"A hot shower. They have one of those wall-hanging propane water heaters."

She gazed longingly toward the bathroom. "Hot water?"

He held out his arms. "Give me the baby. I'll feed her while you shower and change out of those wet jeans. There are clothes in the bedroom."

That was all it took to convince her. She nodded toward the rocking chair. "Sit. Do you know how to feed an infant?"

"How hard can it be?"

"You haven't been around babies much, have you?"

"I was an only child."

Another piece of personal information she didn't need to know. "Here's how it's done. Don't force the nipple into her mouth. Let her take it. She's tired and will probably drop off before she gets enough nourishment. Gently nudge with the nipple. That stimulates the sucking reflex."

She placed Goldie in his arms and watched him. His rugged hands balanced the clear plastic bottle with a touching clumsiness. When Goldie latched onto the nipple, Cole looked up at her and grinned triumphantly. He really was trying to be helpful. She had to give him credit.

"What did you find when you went outside?" she asked. "Is it safe for us to stay here?"

"The men who were after us must have turned back. If they were still on our trail, they would have busted in here by now."

"The blizzard saved us."

"They won't stop looking. Tomorrow, we'll need to move on."

She turned on her heel and went into the bedroom. There was only one thing she needed Cole for: survival. The sooner he was out of her life, the better.

Like the rest of the cabin, the bathroom was well-equipped and efficient. Quickly, she shed her clothes and turned on the steaming water. As soon as the hot spray hit her skin, a soothing warmth spread through her body, easing her tension. She ducked her head under the hot water. One of the benefits of short hair was not worrying about getting it wet. She would have liked to stand here for hours but wasn't sure what sort of water system the cabin had. So she kept it quick.

As soon as she was out of the shower and wrapped in a yellow bath towel that matched the plastic shower curtain, Rachel realized her logistical dilemma. No way did she want to get back into her damp clothes. But she didn't want to give Cole a free show by scampering from the bathroom to the bedroom wearing nothing but a towel.

Her hand rested on the doorknob. *I can't hide in here.* Rachel prided herself on being a decisive woman. No nonsense. She did what was necessary without false modesty or complaint. And so she yanked open the bathroom door and strode forth, *decisively.* She had nothing to be ashamed of.

As she walked the few paces in her bare feet, she boldly gazed at him. In his amber eyes, she saw a flash of interest. His mouth curved in a grin.

She challenged him. "What are you staring at?"

"You."

Her bravado collapsed. She felt very, very naked. He seemed to be looking through the towel, and she had the distinct impression that he liked the view.

Despite her determination not to scamper, she dashed into the bedroom, closed the door and leaned against it. Her heart beat fast. The warmth from the shower was replaced by an internal flush of embarrassment that rose from her throat to her cheeks. If he could decimate her composure with a single glance, what would happen if he actually touched her?

In spite of the burning inside her, she realized that the temperature in the bedroom, away from the propane fireplace, was considerably cooler than in the front room. The double bed was piled high with comforters and blankets. Would she sleep in that bed with Cole tonight? As soon as the question formed in her mind, she banished it. Sleeping with the enemy had no place on her agenda.

Inside a five-drawer bureau, she found clothing—mostly long underwear and sweats—in several sizes. It was easy to imagine a family coming to this weekend retreat for cross-country skiing or ice skating or snowmobiling. When this was over, Rachel fully intended to reimburse the cabin owners and thank them for saving her life.

After she slipped into warm sweats and socks, she eyed the bedroom door. Cole was out there, waiting. Physically, she couldn't avoid him. But she could maintain an emotional distance. She remembered motorcycle man and the flaming leather jacket. Any involvement with Cole would lead inevitably to that same conclusion.

She straightened her shoulders. *I can control myself. I will control my emotions.*

She opened the door and entered the front room. Cole was still sitting in the rocking chair. Without looking up, he said, "I think Goldie's had enough milk."

"How many ounces are left in the bottle?"

He held it up to look through the clear plastic. "Just a little bit at the bottom."

"Did you burp her?"

"I do that by putting her on my shoulder, right?"

"Give me the baby," she said.

When he transferred the swaddled infant to her, their hands touched. An electric thrill raced up her arm, and she tensed her muscles to cancel the effect.

He took a step back. His baggy gray sweatsuit didn't hide the breadth of his shoulders, his slim torso or long legs. His gaze assessed her as though deciding how to proceed. Instead of speaking, he went to the front window and peered through the gap in the green-and-blue plaid curtains. "It's still snowing hard."

"This morning they predicted at least a foot of new snow." A weather report wasn't really what was on her mind.

"It's mesmerizing. I didn't actually see snow falling from the sky until I was nine years old."

"Not so pretty when you're caught in a blizzard." She did a bouncy walk as she patted Goldie on the back.

"I never want to do that again."

"Tomorrow morning, we shouldn't have to walk too far. All we need to find is a working telephone."

Then they could call for help. She and Goldie would be safe. Cole was a different story. When the police came to her rescue, he'd be taken into custody. Would he turn himself in without a fight? Or would he run?

"It's ironic," he said. "This is the first time in years that I've been without a working cell phone."

Had he planned it that way? She needed to clear the air of suspicions. "Cole, I—"

A shuffling sound outside the front door interrupted her, and she turned to look in that direction.

The door crashed open. A hulking figure charged across the threshold. His shoulders and cap were covered with snow. His lips drew back from his teeth in an inhuman snarl.

He had a gun.

Chapter Six

Frank Loeb! Cole barely recognized him. The man should have been dead. He'd been shot. Cole had seen his blood spattered in the snow. How the hell had he made it through the blizzard? Some men were just too damned mean to die.

Frank raised his handgun.

Cole's weapon was all the way across the room on the table. No time to grab it. No chance for subtlety or reason. He launched himself at the monster standing in the doorway. His shoulder drove into the other man's massive chest.

With a guttural yell, Frank staggered backward onto the porch. He was off balance, weakened. Cole pressed his advantage. He shoved with all his strength. His hands slipped against the cold, wet, bloodstained parka. The big man teetered and fell. Cole was on top of him. He slammed Frank's gun hand on the floor of the porch.

Frank released his grasp on the gun. He was disarmed but still dangerous. Flailing, he landed heavy blows on Cole's arms and shoulders. The snow gusted around them. Icy crystals hit Cole's face, stinging like needles.

He drew back his fist and slammed it into Frank's face, splitting his swollen lip. He winced. Blood oozed down his chin.

Cole hit him again. His fingers stung with the force of the blow.

"Wait." Frank lay still. The fight went out of him.

With his arm still cocked for another blow, Cole paused. He knew better than to let down his guard. He'd seen Frank in action. When the big man caught one of the other guys in the gang cheating at cards, Frank broke two of the cheater's fingers. And he smiled at the pain he had inflicted.

"The shooters," Frank said. "They were feds."

That wasn't possible. Though Cole had put in a call for backup, the shooters had appeared within minutes. Even if the FBI had been tracking his movements, the violent assault on the house wasn't standard procedure, especially not when they had a man on the inside. "I don't believe it."

"They were after you." His tongue poked at his split lip. "I heard them talking. They said your name."

"What else did you hear?"

"They reported to somebody named Prescott."

Wayne Prescott was the field agent in charge of the Denver office—the only individual Cole had met with in person. "How did you find us?"

His eyes squeezed shut. Clearly, he was in pain. "Wasn't looking for you."

"The hell you weren't."

"On the run. Just like you," he mumbled. "Went across a field. Saw the lights from the cabin."

Rachel stepped out on the porch. She took a shooter's stance, holding his gun in both hands and aiming at Frank. "Don't move. I will shoot."

There was no doubt that she meant what she'd said. Her voice was firm and her hand steady. She positioned herself far enough away from Frank that he couldn't make a grab for her ankle.

"You're a medic," Frank said. "I need your help."

Cole noticed a flicker of doubt in her eyes. Her natural

instinct was to save lives, not threaten them. Even though he wasn't inclined to help Frank, he couldn't justify killing the man in cold blood.

He stood, picked up Frank's gun and aimed for the center of his chest. "Get up."

Moving slowly and laboriously, Frank got to his knees. Then he heaved himself to his feet and stood there with blood dripping down his chin onto his wet black parka.

Cole instructed, "Rachel, go inside. Keep your distance from him. If he makes a move toward you, shoot him."

After she was safely in the house, Cole escorted his prisoner into the cabin. He saw Goldie sleeping, nestled in blankets on one of the sofas. He had to protect that innocent baby. If Frank wasn't lying, Cole's hope for a rescue from the FBI was disintegrating fast. Agent Wayne Prescott was connected with the men who opened fire on the house. *Houston, we have a problem.*

With the gun, he gestured toward the bedroom. "In there."

Rachel wasted no time closing the front door. Frank had broken the latch, and she had to pull a chair in front of it to keep it shut.

In the bedroom, Cole ordered, "Take off the parka."

Frank peeled off his jacket. A swath of gore stained the left side of his plaid flannel shirt and the left arm. It looked like he'd been shot twice. It was a miracle that he'd made it this far.

The question was whether or not to treat his wounds. They didn't have medical supplies, but Rachel could probably do something for him. Cole hated the idea of her getting close to this dangerous criminal.

Frank groaned. "You had me fooled, man. I thought you were just some punk from Compton. But you've got the feds on your tail. You must have pulled something big-time."

Cole was aware of Rachel standing behind him, listening. He glanced toward her. "Find something to tie his hands and feet."

"We need to clean those wounds," she said. "He could still be losing blood."

"Listen to her," Frank said. "I don't want to die."

"Why should I help you? You crashed through the door with a gun."

"But I didn't shoot."

A valid point. Frank had caught them unawares but hadn't opened fire. What did he want from them?

Cole asked Rachel, "How would you treat him?"

"He needs to go into the bathroom, strip down and get out of his wet clothes. Then he should clean his wounds with soap. Once I can see the extent of the damage, I'll tell you what else is necessary."

"I still want you to find something to tie him up." He turned back to Frank. "Here's the deal. Do exactly as she says, and I won't kill you."

He nodded. This willingness to cooperate was out of character. Maybe he was intimidated by his new idea of Cole's reputation. Maybe the loss of blood had weakened him.

Cole stood in the bathroom door and watched as the big man sat on the toilet seat and pulled off his boots, socks and wet jeans. His skin was raw. His feet had white streaks, indicating the start of frostbite, but the more serious physical problem became evident when he removed his shirt. Blood caked and congealed on his upper chest and left arm. When he turned his back, Cole didn't see an exit wound.

"You need treatment in a hospital," Cole said. "The bullet is still in your chest."

"I'm not going back to prison."

"Jail is better than a coffin."

"Not for me."

After Frank had pulled on a pair of sweatpants and dry socks, he washed the wounds. His left arm wasn't too bad, but the hole in his upper chest was ragged at the edges and slowly bleeding. It had to hurt like hellfire. Cole had never been shot, but he'd nursed a knife wound for three hours without treatment.

Still holding his gun, he tossed Frank a towel. "Press this against your chest, and come into the kitchen."

Frank shuffled forward obediently. His heavy shoulders slouched. His head drooped forward, and his long hair hung around his face in strings. He reminded Cole of an injured grizzly, willing to accept help but still capable of lethal violence.

After he was seated in a straight-back chair, Rachel went into the bathroom to look for first-aid supplies.

"How did you get away?" Cole asked.

"I lay still, played possum. They thought I was dead. When they all went inside, I got up and ran. Two of them went after you and Rachel. They had flashlights."

"You were following them?"

"I was going parallel up the slope behind the house. I thought for sure they'd hear me."

The wind and the fury of the oncoming blizzard had masked the sounds from desperate people climbing through the forest. "You had a gun."

"Nothing like the kind of heat they were packing. Damn feds. They've got the primo weapons."

Not always. "When did they turn back?"

"Didn't even make it to the top of the hill." Frank grimaced. "I kept going. Picked up your trail. Then I got to an open field. The snow was coming down hard. Couldn't see a damn thing. Man, I thought I was going to die out there in the field. Frozen stiff." He barked a laugh. "A stiff. Frozen. Get it?"

Rachel returned with an armful of supplies, which she placed on the table. "I found antiseptic, gauze and surgical tape. I think I can make this work."

When she approached Frank and touched his shoulder, Cole's gut clenched. Though she showed no sign of fear, he knew how dangerous Frank could be. If the big man took it into his head to attack her, Cole couldn't risk shooting him. Not while Rachel was so close. He holstered his gun and took a position behind Frank's right shoulder, preparing himself to react to any threatening move.

Focused on first aid, Rachel lightly probed the wound on Frank's chest.

He inhaled sharply. The muscles in his chest twitched. "What are you doing?"

"Feeling for the bullet," she said. "I'm afraid it's deeply embedded."

"Cut it out of me."

"That's a painful process, and we've got no anesthetic. Not even booze. Plus, you've already lost a lot of blood. If I open that wound wider, you could bleed to death."

"I can take the pain," Frank said.

"But I can't give you a transfusion. For now, I'm going to patch you up and get the bleeding stopped. Later, you can deal with surgical procedures."

"Just do it."

Quickly and efficiently, she dressed the wound on his arm and wrapped it with strips of cotton from a T-shirt she'd shredded. "We're going to owe the people who own this cabin a whole new wardrobe," she said. "All this stuff is saving our lives."

"But no booze," Frank muttered.

She peeled the wrapper off a tampon and removed it from the casing. "I'm going to use this to plug the hole in your chest. It's sterile. And the absorbency will stop the bleeding."

Cole had heard of using feminine products to staunch blood flow but had never seen it done. Frank would owe his life to a tampon. Cole kept himself from smirking.

Frank turned his head away as she packed the wound. "You got to be pretty good friends with Penny," he said.

"We talked." A frown pulled Rachel's mouth.

"What did you talk about?"

"Anything that would take her mind off the labor pains," Rachel said. "Her childhood. Her dreams."

"Her baby's daddy? Baron?"

"I know you guys work for him and think he's a big deal, but I think he's a jerk. Sending his pregnant girlfriend to rob a casino?" She finished taping and wrapping the wound. "What kind of man does something like that?"

Frank's right hand shot forward. He held Rachel's jaw in his grip and pulled her face close to his. "Where did Penny hide the money?"

Cole reacted. He broke Frank's grasp and yanked his arm behind his back. The damage had already been done.

When he looked at Rachel, he saw fear written all over her face. Frank had achieved his objective. He'd showed her that he was someone who would hurt her if she didn't do as he said. Cole hadn't protected her; she'd never trust him now.

Chapter Seven

After checking one more time to make sure Goldie was sleeping peacefully, Rachel sat at the end of the long table in the cabin. She slouched, head bent forward. With her fingernail, she traced the grain of the wood on the tabletop. The unidentifiable aroma of something Cole was cooking on the stove assaulted her nostrils.

Though she tried to focus on simple things, Rachel couldn't dismiss her rising fears. When Frank grabbed her, she hadn't been bruised. But she could still feel the imprint of his fingers. His grip had been ferocious—strong as a vise squeezing her jawbone. He could have killed her. With a flick of his wrist, he could have broken her neck. He'd forced her to look into his dark, soulless eyes. His split lip had sneered when he asked where Penny hid the money.

She hadn't expected the big man to lash out. Not while she was helping him by dressing his wounds. Her mistake had been letting down her guard and getting too close to him. The warmth of the cabin had imbued her with false feelings of security.

She wasn't safe. Not by a long shot.

Trusting Cole was out of the question. His subtle charm was more potentially devastating than a blatant assault. She'd heard Frank say that the FBI was chasing Cole.

Those men with guns who came to the house had been after Cole.

He placed a bowl of the canned chili he'd been heating in front of her. Though she should have been starving, Rachel didn't have an appetite. As she picked a kidney bean from the chili with her spoon, she felt Cole watching her.

"You don't have to worry about Frank," he said. "I've got him tied down in the bedroom."

Though Frank scared the hell out of her, she didn't want to mistreat him. "He should eat something."

"I'm not going to feed him. He'd probably bite my hand off. Besides, he's fallen asleep."

"Or gone into a coma," she said.

"I don't want him to die," Cole said. "I wouldn't wish death on anyone. But I've done all I intend to do for Frank Loeb."

At least he was being honest. She dared to lift her gaze from the chili and look into his face. His cognac-colored eyes gleamed. The color had returned to his roughly stubbled cheeks. It wasn't fair for him to be so handsome. The evil he might have done wasn't apparent in his features.

She shoveled a bite of chili into her mouth. The taste was bland and the texture gooey, but she swallowed and took another bite. If she was going to survive, she needed her strength.

Cole said, "Not the world's best dinner. Would you like a stale cracker to go with it?"

She shook her head, not wanting to get into a conversation with him. Given half a chance, he'd seduce her with his smooth-talking lies.

"You might be wondering," he said, "about some of the things Frank said."

"Not at all." She forced herself to swallow more chili.

"There are a couple of things you need to know, starting with—"

"Stop." She held up her hand. "I don't want to hear it."

"Five words," he said. "Give me five words to explain myself."

"All right. And I'm counting."

"I'm. An. Undercover. FBI. Agent." He shrugged. "Maybe FBI ought to count as more than one word. But you get the idea."

She dropped her spoon. *I didn't see this coming.* "Why should I believe you?"

He grinned. "Are you willing to hear more?"

Not if he was lying. "I want the truth."

"Until tomorrow when we talk to the police, I can't prove my identity," he said. "The mere fact that I'm willing to turn myself in to the cops ought to tell you something. My handler works out of the Denver field office. I contacted him after the shoot-out at the casino, and he told me to stick with the gang."

"Even though Penny was wounded and pregnant?"

"I thought the gang would make a clean getaway. She seemed okay. And I didn't expect her to go into labor."

"But she did. Wasn't it your duty to protect her and her baby?"

"That's why I got you."

"And put me in danger." If he really was an undercover agent, he was utterly irresponsible. "A real FBI agent wouldn't put a civilian in harm's way."

"Think back," he said. "I was doing my best to keep you safe. I kept you from seeing the other members of the gang so they wouldn't think you could identify them. Damn it, Rachel. Before the shoot-out started, I was taking you to your van, helping you escape."

Some of what he was saying backed up his claim to be an undercover lawman, but all she could see when she looked back was Penny, lying dead on the floor after delivering her baby. "She didn't deserve to die."

"I never thought Penny would be harmed. She was the mother of Baron's child. That should have been a guarantee of safety." His smile had disappeared. "But you're right, Rachel. Her death—her murder—was my fault. I failed. I can tell myself that there was nothing I could have done to save her, but it doesn't change what happened. Somehow, I'll have to find a way to live with that."

His regret seemed real. Did she dare to believe him? From the start, she'd sensed that he was a dangerous man. As an undercover agent, that was true. Even if he was on the right side of the law, he had that renegade edge. "Why didn't you tell me before? We were alone in my van when you kidnapped me. You could have told me then."

"If you'd known I was undercover, you would have been in even more danger."

Again, his reasoning made sense. But she couldn't allow herself to be drawn in to this improbable story. "Frank said the FBI was after you. Not the other way around."

"And that could be a big problem." He glanced toward the closed door to the bedroom where Frank lay unconscious. "Usually, I'd dismiss anything Frank said as a lie, but he came up with a name that makes me think twice."

"I'm listening."

"Let me start at the beginning." Ignoring his chili, he leaned back in his chair and stretched his long legs out in front of him. "It was a month ago, give or take a couple of days. The FBI had an opportunity to infiltrate Baron's operation. They recruited me from L.A. because they suspected there was an FBI agent working with Baron. None of the agents in the Rocky Mountain area know me."

"Except for your handler."

"His name is Wayne Prescott. That's the name Frank heard. One of the shooters at the house mentioned Prescott."

"The shooters were from the FBI?"

"I don't think so. Attacking the house with guns blazing isn't the way we do things, especially not when the shooters knew they had an agent on the inside. Before they opened fire, they would have negotiated and offered a chance to surrender."

"Is that always the way they work?"

"In my experience, yes."

His gaze was steadfast and unguarded. His posture, relaxed. He didn't seem to be lying, but an expert liar wouldn't show that he was nervous. "Well, then. How do you explain what happened at the house?"

"The shooters know Prescott, but they have to be Baron's men. Penny told us that he owned the cabin and knew the location. Baron has a reputation for cruelty. During the casino robbery, our gang screwed up by getting into a shoot-out and attracting attention. My guess is that he wanted us all dead rather than in custody."

"All of you? Even the mother of his child?"

"I've been undercover a lot, and I still don't understand the criminal mind. A lot of these guys seem perfectly normal. They have wives and kids. They live in houses in the suburbs and drive hybrids. But they don't think the same way that we do. They don't follow the same ideas of morality. Baron might have a moment of sadness about Penny and Goldie, but he won't let their death stop his master plan."

"Even if he loved her?"

"A guy like that?" Cole leaned forward, picked up his spoon and dug into the chili. "He's not capable of love."

Penny had certainly thought differently. During the time she was in labor, she'd talked about her relationship with Goldie's father. They'd known each other since she was a teenager. Not that they were the typical hand-holding high school sweethearts. Baron was older than she was—much older. The way they'd met wasn't clear to Rachel, but he was somehow connected to her high school.

Penny had talked about the way he swept her off her feet. He drove an expensive car and gave her presents and took her to classy restaurants.

The thought of this older man taking advantage of Penny disgusted Rachel, but she'd kept her opinion to herself. When a woman was in the midst of labor, she didn't need to have a serious relationship discussion.

She asked, "Why did Frank think I knew where Penny hid the money?"

"Do you?"

"She mentioned the hidden cash. It was her insurance policy to make sure the gang wouldn't kill her. But she never said where it was, and I didn't really know what she was talking about."

"It's complicated," he said.

"Explain it." She leaned back in her chair. "We've got time."

Cole took one more bite of chili before he responded. "Baron runs five gangs—maybe more—throughout the Rocky Mountain region. He does the prep work—figures out the site of each robbery and the timing. The gang goes in, makes the grab and gets away fast."

"Always at casinos?"

"Usually not. Casinos generally have better security

than banks. The typical target is a small bank. The heists are nothing clever. Just get in and get out. Then comes the genius part of Baron's scheme."

In spite of her skepticism, she found herself being drawn into his story. "How is it genius?"

"A lot of robbers get caught when they start to spend the money. Sometimes, it's marked. Passing off hundred-dollar bills isn't easy. And the robbers can't exactly take their haul and deposit it in a regular bank account."

"Why not?"

"Think about it," he said. "If somebody like Frank strolls into a bank and wants to open an account with hundred-dollar bills, a bank teller is going to get suspicious."

She nodded. "I see what you mean."

"Baron has a designated person—in our gang, it was Penny—who puts the cash into a package and mails it to a secure location."

"What do you mean by secure location?" she asked. "It seems like Baron would want the money sent directly to him."

"But that would mean that his location could be traced."

"Okay, I get it," she said. "Then what?"

"After a couple of weeks when the heat is off, the designated person either picks up the money and hand delivers it. Or they give Baron the location and he arranges for a pickup. He launders the cash and keeps half. The gang gets paid a monthly stipend, just like a real job."

She could see why the FBI wanted to shut down Baron's operation. "How much money are we talking about?"

"Five gangs pulling off two or three jobs a month. The take ranges from a couple thousand to twenty. I figure it's more than a hundred thousand a month."

"I can't believe all these gangs keep getting away with it," she said.

"You'd be surprised how many bank robberies there are," he said. "Last year in Colorado alone, there were over a hundred and fifty. Most of the time, they don't even make the news. Especially when there's not a huge amount of cash involved and no one is injured."

She finished off her chili while she considered what he'd told her. Baron's scheme sounded far too complicated for Cole to have made it up, but that still didn't prove that he was working undercover for the FBI.

His behavior while she'd been held captive was more convincing. During the whole time Penny was in labor, he'd been a gentleman. Like he said, he'd kept her separate from the other gang members. And he had been helping her escape when the shooters attacked.

She shivered from a draft that slipped around the edge of the front door. Though they'd pushed a chair against it and blocked the air with towels from the bathroom, the door didn't fit exactly into the frame after Frank burst through it.

Rising from the table, she carried her bowl to the kitchen and looked out the uncurtained window. "Still snowing."

"That's a good thing." He reached around her to put his bowl in the sink. "The blizzard will keep anybody from searching for us."

Though they weren't alone in the cabin, she felt as if they were sharing a private moment in the kitchen. Outside the wind rushed and hurled icy pellets at the window, but they were tucked away and sheltered.

When she turned toward him, he didn't back away. Less

than two feet of space separated them. "Why did you tell me all this?"

"I wanted you to know. I'm one of the good guys, and I'm not going to hurt you."

She'd heard that promise before. Other men had assured her that they wouldn't break her heart. The smart thing would be to step away, to put some distance between them. But they were awfully close. And he was awfully good-looking.

Arms folded below her breasts, she tried to shut down her attraction to him. Diffidently, she asked, "Why do you care what I think?"

"I like you, Rachel."

He could have said so much more, could have called her his baby doll and told her she was beautiful. "Is that all you have to say?"

"I like you...very much."

And she liked him, too. In spite of her resolution to steer clear of dangerous men, she unfolded her arms. Gently, she reached up and rested her hand on his cheek. His stubble bristled under her fingers. Electricity crackled between them.

His hand clasped her waist as his head lowered. His lips were firm. He used exactly the right amount of pressure for a perfect kiss.

She pulled away from him and opened her eyes. His smile was warm. His eyes, inviting. *Perfect! Of course!* Guys like Cole—men who lived on the edge—made the best lovers. Because they didn't hold back? Because they took risks in everything?

"That was good," she said.

"I can do better."

He stepped forward, trapping her against the kitchen

counter, and encircled her in a powerful embrace. Through the bulky sweatsuits, their bodies joined. This kiss was harder and more demanding. If she allowed herself to respond, she didn't know if she could stop. In minutes, she'd be tearing off his clothes and dragging him onto her and...

His tongue slid into her mouth, and her mind went blank. Sensation washed through her, sending an army of goose bumps marching along the surface of her skin. She felt so good, so alive. Though she was unaware of moving a muscle, her back arched. Her breasts pressed against his chest, and the sensitive tips of her nipples tingled with pleasure. Her feet seemed to leave the floor as though she was weightless. Floating. Drifting through clouds.

When the kiss ended, she lightly descended to earth. *Oh, man, that was some kiss!* A rocket to the moon.

Still holding her, he leaned back and gazed down at her. She stared up at his face, watching as his lips pulled into a confident smile. He knew his kiss had affected her. He knew that he was in control.

In spite of her dazed state, Rachel realized that she needed to pull back. She'd have to be crazy to make love to him tonight. It wasn't possible. Not with baby Goldie sleeping nearby. Not with psychopathic Frank tied up in the bedroom.

She couldn't manage a single coherent word, but he must have sensed her reticence because he loosened his grasp and stepped back.

"I want to make love to you, Rachel." His voice was low and rough. "I want you. Now."

"Uh-huh."

"But the time isn't right."

She nodded so vigorously that she made herself dizzy. "Not tonight."

"You're a special woman. I want to treat you right."

"Uh-huh."

"And I want you to trust me."

"Okay."

He took her hand and squeezed. "When we're safe and this is over," he said with the sexiest smile she'd ever seen. "It won't be over between you and me. That's a promise."

Chapter Eight

After Cole converted one of the sofas into a double bed and got Rachel and Goldie settled down to sleep, he stretched out on the other sofa on the opposite side of the cabin. Between his side of the front room and Rachel's the gas fireplace blazed warmly. His gun rested on the floor beside him, easily reachable. Though the sofa was too short for his legs, this wasn't the worst place he'd gone to bed. His undercover work meant he sometimes didn't know where he'd be sleeping or for how long.

Over the years, he'd trained himself to drop easily into a light slumber. Never a deep sleep. Not while on assignment. Even while resting, he needed to maintain vigilance, to be prepared for the unexpected threat.

As soon as he closed his eyes, he became aware of aching muscles from their hike and bruises from his fight with Frank. Ignoring the pain, he concentrated on letting go of his tension, keeping his breathing steady and lowering his pulse rate.

He tried to imagine a blank slate. Soft blue. Peaceful. But his mind raced, jumping from one visual image to another. He saw Penny in a pool of her own blood. Saw Frank being gunned down, throwing his arms into the air before he fell. He saw snow swirling before his eyes. Then through the whiteness, Rachel's face emerged. Her startling blue eyes opened wide. He saw Goldie in Rachel's arms. The baby reached toward him with her tiny hands.

No matter what else happened, he had to make sure Goldie and Rachel got to a safe place—a task that should have been easy. He should have been able to make one phone call and rest assured that the FBI would swoop in for a rescue. But he was wary of his connections, and he'd learned to trust his instincts. If he smelled trouble, there was usually something rotten. Special Agent Wayne Prescott?

Cole had only met with Prescott once at a hotel in Grand Junction for a briefing before his assignment. Though dressed in casual jeans and a parka, Agent Prescott had presented himself as a buttoned-down professional with neatly barbered brown hair and a clean-shaven chin. An administrator. A desk jockey. He had passed on the necessary information in a businesslike manner.

Cole had refused his offer of a cell phone with local numbers already programmed in. By keeping his own cell phone, Cole had more autonomy. Not only did his private directory have phone numbers for people he trusted, but his phone also had the capability of disabling the GPS locator so he couldn't be found.

Though his handlers didn't agree, Cole found it necessary at times to be completely off the grid. His current situation was a good example. If Prescott could track his location, they might be in even more danger.

Cole's eyelids snapped open. Though his body was exhausted, his mind was too busy for sleep.

Leaving the sofa, he went toward the kitchen table where he'd left his phone. Shortly after Frank mentioned Prescott's name, Cole had turned off the GPS. But was it really off? His boss in L.A., Agent Waxman, hadn't been pleased about having his undercover agent traceable. Had Waxman programmed in some kind of tracking mechanism?

If Frank had been awake and hadn't been a psycho, Cole would have turned to him for help in analyzing his phone's capabilities. Frank had expert skills with electronics.

For a moment, Cole toyed with the idea of destroying his cell phone. Then he decided against it. Tomorrow when the blizzard lifted, they could use his phone to call for help. *Yeah? And who would he call? Who could he trust?*

Through the kitchen window—the only one without a curtain—he saw the snow continue to fall. His visibility was limited. He couldn't tell if it was letting up—not that it mattered. There was nothing they could do tonight. Trying to fight their way through the blizzard and the drifts in the dark would be suicide. They had to wait until morning. Until then, he needed to sleep, damn it. His body required a couple of hours' solid rest to replenish his physical resources.

He headed back toward his sofa but found himself standing over Rachel. She lay on her back, covered up to her chin with a plaid wool blanket. The light from the gas fireplace flickered across her cheeks and smooth forehead. Her full lips parted slightly, and her breathing was steady.

Hers was an unassuming beauty. No makeup. No frills. No nonsense. Her thick, black lashes were natural, as were her dark eyebrows that matched the wisps of hair framing her face.

Looking down, he realized that she was the real reason he couldn't sleep. He'd made her a promise, told her that they'd have a relationship beyond this ordeal. That was what he wanted. To spend time with her. To learn more about this complicated woman whose livelihood was bringing new life into the world.

He admired her strength of character and wondered what caused her defensiveness. Until she had melted into his arms, she'd been pushing him away with both hands. But she'd kissed him with passion and yearning. No way had that kiss been a timid testing of the waters. She'd committed herself. She'd responded as though she'd been waiting for him to strike a spark and ignite the flame.

He reached toward her but didn't actually touch her cheek. He didn't want to wake her; she needed her sleep. *I didn't lie to you, Rachel.*

But he hadn't been completely honest. A man in his line of work changed his identity the way other people changed their socks. He never knew how long he'd be on assignment and unable to communicate with a significant other. Bottom line: he couldn't commit to a real, in-depth relationship.

Tearing his gaze away from her, he went back to his sofa and lay down. This time, he fell asleep.

It seemed like only a few minutes later that he heard Goldie's cries. He bolted upright on the sofa. His gun was in his hand.

Rachel was already awake. "It's okay," she said. "Don't shoot."

After a quick scan of the cabin, he lowered his weapon. "What's wrong with her?"

"She's hungry." Rachel opened the blanket she used to swaddle the infant and picked her up. Immediately—as if by magic—the wailing stopped. Rachel bent her head down to nuzzle Goldie's tummy. "Most babies wake up a couple of times at night."

He knew that. A long time ago, he had a female partner with a newborn baby boy. She was always complaining about not getting enough sleep. "Anything I can do to help?"

"I'll handle this."

She got no argument from him. Through half-closed eyes, he watched her taking care of the baby. Her movements were efficient but exceedingly gentle as she changed the diaper. Even though Goldie wasn't hers, it was obvious that Rachel cared deeply for this infant. He understood; babies were pretty damned lovable.

As she walked to the kitchen she bounced with each step and made soft, cooing sounds. Her voice soothed him. So sweet. So tender. He closed his eyes and imagined her lying beside him, humming and—

"Cole." Frank's shout tore him out of his reverie. "Damn you, Cole. Get in here."

Cole groaned. He would have much preferred changing diapers to dealing with a wounded psychopath. With his gun in hand, he crossed the room and shoved open the bedroom door. In this room away from the fireplace, the temperature was about ten degrees cooler and it was dark. Cole turned on the overhead light. "What?"

"Untie me. I've got to pee."

The restraints Cole had used on Frank were a combination of twine, rope and bungee cords. There was enough play in the ropes that fastened his wrists to the bed frame on either side of him that he could get comfortable. The same went for his ankles, which were attached to the iron frame at the foot of the bed. Setting him free involved a certain amount of risk. Frank could turn on him; he needed to be handled with extreme caution.

Cole was tired of dealing with men like Frank. Always

trying to stay two steps ahead. Never letting his guard down. He didn't like what his life had become.

He came closer to the bed and unzipped the sweatshirt stretched across his chest. The wound near his shoulder showed only a light bloodstain. Rachel's tampon plug had done its job in stopping the bleeding.

"Here's the deal, Frank. If you give me any trouble, I'll shoot. No hesitation. No second thoughts. Understand?"

"Yeah, yeah, I get it."

One-handed, he unfastened the cords. All the while, he kept his weapon trained on the big man. Once he was free, Frank stretched his arms and winced in pain. He hauled his legs to the edge of the bed. Slowly, he lumbered to the bathroom, where Cole stood watch. Not a pleasant experience for either of them.

When they returned to the bedroom, Frank sat on the bed and reached for the water glass on the bedside table. He swallowed a few gulps and licked his lips. "I'm hungry."

"Too bad."

"You don't have to tie me up, man. I'm not going to—"

"Save it." Cole wasn't taking any chances. Not with Rachel and Goldie in the other room.

With his finger, Frank touched his split lip. "As soon as the snow stops, we should move on. Those feds are still after you."

"Lie down. Arms at your sides. Legs straight."

"You need me. When those guys catch up to you, you're going to want somebody watching your back. Come on, man. I'm a good person to have on your side in a fight. You know that."

There were a few things Cole knew for certain. The first was that Frank enjoyed inflicting pain. The second, he was a bully who couldn't be trusted. Number three, he was smarter than he looked. "You can lie down. Now. Or I'll knock you unconscious. Your choice."

With a low growl, Frank stretched out on the bed. "I've been lying here, thinking. I know what you're up to. You've got leverage. A couple of bargaining chips."

Cole fastened the cords on his ankles. "You just keep thinking, Frank."

"You're going to use the baby to deal with Baron. I mean, Baron is as mean as they come, but he's not going to kill his own kid, right?"

While Cole dealt with the bonds on Frank's wrists, he pressed the nose of his gun into the big man's belly.

"And Rachel," Frank said. "She's going to take you to where Penny sent the loot. Oh, yeah, I got it all figured out. But there's something you don't know."

"What's that?" Cole finished securing the ropes and stepped back. "What don't I know?"

"If I tell you, I'm giving up my own bargaining chip."

As far as Cole was concerned, Frank could keep his information to himself. Tomorrow, after he and Rachel were far away from this cabin, he'd call the local police and give them the location. The cops could take Frank into custody.

Cole turned toward the door.

"Hey," Frank called after him. "I can tell you why the feds attacked. You want to know that, don't you?"

Clearly, Frank was grasping at straws, trying to play him. In other circumstances, Cole might have been interested in his information, but he was weary of these games. "Whether you tell me or not, I don't give a damn."

He wanted to get back to a semblance of normal life, to take Rachel home to California with him and show her his favorite beach. He hadn't seen much of her body, except when she stepped out of the bathroom in a towel, but he thought she'd look good in a bikini.

"It's about the money," Frank said. "Penny told me that she was keeping the place she'd sent the last three packages a secret from Baron. That's got to be close to seventy thousand bucks. Just sitting there. Waiting to be picked up."

"I don't believe you. Penny wouldn't try a double cross on Baron."

"She said that she wasn't going to steal from him. She just wanted to see him. And she knew he'd come for the money."

Though the idea disgusted him, Cole understood Penny's reasoning. Baron wouldn't come to see his pregnant girlfriend or his newborn child. But he'd make an effort for the money. "So what?"

"I'm betting Rachel knows where it is. She and Penny were getting real chummy." He gave a grotesque wink. "We can make her tell us where the money is hidden."

"Go back to sleep."

He closed the bedroom door and stepped into the front room, where Rachel sat in the rocking chair feeding Goldie by the golden light from the gas fireplace. Cole felt as if he'd entered a different world. A better place, for sure. The energy in this room nurtured him and gave him hope.

When Rachel met his gaze and smiled, he wanted to gather her into his arms and hold her close. He needed her honesty and decency. She was the antidote to the ugly life he'd been living.

"How is Frank doing?" she asked.

"I checked the wound. There's very little bleeding."

"He needs to get to a hospital tomorrow."

He wanted to tell her that tomorrow would bring a solution to all their problems. But he couldn't make that promise.

IN THE DIM LIGHT OF DAWN, Rachel stepped onto the porch of the cabin and shivered. The furry bristles of her parka hood froze instantly and scraped against her cheek as she adjusted Goldie's position inside the sling carrier under her parka.

The blizzard had dwindled to a sputtering of snow, but the skies were still blanketed with heavy gray clouds. Cole joined her on the porch and held up his cell phone.

"Still no signal," he said.

"We shouldn't have to go too far." She pointed with her gloved hand toward a break in the trees. "It looks like a road up there. There ought to be other cabins. We should be able to find somebody with a working phone."

From inside the cabin, Frank yelled out a curse at Cole and threatened revenge. His voice was hoarse and rasping. She knew they couldn't trust Frank but felt guilty for leaving him tied to the bed.

As Cole fastened the broken front door closed with a bungee cord, she asked, "We're going to get help for Frank, aren't we?"

"When we talk to the cops, we'll give them the location of this cabin. Frank won't be happy about being rescued and arrested at the same time."

"I almost feel sorry for him."

"Don't."

Before they'd left the cabin, she'd made a final check on Frank's wounds. The bleeding had stopped, and he wasn't in imminent danger. Though the cabin wasn't cold, he'd told her that he was freezing and asked her to cover him up with his parka. She figured it was the least she could do for him.

She fell into step behind Cole. The oversize backpack on his shoulders blocked the wind. Though this area had been sheltered from the full force of the storm by trees, the new-fallen snow was well over her boots—probably a foot deep. On the north side of the cabin, the drifts reached all the way to the windowsill.

Cole led the way to a log structure that looked like a garage. He shoved the door open and ushered her inside.

"Which do you prefer?" he asked. "Cross-country skis or snowshoes?"

"What are you thinking?" He claimed to be one of the good guys but he acted like a thief. "We can't just walk in here and help ourselves. We've already destroyed the front door on the cabin, made a mess and eaten their food."

"Don't worry. It hasn't escaped my attention that this well-equipped little cabin saved our lives. I fully intend to pay the owners back."

"Did you leave a note?"

"It kind of defeats the purpose of being undercover if I start handing out my address."

"How about money?" she demanded. "Did you leave cash?"

"I'm sending people back here for Frank. If I left cash, somebody else would pick it up. Don't worry, I'll pay for the damages."

In an unconscious gesture, he patted the left side of his jacket then pulled his hand away. She was beginning to understand the sneaky undercover side to his personality. Every twitch had a meaning. She asked, "What's in your pocket? Are you hiding something from me?"

"Do you have to know everything?"

"Yes."

"Fine," he said. "I've got nothing in my pocket, but there's a pouch with cash, a switchblade and a new identity sewn into the lining."

"Impressive."

"In spite of this disaster, I'm good at my job. The hardest part of an undercover op is getting out in one piece." He sorted through the array of skis and snowshoes. "What's best for moving through the snow?"

She still didn't want to steal the equipment. If somebody took her cross-country skis, she'd be furious. "Why can't we just hike up to the road? Even if it hasn't been cleared recently, the snowplows will be coming through."

"We aren't taking the road."

"Why not?"

He held a set of snowshoes toward her. "The shooters—whether they're FBI or Baron's men—are going to be looking for us."

His gaze met hers. Even in the dark garage, she could see his tension. If they were found, they'd be killed. Normal rules of conduct didn't apply. She pulled off her gloves and took the snowshoes.

Chapter Nine

After a bit of trial and error, Cole figured out how to walk in the snowshoes with minimal tripping over his own feet. Even using the ski poles for balance, he'd fallen twice.

From behind his back, Rachel called out, "You're getting the hang of it. Don't try to go backward."

He muttered, "It's like I've got tennis rackets strapped to my shoes."

"That's still better than plowing through two feet of new snow."

Or not. The winter sports he enjoyed involved speed—racing across open terrain on a snowmobile, streaking down a slope on downhill skis or a snowboard. A clumsy slog through deep snow was the opposite of fun—another reason to hate Colorado. After last night's blizzard, he'd lost any appreciation he might have had for the scenic beauty of a winter wonderland. All this pristine whiteness depressed the hell out of him. Never again would he take an undercover assignment in the mountains. A tropical jungle filled with snakes and man-eating lions would be preferable.

Though they weren't on the road, he stayed on a trail through the forest that ran parallel to it. The worst thing that could happen now was to get lost in this unpopulated back country. They'd been hiking on snowshoes for nearly half an hour—long enough for him to freeze the tip of his nose—and they still hadn't sighted a cabin.

The dawn light was beginning to brighten, and the snowfall lacked the fury of the blizzard. On the opposite side of the road, he could see the outline of a tall ridge through the icy mist. What lay beyond? He'd lost all sense of direction.

"Hold up." He laboriously maneuvered his snowshoes to face Rachel. "Do you have any idea where we are?"

"Let me check my GPS. Oh, wait, I don't have a GPS. Or a map. Or a satellite photo."

He preferred her snarky attitude to fear. It was better for her not to know how much danger they might be in. "I want to get a general idea. When I picked you up, what was the closest town?"

"We were near Shadow Mountain Lake. There are a couple of resorts there but nothing resembling a town until Grand Lake."

"In terms of miles, how far?"

With her glove, she brushed a dusting of snow off her shoulder. "Hard to say. As the crow flies, only about five miles or so. But none of these roads are straight lines."

They could be winding back and forth for hours and making very little progress. "I hate mountains."

"A typical comment from a Southern California boy."

"Yeah? What have you got against palm trees and beaches?"

"Real men live in the mountains."

Though tempted to yank her into his arms and show her that he was a real man, he took his cell phone out of his pocket. Miracle of miracles, he had a signal!

"What is it?" Rachel asked.

"The phone works. Finally." He peeled off his glove, accessed his directory and called Agent Ted Waxman in Los Angeles. California was an hour earlier and it was before seven o'clock here, but his primary FBI handler was available to him 24/7.

Waxman's mumbled hello made Cole think the agent was still in bed, warm and cozy under the covers.

"It's Cole. I need to come in from the cold. Literally."

"Where are you?" Waxman's voice had gone from drowsy to alert. "Do you have your GPS locator turned on?"

He wanted to believe he could trust Waxman. They weren't buddies; undercover agents didn't spend much face time inside the bureau offices. But Waxman had been his primary contact for almost four years.

Cole's phone didn't have much juice; he didn't waste words. "Give me an update. Fast."

"Turn on the GPS and go to a road," Waxman instructed. "We'll find you."

His suspicions about Agent Wayne Prescott and his possible involvement with the shooters from last night warned against giving away their location. "Who's looking for us?"

"Every law enforcement official in the state of Colorado, especially the FBI."

"Why? Give me the 4-1-1. What's going on?"

His pause spoke volumes. Waxman was a by-the-book agent who followed orders and trusted the system. If he'd been given instructions to withhold info, it would go against his nature to disobey. At the same time, he was Cole's handler, and it was his duty to protect his agent.

"Turn yourself in," Waxman said, "and we'll get this straightened out."

Turn myself in? That sounded like he was wanted for

committing a crime. "The last time I contacted anybody was after the casino robbery. Prescott told me to stick with the gang. What's changed since then?"

Another pause. "Activate the damn GPS, Cole."

While he was at it, maybe he ought to paint a bull's-eye on his back. "Give me a reason."

"Don't play dumb with me. Three people are dead. And you're on the run with two of the gang members. You're considered to be armed and dangerous."

That description justified the use of lethal force in making an arrest. Cole saw their chances of a peaceful surrender disappearing. "Two other gang members?"

"One male and one female."

Somehow Rachel had been labeled as part of the gang. "You've got that wrong. The woman with me is—"

"Damn it, Cole. You kidnapped a baby."

The worst kind of crime. Violence against children. Cole was in even more trouble than he'd imagined. "Here's the true story. I'm close to identifying Baron, and he's running this show. Don't ask me how, but he's got people inside the Denver FBI office."

"A newborn infant." Waxman's voice rasped with anger. "You're using a baby as a hostage."

There would be no reasoning with him. Cole ended the call and turned off the phone, making sure the GPS wasn't on.

Rachel stared at him. Her eyes filled with questions. He didn't have the answers she'd want to hear.

RACHEL LISTENED WITH RISING DREAD as Cole recounted his conversation with Agent Waxman. They were the subjects of a manhunt? Considered to be dangerous? The FBI thought they had kidnapped Goldie?

"No," she said firmly. "People around here know me. They'd know those accusations are wrong. As soon as they heard my name—"

"It's not likely that they've identified you."

"If they show my picture—"

"They won't."

In normal circumstances, she'd be missed at work. But this was her vacation; nobody would be looking for her. "The van," she said. "When I don't return the van to the clinic, the women I work with will know that something's wrong. I can contact them and get this all cleared up."

"Not a good idea."

"Why not?"

His face was drawn. His eyes were serious. "You saw what those men did last night at the house. It's best if we don't get anyone else involved."

"Are you saying that they'd go after my friends? My coworkers?"

"Not if they don't know anything."

She'd been cut off from anything resembling her normal life. The only person she could turn to was Cole, and she barely trusted him. "What's going to happen to Goldie?"

"We need to get her to a safe place. If we can find a cabin with reliable people, we'll leave her in their care."

She peered through the trees at the surrounding hillsides, which were buried in drifts and veiled in light snowfall. "We can turn ourselves in at the same time."

"It's not safe for us to be in custody. Not until we know who's working with Baron."

Inside her parka, she felt Goldie shift positions. The most important thing was to get the baby to safety. "Grand Lake. We need to go to Grand Lake. Penny told me that her mother was staying there. We'll take Goldie to her grandmother."

Cole reached out with his gloved hand and patted her shoulder. "You're a brave woman, Rachel. I'm sorry I got you into this mess."

"As long as you get me out of it, I'll be fine." She nodded toward the path ahead of them. "Make tracks."

She followed him, tramping through the snow on the path through the forest. The crampons on the snowshoes gave her stability, but the hike was exhausting. Though she couldn't see the incline, she knew they were headed uphill because of the strain on her thighs. Still, she was glad for the physical exertion. If she slowed down, she'd have to face her fear.

As an EMT, she'd worked with cops. She knew what "armed and dangerous" meant. She and Cole wouldn't have a chance to explain or defend themselves. The people looking for them would shoot first and ask questions later.

They approached a crossroads with open terrain on each side. The road was barely discernable under the mounds of snow, but a wooden street sign marked the corner.

Cole halted and squinted at the sign. "The road we're on is Lodgepole. The other is Lake Vista. Ring any bells?"

"Please don't ask me for directions." Grand County was huge, nearly two thousand square miles. Her condo was in Granby, which was forty-five minutes away from here. "I don't know this territory. I've only been to Grand Lake five or six times."

He looked over his shoulder at her. "It makes sense that the Lake Vista road will lead to water. We'd be more likely to find cabins at lakeside."

"But the other road goes uphill," she pointed out. "It offers a better vantage point."

She tilted back her head, looked up and glimpsed a hint of blue through the pale gray clouds. Good news: the snowfall was ending. Bad news: they were more exposed to the people who were searching for them.

"Do you hear that?" Cole asked.

"What?"

He sidestepped deeper into the forest. "Get back here."

Though she didn't hear anything, she did as he said, remembering how he'd sensed the attack at the house before the shooting started. She shuffled forward, taking cover behind the trunk of the same tree he stood behind.

Cole shifted his feet in the snowshoes so he was facing her. Quickly, he shed the huge backpack from his shoulders and moved closer to her.

She heard the sound of a vehicle. *They were coming.*

A black SUV crested the hill above the crossroads and ploughed a trail through the snow that covered the road. There were no markings on the vehicle; it wasn't a police car. She held her breath, waiting for them to pass.

The SUV drove past them, headed toward the cabin.

Cole took his cell phone from his pocket. Quickly, he dialed.

She heard his end of the conversation. "Waxman, this is Cole. There's a wounded man in a cabin on Lodgepole Road. He's tied down, helpless. The cabin isn't far from the house where we stayed last night."

He ended the call and put away his phone.

If the men in the SUV were the same shooters who attacked last night, Frank didn't stand a chance. Last night, she'd patched him up. Today, he could be murdered.

When she looked up at Cole, she felt a tear slip from the corner of her eye. "I wish things were different."

"There's nothing we can do for Frank." With his ungloved hand, he stroked her cheek and wiped away the tear. "They're close, Rachel. They'll be able to follow our tracks through the woods. We need to move fast."

There was no time for regret or recrimination. All her energy focused on pushing forward. They stayed in the trees, avoiding the road, but the forest was beginning to thin. Many of these trees had been lost to the pine beetle epidemic. The bare branches looked like gnarled fingers clawing at the snowy mist.

Rounding a boulder, Cole stopped so suddenly that she almost ran into him. She peered around his shoulder and saw the frozen expanse of Shadow Mountain Lake. Untouched, white and spectacularly beautiful, it was covered with snow, and the drifts swirled like vanilla frosting on a cake. Heavy clouds prevented her from seeing all the way to the opposite side.

"How wide is the lake?" Cole asked.

"It varies."

"How far from the town?"

"At the north end, it's only about a mile and a half farther to Grand Lake."

"If we cross it, we've got no cover," he said. "But we're running out of path. As soon as they pick up our trail, they'll know we're following the road."

She assumed the lake was frozen solid, but she didn't know for sure. If they broke through the ice, it would be over for them. And for Goldie. She imagined the dark, frigid waters beneath the pristine surface—waters that could suck them down to a terrible death.

Cole made a turn-around on his snowshoes and looked down at her. His eyes were warm. "We can do this."

"Or we could keep looking for a cabin." Hiking through a blizzard was one thing. Walking on a frozen lake—even when it appeared to be solid—was a risk. "I'm not sure this is safe."

"It's our best chance, Rachel."

He was right. She swallowed hard and nodded. "You go first."

They climbed down the incline leading to the frozen lake. As Cole stepped onto the surface, his snowshoes sank three or four inches into the snow. She clenched her jaw and listened for the cracking sound of ice breaking.

He strode ten feet onto the lake, breaking a path for her to follow. He turned back toward her and held out his gloved hand. "It's all going to be all right."

"How do you know?"

"I'm taking a leap of faith."

Cautiously, she stepped onto the lake. The snow sank beneath her snowshoes, and she caught her breath. Was it solid? Would it hold?

Cole caught hold of her gloved hand and squeezed. "Stay close."

"Do I have a choice?"

Lowering her head, she concentrated on putting her shoes in his tracks. One foot after the other, she followed. With every step, she prayed that the ice would hold.

For what seemed like an eternity, they made their way forward. Without the shelter of the forest, the fierce wind bit the exposed skin on her face. Inside her parka, she was warm. Goldie was protected by her body heat.

"I can see the other side," Cole said.

Looking back over her shoulder, she saw the long trail they'd left in the snow. The point where they'd started was barely visible through the snowy mist.

She saw something else.

A volley of gunfire exploded behind them.

Chapter Ten

The shooters had found them. The bursts from their semi-automatics boomed across the frozen landscape. Cole estimated they were over four hundred yards away on the other side of the lake—out of range unless they had a sniper rifle with a high-tech scope. Even with a more accurate weapon, their visibility would be hampered by the icy mist.

As he watched, the SUV lurched off the road. They were driving onto the lake.

He drew his handgun, ready to make a stand even though he was outmatched in terms of men and firepower. "Rachel, keep going."

"I can't leave you here."

"You need to get Goldie away from here."

Her internal struggle showed in her eyes. She didn't want to desert him, but the SUV was coming closer. The baby's safety came first.

"Don't die," she said. "I wouldn't be able to stand it if you—"

"Just go."

In her snowshoes, she rushed forward. The shoreline was so damned close. She had to make it into the forest. The bare limbs of trees reached toward her with the promise of shelter.

He looked back toward the SUV. They were coming closer, but their forward progress was slow. The heavy vehicle sank down into the new snow. The drifts piled up higher than the hubcaps.

One of the gunmen leaned out a window and fired off another round—a sloppy tactic typical of a drive-by shooter who figured if he sprayed enough bullets he'd eventually hit something. These guys weren't trained to attack in open terrain, and they sure as hell weren't FBI.

These were Baron's men. Lethal. Bent on murder.

Cole shrugged off his huge backpack and dropped it onto the snow in front of him. The canvas pack and light-weight aluminum frame wasn't enough to stop a bullet, but it was something. Not taking off his snowshoes, he ducked behind the pack and waited. When they got closer, he'd aim for the windshield on the driver's side. If he could take out the man behind the wheel, he might slow them down long enough to make his escape.

The engine of the SUV whined as the tires failed to gain traction on the ice. Snow had accumulated in front of the SUV. The driver had to back up in his own tracks and push forward again.

From the trees, Rachel called to him. "I made it."

"Go deeper into the forest."

"Not without you."

The SUV jerked forward and back. The wheels were stuck. Two men emerged from the vehicle and staggered through knee-deep snow to the front bumper, where they started digging.

The weight of the SUV had to be close to two tons. Heavy enough to break through the ice? That was too much good luck to hope for.

For now, he should take advantage of the situation. They

were distracted by being stuck. He might have enough time to make his escape before they started shooting again.

He slung the pack onto his shoulders, grabbed his ski poles and rushed along the trail Rachel had made through the snow. He reached the forest. Gunfire erupted. Cole dodged behind a boulder, where she stood waiting.

Breathing hard, he rested his back against the hard granite surface.

"We're good," Rachel said. "Even if they get themselves dug out, there's no access to a road on this side."

The muscles of his face tightened as he grinned. They just might make it to safety. "We got lucky."

"It's more than that."

"Yeah, those guys are idiots."

"And we were prepared," she said. "After all your complaining, I'll bet you're glad you have those snowshoes."

"Hell, yes. I'm thinking of having them permanently attached to my feet."

"You might be a real mountain man, after all."

Another wild blast of gunfire reminded him that they needed to keep moving. Even idiots were dangerous when well-armed. He shoved away from the rock. "When we get to the town, do you know how to find Penny's mother?"

"I do, indeed."

Until now, Rachel had been hesitant about giving directions. "What makes you so certain?"

"Penny called her mom after the baby was born and got the address, which she repeated several times."

"Why didn't she know her own mother's address?"

"Her mom doesn't actually live in Grand Lake. She's house-sitting for a friend who has a business in town. The house is around the corner from her friend's shop on the main street."

They'd be marching through the center of town. With every law enforcement officer in the state of Colorado looking for them, this might be tricky. "What kind of shop?"

"One that's closed in the winter," she said. "An ice cream parlor."

THEIR TREK INTO GRAND LAKE went faster than Rachel expected. It was still early, and the locals were just beginning to deal with the aftermath of last night's blizzard. A few were out with shovels. Others cleared their driveways and sidewalks with snowblowers. None of them paid much attention as she and Cole hiked along the road in their snowshoes.

The main tourist area was a rustic, Old West boardwalk with storefronts on either side. She spotted Lily Belle's Soda Fountain and Ice Cream Shop with a neatly lettered sign in the window: Closed for the Season.

In minutes they'd be at the house where Penny's mom was staying. Rachel was glad to be dropping Goldie off with someone who would care for her, but she wasn't looking forward to telling Penny's mom what had happened.

A young man with a snowblower finished clearing the sidewalk leading up to a two-story, cedar frame house. He turned toward them and waved. She waved back and yelled over the noisy machine. "Does Pearl Richards live here?"

He nodded and continued along the sidewalk to dig out the next house on the street.

Cole gave her a glance. "Penny's mother is named Pearl?"

"Pearl, Penny and Goldie," she said. "I guess they're all material girls."

Standing on the porch, they took off their snowshoes

and knocked. A woman with curly blond hair pulled back in a ponytail opened the door a crack and peeked out. "Do I know you?"

"Penny gave me your address," Rachel said.

She pulled the door open, revealing a brightly colored patchwork jacket over jeans and a turtleneck. Though it was early, Pearl was fully dressed and wearing hiking boots as though she was prepared for action.

Pearl stepped back into the dim recesses of an old-fashioned looking parlor with drawn velvet curtains, an Oriental rug and an uncomfortable looking Victorian sofa with matching chaise. Pearl went to a claw-footed coffee table and picked up her revolver. Like Penny, she was a small, slight woman who needed both hands to aim her weapon.

Rachel should have been alarmed, but this greeting was so similar to the way she'd met Penny that she almost laughed out loud. Apparently, the women in this family routinely said hello with a gun.

"Close the door," Pearl said. "Young man, take off that backpack and that ridiculous leather jacket. You're dripping all over the floor."

As Cole removed his jacket, he said, "I'm armed."

"I expected as much." Pearl leveled her gun at the center of his chest. "Using your thumb and forefinger, place your weapon on the floor and step away from it."

Though Rachel suspected that this wasn't the first time Pearl had confronted an armed man, she still wasn't afraid. Either she was growing accustomed to having her life threatened or she sensed a basic goodness in this curly haired woman who didn't look like she was much older than thirty.

"Both of you," Pearl said, "come through here to the kitchen. No sudden moves."

Rachel did as she was told. The huge kitchen, painted a sunny-yellow, had professional quality appliances and gleaming marble countertops. In no way did it resemble the antique parlor.

"The gun isn't necessary," Rachel said.

"I'll make that decision, missy. My daughter got herself tangled up with some bad folks. I'm not taking any chances."

"I'm a midwife," Rachel said. "I helped Penny deliver her baby."

Pearl's big brown eyes softened. "Goldie."

"She's right here." Rachel unzipped her parka and took it off to reveal the sling holding the infant. "And she's hungry."

"My granddaughter." Pearl's gun hand faltered. "But where's… Oh, no. Penny's dead, isn't she?"

"I'm sorry," Cole said.

He stepped forward, smoothly took the gun from Pearl and helped her into a chair at the kitchen table where she sat, stiff as a rail. Her unseeing eyes stared at the empty space opposite her.

"I knew this day would come." Pearl's voice dropped to a whisper. "Penny was always wild. Careless. I encouraged her to be a free spirit and to express herself, but she should have had more controls, more rules."

"I'll get you a glass of water," Cole said.

"Make it orange juice."

"Orange juice it is."

"With a shot of vodka. The booze is in the cabinet over the sink."

While he went to do Pearl's bidding, Rachel lifted

Goldie out of the sling and set her down on the counter-top to take off the purple snowsuit. The baby waved her arms, kicked and cooed. She was full of life, deserving of a chance at happiness.

Rachel hoped Pearl would be able to care for her grand-daughter. "Penny said you were house-sitting. Where do you live?"

"I have a studio in Denver."

"You're an artist?"

"I do some painting. And I design jewelry. For a while, I had a shop in Grand Lake. When Penny was in her teens, I moved up here. I wanted to get her away from bad influences in the city." She paused. "That didn't work too well."

"I only knew Penny for a short time," Rachel said. "No matter how many unfortunate decisions she might have made in her life, she did the right things during her pregnancy. She wanted to give birth without drugs, wanted the best for her baby."

"I had natural childbirth, too. I was only eighteen." A thin smile played on Pearl's full lips. "I wasn't ready to settle down, drifted from place to place, fell into and out of love. But I always did right by my daughter. She was more precious to me than air. That's not to say we didn't fight. The last time I saw her, I was so angry."

"Did you know what she was doing?"

"I knew it wasn't good. The fellow with her was a thug. I believe his name was Frank. He's not the father, is he?"

"No," Rachel said quickly.

"Thank God." Pearl slowly shook her head. "I went looking for my daughter. Found her at a casino in Black Hawk. She stood there in the middle of all those slot machines with her belly bulging. I wanted to take her home with me, but she refused. I had hoped that when she was a mother, she'd understand."

"I believe she did. When she saw Goldie for the first time, she glowed from inside. It was as though she'd swallowed a candle."

Cole placed the vodka and orange juice on the table. "Penny couldn't stop smiling. She was beautiful."

Pearl lifted the glass to her lips and took a sip. Thus far, she had avoided looking at her grandchild. Glass in hand, she stood and snapped at Cole. "Come with me into the other room. I want to know what happened to Penny. Tell me everything."

They left the kitchen, but Cole returned almost immediately with the backpack. "You need to get Goldie changed and fed. I don't think we can leave her here."

"Penny wanted her mother to take the baby."

"I'm not sure Pearl can handle an infant."

An aura of sorrow veiled his features, and she knew that he was feeling guilt for Penny's death. Rachel understood. Logically, he'd know that her murder wasn't his fault. He hadn't pulled the trigger. He hadn't put Penny in danger. But he'd take responsibility the same way she'd blamed herself when she lost a patient.

He stood and straightened. When he walked back to the parlor, he looked stoic as though preparing to face a firing squad. His conversation with Pearl was going to be difficult, but it had to be done.

She looked down at Goldie and smoothed the fringe of downy brown hair that framed her round face. "What are we going to do with you?"

The baby gurgled in response. Her shining eyes fixed on the light from the window above the yellow café curtains.

Dragging this darling infant all over the frozen countryside simply wasn't an option. They'd been lucky so far; Goldie had stayed safe and warm, snuggled against her chest. But so many things could have gone wrong. If Penny's mother couldn't take the baby, they'd have to risk going to the police and handing Goldie to them.

As Rachel went through the procedures of preparing formula, she tried to imagine what would happen if they turned themselves in. Cole was in far more danger than she was. As soon as her identity was verified, she ought to be all right. After all, she had an alibi for the time when the gang was on the run. She'd been delivering a baby. *Jim Loughlin's baby.*

She caught her breath. Oh, God, why hadn't she thought of this before? Big Jim Loughlin was a deputy. She could call on him to help her.

The yellow phone hanging on the wall by the kitchen cabinets beckoned to her. Though she didn't know the Loughlins' phone number off the top of her head, information would have it. But if she used this phone, it would pinpoint her location. Other people could track them down to this house.

Deputy Loughlin was the answer to all their problems. She couldn't wait to tell Cole.

When he returned to the kitchen with Pearl, Rachel was glad to see that the vodka and orange juice had barely been touched. The older woman came directly to her. "I'm ready to meet Goldie."

Rachel placed the baby in her grandmother's arms. The bonding was instantaneous. The pained tension on Pearl's face transformed into adoring tenderness, and she exhaled in a sweet, soft hum.

Rachel exhaled a sigh of relief. Goldie was going to be just fine with her grandma.

Chapter Eleven

While Pearl settled down on the parlor sofa to feed Goldie her bottle, Rachel took Cole into the kitchen. She kept her voice low, not wanting to disturb the moment of bonding between grandma and baby. But she felt like singing. Their problems were all but over.

She beamed at Cole. In his black turtleneck and still-damp jeans, he looked big, rough and intimidating, until he smiled back and she saw the warmth in his eyes. He came closer. With his thumb, he tilted her chin up, and she thought he was going to kiss her again.

His voice was a whisper. "What's going on? You look like you just found the pot of gold at the end of the rainbow."

"Jim Loughlin," she said. "Deputy Jim Loughlin. He'll help us."

"Why do you think so?"

"Don't you see?" Excitement bubbled through her. "This is the perfect solution."

He rested his palm on her forehead. "That's funny. You don't feel feverish."

"I'm not delusional." She took a step back. "Once I contact Jim, we'll be in the clear. In fact, the police will probably thank us."

"Before you schedule our ticker tape parade, take a breath. Sit down."

"Why are you being so negative?"

"Start at the beginning. Who's Loughlin?"

She plunked into a chair at the kitchen table. "The house I was at before you kidnapped me belongs to Jim and Sarah Loughlin. Jim happens to be a deputy sheriff. If I call him, he can arrange for us to turn ourselves in."

"You believe that you trust him."

"One hundred and ten percent," she said confidently. "Jim would do anything for me. I just went through the labor-and-birthing process with him and his wife. They think I'm pretty terrific."

"Which you are."

"Thank you."

He wasn't responding with the enthusiasm she'd expected. As he took a seat beside her, his forehead furrowed. His cognac-brown irises turned a deeper, darker shade. "Let's think about it before you call him."

"What's to think about? We turn ourselves in, and he calls off the manhunt."

"After which," Cole said, "your friend will be ordered to turn us over to Wayne Prescott and the FBI."

"Not necessarily."

"It's his job. Even if Loughlin thinks you walk on water, he can't go against orders. Prescott is calling the shots."

She hadn't thought that far ahead. "But the Loughlins know I'm innocent. They're my alibi. I was with them when you were on the run. They know I'm not a criminal."

"Neither am I." Gently, he took her hand. "But Prescott has somehow managed to turn my FBI handler against me."

"I still want to call Jim," she said. "Your cell phone doesn't have GPS tracking, right?"

He took it out of his pocket and placed the phone on the table. "Give it a shot. Put the call on speaker so I can hear."

She'd already used Pearl's phone to call information and get the home number for the Loughlins. She punched it into Cole's cell. *This plan will work. It has to work.*

As soon as Jim answered, she said, "This is Rachel. How's the baby doing? Do you have a name yet?"

"Caitlyn," he said. "She's beautiful."

"And Sarah?"

"I didn't think it was possible to love my wife more than the day we were married, but I'm in awe of this woman— the mother of my child."

He was the kind of guy who renewed her faith in the goodness of humanity. She felt guilty about intruding on his happiness with her problems. "What have you heard about the casino robbers?"

"There's a big-deal manhunt. Everybody on duty is looking for the three that got away. They've got roadblocks set up. They were trying to monitor the on-the-road cameras, but a lot of them got messed up by the snow. Why do you ask?"

"The woman fugitive," she said. "The supposed woman fugitive is me."

There was a silence. He cleared his throat and his deep voice dropped all the way into the cellar. "What are you talking about?"

"After I left your house, I was kidnapped by the robbers to help a woman in the gang deliver her baby. You must have suspected something. My van was at the house where the three people were killed."

"I haven't heard anything about your van. As far as I know the three victims were found by the FBI in a clearing right before the blizzard hit."

"Not in a house?"

"No."

A cover-up. She should have expected as much. Penny had told her that the house belonged to Baron; he wouldn't want to be associated with them.

Quietly, Cole said, "Tell him you have an address."

She spoke up, "I can give you the location of—"

"Is somebody with you?" Jim asked.

"Yes." She wouldn't lie. "I'm with a man who was part of the gang, but he's really an undercover FBI agent. A good guy. He saved my life. And the baby's."

"You have the baby with you," Jim said.

"If we'd left her behind, they would have killed her. You have to believe me."

"Where are you, Rachel?"

She looked at Cole, who shook his head. Sadly, she agreed with him. If she told Jim where she was, the police would be at the door, and they'd be handed over to the people who wanted them dead.

"I can't tell you. There's a conspiracy going on that's too complicated to explain. If I'm taken into FBI custody, I'll be arrested or made to disappear. Or killed."

"Is that what this undercover fed told you? Rachel, you have to get away from him. He's no good."

"Deputy Loughlin," Cole said with calm authority, "you know Rachel isn't a criminal. She's a healer. To protect her, it's imperative that you tell no one about this phone call."

"Don't tell me about protecting Rachel." Jim's voice rumbled. "I'd do anything for her."

"I'm counting on your silence," Cole said. "I'm going to give you an address. It's the house where the murders took place. Even if the blood has been cleaned up, there will be evidence of a shoot-out. Check the property records and find the name of the owner. Tell no one what you're doing."

"I won't help you. That's aiding and abetting."

"Please," Rachel said. "I need your help, Jim."

Cole gave him the address. "We'll call you back."

As he disconnected the call and slipped the phone into his pocket, Rachel felt her high hopes come crashing to the ground. She couldn't trust anyone. Not even Jim.

COLE PULLED OPEN the heavy velvet drapes in the front parlor and looked outside. Above the snow-laden rooftops, he saw the clouds breaking up and the sky turning blue. Sunlight glistened on mounds of snow piled beside the sidewalks. Kids in parkas and snow hats were having a snowball fight. People waved to each other. A four-wheel-drive vehicle bounced along the plowed street in front of the house.

His undercover work generally led him into rat-infested back alleys and strip joints. Not here. Not to small town America, where you couldn't see the criminals until they held a knife to your throat.

He turned away from the window.

The scene inside the house was equally charming. Rachel and Pearl sat beside each other on the fancy Victorian sofa. Their heads bent down; the curly blond bangs on Pearl's forehead almost touched Rachel's sleek dark hair as they fussed over the baby.

There wasn't time for cooing infants and cozy musing after the storm. He and Rachel had managed to find Penny's mother without too much difficulty. Sooner or later, Baron's men would do the same. They could be surrounding the place at this very moment.

"Ladies," he snapped.

Pearl looked up at him. Though her lips smiled, her expression was flat. Something inside her had died. When he'd talked to her earlier, she had demanded the truth about her daughter's death. He'd tried to be gentle, but as he spoke, he'd seen the cold embrace of despair and sorrow squeeze the light from her eyes.

Beside her, Rachel had slipped into an attitude of outward calm that masked her internal tension. She'd looked the same way when she directed Penny through the last stage of labor.

These two women weren't kidding themselves. No matter how unflustered they looked, both were aware of the tragedy and the danger. They needed him to point the way.

"Here's what we're going to do," he said. "First we get Pearl and Goldie to safety."

"Agreed," Pearl said. "I can't stay here. Too many people in town know that I'm house-sitting."

"Deputy Loughlin said there were roadblocks and surveillance cams, but they won't be looking for you. Take Goldie and get onto the highway as soon as possible."

"You need a car seat," Rachel said.

"Not a problem. The woman who owns this house has a couple of car seats in the closet of the guest bedroom for when her grandchildren come to visit in the summer." She looked down at the sleeping baby on her lap. "Don't worry, little one. Grammy Pearl is going to take good care of you."

"You shouldn't return to your home in Denver," he said. "Not until we know it's safe."

When she nodded, her curly blond ponytail bounced. "Maybe I can stay with a friend in Granby. She was Penny's favorite teacher in high school. Taught economics and history."

"Does she still teach there?" Rachel asked. "I might know her. I do health programs at the high school."

"Jenna Cambridge."

"A teacher?" Rachel lifted an eyebrow. "Penny talked about Jenna as though she was more of a friend."

"That boundary might have gotten a bit fuzzy. Jenna was new in town and lonely. Plain as dishwater. She liked to go out with Penny." Her lip trembled. "My daughter attracted attention wherever she went."

Though Cole had known Penny for less than a month, he had to agree. Even nine months pregnant, Penny was a firecracker. "Did Jenna know Penny's boyfriends?"

"More than I did." Pearl swiped a tear from the corner of her eye. "Penny didn't tell me much about the guys she dated."

Gently, Rachel said, "One of them might be Goldie's father. Penny said they started dating when she was in high school. He was an older man."

"How much older?"

"He took her to a classy places, bought her expensive gifts." Rachel circled her wrist with her fingers. "A diamond tennis bracelet."

"Those were real?"

"According to Penny."

"How could I miss that? I'm a jewelry designer." Pearl's features hardened. Anger was beginning to replace her sadness. "Not that I work with precious gems. Amethyst is about as fancy as I get. And pearls, of course."

He noticed that she was wearing silver teardrop earrings and a ring with three black pearls. Her only bit of artistic flamboyance was her colorful patchwork jacket. He liked her flair and her earthy sensibility.

Rachel cleared her throat. "Does the name Wayne Prescott mean anything to you?"

She frowned as she considered. Her hand absently patted Goldie's backside. "I don't know him. Is he the father?"

"I don't know."

"Tell me more about this older man."

"Penny didn't actually say how they met, but I got the idea that he was somehow connected to her school. Not a teacher, though. Maybe the father of another student. She said that Jenna told her he was Penny's Mister Big—the man she'd spend the rest of her life with."

"Jenna knew? All of a sudden, I don't want to see her or talk to her. Why wouldn't she tell me?"

"Penny probably asked her not to."

"I never guessed that Penny was dating an adult man. She was only seventeen when she waltzed through the door with that bracelet." She shot a hard glance at Cole. "If she was sleeping with him, that's rape, isn't it?"

He nodded. "This older man is the mastermind behind the gang and the robberies. They call him Baron."

Still holding Goldie, she surged to her feet. "And he's the father."

"Yes."

"I want you to catch this bastard."

Cole had come to the same conclusion. He and Rachel couldn't run forever. The only way they'd be able to turn themselves in to the cops would be if they had solid, irrefutable evidence against Baron. They needed to go on the offensive.

"We can start by talking to Jenna," he said. "She might know Baron's real name."

"I'll make the call," Pearl said as she handed the sleeping baby to Rachel.

In the kitchen, Cole went over a few things Pearl needed to avoid mentioning. Obviously, she couldn't tell Jenna about him or Rachel. And it was best not to mention that she had Goldie with her. Penny's high school teacher had already kept one secret from Pearl. "She's not entirely trustworthy."

"You can say that again." Pearl gave a brisk nod. "Listen, Cole. I'm a pretty good actress. Just tell me what to say."

"You want to get the father's name. That's number one."

"Got it."

"Pretend that you never saw us. Say that you had a call from Penny and she had her baby." He glanced at the clock on the stove. "It's after nine. Will Jenna be at work?"

"Not today. The kids are out of school because of the blizzard."

He handed Pearl his cell phone, which had been recharging for the past hour. "Make the call. Put it on speaker."

Jenna answered on the third ring. Her greeting was overly effusive—as giggly as the teenagers she taught. "I haven't seen you in ages, Pearl. How are you?"

"I'm worried," she said. "Penny called last night and said she had her baby, but I haven't been able to get in touch with her. Did she call you?"

"Boy or girl?"

"Girl. Her name is Goldie," Pearl said.

"Congratulations, grandma. You must be so happy."

"Must be." Sadness tugged at the corners of Pearl's lips, but she kept her voice upbeat. "I sure wish I knew the baby's daddy. I think it was somebody she dated in high school. Did she mention him to you?"

"Penny has so many boyfriends. I can't keep track."

"This one was special. He gave her that sparkly tennis bracelet."

"Sorry. I don't remember."

Cole didn't believe Jenna. Penny would have been sure to brag about her diamonds, and she'd told Rachel that Jenna was her confidante.

Pearl said, "She called him Mister Big."

"Like *Sex and the City*." She giggled. "I guess Penny is the Granby version of high fashion."

"Are you sure," Pearl said, "that you don't remember him?"

"Not at all, but I'll let you know when Penny contacts me. I'm sure she'll turn up. Like a bad penny."

"Why?" Pearl's voice betrayed her rising frustration. "Why are you so sure she'll contact you?"

"For one thing, we're friends. For another, she's been sending me these mysterious packages to hold for her."

Jenna was the contact.

Penny had been using her high school teacher as the drop-off person after the robberies. She'd been sending Jenna bundles of loot.

Chapter Twelve

As hideouts went, the office in the back of Lily Belle's Soda Fountain and Ice Cream Shop was okay. At least, Rachel thought so. She would have preferred staying in the house, but too many people knew Pearl was living there. Lily Belle's was empty, closed for the season and it had an alarm system.

She and Cole would stay here until nightfall. According to his FBI training, the first twenty-four hours were considered to be the most crucial in a manhunt. After that, the intensity would let up, and they'd make their move.

Rachel slipped off her parka and lowered herself onto the mint-green futon. After sending Pearl on her way with Goldie and the massive backpack filled with baby supplies, she felt unencumbered and a hundred times less tense. All she had to worry about was her own safety and Cole's.

After closing the office door and placing their food supplies on the coffee table in front of the futon, he prowled around the windowless, peach-colored room. The top of the cream-painted desk was empty except for a day-by-day calendar, a pencil jar that looked like an ice cream cone and a couple of framed photographs of smiling, blue-eyed kids. Lily's grandchildren, no doubt. A row of three-drawer cabinets in pastel colors lined the back wall. Bouquets of fake flowers in matching pastel vases sat atop them. A light coat of dust covered every surface. Otherwise, the office was clean. The lingering scent of vanilla and buttery cream hung in the air.

"Too cutesy," he muttered.

"Like Willie Wonka. But with ice cream."

He checked the thermostat. "Good thing we brought blankets. It's set at fifty-two degrees."

"Sounds about right. Warm enough to keep things from freezing but not wasteful. Nobody is supposed to be here until the summer season."

He sank onto the futon beside her. "Take off your shoes."

"Why?"

"We should explore this place, and I don't want to leave wet footprints in case somebody looks through the front window."

With a groan, she wiggled her butt deeper into the futon cushion and stretched her legs out in front of her. Her thigh muscles ached after their crack-of-dawn trek across Shadow Mountain Lake in snowshoes. "What's the point of looking around? Nobody knows we're here. We're safe."

"Are we?"

"Please let me pretend—just for a moment—that crazy people with guns aren't trying to kill us."

"That's not your style," he said. "You're realistic. Practical. You don't delude yourself."

His snap analysis was pretty much on target, but she didn't want him to get cocky. "What makes you think you know me?"

"I'm a trained observer."

She supposed that was true. "In your undercover work, I guess you need to be able to figure out how people are going to act. To be thinking one step ahead."

"That's right."

"But that's on the surface. On a deeper level, you don't know me at all."

He dropped his boots onto the pink-and-green patterned area rug. "I've had a chance to observe your behavior in high-stress situations. I know how you'll react."

"But you don't know why," she said. "You can't tell what I'm thinking. You don't know what's going on inside my head."

He turned toward her and stared—stared hard as though he could actually see her brain working. The two days' growth of stubble on his chin and his messy hair made him look rough, rugged and sexy. Her gaze shifted from his eyes to his lips.

The corner of his mouth twitched into a grin. Then he came across the futon and leaned in close. The suddenness of his kiss took her breath away.

Without thinking, she wrapped her arms around his torso and pulled him against her. His mouth worked against hers. His tongue pushed through her lips.

In spite of her exhaustion, her body responded with a surge of excitement. She didn't feel the chill in the room, didn't look for an escape, didn't want to do anything but prolong this contact.

Ever since their kiss in the cabin, she'd been waiting for this moment—a time when they were finally alone. She had every intention of making love to Cole, but she didn't want to give in too fast. She wanted him to work for it.

Abruptly, she ended the kiss and pulled away from him. But only a few inches away. His face filled her field of vision, and she was captivated by the shimmer in his light brown eyes.

He murmured, "Is that what you were thinking?"

Was she that obvious? Did she radiate a vibe that told him she was a single, thirtysomething woman who needed a big strong man? "You tell me."

"You kissed me back," he said.

"Just being polite."

"Here's what I know about you," he said. "You're smart, competent and pretty. You're at a good place in your life, and you love your work."

"I sound good," she said. "You're lucky to be in the same room with me."

"You're brave. But you're also scared."

Apparently, the compliment train had come to an end. The gleam in his eyes sharpened as he assessed her. He said, "You've been hurt."

"Who hasn't?"

As smoothly as he'd pounced on her, he adjusted his position so he was sitting beside her. "Who hurt you, Rachel? What happened?"

She thought of the men who had passed through her life, ranging from motorcycle man to a rocker with more tattoos than brains. That array of losers wasn't her greatest hurt.

"A six-year-old boy," she said.

She had never talked about this. *Never.* The memory was too painful, too devastating. Her memory of that boy sucked the air from her lungs.

"His name," she said, "was Adam."

He held her hand. "Go on."

"I'd rather not."

After this crisis was over, she didn't honestly expect to see him again. He would go back to California and be an undercover fed. She'd stay here and continue with her midwife career. They were like the proverbial ships passing in the night—if ships were capable of stopping at sea and having hot sex. Bottom line: she didn't need to reveal the dark corners of her soul to him.

He squeezed her hand. "Do you want to talk about what happened with Adam?"

"You're not going to give up on this, are you?"

"No pressure." He sat back on the futon and turned his gaze away from her. His profile was relaxed and calm. He was waiting; his message was clear.

If she wanted to talk, he'd listen. If not, she could keep her secrets buried. It certainly would be less complicated to grab him and proceed with the passion they were both feeling, but the words were building up inside her. If she didn't speak, she might explode.

"I'd been working as an EMT for a year and a half," she said. "I'd seen a lot. Traffic accidents. Heart attacks. Gunshot wounds. The work was getting to me. I was on the verge of a burnout."

She remembered the sunny summer day in Denver—the kind of day when you should be taking a puppy on a walk through a grassy green park. "We got the call and responded. It was a fire and an explosion in an apartment complex."

"Meth lab?"

"I don't know how it happened. Somebody probably told me, but the facts went out of my head."

The details blurred in her memory, but she felt a stab in her gut as she recalled the scene in a central courtyard with three-story buildings on all four sides. The smell of grit and smoke and blood came back to her.

"When we got there, rescuers were pulling people out of the buildings. Other ambulances had already arrived, and a senior EMT had taken charge. He assigned me to triage the wounded while my partner loaded the ambulance and took the more serious burn victims to the nearest hospital."

In minutes, her uniform had been covered in greasy soot and blood as she tended to the survivors. First-, second- and third-degree burns. Wounds caused by the shrapnel from the explosion. Someone had fallen down a flight of stairs.

"That's when I met Adam. A sweet-faced kid. He was lying on a sheet on the ground, and he didn't seem to be badly injured. His head was bleeding. The laceration didn't appear to be deep. When I started working on him, he looked up at me and smiled. He told me his name, and he promised he'd be all right. His exact words were...I'm not going to die."

A swell of emotion rose up inside her. She told herself that not everyone could be saved, but that truth did little to assuage the pain of her sorrow. She'd been hurt. God, yes, she'd been hurt. Not by a person but by life.

When Cole wrapped his arm around her and pulled her close, she didn't object. Her cheek rested against his chest; his solid presence comforted her.

In a whisper, she continued, "I left Adam. Went to deal with other victims. A woman with a broken leg called out Adam's name. His mother. Somehow, they'd gotten separated. She was frantic."

Rachel hadn't wasted time trying to calm Adam's mother. She'd gone back to the boy. His injuries had seemed less traumatic. She'd thought she could carry him and reunite the boy with his mother. "He was dead."

She'd tried to resuscitate the child. CPR. Straight oxygen. Mouth-to-mouth. Nothing worked. "I couldn't bring him back."

"Is that when you changed jobs?"

"Shortly after that." She shrugged. It wasn't necessary to talk about the months of debilitating depression and anger. The important thing was that she'd fought her way through to the other side. She'd learned how to cope. "You asked me what I'm afraid of, and this is it. I'm scared of losing someone I care about."

"Given that fear," he said, "you don't fall in love easily."

"No, I don't." She lifted her chin. "You?"

"Not so much." He kissed the tip of her nose. "Let's get moving. I want to check this place out. Your shoes."

She appreciated the lightning-quick change of subject. After baring her soul to him, the last thing she wanted was to wallow in grief. She'd said her piece. Time to move on.

When she caught his gaze, she wondered if Cole had known this would be her reaction. God, she hated being predictable. "What about my shoes?"

"Take them off."

She raised a questioning eyebrow. "Only the shoes?"

"Later, I'll take your socks, your hat and your belt. I'll unbutton your shirt. Unsnap your jeans." He rose from the futon. "For now, just the shoes. We'll take a look around."

In her stocking feet, she padded behind him on the concrete floor of the kitchen area in the back of the ice cream parlor. Like the office, there weren't any windows. When Cole turned on the overhead light, she saw an array of shelves, drawers, stainless steel counters and a commercial-sized sink, as well as machines of varying size and shape.

"Lily must make her own ice cream," she said. "What's your favorite flavor?"

"Rocky Road," he said.

"That figures."

He opened the door to a pantry. The shelves were all

cleaned out. Likewise for the freezer unit. A closet by the back door was filled with cleaning supplies.

She asked, "Is there something special we're looking for?"

"I'm visualizing. If somebody breaks in here, I want to know where I'm going."

"There's a burglar alarm," she reminded him. "We'll have time to escape."

"Not if the alarm is short-circuited."

She folded her arms and leaned against a counter. "It must be a drag to always focus on the worst-case scenario."

"Yeah, yeah, poor me. Living the hard life of an under-cover agent. When you walk into a room, you always look for the exits. You check out everybody you meet, looking for concealed weapons."

"You sound bored with it."

"I'm ticked off. Usually, I'm on my own. Making my own decisions and deciding my own actions. I get a lot of grief for being a lone wolf. And now, when I call on my handler for help, Waxman turns his back on me."

The front area of Lily Belle's was a typical ice cream parlor and soda fountain with sunlight pouring through the front windows onto the white tile floor. The color scheme was—surprise, surprise—pastel. And the far wall was decorated with a fanciful painting of an animal parade. Pink lion with a top hat and baton. A lavender bear in a tutu. Green and blue squirrels blowing bubbles from their trumpets.

Wrought-iron white chairs and tables were stacked against the walls. Padded stools lined up at a typical soda fountain counter, and there was a long row of empty cool-ers where the ice cream would be stored in the summer.

"FYI," he said, "if we get attacked, come this way.

There's room to hide behind the counter and the coolers. If worse comes to worst, you can bust through the windows. In the back, there's only one exit."

"Lovely." She smiled at him. "You know what makes me really sad?"

"What's that?"

"Looking at all this, I'm dying for some ice cream. Maybe a fudge sundae with whipped cream on top."

"Sounds like you need a little sweetness."

He slung his arm around her waist and yanked her toward him with such force that her feet came off the floor. He pressed her tightly against him and kissed her hard. There was nothing tentative about his approach; the idea of making love was a foregone conclusion. He was aggressive, fierce, demanding.

And she liked it.

Chapter Thirteen

The creamy pastel ambience in the office contrasted the hot red fire of their passion. Rachel felt like she ought to turn the desktop photographs of Lily Belle's grandchildren facedown so they wouldn't be traumatized. Her spirits rose and her excitement soared as Cole tore off her panties.

Breathing hard, she wrapped her arms around his neck and clung to him. Her right leg coiled around his, and she pressed herself against his erection.

His hand grabbed her butt and held her in place. He arched his neck and tilted his head back. For a moment, she thought he might start howling like a wolf. Then he lowered his head and consumed her with a kiss. His hands explored her body with rough caresses.

She felt herself turning into a quivering mass of jelly, unable to stand. They slid to the floor. On the pink-and-green patterned carpet, he straddled her and sat back, looking down.

His body amazed her. Muscular arms. Lean torso. Smooth chest. When she reached toward him, he cuffed her wrists in his grasp.

"No fair." She gasped. "I want to touch."

"How bad do you want it?"

She tried to pull her hands free, but he held her wrists firmly. He was in complete control. Or so he thought.

She widened her eyes and softened her voice. "Please, Cole. You're hurting me."

Concern flashed in his eyes. Immediately, he released his grasp.

And she took advantage. She rose up and twisted her body, throwing him off balance. Now she was on top. "Gotcha."

"You win."

He lay on his back with his arms sprawled above his head while she fondled, stroked and pinched. Her fingers glided along the ridges of his muscles. Leaning down, she nuzzled his chest and torso. Her excitement was building to a fever pitch. She didn't want to wait for one more second.

"Condom?" she asked.

"Wallet."

She crawled across the carpet to where he'd discarded his jeans. Was it really necessary to stop for a condom? Of course, it was. She gave lectures on the importance of protected sex. She had to do this.

After clumsy fumbling, she held the tiny see-through package in her hand. "It's blue."

"The only ones they had in super, gigantic, extralarge."

He took charge again, and she let him. When he plunged into her, she gave a sharp cry. Her last coherent thought was that this was the best sex she'd ever had. Then she abandoned herself to the sheer physical pleasure of their lovemaking.

When it was over, she was shivering from head to toe. Not because it was fifty-two degrees in the room. This was a sensual release that had been building in her for years.

For the first time, she wondered if there might be a future for her and Cole.

Cole wanted to spend the rest of the day making love to Rachel. Their hideout in the office of the ice cream parlor seemed insulated from the rest of the world. After he converted the futon into a bed and spread out blankets, they were cozy and comfortable.

He lay on his back, and she snuggled her head against his shoulder. Cuddling had never been one of his favorite things, but he was betting that this cuddle would lead to something more.

"I only had the one rubber," he said.

"That could be a problem." She rose up on an elbow and looked down at him. "I'm guessing that Lily Belle doesn't keep a condom supply in her desk."

He looked up at her, memorizing every detail. Until now, she'd been so bundled up in turtlenecks and sweaters that he hadn't been able to appreciate her. From the neck down, she was firm but not too muscular and surprisingly graceful from the arch of her back to the crook of her elbow. Her throat was as smooth as ivory. He liked her short hair; it suited her face. Her high forehead balanced a strong, stubborn jaw. And her eyes? Those big blue eyes sparkled with humor and excitement.

He already wanted her again. "Would it help if I told you I recently had a physical, and I'm clean?"

"I give health lectures about bad boys like you. You wouldn't believe the stories high school boys come up with when they're trying to get their girlfriends to say yes."

"Actually, I'm familiar with those stories."

She traced a line down his nose and across his lips. "You and me? We're not in high school. Nothing you could say would convince me. It's my decision whether or not I take a risk."

They had bigger threats to worry about than unprotected sex. Armed killers could burst through the door at any given moment. He needed to deal with that situation.

Reaching toward the coffee table, he picked up the cell phone and turned it on. "I want to check in with Pearl and see how she's doing."

"Put it on speaker," Rachel said.

Pearl answered right away on her hands-free phone. Her voice was chipper. "I got on the highway with no problem. The snowplows have been out, and I'm making good time."

"Any roadblocks?"

"None that I've seen. But there were a whole lot of police cars on the road when I was leaving Grand Lake."

"Are you headed to Jenna's house?"

"Certainly not. I'd rather camp in the forest than see that lying little snake again. I'm staying with a friend in Denver. She has a penthouse condo in a secure building. We ought to be safe."

He was glad to hear that Pearl was taking the threat seriously.

Rachel piped up, "How's Goldie?"

"Sleeping in the car seat, snug as a bug. I might have to stop and give her a bottle, but I want to get out of the high country. There's more bad weather coming in."

"How bad?" he asked.

"Another eight to ten inches. On the radio, the ski areas are whooping and hollering about great conditions."

More snow presented an obstacle. He wanted to drive to Granby tonight, to talk with Jenna Cambridge and take possession of the packages Penny had sent to her. "Take care of yourself, Pearl. We'll call again later. Don't tell anyone else where you are."

"I understand."

"Give Goldie a hug," Rachel said.

He disconnected the call and looked toward her. She was sitting up on the futon, wide-awake and alert, with a blanket around her shoulders to keep warm. He asked, "How are you at driving in snow?"

"Better than you, California boy."

"I'm good in a high-speed chase."

"What about black ice?"

"Have I mentioned how much I hate the mountains?"

"Seriously," she said, "the highway ought to be okay. The real problem will come when we get to Granby. Side roads don't get cleared too often. Since Pearl took the four-wheel drive SUV that belongs to Lily Belle, we're driving her little compact—not the best vehicle for deep snow."

"Do you think we can make it?"

"I don't know," she said. "If we run into trouble, we're caught."

It wouldn't be too bad to stay here overnight. He and Rachel could find plenty of ways to amuse themselves. "Let's call your cop buddy and see what he's found out."

Like Pearl, Deputy Jim Loughlin was quick to pick up. Had he been hovering by the phone, waiting for their call? Cole wanted to trust this guy because Rachel did, but he was realistic about the responsibilities of a law enforcement officer. At some point, Loughlin would have to obey orders. His tone was anxious. "Are you all right? Can you tell me if you're all right?"

"I'm good." She gave Cole a sultry smile. "Better than you'd expect."

"I went to the address you gave me," Loughlin said. "You were right. There was blood all over. Bullet holes. Looked like a semiautomatic weapon."

"Did you report it?" she asked.

"I should have, but I didn't." He grumbled, "I couldn't

figure out how to tell the sheriff without mentioning that I'd been in contact with you."

"Sorry to put you in this position," Cole said.

"Not your fault. There's something about this manhunt that just doesn't ring true. For starters, Rachel, you're obviously not a criminal."

"Thanks," she said. "What else bothers you?"

"The sheriff stopped by to see the baby. By the way, Sarah appreciates those instructions you left behind about breast-feeding. My mom kept telling her that the bottle was better, but Sarah won't hear of it."

"Good for Sarah."

Cole told himself to be patient while the deep, rumbling voice of Deputy Loughlin talked about being a new daddy. His chat about breast-feeding made a strange counterpoint to the massacre of the gang, but it was best to let Rachel's friend take his time.

"Anyway," Loughlin said, "there was an FBI agent with the sheriff. A guy by the name of Prescott."

Son of a bitch. Cole could think of only one reason why Prescott would be there. He knew about Rachel and wanted to get a lead on her whereabouts. It was looking more and more like Agent Wayne Prescott was a link to Baron.

Rachel asked, "What did Prescott want to know?"

"Here's the funny thing about him. He claimed that he doesn't know this area, but he used the names of local landmarks. Things like Pete's Pie Shack and Hangman's Tree. Stuff you wouldn't find on a map."

"You thought he was fishy?"

"Something about him didn't smell right," Loughlin said. "Then he asked me about you and the clinic. He mentioned your vacation and asked if we knew where you were going. But he never identified you as the female fugitive. The only name that's been given is Cole Bogart."

She shot him a questioning glance. Bogart wasn't the name he'd told her; that was his undercover identity.

Loughlin continued, "You're both described as being armed and dangerous based on the murders of those three people. But if you killed them, how did you remove the bodies? And why?"

"Somebody wants to keep the house where they were killed a secret," Cole said. "Did you check the records to find the owner?"

"It's a corporate group called Baron Enterprises. The primary name is Xavier Romero, who happens to be the owner of the Black Hawk casino that got robbed."

Cole knew that name, knew it well. Xavier Romero had been a small-time operator in the Southern California gambling scene. He was also a snitch—a likable old guy but shifty as a snake. Cole hadn't known that Romero owned the casino they hit.

Deputy Loughlin cleared his throat. "This just doesn't add up. Why would the gang hide in a house that belongs to the guy they robbed?"

Xavier Romero had to be in on the plot. Cole asked, "How much does Romero claim was stolen?"

"Over a hundred thousand."

Cole shook his head. "It wasn't half that much."

"The robbery report stated the higher amount," Jim said, "which means the insurance company will pay out the hundred thousand to the casino."

"Unless we can prove fraud," Cole said. "We need to find that money."

"We're talking about a lot of cash." The deputy's voice took on a note of suspicion. "I've never met you, Cole. I'm putting a lot of trust in you based on what Rachel says. Don't let me down."

"I won't," he promised.

"Thank you, Jim," Rachel said. "We'll be in touch as soon as we know anything else. Give Caitlyn a kiss from me."

She ended the call and turned to him. "Is that the answer you were looking for? Is Xavier Romero really the Baron?"

"Not possible. Romero is close to seventy. A potbellied old man with thinning white hair and thick glasses. His hands look arthritic, but he can make the cards dance when he's dealing poker."

"He must be Baron's associate. They're part of the same group that owns the house. And it sounds like he intends to commit insurance fraud with Baron's help."

"Right on both counts, partner."

She shook her head. "I'm not your partner in crime. Or crime solving. I'm not cut out for this undercover life."

"It's a gift," he said.

"Is it, Mister Bogart?"

"That's my undercover name. Cole Jeremy McClure is the name on my birth certificate."

"You didn't lie to me." She snuggled down beside him. Her flesh molded to his. "That makes me feel good."

He pulled her close. There were a number of things he ought to be thinking about: logistical problems in driving through another damn blizzard to Granby at night and the usefulness of calling Waxman with the new information about Xavier Romero. But his brain was clouded by her nearness. The scent of her body made him stupid. And happy.

He brushed his lips across her forehead and looked into

her eyes. "How do you feel about making love *sans* condom?"

"I'm for it," she said.

"What if you get pregnant?"

"This is something I never thought I'd hear myself say. Never. Do you understand? Never."

"I get it."

"But the truth is that I wouldn't mind getting pregnant. At this point in my life, I'm ready to have a baby."

His heart made a loud thud. His pulse stopped. He was lying naked with a woman who wanted a baby. *Danger, danger, danger.* "Excuse me?"

She laughed. "I've never seen the blood drain from someone's face so fast. Are you going into shock? Should I start CPR?"

"I'm cool."

"If I should happen to get pregnant, I wouldn't saddle you with any responsibilities. Being a single mom isn't my first choice. But I'm in my thirties, and I want kids. I love kids. And it's entirely possible that I'm not cut out for the whole marriage thing."

"Marriage?" He choked out the word. Was she trying to give him a heart attack?

"Don't worry, Cole. I'm not looking for a relationship with you. How could I? You live in California. And you have an incredibly dangerous job. Frankly, I wouldn't marry you on a bet."

His mood swung one hundred and eighty degrees. Because she said she'd never marry him, he had an urge to propose. "Are you giving me a preemptive rejection?"

"Absolutely. Long-distance relationships hardly ever work. And your undercover work scares me."

"Doesn't seem fair," he muttered.

"Don't feel bad. I consider you to be an excellent sperm donor. You're intelligent, and you seem to be healthy. There aren't any weird genetic diseases lurking around in your DNA, are there?"

"Not that I know of."

She slipped her fingertips down his chest. "I don't think we need to worry about not having a condom."

When he kissed her, he was thinking of more than her slim, supple body. In his mind, he visualized a home with Rachel. She'd be wearing his grandmother's wedding ring and holding his baby in her arms. Not a typical fantasy for making love. But he found the thought of being with her—long-term and committed—to be intensely arousing.

Chapter Fourteen

Though Rachel didn't want to get dressed, she shoved her arms into her sleeves and pulled on her turtleneck. Hours had passed since they'd entered the windowless office behind the ice cream parlor, but the time had gone faster than the blink of an eye. She wished these moments could stretch into days, months, years.

In a way, it felt like she'd known Cole forever. There was something so familiar about him. In spite of being opposites, they were well-matched, like a hook and an eye. A bolt and a screw. She chuckled to herself. Best not to think about screws or she'd never get her clothes on.

Their passion was wild. It was crazy. And she knew better. She was an adult—a thirtysomething woman who had her life on track. Why had she abandoned all restraint? Was it the intensity of being chased? Did she cling to him because she was terrified that she wouldn't survive this ordeal?

Reluctantly, she zipped her jeans. Maybe the answer was Cole himself. He was different from all the other bad boys she'd known. True, he had an edge. The man earned his living by deception. But he also made her laugh. And he was capable of incredible tenderness.

He smacked her butt and said, "Get your jacket on. If it's not snowing too hard, we need to get on the road."

She was praying for a blizzard. "I don't want to go."

He yanked her into his arms and held her tightly against him. She liked the rough-and-ready way he handled her. He treated her as an equal, not a porcelain figurine that might shatter and break.

"Rachel, beautiful Rachel." His voice dropped to a low, intimate level. "If we had a choice, I'd keep you here forever. I'd burn your clothes so you could never get dressed."

The way she'd burned motorcycle man's leather jacket? "Do you ride motorcycles?"

"Only Harleys."

"Figures."

Pulling away from him, she shrugged into her parka. The superwarm coat felt empty without the added burden of Goldie snuggled against her chest. "Do you think Pearl is okay?"

"We checked with her an hour ago. She was at her friend's condo, feeding the baby."

"That's not what I meant."

He nodded. "It's going to be a long time before she's okay. She lost a daughter and gained a granddaughter. In the space of a day, her whole life got turned upside down."

Like mine. "I'm dressed. What's next?"

"Come with me." He took her hand. "I'm not going to turn on any lights. Somebody might notice."

A shiver trickled down her spine. "Do you think they're watching?"

"Don't know."

They left the office, and he closed the door behind them. For a moment, they stood in the kitchen area and waited for their eyes to become accustomed to the darkness. The empty area with stainless steel fixtures felt cold, even with her parka. She held Cole's hand as he moved toward the front of the shop.

The glow from a streetlight fell softly through the wide, snow-splattered front windows. They circled the serving counter and crossed the white tile floor until they stood at the glass, looking out.

Though it was only nine o'clock, there was no traffic on the main street running through Grand Lake. Snow piled up three feet high at the curb, and a car parked at the side of the road was completely buried. The sidewalk had been cleared enough that two people could walk abreast. On the opposite side of the street, the storefronts were all dark. The town had closed down early.

The light snowfall disappointed her. She'd been hoping for a raging storm that would force them to cancel their plan.

"Looks peaceful," Cole said.

"These blizzards can be real deceptive. I vote to stay here until morning."

He stepped behind her and slipped his arms around her waist. She leaned back against his chest, feeling cozy and protected in his embrace.

"It's pretty," he said. "Maybe your mountains aren't so bad, after all."

She closed her eyes and thought about spending time with him in a ski lodge with paneled walls, a fireplace and a mug of hot buttered rum. "There's nothing as beautiful as a blue sky day with the sun sparkling on champagne powder snow."

"A full moon on a white, sandy beach," he said.

"Mountain streams."

"Palm trees waving in the breeze." He hugged her.

"When this is over, I want to take you to California. You can vacation with me."

Her heart took a happy little leap. *He wants to spend more time with me.* Immediately, she pushed the thought aside, not wanting to get her hopes up. "You're just trying to convince me that we should make this drive tonight."

"We'll exit through the back. Then we'll head down the street to the garage behind Pearl's house." He kissed the top of her head. "If everything goes well, this could be over in a matter of hours."

With a sigh, she gave in and followed him through the door at the front of the ice cream parlor into the darkness of the kitchen area.

Cole came to a sudden halt. She couldn't see what he was doing, but she sensed his movement as he raised his gun.

"What's wrong?" she asked.

"The green light on the alarm box is off."

"It must be a malfunction."

"Let's hope so."

They hadn't heard the alarm go off. Though she couldn't see far into the darkness, she surely would have sensed the presence of another person. "There's nobody else in here."

"It's too dark back here," he muttered. "We'll go out the front entrance."

She turned and retraced her steps. He stayed with her, close enough that she felt his arm brush against hers. As she reached the open doorway, the light through the front windows gave her more visibility. She glanced over her shoulder and saw Cole facing backward, toward the kitchen.

When she passed the doorway, she looked toward the front counter to her right. And she froze. The dark silhouette of a huge broad-shouldered figure stood out against the pale pastel of the wall.

His arms flung wide. "He-e-e-re's Frankie."

He charged toward her, more stumbling than deliberate. His hands slid under her arms and he lifted her off her feet. His forward momentum carried her beyond the counter toward the far wall.

She kicked hard. Her foot tangled with his legs, and she could feel him losing his balance. If he fell, he'd land on top of her with his full weight. He'd crush her.

The instant her boots touched the floor, she threw her weight toward his left. His left shoulder was the one that was injured—the weaker shoulder. The bullet was still in there, probably turning septic.

Frank crashed to the floor, pinning her legs. She struggled to free herself. Frank sat straight up, grabbed her arm and yanked her around so she was sitting in front of him on the floor. Light reflected off the barrel of his gun.

"Don't move," he said. "Neither one of you."

Cole stood only a few feet from them, looking down. His gun aimed at Frank's forehead. "Let her go."

"Yeah? Then you'll drill a hole in my head?"

"If I wanted to kill you," Cole said, "I would have done it back at the cabin."

"You left me there." He coughed. Phlegm rattled in his throat. "Left me to die."

His stench—stale sweat, blood and grit—turned her stomach. A feverish heat emanated from him, and he was shaking. It was clear to her that he was feeling the effects of the gunshot wounds, loss of blood, shock and exposure. He was weakened and losing control. That made him even more dangerous.

Keeping the fear from her voice, she said, "You need a doctor, Frank."

"I need for you to shut the hell up." He pressed the nose of his gun against her temple. "I can't see a damn thing in here. Turn on the lights, Cole."

"Will the light be a signal for your friends? The murderers you hooked up with at the cabin?"

"I ditched those guys as soon as I got into town."

A spasm shook Frank's body. His gun hand twitched. She was afraid he might kill her by accident. Rachel said, "Do as he says."

"That's right," Frank growled. "I'm in charge."

Cole backed up a few paces, heading toward the light switch by the door. "How did you find us?"

"I met Penny's mom in Black Hawk at the casino. Pearl Richards. She said she was living in Grand Lake. I asked around. Found her house. Went inside. And then...I don't remember. It was warm. Must have gone to sleep."

His grip on consciousness was fading. She wanted to keep him calm and placated. "Finding Pearl was smart, Frank. Why don't you put the gun down and—"

"I'm a hell of a lot smarter than you know," he said. "Ask Cole. I'm good with electronics. Disconnected the alarm to this place. No problem."

"Why did you come here? To the ice cream parlor?"

"Found a business card. I got inside. Easy does it. Then I got dizzy. Shhhhh." He slurred, "Had to s-s-s-sleep."

From the corner of her eye, she saw the gun drooping in his hand. He was on the verge of passing out.

"Let me bring you something to drink," she said gently. "Something nice and cool. You'd like that, wouldn't you?"

His body stiffened as he forced himself awake. "Turn on the damn lights."

When Cole flicked the switch, light flooded the room. The cheerful, pastel décor mocked the hopelessness of her situation. Two men with guns faced each other, and she was in the middle.

Frank shook her arm and ordered her to stand up. "Slow. Move real slow."

She was tempted to bolt. Frank was suffering; his reactions would be slowed. She remembered what Cole had told her earlier. If attacked, hide behind the counter.

"Move," Frank barked.

She did as he said, and he maneuvered into position behind her, using her as a shield. He held her left arm to keep her from running. His gun jabbed her ribs.

When she flinched, Cole reacted. His movements were slight, not enough to spook Frank. But she saw the tension in his jaw and noticed that he had moved a few inches closer.

Like her, he kept his tone level and calm. "You don't want to hurt Rachel. She's the one who's going to lead you to all that money."

"Penny sent the cash here to her mom," Frank said. "It's close. I can smell it."

"You're wrong," she said. "But I'm sure you already know that. You must have searched in the house before you came here."

"Where is it?"

She looked toward Cole, who gave her a nod. Then she said, "Penny sent the money to a friend in Granby. We have to drive to get there."

"If you're lying, I'll kill you." He poked her again. "Cole, put your gun on the floor and step back."

She could guess what would happen if Cole disarmed himself. Frank was desperate, half crazed. He thought he needed her to lead him to the money, but he had no further use for anyone else. He'd shoot Cole in a minute.

She couldn't stop herself from crying out. "No, Cole. Don't do it."

Frank dragged her by the arm. He edged toward the windows as though he was planning to walk out the front door. Was it unlocked? Had he entered through that door?

"Listen to me, Frank. We'll take you with us," Cole said. "We'll drive together and take you to the money."

"Drop your weapon. Or I'll shoot her in the gut."

"You need her. She's the only one who—"

"Drop it."

Cole placed his gun on the floor.

"That's real good," Frank said. "Kick it over here."

She watched in horror as the automatic weapon slid across the white tile floor into the corner under the painting of the dancing lavender bear in a tutu. This shouldn't be happening. Not here. Lily Belle's Ice Cream Parlor wasn't the place for a showdown.

With a satisfied grunt, Frank pulled the gun away from her side and aimed at Cole. Though his hand wobbled, he couldn't miss from this distance.

She didn't plan her move. All Rachel knew was that she had to do something. She bent forward from the waist. Before Frank could yank her back into an upright position, she flung her head back as hard as she could. Her skull banged against Frank's wounded left shoulder.

He screamed in pain. His grip on her arm released.

She made a frantic dash.

Chapter Fifteen

The gutsy move by Rachel gave Cole the chance he needed.

There wasn't time to reach his gun. Every second counted. He took two quick steps and launched himself in a diving tackle. His shoulder hit the solid mass of Frank's chest, and the big man went down with a thud. Still, he managed to fire two shots. He didn't lose his grip on the weapon.

On the floor, Cole struggled for the gun. From the corner of his eye, he saw Rachel dive across the countertop. She was out of sight. Out of range. Good.

With a yell and a ferocious surge, Frank threw Cole off him and staggered to his feet. He braced his legs, wide apart. His shoulders hunched as he groped the empty air. He squinted. His eyes seemed unable to focus. Like a wounded beast, he swung his long arms, waving the gun back and forth.

Cole squared off with him. A one-two combination to the gut drove Frank backward. Cole flicked a stinging blow to the center of Frank's face, snapping his head back.

His arms flew wide. His fingers loosened. The gun clattered to the floor. This fight was all but over.

Frigid air rushed into the ice cream parlor as the front door opened. A man with a gun entered. Frank had brought backup, and Cole couldn't handle two of them.

Following Rachel's example, he pivoted and leaped across the soda fountain counter, where he found her crouched on the floor in a tight little ball. "Are you all right?"

She nodded. "You?"

"Been better."

Three gun shots erupted.

Cole peered over the edge of the counter. Frank sprawled on the floor. His blood splattered the white tile floor.

The gunman flipped back the hood of his parka and said, "It's over. You can come out."

Agent Wayne Prescott.

Slowly, Cole stood. When he'd been looking down the barrel of Frank's gun, he felt less threatened than when Prescott came toward him and extended his hand. There was every reason to believe that this man had betrayed him and put him in lethal danger. Should he shake that hand? Why not just stick his arm down a wood chipper?

"Agent McClure," Prescott said, "you're a hard man to find."

"You've got me now." There was no choice but to play nice. He reached across the soda fountain counter and gripped the traitor's hand. In spite of his years as an undercover operative, he couldn't force himself to return Prescott's smile. "Rachel, this is Agent Wayne Prescott."

His supposedly disarming smile extended to her. "I apologize, Ms. Devon. It's unfortunate that you were caught up in this situation. I assure you that this isn't the way the FBI does business."

Her lips pressed tightly together. With wide, unblinking eyes, she stared at Frank's body. "Is he dead?"

"He's not going to hurt anybody."

Cole knew that her EMT training and instincts wouldn't

allow her to ignore a victim. He wasn't surprised when she straightened her shoulders, walked around the counter and knelt beside Frank.

Watching her check for a pulse gave Cole a renewed respect for her. She valued human life—even the miserable existence of someone like Frank Loeb, a man who had tried to kill her. Rachel was a good woman. The best.

She looked up and shook her head. "No need to call for an ambulance."

When Prescott moved closer to her, Cole vaulted over the counter and inserted himself between them. Even though Prescott had holstered his gun, he couldn't be trusted. He looked like one of the good guys with his barbered black hair and clean-shaven jaw. His manner was calm. His expression showed no emotion, typical of a trained agent. Pulling information from him wasn't going to be easy.

Cole helped Rachel to her feet and guided her to one of the padded turquoise stools in front of the counter. When she was seated, he turned toward Prescott, waiting for him to speak first.

Unfortunately, Prescott employed the same negotiating tactic. He stood beside Frank's body as though he was a hunter with a fresh kill waiting to have his photograph taken. The corner of his mouth twitched. Cole could tell that there was something Prescott wanted to know, a burning question that would break his silent facade.

"The baby," Prescott said. "Is the baby all right?"

Cole hadn't expected him to ask about Goldie. If he was right about Prescott working with Baron, the first question should have been about the money.

Rachel answered, "Goldie is doing very well. She's with Penny's mother."

"Where?" Prescott demanded.

Before Rachel could answer, Cole said, "In a safe place."

"I need to see the baby before I can call off the search."

"That doesn't make a hell of a lot of sense," Cole said. "You know we're not armed and dangerous fugitives. You shook my hand. Apologized to Rachel. You put your gun away."

"I'm not the one who made the call for a manhunt," Prescott said. "Somebody higher up said you'd lost it. You know how often that happens with undercover ops."

"Not with me."

"There were three dead bodies. One of them, a woman who had just given birth."

"Who called for the manhunt?"

"The director gave the order. I don't know who talked to him."

A lie? Prescott had jammed his hands into the pockets of his parka so he wouldn't betray any nervousness with his gestures. His forehead pulled into a frown that might indicate concern or confusion. Or else he was hiding something. His dark eyes were steady, but his lips thinned. *Was he lying?*

"You called me in on this investigation," Cole said. "You suspected someone in your office of working with Baron."

"I still do."

Cole continued as though he hadn't spoken. "Then you show up here with Frank."

"Hold it right there. Frank Loeb and I weren't working together. I was following him." He paused. "I didn't know Frank was so skilled at electronics. It didn't take him ten minutes to bypass that burglar alarm."

There was something cruel about discussing Frank's

skills while the man lay dead at their feet. Though Rachel was no stranger to violent death, he wanted to get her away from this horror.

Less than an hour ago, they'd been lying in each other's arms. The world had been sweet. He had been happy. No more.

His life didn't have room for a normal relationship. He lived on the razor's edge.

"Call Waxman," Cole said. His handler needed to be apprised of the situation.

Prescott's scowl deepened. "Waxman might be the one who betrayed you. When he assigned you, he warned me that you were a loose cannon. He said that when you go undercover, you cut all ties."

That policy had served Cole well. If Prescott had been able to track him with GPS, he and Rachel would have been caught. "You're saying that Agent Waxman is the traitor."

"I'm not accusing anybody."

But he was pushing suspicion away from himself, which seemed like a blatant ruse. Cole needed to be careful in dealing with this guy. If Prescott had been working with Baron, he had a lot to lose. Not only would his payoff money stop coming, but he'd also lose his job, his reputation and his freedom. The feds dealt harshly with those who conspired against them.

"Think about it, Cole." Prescott's hands came out of his pockets. He held them open, showing that he had nothing to hide. "I'm not the bad guy. If I wanted you dead, I could have killed you when I walked through this door."

A threat? "Don't underestimate me."

It had been a while since he'd killed a man with his bare

hands. The years had taught him patience. He was smarter now than when he first started.

"Here's the deal." Prescott's hands went back into his pockets. "If I call off the manhunt, I have to take you and Rachel into custody."

He looked toward her. She hadn't made a peep. Until now, she hadn't been shy about making her needs and desires known. What was going on behind those liquid blue eyes?

He glanced at Prescott. "Excuse us for a moment."

Taking her arm, he led her toward the door into the rear of the shop. He stood just inside, where he could keep an eye on Prescott while they held a whispered conversation. "Why so quiet?"

"I was watching you," she said. "When you're negotiating, you become a different person."

"How so?"

She lifted her hand as though she wanted to touch him. But she held back. "You know how much I like a bad boy. That element of danger is… Well, it's a turn-on. But you're not the same man who made love to me all day."

"I'm not?"

"You're more like the guy in the ski mask who kidnapped me in my van and stuck a gun in my face."

Though he wanted to give his full attention to Rachel, his gaze focused on Prescott, who stood at the window, staring out at the snow. "That was my undercover identity. You know, like an actor playing a role."

"Actors don't carry real guns."

"True," he conceded.

He wasn't an actor following a safe little script that led to the inevitable happy ending. When he went undercover, he took on another identity. From the way he combed his hair to the way he handled his weapons, he was different. He couldn't risk showing a single glimpse of himself, and he never knew how it would all end.

"You're scaring me, Cole. You're so closed off, so tough, so cold. Your eyes don't even reflect the light. You're dangerous. And it's a real danger, the kind that got Penny killed."

He could feel her pulling away as though she was walking backward into a mist, fading into a memory. "I don't want to lose you."

"I'm not blaming you. It's your job. It's what you do."

He'd work this out with her later. "We have to make a decision. Do we turn ourselves in?"

"Is it safe?"

"I'd feel better if I knew Baron's identity. I'd have a bargaining chip."

Thus far, his undercover assignment was shaping up to be an unmitigated failure. Four people, including Penny and Frank, were dead. And he was only a few inches closer to finding the mastermind who caused those deaths and engineered a chain of robberies throughout the west.

"You hate to quit," she said.

"Right, again."

"And you promised Pearl that you'd find the man responsible for Penny's murder."

He nodded. "The only way we'll really be safe is when Baron is found, and the traitor in the FBI is identified."

A grin lifted the corners of her mouth. He knew she wasn't trying to be sexy, but that energy emanated from her. "I say the hell with Prescott."

"I've never wanted to kiss somebody so much in my life."

"Kiss me later. Right now, we need to get away from here."

As they returned to the front of Lily Belle's ice cream parlor, a plan was already taking shape in his mind. He confronted Prescott. "Where were we?"

The pinched eyebrows and the scowl had become a permanent fixture on Prescott's face. "I want an update on your investigation."

"You'll have to wait."

Prescott glared and looked him straight in the eye in an attempt to assert his authority as the higher ranking agent. "You need to start cooperating with me. Tell me what you've learned about Baron."

Cole had two options: keep quiet or dribble out just enough information to get a response. This was a chess game played with hubris and cunning. Spending years undercover gave Cole the clear advantage; he knew how to manipulate people to get information.

He made the first move, starting with the truth. "Baron is the baby's daddy."

Without admitting or denying, Prescott asked, "Will DNA confirm that relationship?" It was a sideways move.

"Penny named him. She grew up in this area."

Prescott's nod was a signal of confidence. "I have background on her. She went to high school in Granby."

"Is that how you tracked her mother?"

"Finding Pearl Richards didn't take any complicated sleuthing." Prescott moved toward bragging. Clearly, he thought he was winning this game. "She had her mail forwarded to the house in Grand Lake."

Cole shot him down. "But you didn't know that the owner of the house also owned the ice cream parlor."

"No, I didn't."

"But you're familiar with the Grand County area," Cole said, remembering what Deputy Loughlin had told them.

"I've been up here a couple of times. I used to be the information liaison for the FBI in Colorado."

A piece of new information. How did it fit? "You did public relations?"

"Checking in with the locals. Giving Q-and-A talks. Creating an FBI presence. In some of these remote areas, weirdo militia groups can take root. It's good if the local people have someone they've met and can talk with."

"So you know people around here." That could be a useful attribute if he was working with Baron. Cole pushed with a more aggressive move. "Is there a more personal reason you've spent time around here?"

"No."

Prescott had hesitated slightly before answering; Cole knew that he'd hit a nerve. The game shifted to his advantage. "Ever owned property in Grand County?"

"This isn't about me." An edge of anger crept into his voice.

"I think maybe it is."

"Damn it, McClure. I offered you a deal to go into custody. I'll take care of you. Trust me."

"I never trust anybody who uses those words."

"My actions speak louder." A red flush colored Prescott's throat. He was getting angry, losing control. "I'm here to help. I didn't kill you when I had the chance."

"You never had that chance." He gestured for Rachel to stay back, out of harm's way.

"Get real, McClure. Frank was charging after you like a wounded grizzly. I had a gun, and you were unarmed."

It was time to take Agent Wayne Prescott down. This was the endgame.

Since they'd both had the same FBI training in H2H, hand-to-hand combat, Cole decided to avoid a real fight. His plan wasn't to hurt Prescott. Just to show him who was boss.

A pat on the shoulder and a light slap on the ear distracted Prescott enough for Cole to slip his gun from the holster and drop it on the floor. Likely, Prescott was carrying other weapons. Probably had a knife in those pockets where he kept hiding his hands. And an ankle holster.

He blocked a punch with his forearm and waded in closer. Cole ducked. When he popped up, he spun the agent around and pulled off his jacket. He had him in a choke hold.

The whole altercation took less than a minute.

"Here's the deal," Cole said. "I want your vehicle."

"Why?"

Cole released him. "You have to stay here and deal with poor old Frank. And I have someplace to go."

"I'm urging you to turn yourself in. I can't call off the manhunt. Every cop in the state is looking for you, and they are authorized to use force."

"I'm not walking away from this assignment until it's done," Cole said. "Now it's time for you to trust me."

When Prescott leaned down to pick his parka off the floor, he reached for his ankle holster.

Anticipating the move, Cole already had the gun he'd slipped from Prescott's holster pointed in his face. *Checkmate.*

Chapter Sixteen

Fat snowflakes splatted against the windshield of Prescott's four-wheel-drive SUV. A nice vehicle for driving in the snow; Cole understood why Prescott was willing to fight instead of handing over the keys.

As soon as they got into the car, he'd searched the glove box and found nothing but a neat packet containing registration and proof of insurance. Prescott was a careful man. A career agent. He hadn't given up any information, except the part about him being a liaison and knowing people in the area. Somehow that had to be useful.

Though this storm was nowhere near as violent as the blizzard, Cole hated driving through it. He gripped the steering wheel with both hands, willing the tires not to slip on the snow-packed road leading away from Grand Lake. On the plus side, the bad weather was keeping cars off the road. If anybody followed them, the taillights would be easy to spot.

Rachel held his cell phone but hadn't yet dialed. "I don't want to drag Jim Loughlin into this mess. Cole, it's getting worse and worse. You assaulted a federal officer."

"I *am* a federal officer," he said. "A damn better one than Prescott. And we need your friend to help us."

"Why?"

"I'm pretty sure this nice SUV has GPS. Prescott can track our location."

His plan was to drop off Prescott's car at the house where they were attacked. Like it or not, the feds and the cops would be forced to look at that house and to realize the murders had been committed there. Even a rudimentary crime-scene analysis would show evidence of a major assault. Their investigation would take a different direction—leading *away* from them.

Unfortunately, when the cops checked the property records, they'd see the connection between Xavier Romero and Baron. If Cole wanted to get information from Romero, he needed to contact him before Prescott and his men closed in.

Rachel asked, "What do you want Loughlin to do?"

"Ask him to meet us at the house. He's already been there so he knows the location. I want him to give us a lift."

"Where to?"

"How much he wants to be involved is up to him. Make the call, Rachel. The alternative is another hike through the snow." He dared to take his eyes off the road for an instant to glance at her. "You don't want that, do you?"

As she made the call, he followed the route that he vaguely remembered from the first time the gang went to the house where three of them had died. Navigating in the mountains on these twisting roads that were half-hidden by snow took 90 percent of his concentration. With the other 10 percent, he figured out what they should do next.

Initially, he'd thought they would find Penny's friend, Jenna Cambridge, in Granby and pick up the bundles of cash to use as evidence. Now, it was more imperative to hightail it over to Black Hawk to see Xavier Romero. In the past, the old snitch had helped Cole out with information. Romero might be able to cut through the crap and give him Baron's name.

It was becoming obvious that the only way Cole would end this assignment successfully was to apprehend Baron by himself and turn him over to the cops.

"Okay," Rachel said, "Loughlin will meet us at the house."

"Good." He made a left turn. Was this the route? He wished like hell that he was driving on a clean, paved, well-marked California freeway.

"What's going to happen next?"

"I'm going to have a talk with Xavier Romero."

"In Black Hawk? You can't ask Loughlin to drive all the way to Black Hawk."

"I'm hoping he'll loan us his car."

"That's a lot to ask," she said. "He could be charged with aiding and abetting fugitives."

"If we were criminals, he'd be in trouble. But we're not. Remember? We're the good guys."

"I'm an upstanding citizen, but I'm not so sure about you."

That wasn't the way she'd felt when they were lying in each other's arms. She'd snuggled intimately beside him. They were one. Not anymore.

In the real world—the one where she lived in snow-ridden Colorado and he resided in sunny California—he and Rachel were very different people. He lived by deception, and she couldn't tell a lie to save her life. He was no stranger to violence; she was a healer. Different.

And yet, there was a level where they matched perfectly. He didn't quite understand the connection. In a way, she filled in the places where he was lacking. And vice versa.

She gave him a solid grounding. He gave her...excitement.

She'd never admit it, but he'd seen the fire in her eyes. Every time they'd been at risk, she had risen to the challenge. He wanted her with him, didn't trust her safety to anyone else, not even Loughlin. But he couldn't ask her to continue on this dangerous path. He needed to do what was right for her.

When he recognized a road sign, he almost cheered. They were headed in the right direction. "This might be a good time for you to take shelter. When I go to Black Hawk, you could stay with the Loughlins."

"Are you trying to get rid of me?"

"I'm trying to keep you safe. Think about it."

Their tire tracks blazed the first trail through the new snow piling up on the road. He would have worried about being followed if that hadn't been his intention; he wanted the cops to come to this house.

"I'm thinking," she said. "If I stay with the Loughlins, I'm putting them in danger. Those guys who attacked the house are still out there."

"The odds are in your favor. Nobody has reason to suspect you'd be with a deputy sheriff."

"But if they guess…" She exhaled a sigh. "This isn't about being safe and smart. Here's the truth. I want to come with you."

He didn't understand, but he liked her decision. "Because?"

"Are you going to make me say it?"

"Oh, yeah."

"I care about you, Cole. I can't imagine being apart from you, sitting around and worrying. Too much of my life has been wasted with sensible decisions. I'm going to follow my heart and stick with you."

He couldn't remember another time when he'd been a heartfelt choice. "I care about you, too."

"Besides," she said, "I can help. You need a partner."

"I've always worked alone."

"Things change."

He made the last turn into the driveway outside the house, put the car in Park but left the engine running. He turned toward her. In the dim illumination from the dashboard, he saw her smile. "Clearly, you've lost your mind."

"Clearly."

He unfastened her seat belt and pulled her toward him. "I'm so damn glad."

WHEN JIM LOUGHLIN pulled up in his four-wheel-drive Jeep, Rachel made a quick introduction. Cole sat in the passenger seat, and she got into the back. During their time on the run, she'd grown accustomed to the way they looked. Their clothes were filthy, bloodstained and torn from catching on branches. Cole's stubble was turning into a full beard. They might as well have the word *fugitive* branded across their foreheads.

Loughlin glanced over his shoulder at her and shook his head. "Hard to believe you're the same woman who helped my sweet Caitlyn into this world."

A lot had changed since then. "How's she doing? Is Sarah okay?"

"They're both great, especially since my mom went home." He put the Jeep in gear and pulled away from the house where the killing had taken place.

Cole said, "I appreciate your help."

"I'd do just about anything for Rachel." He expertly swung onto the road. "She seems to like you. That makes you okay in my book. But I'm hoping you've decided to turn yourselves in and end this."

"I'd like to pack it in," Cole said, "but we're still not

safe. There's a traitor in the FBI network. He's working with Baron, and he's not going to let us live. We know too much."

From the backseat, Rachel said, "We need a favor. You don't have to say yes. I'm only asking."

Loughlin drove for a long minute in silence while he considered. She knew this was a hard decision for him. On one hand was his duty as a deputy. On the other was his innate sense of what was right and wrong. Did he believe in her enough to go along with them?

In his deep rumbling voice, Loughlin said, "Name it."

"We need to get to Black Hawk," she said. "We have to talk to a man who—"

"Don't tell me why. I don't want to know." He held up his hand to forestall further conversation. "I can't take you there on account of I need to stay with Sarah and the baby. But you can use my car."

"There's one more thing," Cole said. "We need clothes."

"You're right about that," Loughlin said. "When we get to my house, I'll pull into the garage. You stay here in the car, and I'll bring some stuff down to you. I haven't told Sarah about any of this, and I don't intend to."

"Thanks," Cole said. "I'd be happy to pay you."

"Don't want your money," he grumbled. "Use it to make a donation to Rachel's clinic."

She unhooked her seat belt, leaned forward and gave Loughlin a kiss on the cheek. "You're a good guy."

"Or a crazy one."

She grinned. "There seems to be a lot of that going around."

Settling back into her seat, Rachel realized that she was feeling positive. Crazy? Oh, yeah. Ever since Cole kidnapped her, she'd been caught up in a sort of madness—an emotional tempest that plunged to the depth of terror and then soared. Their passion was unlike anything she'd ever experienced. She wanted to be with him forever, to follow him to the ends of the earth, in spite of the peril. *The very real peril.* She couldn't let herself forget that they were still the subjects of a manhunt, not to mention being sought by Baron's murderous thugs. And they were on their way to chat with a snitch.

None of the other bad boys she'd dated came close to Cole when it came to danger. Why was she grinning?

She only halfway listened to the conversation from the two men in the front of the Jeep. Cole was telling Loughlin about Prescott's role as an FBI liaison.

"He claimed," Cole said, "that he'd met a lot of people in Grand County."

"I recall that some years back there was an FBI agent who talked at a couple of town councils when we had a problem with militia groups setting up camp in the back country."

"Can you think of any other connections he might have?"

"Maybe church meetings. Or Boy Scouts. The idea is to give folks a face—a real live person they can call at the FBI. We do the same thing at the sheriff's department. Right now, we've got a program to get teenagers off their damn cell phones when they're driving."

Rachel had a brain flash. "The high school."

"What's that?" Cole asked.

"Prescott could have given an informational talk at the high school. I do those programs all the time. The teachers love it when I show up. It gives them a free period."

If Prescott had come to Granby High School when Penny was a student there, he could have met her. Through Penny, he might have linked up with Baron.

In deference to Loughlin's wishes not to know any more about what they were doing than absolutely necessary, she said nothing more, but her mind kept turning.

As soon as they were parked in Loughlin's two-car garage and she was alone with Cole, she said, "What if Prescott met Penny at the high school? Then she introduced him to Baron."

"Interesting theory. But I don't think Penny was a teenage criminal mastermind."

"From what she told me and what her mother said, she was wild. The kind of kid who gets into trouble."

Instead of pursuing her line of thinking, he grinned. "They say it takes one to know one. Were you a wild child?"

"I had my share of adventures," she admitted. "And really bad luck with the guys I dated."

"Bad boys. Like me."

He left the passenger seat and came around to open her door. In the glare from the overhead light, she realized how truly ratty and beat up his clothes were. In spite of the grime and the scruffy beard, she liked the way he looked. One hundred percent masculine.

She slid off the seat and into his arms. Looking up at him, she said, "You're not a bad boy. Dangerous? Yes. But not bad."

His long, slow kiss sent a heat wave through her veins. Definitely not bad.

Before their kiss progressed into something inappropriate, Loughlin returned to the garage with fresh clothing. He set the pile of coats, shoes and clothing on his cluttered workbench against the back wall and turned to Rachel. "Could I talk to you in private?"

She went with him through the garage door into a back hallway. "What is it?"

He took both her hands in his and leaned down to peer into her eyes. In a low whisper, he asked, "Is this really what you want? To go with Cole?"

"Yes."

"Rachel, you could get hurt."

"It's worth the risk. *Cole* is worth it."

"You just met this man a couple of days ago," Loughlin said. "You've only known him for a matter of hours."

But she wanted to believe that Cole was the man she'd been looking for all her life. She'd gone through a string of losers—so many that she'd almost given up on men altogether. If she didn't take this chance, she'd regret it. "I'm sure."

He pulled her into a bear hug. "I trust your instincts, girl. Try to be careful."

"I will." His concern touched her. He and Sarah and their baby were like family to her. "Your friendship means a lot."

"Just don't wreck my car. Okay?"

She returned to the garage to find Cole dressed in fresh jeans and a cream-colored turtleneck. Though Loughlin was heavier than Cole, they were the same height. The new outfit was a decent fit.

"A major improvement," she said. "Except for the scruffy beard."

"I thought you liked the rugged mountain-man thing."

"But you're not a mountain man. You're a clean-shaven dude from California."

"Apparently, your friend thinks so, too." He held up an electric razor. "I'm not sure if I should shave. The cops have probably circulated ID photos of me. I don't want to be recognized. On the other hand, a beard could attract closer scrutiny. It's an obvious disguise."

She hadn't considered photos. "Will they have a picture of me?"

"It's possible. But, as you pointed out before, a lot of people in this area know you. If they saw your photo, they'd suspect something was wrong with the manhunt."

"I hope you're right. There's nothing I can do with my short hair except put on a wig or a hat."

He held up a wool knit Sherpa hat with ear flaps. "Ta da."

"I love these." She grabbed it and put it on. "Mmm. Warm."

"Warm and damn cute." He gave her a grin. "I was thinking about your theory of Prescott meeting Penny at the high school."

"And?"

"What was the first thing he asked when he found us?"

He had wanted to know about Goldie, wanted to know that she was safe. His concern for the infant was apparent. "The baby."

"Why? Why would that be his first question?"

"He could be the father."

Agent Wayne Prescott might be Baron.

Chapter Seventeen

As they drove to a lower elevation, they left the snowstorm behind. Rachel gazed through the passenger-side window at pinprick stars in the clear night sky. Leaning back in the comfortable seat, she listened to the hum of the Jeep's tires on clear pavement. The only sign of the blizzard that had paralyzed Grand County was a frosting of white on moonlit trees and the rocky walls of the canyon leading to Black Hawk.

The more temperate weather had an obvious effect on Cole, the California guy. His mood was more contemplative. His death grip on the steering wheel had relaxed. The worry lines across his forehead smoothed, and he was almost smiling. With his left hand, he massaged his clean-shaven jaw. Losing the beard made him appear less ferocious and more handsome.

Jim Loughlin had been right when he said she didn't know much about Cole. Even when they were making love, he hadn't talked about his past. Did she want to know? Did she really want to see Cole as more than a casual affair?

Connecting to him on a deeper level was dangerous. He hadn't represented himself as relationship material. Sure, there were the occasional hints that he'd like to see more of her. But nothing he'd said—not one single word—resembled a commitment.

On the other hand, she had taken the ultimate risk when she had unprotected sex with him. Caught up in the whirlwind of their passion, she'd made that decision. Maybe not the smartest thing she'd ever done. Didn't she give lectures to high school classes on exactly this topic? No condom means no sex.

She'd broken her own rule.

For the first time.

Wow.

With other boyfriends, even men she thought she was in love with, she had never once taken that chance. Clearly, there was something special about Cole and she needed to know more about him.

Clearing her throat, she asked, "Did you grow up in California?"

"Mostly."

Not a very revealing answer. She'd have to be more specific. "Where were you born?"

"Vegas."

Now they might be getting somewhere. Cole was in his thirties. When he was born, Las Vegas had been more decadent and edgy than it was now. "Did your parents work in the casinos?"

"Nope."

Another one word response. *Great.* "How long did you live there?"

He turned his head toward her. Moonlight through the windshield shone on the sculpted line of his jaw. "There's no need for you to go on a fishing expedition. If there's something specific you want to know about me, just ask."

"I'm curious," she said. "I want to get an idea of where

you came from. How did you grow up to be an undercover FBI agent? What were you like as a kid?"

"I always played with guns." He grinned. "My mom wouldn't let me or my younger brother bring our violent toys into the house. She was a pacifist. A grade school teacher."

"And your father?"

"Dad was a preacher in Vegas—a reformed gambler who started his own church. I can't remember the name of it, but there was a lot of 'repent and be saved' going on."

"You were a preacher's kid." She wouldn't have guessed that background. "If the stereotypes hold true, that means you were either annoyingly perfect or a holy terror."

"I didn't have time to get settled into either personality. I was only five when my parents split up. Marrying my mother and having kids went along with Dad's preacher identity. But it didn't last."

"He went back to gambling," she guessed.

"It turned out that he had a lot of loyal followers, and they donated bundles of cash to build a new rec hall for the church. Dad thought the Lord might help him find a greater contribution in the casinos. Apparently, God was looking the other way."

"He lost the money."

"Not all of it, but a significant portion. The crazy thing was that he admitted what he'd done, and his followers forgave him. Mom wasn't so easy to con. She divorced him and moved us to Los Angeles."

"Did your dad stay in Vegas?"

"For a while. After he paid back the money, he handed over the church to his assistant and devoted himself full-time to gambling. He does okay. He paid child support and stayed in touch with the family. Whenever he showed up, he always had big extravagant presents."

She was beginning to have a context for understanding Cole. "Were you more like your dad or your mom?"

"I've got a bit of the con man in me," he admitted.

"Which is why you're so good at going undercover."

"But I get my sense of fair play and loyalty from my mom. I never once heard her say a bad thing about my father. She remarried several years ago and moved to Oregon."

"And your brother?"

"He's a fireman. Happily married with two little girls whom I love to spoil."

"By showing up with big extravagant presents?"

He shot her a glance. "I never thought of it that way. Maybe I'm more like my dad than I realize."

"Do you gamble?"

"I'm a hell of a good poker player, but I don't have the sickness. I hate losing too much."

They were on the last curving stretch of road through the canyon that led to Black Hawk. The roads were pristine—well-maintained by casino and hotel owners who wanted to make the trip easy and smooth.

"What we're doing right now is a gamble," she pointed out. "You're taking a chance on being recognized at a casino where you committed a robbery."

"I was wearing a ski mask. Nobody saw my face."

"What if the police put out a photo of you?"

"I've got new identification from the papers I had sewn inside my leather jacket." He shrugged. "If somebody thinks they saw me before, I can talk my way around it."

She wished she had half his confidence. If somebody

accused her of being one of the fugitives the FBI was looking for, she'd fall apart. "And what should I do?"

"Say as little as possible. I'm going to introduce you as my associate, even though most FBI agents tend to wear more conservative attire."

The clothing she'd borrowed from Sarah Loughlin was a size too small. The jeans hugged her bottom, and the pink knit top stretched tightly across her breasts. Even the lavender parka was fitted at the waist. Rachel missed her oversize practical parka. "Too cutesy?"

"Not if you put on the cap with the ear flaps."

"Then I would definitely be too dorky," she said. "Should I have a different name? Can I be Special Agent Angelina?"

"It's better if you have a name you can relate to. Do you have a nickname?"

"My youngest brother calls me Rocky."

"Short for Rachel. I like it. For the last name, let's use the street where you lived as a kid."

"Logan. Call me Special Agent Rocky Logan."

He grinned. "Xavier thinks my name is Calvin Spade. I met him a long time ago, probably eight years, when he was involved in an illegal gambling operation in Culver City. I went in as a card shark, and I did okay in a couple of tournaments. Then I recruited Xavier as a snitch."

She was beginning to feel apprehensive. "I've never been good at lying. Maybe my identity should be something more familiar. Like a nurse."

He reached over and stroked her cheek. "Don't try to play a role. Just be yourself. Go along with whatever I say."

"Roll with the punches."

"Let's hope it doesn't come to that."

The lights of Black Hawk glittered against the dark

slopes and the surrounding forest. Extralarge new casinos and parking structures bumped up against the older buildings that had been part of the historic town before limited stakes gambling was legalized here and in neighboring Central City.

Xavier's casino—the Stampede—was at the quiet end of town away from the new casinos. Cole parked at the far end of the half-full lot. On a weekday night at eleven o'clock, there weren't many cars.

He killed the headlights and turned to her. "If you want, you can stay in the car. I don't expect this to take too long."

Pulling off an undercover identity was daunting, but she wanted to do it. The best way to understand Cole was to see him in action. "I'm ready. Let's go."

As they walked through the crisp night to the casino that appeared to be in a renovated barn, she noticed his sense of humor falling away from him. His posture shifted. His shoulders seemed wider. His height, more impressive.

Trying to match his cool attitude, she narrowed her eyes to a squint. *Agent Rocky Logan is on the job. Bad guys, beware.*

The interior of the casino was similar to an Old West saloon. Rows of slot machines blinked and made clinking noises as though money was pouring out of them. In truth, there were only a few people at the slots. Most of the patrons were huddled around the poker tables.

Cole strode up to the bar. He ordered a couple of beers and asked the bartender—who sported an old-fashioned handlebar mustache—where he could find the old man, Xavier Romero. "Tell him Calvin Spade wants to talk."

The bartender left his post and went through an unmarked door at the rear of the casino. Her apprehension was turning into full-blown anxiety. Her hand trembled as she lifted the beer to her lips. What if Xavier was calling the cops? What if Baron's armed thugs charged out of the back room?

Cole gave her arm a nudge. When she looked up at him, she saw a flash of the familiar Cole—the guy she knew and trusted. He gave her a wink. "It's going to be all right."

She wanted to believe him, but she'd used those very words often when she was dealing with a difficult labor. *It's going to be all right.* An empty reassurance. The pain always got worse before it got better.

When the bartender returned, a short man with white hair and black-rimmed glasses trotted at his heels. He was solidly built but light on his feet. He came to a stop in front of Cole and did a two-fisted handshake. When he smiled, she saw the gleam of a gold tooth.

"It's been a long time." Xavier's voice was a whisper. He swung toward her. "Who's the broad?"

"My associate, Rocky Logan," Cole said. "This is Xavier Romero."

He took her hand and raised it to his lips. "Charmed. When he says 'associate' does he mean you're—"

"We work at the same place," Cole said. "I want to talk to you in private."

Xavier stepped back and gave them both a golden grin. "Take a look around, buddy boy. Finally got my own place. And it's legit."

"The Stampede," Cole said drily. "I never figured you for a cowboy-themed casino."

"Yippee-ki-yay."

Cole said, "I didn't come to talk about the decor."

"We had some good times, you and me. Remember that Texas Hold 'em tournament in Culver City? When I was dating that sweet little redheaded dealer?"

"Didn't come to reminisce, either."

"You were always impatient. Good things come to those who wait. I'm living proof. Seventy years old, and my dream finally comes true."

If she hadn't known that Xavier was involved with Baron and in the midst of a scheme to defraud his insurance company, she would have liked the old man.

Cole pushed away from the bar. "We'll go to your office. Giddyap."

Though she thought he was being unnecessarily rude, Rachel fell into step behind him. There wasn't enough room between the tables and the slot machines to walk side by side. Xavier hustled to the front of their little parade. He used a key card to open the door and ushered them into a wide hallway with paneled walls and framed sepia photographs of old-time Black Hawk and the gold rush prospectors who populated the town.

The door to his office was open, and Xavier guided them inside. In addition to his cluttered desk, there were a couple of leather sofas and an octagonal poker table covered in green felt. The scent of cigar smoke hung in the air, and she suspected that smoking wasn't the only law that had been broken in this room.

The overhead light, unlike the dimness of the casino, showed a road map of wrinkles on Xavier's face. He sat at the poker table and picked up a deck of cards. "Have a seat."

Cole positioned himself facing the door. "Tell me how you know Baron."

Xavier shuffled the cards with stunning expertise. "Let's play a little five-card stud. No reason we can't be civilized while we talk."

"The last time I played you," Cole said, "I won."

"Give me a chance to get even. If you win again, I'll tell you whatever you want to know."

Cole took the cards from his hand and passed them to her. "Rocky deals."

She knew how to play poker but wasn't an expert. If Cole was expecting her to cheat and give him winning cards, he'd be sorely disappointed. She cut the cards twice and palmed the deck. "Five cards, facedown."

Xavier fixed her with a steady gaze. "Have you been with Calvin long?"

Calvin? Oh, yeah, that was Cole's alias. "Long enough," she said as she dealt.

He tapped his gold tooth with the tip of his index finger. Unlike his weathered face, his hands were smooth. His fingernails, buffed to perfection. "I'm surprised," he said, "to see Calvin with a partner. He usually works alone."

"Things change," Cole said.

"Indeed." Xavier chuckled. "I used to be a petty crook. Now I'm a casino owner."

"Hard to believe that a wheeler-dealer like you is completely legit." He glanced at his cards and turned them facedown on the table. "How did you put together the money to open this place?"

"I know people."

"Baron?"

Xavier checked his cards, pulled out two and slid them toward her. "Hit me."

Cole held up his hand, indicating that he didn't need any more cards. "I'm thinking that you might have used property for collateral to raise cash. A house near Shadow Mountain Lake."

"Or maybe I gambled big in the big game, the stock market. And maybe I was smart enough to get out before the crash." Xavier's wrinkles settled into an expression-less poker face. "If you win this hand, I'll tell you one fact. Then we can play for another and—"

"All or nothing," Cole said. "You don't have much time. All I want is information on Baron. The feds that are going to show up here after me won't be so gentle."

"You? Gentle?" He shook his head. "If I win this hand, you tell me what you know. Then get the hell out."

"I don't lose." Cole's hands on the table were steady. His deep-set eyes radiated confidence. "I'll tell you this for free. Your house near Shadow Mountain Lake was being used as a hideout. People were killed there."

Xavier blinked. "The idiots who robbed my place?"

"The gang was at your house. Not even the dumbest pencil-pushing fed is going to believe that was a coinci-dence. You were in on the robbery."

"This isn't happening." The old man shook his head slowly. "You're lying. Trying to bluff me."

"Not this time."

Cole turned over his cards. Full house, jacks over tens.

Chapter Eighteen

The only sure way to win at poker was to cheat, and Cole had been learning card tricks from his less-than-holy father before he could read and write. When he'd taken the deck from Xavier, straightened the edges and passed it to Rachel, he'd palmed the cards necessary to play a winning hand.

A simple move. Cole assumed Xavier had been planning to deal himself a winner from the bottom of the deck, so he took those five cards. Voilà! A full house.

Winning was convenient, but he didn't really need that nudge. Xavier was ready to talk; the threat of an FBI investigation into his connection to known criminals had already loosened his lips. He readily admitted that he'd been in touch with Baron when he set up his initial financing. Further, he said that he'd agreed to the casino robbery, knowing that he could claim his missing cash from the insurance company.

"Then everything went wrong," Xavier said. "One of my moron security guards—a guy who's usually asleep in a back room—got trigger happy. Somebody else pulled the alarm."

Cole knew how badly the robbery had been botched.

He'd been there. "On the surface, the shoot-out makes it look like you double-crossed Baron."

"It wasn't my fault. I swear it."

Having experienced Baron's wrath when his men peppered the Shadow Mountain Lake house with bullets, Cole was surprised that Xavier wasn't already dead. "There's another piece to the robbery. You're running an insurance scam of your own. You put in a claim for double the amount that was stolen."

"What?"

"You heard me."

Xavier's poker face crumpled. "There's only one way you could know how much was stolen. You were part of the gang."

In order to extract information, Cole needed to balance truth with deception. He had to apply the right amount of pressure and not show his own disadvantages.

Leaning across the table toward Xavier, he said, "You weren't surprised to see me when I walked in the door. You already knew I was one of the robbers. The feds have already sent you my mug shot."

A twitch at the corner of Xavier's mouth confirmed the statement. *He knew.*

Cole continued, "I infiltrated the gang. I was working undercover."

Though confident in his ability to manipulate the old man, Cole had a weak spot, and her name was Special Agent Rocky Logan. Rachel had already told him that she was a lousy liar. He couldn't predict what she'd say.

Apparently, Xavier realized the same thing. He turned toward her and glared through his thick glasses. "What about you, pretty lady? Where do you fit in?"

She narrowed her big blue eyes to a squint—an expression that she probably thought made her look tough. Cole thought she was adorable.

"I advise you to listen to my partner," she said. "He's trying to help you."

"Is he?"

Cole said, "I've got a soft spot when it comes to you, Xavier. A long time ago, you pointed me in the right direction. Do the same thing now. Tell me about Baron."

Xavier leaned back in his chair. "I've never met the man in person. I couldn't ID him if he walked through the door right now. And I don't know where he lives. When I talked to him on the phone, the calls were untraceable."

"It's hard to believe you set up complicated financial dealings without a meeting."

"His secretary handled the paperwork."

Secretary? "You met the secretary?"

"Sure did, but I can't give you a good description. She was wearing a wig and a ton of makeup. Nice breasts, though. She showed plenty of cleavage."

The makeup sounded like Penny. She applied it with a trowel. "How about her age?"

"The older I get," Xavier said, "the younger the ladies look to me. I'd guess that she was in her thirties."

"When did you see her last?"

"A couple of weeks ago. She was with a pregnant woman."

Therefore, the secretary was *not* Penny. Then who? Cole had been part of the gang at that time, but he'd never come to Black Hawk with Penny. A memory clicked in the back of his mind: Pearl had mentioned meeting her daughter here.

Was Penny's mother working for Baron? He didn't want to believe that he'd been so blinded by guilt about Penny's murder that he'd handed over the baby to another crook. When he'd looked into Pearl's eyes, he hadn't seen a hint of deception. She'd been heartbroken about her daughter's death and ecstatic about her new grandbaby. "Did she wear jewelry? Maybe a string of pearls."

Rachel gasped. If she hadn't been thinking of Pearl, she was now.

Xavier pointed to his nicely manicured hands. "Just an engagement ring. A diamond. Not too flashy."

That didn't sound like Penny's mother. She hadn't been wearing an engagement ring when they saw her. Who was this mystery woman? Finding her was the key to finding Baron.

"I played square with you," Xavier said. "What are you going to do to help me?"

"I suggest you call your insurance company and tell them you made a mistake about the amount of money stolen. They haven't made a payout yet. They might let you off the hook."

"Or refuse to pay." Behind his glasses, his eyes darkened. "I need that money to keep going. The whole gang is dead except for you. If you could see your way clear to—"

"Can't do it," Cole said. "We have the loot."

The lie slipped easily off his tongue. But Rachel wasn't so calm. She fidgeted.

And Xavier noticed her nervous move. He zeroed in on her. "Do you? Have the money?"

Before she could stammer out an unconvincing answer, Cole rose from the green felt table. "We're going."

Rachel dropped the cards and stood. Her hands were trembling.

"You don't have the cash," Xavier said. "Baron's procedure is to get the money away from the robbers as soon as possible so they won't get greedy."

"We know where it is," Rachel said. "In a safe place."

The old man sprang to his feet with shocking agility for a man of his years. "Take me with you. If I can turn in the money and prove that I'm working with the good guys, I could get out of this okay."

"Not a chance," Cole said.

"For old times' sake," he pleaded. "We've got history together. I know your friends. Whatever happened to your buddy from Vegas? That old guy named McClure?"

Moving swiftly and deliberately, Cole came around the table and took Rachel's arm. As soon as he touched her, he knew he'd made a mistake. Xavier would see that his relationship to her was more than a professional association.

He rushed her toward the door. To Xavier, he said, "I'll take care of you."

Instead of making their way through the tables and slot machines in the front of the casino, Cole went to the rear. He pulled Rachel with him through a back door, setting off a screeching alarm.

They ran to Loughlin's Jeep, dove inside and pulled out of the parking lot. As they were driving away, he saw the local police converge on the Stampede casino.

RACHEL HELD HER BREATH as Cole eased out of the casino parking lot with his headlights dark. How could he see? Moonlight wasn't enough.

Sensing a turn, he whipped onto a side road that led past a row of houses. He turned again and headed uphill. The headlights flashed on. He took another turn and another, still climbing. Without snow on the road, his driving skills were expert but scary. She averted her gaze so she couldn't see the speedometer as he fishtailed around a hairpin turn and started a descent. He flew down the narrow canyon road as fast as an alpine skier on the last run of the day.

Across an open field, he drove into forested land. The tall pine trees closed around them, and he slowed.

She exhaled. "How many times in your life have you made dramatic getaways?"

"Often."

Her heart thumped so furiously that she thought her rib cage might explode. Her fingers clenched in a knot. Her skin prickled with an excess of adrenaline. Clearly, she wasn't cut out for undercover work.

Not like Cole. He didn't show the least sign of nervousness. Not now. And not in the casino. The whole time he'd been baiting Xavier, his aura of cool confidence had been unshaken. "How do you do this?"

"Not very well," he muttered.

"You're kidding, right? You were like an old-time riverboat gambler. Sooooo smooth. Always one step ahead, even in that weird poker game. You cheated, right?"

"Yeah."

"If I wasn't familiar with the facts, I wouldn't have known when you were lying and when you were telling the truth. How did you learn to bluff like that?"

"Blame it on genetics. When I first joined the FBI, one of the shrinks told me that I was uniquely suited to undercover work because of my innate behavioral makeup. He gave me a battery of tests, including a lie detector, which I faked out."

"Not surprised," she muttered.

"It seems that I'm a natural born risk-seeker. Most people are risk-averse, more cautious."

"That would be me," she said.

"Not from what you've told me about your boyfriends."

"Okay, maybe I have a risk-seeking lapse when it comes to men. But I'm careful in every other area."

"Being an EMT? Riding in an ambulance?"

"I left that work." Because she couldn't stand the pain of failure. "In every other way, I'm careful."

"And yet, you're riding in a getaway car. You could have backed out at the Loughlins', but you chose to come with me."

She had to admit that he had a point. They weren't total opposites but definitely not peas in a pod. For one thing, she couldn't tell a convincing lie to save her life. "The way you handled Xavier was amazing. You played him."

"But I slipped up," he said. "When we were leaving the room, I took your arm. That's not the kind of gesture I'd use with another FBI agent. And you can bet that Xavier saw that I wanted to protect you. He's no dummy. The old guy knows you're important to me."

"And that's a bad thing?"

"It's a tell," he said. "Like in poker. You never want your opponents to know what you're thinking. I let him see that you're important to me."

In a way, she was touched. In spite of the con, he couldn't keep himself from responding to her. She looked down at her lap and pried her fingers apart. Then she reached toward him. When her hand touched his smoothly shaven cheek, he glanced toward her and grinned.

In that instant of eye contact, she saw his defenses slip away. He really did care about her. She whispered, "What are we going to do for the rest of the night?"

"There are plenty of hotels in Black Hawk and Central City, but they're well-run and organized. The desk clerks might have my photo posted in front of their computers, especially after our escape from the Stampede."

"Right." She frowned. "Why exactly did you rush me out the back door?"

"I had an edgy feeling. When we first saw Xavier, he seemed to be stalling. Maybe he called somebody."

"But when we left, he wanted to come with us."

"I changed his mind," Cole said. "For tonight, I'm thinking of a small motel, a mom-and-pop operation."

Though she was glad that he wasn't planning to drive straight through to Granby and confront Jenna Cambridge, she asked, "Should we go after the money tonight?"

"Too tired. My slip with Xavier showed me that I'm not at the top of my game. I've got to be sharp when we go back to Granby."

Granby. Her home base. She would have loved to take him to her comfy condo, but she was well aware that her home was dangerous. The hunt for them was still active.

"I'm thinking," he said, "that Jenna might be Baron's mysterious secretary."

The same idea had occurred to Rachel. "It makes sense. Penny said that she met Baron at the high school where Jenna teaches."

"If she's the secretary, we could be walking into a trap at her house. Tomorrow is Friday. Jenna will be at the high school, and we'll have a chance to search her place for evidence without interference."

When Penny had talked about her supposed friend, she'd never mentioned a connection with Baron. Though Rachel hated to think ill of the dead, Penny hadn't been very perceptive. She'd cast Jenna in the role of a homely girl who needed advice on makeup and clothing—a nonentity, a sidekick.

The pattern was familiar. A flashy blonde like Penny always seemed to have a dull-as-dishwater friend tagging along. An accurate picture?

Penny's mother also considered Jenna to be a friend, until she found out that Jenna encouraged her daughter's relationship with Baron.

Cole cleared his throat. "There's another woman I suspect."

"Pearl."

Rachel hated that alternative. "If Pearl was working with Baron, why wouldn't she have told him we were hiding at Lily Belle's? We were there all day. His thugs could have attacked us at any time."

He nodded. "My gut tells me Pearl is innocent. But that might be wishful thinking. I've got to believe that Goldie is safe."

"Pearl won't hurt the baby," she said with certainty. "As soon as she took Goldie into her arms, she was in love, and there's nothing stronger than the bond that forms with an infant."

"I'll call her tomorrow morning," he said. "If she's working for Baron, I'll find out."

"How?"

He shrugged. "It'll come to me."

In other words, he would come up with a convincing lie. His talent for deception and manipulation was a bit unnerving; she couldn't be certain of anything he said to her. "Can you teach me how to lie?"

"Why would I do that? I like your honesty."

She wasn't so sure. The truth might be her downfall.

Chapter Nineteen

The adobe-style motel with a blinking vacancy sign promised low rates for skiers. Since nearby Eldora was one of the closest ski runs to Denver, not many people stayed in the area overnight. There were only four other vehicles parked outside the twelve units.

When Rachel entered room number nine, she felt oddly shy. Though she and Cole had spent the afternoon making passionate love, staying at a motel was different—not because there was a comfortable-looking bed or a shower with hot water. Tonight was planned; they intended to sleep together, and she couldn't claim that she'd been carried away by the drama of the moment. Being here with him represented a deliberate choice. A decision she'd regret?

Every step closer to him deepened the feelings that were building inside her, and it was hard to keep those emotions from turning into something that resembled love. She couldn't make that mistake. Cole wasn't made for a serious relationship. Ultimately, he'd go back to California and leave her in the mountains. They had no future. None at all.

While she opened a greasy bag of fried chicken they'd picked up at a drive-through, Cole did a poor man's version of surveillance and security. He checked the window in the small but clean bathroom to make sure they had an escape route. Then he shoved the dresser in front of the door.

"What if the bad guys climb in through the bathroom window?" she asked as she pulled out a bag of fries and a deep-fried chunk of white meat.

"They won't," he said. "The lock on the front door is so pitiful that a toddler could kick it open."

"Hence the dresser blockade."

He posted himself at the edge of the front window curtain to watch the parking lot. "Pass me a thigh."

"I had you figured for a breast man."

"I start with the thigh and savor the breast." He tossed her a grin. "But you already know that."

Earlier when they'd made love, she noticed that he paid particular attention to her breasts. The memory tickled her senses. "Have you always been that way? I mean, with other women?"

"You're starting again with the questions." He mimicked her tone and added, "Do you always give men the third degree?"

She washed down a bite of chicken with watery soda. "In the normal course of events, I don't jump into bed with somebody I've only known for a couple of days. There's a period of time when we talk and become familiar with each other."

"Is that so?"

"You might have heard of the concept. It's called dating."

"Touché."

Even though he spent a lot of time undercover, it was hard to believe that a good-looking, eligible guy like Cole hadn't gotten himself hooked once or twice. She asked, "Have you ever had a serious girlfriend? Someone you lived with?"

"You mean like settling down? It's not my thing."

"You must have a home base. A bachelor pad."

"I pay rent on an apartment, but I hardly ever spend time there. It took me over a year to hang pictures on the walls."

She knew exactly what he was talking about. One of her brothers was the same way. He lived in a square little room with a beat-up futon and used pizza boxes for a coffee table. "Sounds lonely."

"Sometimes." He peeked around the edge of the curtain and sighed. "I wish I could have a dog."

Great! His idea of a long-term commitment was canine. "What kind of dog?"

"Border collie," he said without hesitation. "They're smart and fast. And would come in handy if I ever wanted to herd sheep."

Dragging information from Cole was like trying to empty Grand Lake with a teaspoon. "Is that a secret fantasy? Being a shepherd?"

"There are times when I wouldn't mind having a ranch to tend and a couple of acres. Not heavy-duty farming but a place away from the crowds. A quiet place. Peaceful. Where I could raise…stuff." He gnawed at his chicken and avoided looking her in the eye. "Someday, I want to have a family. When I hang out with my nieces, I get this feeling. An attachment."

She remembered his look of wonderment when Goldie was born and his gentleness when he fed the baby her bottle. Maybe this undercover agent wasn't such a confirmed loner, after all. If so, she was glad. Cole was a good man who deserved the comforts of home—a safe haven after his razor-edge assignments.

But was that what he really wanted? A niggling doubt skulked in the shadows of her mind. He might be lying, saying words he knew she wanted to hear. Deception was second nature to him, innate.

Fearful of probing more deeply, she changed the subject. "How long are you going to stand at the window?"

He checked his wristwatch. "Another twenty minutes. There was a sign posted in the office—Open Until Eleven. If they turn out the lights and go to bed, I reckon we're safe until morning."

She finished off her chicken and retreated to the bathroom. Not the most modern of accommodations but the white tile and bland fixtures were clean. She shed Sarah Loughlin's clothes, turned on the hot water and stepped into a bathtub with a blue plastic shower curtain.

The steaming hot water felt good as it splashed into her face and sluiced down her body. Warmth spread through her, and the tension in her muscles began to unwind. She closed her eyes. The bonds of self-control loosened as she relaxed.

Big mistake. As soon as she let her guard down, her mind filled with images she didn't want to remember. Too many bad things had happened. They played in her head, one after another. Gruesome. Horrible. Sad.

Her eyelids popped open. She tried to focus. Through the plastic shower curtain, the bathroom was a blur.

When she held her hand in the shower spray, she imagined crimson blood oozing through her fingers. Frank's blood when he lay on the floor of the ice cream parlor. The blood that came when Goldie was born. Penny's blood when her life was taken.

More blood would spill before this was over. They were getting closer to Baron. The threat was building. Danger squeezed her heart. Not Cole's blood, she couldn't bear to lose him. Not like that.

A sob crawled up her throat, and she realized that she

was crying. Her tears mingled with the hot, rushing water. If only she could wash her memory clean and erase her fears.

Her knees buckled, and her hand slid down the white tile wall. With a gasp, she sat down in the bathtub. The shower pelted down on her. The steam clung to her pores.

She heard the bathroom door open. Cole asked, "Are you all right?"

Had she been weeping out loud? "I'm fine."

"The lights in the office are out."

"Great. Close the door."

She didn't want him to see her vulnerability. So far, she'd done a pretty good impression of somebody who could keep it together no matter what. She didn't want him to know that she was afraid. Or needy. That was the worst.

He closed the door but didn't leave the bathroom. "Rachel? Talk to me. You can say anything."

The tenderness in his voice cut through her like a knife. She doubled over into a ball with her head resting on her knees. "Go away."

He eased open the shower curtain. Humiliated by her weakness, she refused to look up at him.

"It's okay," he murmured. "You're going to be okay."

He turned off the shower and draped a towel around her shoulders. The cool air made her shiver. She wanted to move, to pull herself together. But she couldn't pretend that she was fine and dandy. She'd witnessed murders, had been attacked and pursued. Right now, it felt like too damn much to bear.

"You need to get into bed," Cole said as knelt on the floor beside the tub. "Under the covers where it's warm."

"Leave me alone."

His arm circled her back. With a second towel, he dried her face. She batted his hands away.

"Let me help you, Rachel. You're always helping others. It's your turn." His low voice soothed her. "When you're with a woman in labor, you guide her through the pain. That's your job, and you're good at it."

"So?"

"This is my job. The violence. The lies. The fear. And the guilt. It's not easy. If you take my hand, I can help you through it."

She allowed him to guide her into the bedroom, where she slipped between the sheets. Fully dressed except for his boots, he lay beside her and held her.

Though she snuggled against him, she was afraid to close her eyes, fearful of the memories that might return in vivid color. How would she sleep tonight without nightmares?

"I'll tell you a story," he said. "A long time ago, almost ten years, I went on my second undercover assignment. Shouldn't have been complicated, but things went wrong. Some of it was my fault, my inexperience. Anyway, the situation turned dangerous. A man was killed and—"

"Stop." She shoved against his chest. "I really hope this isn't your idea of a cozy bedtime story."

"There's a happy ending," he promised.

"Get to it." She ducked her head under the covers. Her hair was still wet from the shower and she was dripping on him and on the pillow.

"After the assignment, I fell apart. Couldn't sleep. Didn't want to eat. Every loud noise sounded like gunfire. And there were flashbacks. I shed some tears, but mostly I was angry. Unreasonably angry."

"But you're always so cool and controlled."

"I lost it. This little two-tone minivan stole my space in a parking lot, and I went nuts. Slammed on my brakes, grabbed my tire iron. I charged the van, ready to smash every window. Then I saw the driver—a petite lady with panic in her eyes. There were two toddlers in car seats." He shuddered. "Probably scared those kids out of a year's growth. I got back in my car and drove directly to a shrink."

"You got help."

"Yeah." He pulled her closer. "Having a reaction to what you've been through in the past couple of days is natural. It's all right to cry or yell."

Or curl up in a fetal position in the shower? She appreciated his attempt to let her know she wasn't crazy, even though she still felt like a basket case. "When do we get to the good part of your story?"

"Eventually, you learn to live with it."

"What kind of happy ending is that?" She drew back her head so she could look him in the eye. "I want sunshine and lollipops."

"The truth is better."

"That's my line," she said. "I'm the big stickler for the truth."

His mouth relaxed in a smile. "If you want to cry, go ahead. I understand. And if you want to hit somebody, I can take it."

"Are you sure about that? I hit pretty hard."

"There's no need for you to put up a front, Rachel. You're brave. You're smart. There's nobody I'd rather have for a partner."

As she gazed at him, she realized that she didn't need to explode with tears or screams. She wanted him. To connect with him. To make love.

When she leaned down to kiss him, she dared to close her eyes. She wasn't afraid. Not right now.

His caresses were gentle at first. He tweaked her earlobe and traced the line of her chin. His hand slid down her throat. He cupped her breast, teased the nub, lowered his head and tasted her.

A powerful excitement crackled through her veins, erasing every other emotion. She was torn between the desperate need to have him inside her and a yearning to prolong their lovemaking for hours. Somewhere in between, they found the perfect rhythm. He scrambled out of his clothes and their naked bodies pressed together.

This was the kind of happy ending she'd been looking for.

When she first came to bed, Rachel hadn't thought she'd be able to sleep. The bloody culmination of everything that had happened to them haunted her, and she was afraid of the nightmares that might come.

But after making love, her fears dissipated and exhaustion overwhelmed her. She had slipped into a state of quiet unconsciousness.

She awakened gradually. Last night, she and Cole had once again made love without a condom. Her hand trailed down her body and rested on her flat stomach. Had his seed taken root inside her? Was she pregnant? Other women had told her that they knew the very moment of conception, but she didn't feel any different.

The thought of having a baby—Cole's baby—made her smile. For her, it was the right time. Even if he wasn't the right mate, even if she never saw him after Baron was in custody, she'd be glad finally to be a mother.

She rolled over and reached across the sheets, needing to feel him beside her. But he was gone. "Cole? Cole, where are you?"

"Here."

She saw him standing at the edge of the front window—his sentry position, where he kept an eye on the parking lot outside the motel. The thin light of early morning crept around the curtain and made an interesting highlight on his muscular chest.

"What are you doing all the way over there?"

He sauntered back to the bed and returned to his place beside her. When they touched, her heart fluttered. In spite of her independence, she never wanted to be apart from him.

"I called Waxman," he said.

The last time he talked to his handler in Los Angeles, the man had thrown them under the bus, refusing to help and telling them to turn themselves in. "What did he say?"

"He's coming around." His voice was bitter. "After working with me for years, it finally occurred to Waxman that he could trust me."

"That's good news, right?"

"Not entirely. Without solid evidence, there's nothing Waxman can do about the local feds. Prescott is still running this circus." He ruffled her hair. "Do you like road trips?"

"It depends on where I'm going."

"California," he said. "I want to pick up the loot from Jenna's house, drive to Denver, get a rental car and go home, where Waxman can offer us real protection."

He wanted to take her home with him. She loved the idea. "I'm ready for a trip to the beach."

Chapter Twenty

"In other developments," said the TV anchorman on the early morning local news, "the police in Grand County are still on the lookout for two suspects in the Black Hawk casino robbery."

Cole groaned as his mug shot flashed on the motel room television screen.

The anchorman continued, "If you see this man, contact the Grand County Sheriff's Department. And now, let's take a look at sports. The Nuggets…"

Using the remote, Cole turned off the TV. Apparently, the manhunt was still active but didn't rate headline status. He figured the Grand County cops were plenty busy, processing the crime scene at the Shadow Mountain Lake house and investigating Frank's death—a murder that Prescott would undoubtedly try to pin on him.

Rachel emerged from the bathroom looking fresh and pretty. He liked the way her wispy hair curled on her cheeks when it was damp. Her blue eyes were bright and clear. For the moment, she seemed to have recovered from last night's meltdown, but he knew it would take more time for her to fully cope with the trauma of the past couple of days—trauma that was all his fault, one hundred percent. He'd kidnapped her and dragged her into this mess.

Somehow, he had to make it better.

She'd seemed pleased when he mentioned the road trip. While they were in California, he'd take real good care of her. They'd go for walks on the beach. Or surfing. Or a sailing trip. Or maybe they'd visit his brother. His nieces would love Rachel. He'd show her why living near the ocean was preferable to these damned mountains.

She rubbed her index finger across her teeth. "I brushed with a washcloth and soap. Disgusting."

"As soon as we're on the road, we'll buy toothpaste."

"Or we could stop at my condo when we get to Granby. I actually own a toothbrush. Might even have a spare for you."

He pulled her close and gave her a kiss. Her mouth tasted like detergent, but he didn't complain. "We can't go to your condo. That's the most obvious place for Prescott to arrange for surveillance. And the cops are still looking for us. I just saw my picture on TV."

"What about me? Was I on TV?"

He shook his head. "No mug shot."

"I'm kind of surprised. When the sheriff's men went to the Shadow Mountain Lake house, they must have found my van in the garage. They've got to know my identity."

"They might consider you a hostage." He urged her toward the door. "When we're on the road, you need to turn up your collar and wear the hat with earflaps to hide what you look like. Never can tell where traffic cams might be located."

He was glad to be driving away from the motel. Though the owner hadn't recognized him last night, the guy might remember after seeing the photo on the news. And he might be suspicious if he noticed that Cole had transposed two digits on the license plate when he checked in. He hadn't wanted to leave a record of Loughlin's car being here; no point in getting Rachel's friend in trouble.

In the passenger seat, she stretched and yawned. "It's early."

"Not a morning person?"

"But I am," she said. "I like to start the day with the sun. Look at that sunrise."

To the east, the sky was colored a soft pink that reminded him of the inside of a conch shell. Overhead, the dawn faded to blue with only a few clouds. The morning TV news program had said the weather throughout the state was clear.

He wasn't looking forward to returning to the mounds of snow left behind by the blizzard in Grand County. "How long do you think it'll take us to get to Granby?"

"A couple of hours," she said. "Jenna probably leaves for school around nine. We'll get there a little after that."

Morning was a busy time in most neighborhoods with people going to work and getting started with their day. Since they were going to break into Jenna's house, he preferred to wait until after ten when people had settled into their routines. "We've got about an hour to kill."

"What should we do?"

"Lay low." On the road, they risked being seen on cameras. If he went into a diner or a store, he might be recognized.

"My picture wasn't on TV," she said. "Pull into the next store that's open, I'll run inside and get supplies. Then we find someplace secluded and park until it's time to go."

As good a plan as any.

After a quick stop in Nederland at a convenience store, he left the main road and drove to a secluded overlook that caught the morning sun. One positive about the mountains: it was never hard to find solitude.

Rachel passed him a coffee cup and opened her car door.

"What are you doing?" he asked.

"Come with me."

Grumbling, he unfastened his seat belt and left the warmth of the car. The mountain air held a sharp chill, but he couldn't retreat without looking like a whiner. At least, there wasn't much snow—only pockets of white in the shadows.

He followed her as she climbed onto a flat granite rock and walked to the edge. Stepping up beside her, he took a sip of his hot black coffee.

She inhaled the cold air and smiled as she looked down from their vantage point. The sun warmed her face. She was beautiful, at peace with herself and the world. No hidden motives roiled inside her. Seldom had he known anyone who lived with such honesty. When Rachel was scared, her fear came from a natural response to a threat. When she laughed, she was truly amused. The woman spoke her mind.

Being with her was the best time he'd had in his life.

Resting his arm on her shoulder, he accepted her vision. Jagged, rocky hillsides filled with trees spread before them. They could see for miles. Sunlight glistened on distant peaks that thrust into the blue sky. Her mountains. Beautiful.

Rachel leaned her back against his chest as she drank her coffee. She said nothing, and he appreciated her silence. No need for words. The experience was enough.

In this moment, he knew. There was no denying the way he felt. He loved this woman.

BEFORE THEY HEADED INTO the high country, Cole needed to make one more phone call. There was, after all, the possibility that they ought to go to Denver instead of Granby. He'd been operating under the theory that Jenna Cambridge was Baron's secretary, but there was another woman in the picture.

He leaned against the driver's side door and punched numbers into his cell phone. She answered on the fourth ring.

"Hello, Pearl," he said. "How are you doing?"

"Dog tired. I forgot how much work it was to take care of an infant. Goldie was up twice last night for feedings. If she wasn't the most adorable creature in the whole world, I'd be really mad at her."

"We had some trouble at Lily Belle's." His vast understatement didn't begin to describe Frank's attack on them and his murder. "The feds might try to contact you."

"Well, then, I'm not going to answer the phone unless it's you. Nobody knows where I'm staying."

"It's smart to keep it that way."

Her instinct to avoid law enforcement reassured him. If Pearl had been Baron's secretary, she'd know about the traitor in the FBI, and she'd use that contact to keep herself out of trouble.

"I miss Penny." Pearl's voice cracked at the edge of a sob. "I keep telling myself that she's an angel in Heaven, looking down and smiling. But she's not here. It's not fair."

"It's not," he agreed.

"You said you'd get the man responsible for my daughter's murder. I'm holding you to that promise."

He wanted nothing more than to see Baron pay for his crimes. "I need to ask you about the last time you saw Penny in Black Hawk. Was there a woman with her?"

"Not that I noticed. That big thug was hanging around, but nobody else."

"What casino were you at?"

"The Stampede. That's the one that got robbed."

Though Cole didn't think Xavier's description matched Pearl, he had to ask about the engagement diamond. "Were you wearing any jewelry?"

"I always wear jewelry. It's free advertising for the stuff I design. But I don't recall what I had on. A couple of rings, some earrings."

"A diamond?"

"Definitely not. I don't use precious gems in my designs."

He switched topics. "Have you ever noticed Jenna wearing an engagement ring?"

"Jenna." She growled the name. "That girl isn't married and is never likely to be. She called me last night, and demanded to know why I hadn't come to her house with the baby. Let me tell you, I gave her a piece of my mind. She should have told me about the older man Penny was dating."

"Did she say anything about him?"

"Not a word. She said she didn't want to betray Penny. I never should have allowed my daughter to spend time with her. It was inappropriate. Why would a high school economics teacher want to hang out with one of her students?"

Why, indeed. "Jenna seems to have a lot of secrets."

"I never thought so before, but you're right. She threatened me on the phone, told me that I wouldn't get custody of Goldie because the baby belongs with her father. That's not true, is it?"

Not if the father was Baron, a criminal mastermind. "I don't think you'll have a problem keeping Goldie."

He passed the phone to Rachel so the two women could talk about the wonderful world of baby care. The fact that Jenna had checked up on Pearl gave him cause for worry. Was she acting for Baron? Was he looking for his child?

No way in hell would Cole allow that bastard to touch one precious hair on Goldie's head. Her survival was a miracle. She had to be kept safe.

When Rachel finished talking, she handed him the phone and gave him a familiar kiss on the cheek. "Pearl and Goldie are okay."

"For now," he said.

She stepped back and regarded him. Her head cocked to one side. Her fists planted on her hips. "Why so ominous?"

"Baron might take it into his head that he wants Goldie. Think about it. The first thing Prescott asked about was the baby. Now Jenna wants to get her hooks into Pearl."

"We can't let that happen." Rachel shuddered. "We have to end this now."

They got back into the Jeep and drove. Though he was glad for the beautiful clear skies, the weather provided nothing in the way of cover. They were exposed. But no one knew they were driving Loughlin's car. With their collars turned up and hats pulled down, he doubted there would be facial recognition on traffic surveillance cams.

When he turned onto U.S. 40, Rachel said, "I have a theory about the engagement ring."

"I'm listening."

"Penny told me that Jenna referred to Baron as Mister Big. A powerful man. An attractive man. Maybe Jenna is more than a secretary. What would you call it? A secretary with benefits? She might be having an affair with Baron, and the ring is wishful thinking."

"If that's true, she would have hated Penny."

"Exactly," Rachel said. "She might be the one who sent those guys to shoot up the house near Shadow Mountain Lake."

Her theory was sound until she got to the shoot-out.

"She wouldn't go against Baron. He's vicious with people who don't follow his orders."

"Then why?" she asked. "Why would he send his men to kill the gang at the hideout?"

"The gang screwed up. Almost got caught."

Baron ran his organization according to strict rules: do as you're told, and you'll profit. Make a mistake, and you'll pay.

"But he almost got his own child killed," she said. "He must have cared something for Penny and she was murdered."

"Collateral damage."

He didn't expect Rachel to understand the workings of a criminal mind. A man like Baron made up his own rules. Penny's murder sent a powerful message to the other people who worked for him. Nobody—not even his pregnant lover—got in his way.

"When you're around someone like that," she said, "how do you keep yourself from showing your emotions?"

"It's my job."

He couldn't explain why he was good at undercover work or why he could beat a lie detector test without breaking a sweat. The FBI shrinks called it a skill. Cole was beginning to think he was cursed.

"Okay." She shrugged. "What do you think about my theory? That Jenna is in love with Baron?"

"I like it." He grinned. "You're one smart detective, Special Agent Rocky Logan."

"It's about time I did something to prove my worth."

"You're the most valuable part of my investigation. Without you, I could never have saved Goldie. It was your connection with Loughlin that got us this transportation. You've helped me. More than you will ever know."

She leaned back against her seat. "This is turning into quite a vacation for me. I can't wait to get to California."

"I have plans for what we'll do when we're there."

In general, Cole considered himself to be good at interrogation and not so much when it came to small talk. But he went at length, telling her about the places he would take her to see and the foods they would sample. "And a sailboat ride on a balmy night. There's nothing like making love at sea."

For once, she didn't counter with a comparison about how the mountains were better. Instead, she beamed a smile. "I know I'll love it."

The long drive into the snow passed quickly. Before he knew it, they were entering the Granby area. He clammed up. Time to put his game face on.

As he drove along the street where Jenna's house was located, Rachel pointed to the address. "That's a nice little place. If I stay in Granby, I might look for something like that."

"If you stay?"

"I'm keeping my options open."

Jenna's cedar frame house with a two-car garage in front was nothing spectacular. An evergreen Christmas wreath hung on the door, and Jenna hadn't yet taken down the string of lights that decorated the eaves.

Cole would have preferred a more secluded location. The house stood on the corner in a residential area with large lots, but the house across the street had a window looking directly at Jenna's front door. The sidewalk and driveway were shoveled, but there was no way they could sneak up on the house through the mounds of snow left behind by the blizzard.

He braked for the stop sign, and then drove on. Though

there were no other cars on the street, he had the sense that they were being watched.

"What's the plan?" Rachel asked.

"I'm not sure yet."

He'd rather not risk being seen, but there didn't seem to be any approach other than parking in the driveway and marching up to the door. If she didn't have an alarm system, he could pick the lock.

Circling the block, he checked his mirrors. Two blocks away, he saw a truck cross an intersection. Nothing else seemed to be moving in this quiet neighborhood. Still, he decided to retreat and consider their next move.

Several blocks away, he backed into a parking space in a lot outside a supermarket. The snow that had been cleared from the lot made an eight-foot-high pile at the far end. Damn this Colorado snow.

He passed his cell phone to Rachel. "Call Jenna and make sure she didn't stay home from work."

"You think we might be walking into a trap."

"Something isn't right."

"I trust your instincts," she said. "I still remember how you sensed the attack on the hideout before a single bullet had been fired."

Before she could make the call, a red SUV pulled up in front of them, trapping them in the parking space.

The back door swung open, and Xavier stepped out. His heavy-duty parka was as red as his vehicle. Stealth had never been his strong point.

He opened the back door to their Jeep and climbed in.

"Hi, kids." His gold tooth flashed when he smiled. "Did you miss me?"

Chapter Twenty-One

Wearing her hat with the earflaps, Rachel doubted she could pull off her supercool undercover identity as Special Agent Rocky Logan. She turned around in her seat and glared at Xavier. "How did you find us?"

"A good poker player never tells his secrets."

Without turning around, Cole growled, "He must have planted a GPS tracker."

"Where?" she demanded. "How?"

Xavier chuckled. "Under your collar, sweetheart."

Leaning forward, he patted her shoulder, slid his hand up toward her neck and detached a tiny circular object from her parka. Like a magician, he held it up so she could see. "Ta da!"

Though she didn't remember him touching her at the casino, the evidence was there. He had bugged her parka.

She drew the logical conclusion. "That's why we didn't see you tailing us. You knew where we were all the time."

Xavier pocketed the device. "If I'd thought you two were going to stop for the night at a motel, I could have arranged for classier accommodations. But then, you might be seen and recognized. Other people wouldn't be as understanding as I am about harboring a fugitive."

"What do you want?" Cole muttered.

"To get my money back. The insurance company isn't going to be understanding about my losses in the robbery, and I can't afford to be out forty-two thousand bucks."

"Is that right?" She heard the anger in Cole's voice. "Why should I do you any favors?"

"For old times' sake. We go back a long way, buddy boy. You know things about me that nobody else does. And vice versa."

"You don't know squat."

"Come on, now. There's no need to be hostile."

Cole stared through the windshield at the red SUV, and she followed his gaze. The driver was visible through the front window, but she didn't see anybody else. "How many men did you bring with you?"

"Only two. It was never my intention to overpower you. I've seen you in action, and I'm too old to recover from a busted kneecap." Xavier turned to Rachel. "He can be a dangerous fellow. Are you aware of that?"

Since he wasn't treating her like an FBI agent, there was no reason for her to try to outbluff this canny old man. "I know him well," she said. "He's only dangerous with people who need to be taken down."

Behind his glasses, his beady little eyes narrowed. "Be careful about standing too close to the flame, my dear. You might get burned."

Cole turned in his seat to face Xavier. "I don't like the way you followed us. And I'm not making any promises about what happens to the money. But the truth is, I could use some backup."

The old man massaged his chin while he considered. Then he said, "Fine. I scratch your back and you—"

"Here's the deal," Cole said. "Rachel and I are going to

break into a house. You and your men wait outside. If we don't come out in ten minutes, it means we need your help."

"I'll do it, and we'll settle up afterward. Aren't you lucky that I turned up when I did?" Xavier opened the car door. "You never appreciated all that I did for you back in the day. It takes guts to be a snitch."

"Guts and greed," Cole said. "Follow us and don't be too obvious."

"By the way." A wide grin split the old man's wrinkled face. His gold tooth gleamed. "How's your wife?"

His wife?

The inside of her head exploded.

Cole was married?

She watched Xavier scamper to his red SUV like an evil leprechaun. She couldn't trust a word he said. He wanted to get back at Cole, to cause him strife.

Desperately wanting to believe that Xavier had been lying, she turned her gaze on Cole. His cognac eyes held a seriousness that she had never seen before.

"Rachel," he said, "I've never lied to you."

That wasn't an answer. She'd asked him dozens of questions about his prior girlfriends and relationships, but she had never actually asked if he had a wife. "Are you married?"

"I can explain."

He hadn't denied it, and she didn't want to be sucked into whatever deceptive ruse he was playing. The man lied for a living. He changed identities every other day. "Yes or no?"

"It's a technicality. No big deal."

She repeated, "Yes or no?"

"Yes."

Anger and hurt knotted in her gut. A flush of heat

crawled up her throat and strangled her. Once again, she'd fallen for a bad boy—another man in the long line of dashing, sexy, handsome jerks who ultimately betrayed her. "Don't say another word. I don't want to hear your phony explanations. Let's get this over with and say goodbye."

"Is that what you want?"

"Damn right."

She held up his cell phone and tried to remember how to contact Jenna Cambridge. Pearl had given them the phone number. Was it in the memory? She thrust the phone toward Cole. "Get Jenna on the line."

"I should make this call," he said.

"Because I'm not a natural born liar like you? Because you don't think I can pull it off?"

He grasped her arm near the wrist and pulled her closer, forcing her to confront him. "Settle down, Rachel. If we're going to get through this in one piece, you need to concentrate."

"Don't tell me what I need."

She locked gazes with him. His eyes were intense, volatile. He was nearly as angry as she was, and that was just fine with her. She was done with him and his lies.

With a strength born of fury, she yanked her arm away from him. "Go ahead and call her. I don't care."

While he made the call, she stared through the windshield at Xavier's red SUV. She could see the old man's face in the window of the backseat. He was laughing and she knew the joke was on her.

COLE DROVE INTO Jenna's quiet, residential neighborhood where every sidewalk was shoveled. No one was outside. Nothing seemed to be moving. Beams of sunlight glistened and slowly melted the snow.

He hadn't been able to reach Jenna on the phone, but he'd called the high school and been informed that she was teaching her senior economics seminar and couldn't be disturbed. She wasn't at home; that was all he had to know.

There were still obstacles to breaking into her house. She might have an alarm system or a guard dog or a lock he couldn't pick. *Logistics.* He needed to concentrate on logistics. In normal circumstances, that wouldn't have been a problem. He was good at honing in with sharp focus, doing what had to be done. But Rachel had distracted him.

He glanced over at her. In defiance, she'd torn the cap with earflaps off her head, and her short hair stood up in spikes. A feverish red flush colored her throat and cheeks. Anger sizzled around her like static electricity.

Later, he'd explain about his alleged wife. He should have said something before, but he wasn't accustomed to baring his soul. Damn Xavier for bringing up his wife and making him out to be a liar. Or an unfaithful husband.

Why the hell had Rachel jumped to the worst possible conclusion? It was almost as though she'd been looking for a reason to cut him off at the knees and end this thing that was growing between them. They had a connection, a relationship.

Oh, hell. He might as well face it. He loved her. And she loved him back. But she was as scared of commitment as he was. Why couldn't she understand? He wasn't like all the other creeps she'd dated. He was one of the good guys, damn it.

He shook his head. For now, he had to maintain a single-minded objective. *Get into Jenna's house and find the money.*

In the rearview mirror, he saw the red SUV following them. Tersely, he said, "You should stay outside with Xavier. I'm not sure what I'll find in the house."

"I'm going with you."

"It could be a trap."

"Do you really think so?"

He considered. The evidence connecting Jenna to Baron was largely circumstantial. The only thing they knew for certain was that Penny had sent Jenna the bundles containing the haul from the casino robbery. "Even if she is Baron's secretary, she has no reason to suspect that we're coming after the money."

"So we ought to be fine," Rachel said. "And I'm coming with you to search. Two sets of eyes are better than one."

He pulled into Jenna's driveway and parked. "I go first. If I tell you to run, do it. No questions."

"You're the boss."

"I'm not kidding around," he said.

"You don't need to remind me about the danger." She kept her head averted as though she couldn't stand the sight of him. "I've seen Baron's men in action."

They got out of the car and followed the shoveled path through the snow to the front porch. He saw no indication of an alarm system, but that didn't mean much. Most of these systems were invisible. "We've got five minutes to get in and out. If she has a silent alarm that rings through to a security company, it'll take that long for them to get here."

He pressed the doorbell and listened for any sound coming from inside the house.

Rachel moved along the porch to the front window. "I can't see inside. The drapes are closed."

"Any of the windows open?"

She shook her head. "Triple pane casement windows. They're sealed up tight."

The lock on Jenna's door was a piece of cake, but she also had a dead bolt, which could be a pain in the butt. He squatted so he was eye level with the door handle and went to work.

"Of course," she said, "you carry a lock pick."

"My version of a Swiss Army knife."

He had the lower lock opened in a couple of minutes. When he pushed on the handle, the door swung open. Jenna hadn't bothered with the dead bolt.

"Five minutes," he reminded her as he took his gun from the holster and stepped inside. "You go left. I'll go right."

He was only halfway down the hallway to the bedrooms when he heard her call out. "Cole."

Something had gone wrong. He whipped around, raising his gun to shoot. A man with a shaved head held Rachel by the throat. His gun pointed to her head.

Cole sensed someone behind his back. A deep voice with a Western twang said, "Drop your weapon or she dies."

If he'd been alone, he might have taken his chances with these two. But he couldn't risk Rachel's life. He set his weapon on the floor and raised his hands. "We're not going to cause trouble."

"Too late," the guy behind him said. "We've been chasing you two all over the damn mountains. We halfway froze to death."

If these were the same guys who chased them onto Shadow Mountain Lake, they'd talked to Frank. What had he told them? Cole had to come up with a story that would convince these guys to let them go. Was it better to tell them he was a fed, and the full force of the law would be after them? Should he act like he was still a loyal member of the robbery crew? His mind raced.

He came up with...nothing. No bargaining chip. No leverage. No believable threat. Nothing. Nada. His entire focus was on Rachel. He had to get her out of here. Somehow, he had to save her.

The man behind him shoved him against the wall in the hallway, yanked his arms down and cuffed his hands behind his back. Then, he did a thorough pat down. When he was satisfied that Cole had been disarmed, he stepped back. "Turn around and walk into the bedroom. I'd advise you not to make any sudden moves."

Cole rooted himself to the floor. No matter what happened to him, he wouldn't leave Rachel alone with these two. "She comes with me."

"Don't you worry none. She's going to be with you. Until death do you part."

The man holding Rachel moved toward them. His arm at her throat was tight.

They went through Jenna's bedroom into the master bathroom. As soon as they were inside, the door closed.

They weren't alone.

Agent Prescott curled up on the floor beside the free-standing bathtub. When he heard them, he opened his eyes and struggled to sit up. Blood from a head wound caked in his hair.

He croaked out one word. "Sorry."

Chapter Twenty-Two

Rachel's nurturing instinct should have sent her running across the bathroom toward Prescott. The man was clearly in need of first aid.

But she wasn't a paramedic anymore. She was the one in imminent danger. She turned toward Cole and placed the flat of her hand on his chest. *Until death did them part?* They weren't going to get out of this alive. The guys who nabbed them were the same merciless bastards who mowed down the gang at the Shadow Mountain Lake house. "Why didn't they kill us when we walked in the door?"

When he looked down at her, his gaze was so warm and full of caring that her heart ached. "Murder leaves a mess," he said. "That's why we're in a bathroom. If they kill us here, they can swab down the tiles and get rid of the evidence."

"That can't be right."

"Why not?"

How could she be discussing the circumstances of her own death? With ridiculous calm, she said, "There'd still be evidence. The CSI shows on TV always find traces."

"I seriously doubt the Grand County Sheriff's Department has a mass spectrometer or instant DNA analysis."

"But you and Prescott are FBI. You guys have all the forensic goodies."

He gave her a sad smile. Then he looked at Prescott. "You're in the Denver office. Do you think they're good enough to figure out who killed us?"

Using the edge of the tub, Agent Prescott forced himself to stand. His breathing was shallow. Even from a distance, she could tell that his pupils were dilated. "You're in shock," she said. "You're probably concussed and should be in a hospital."

He reached up and touched the wound on his head. His fingers came away bloody. "Tell me about Goldie. Is my baby girl safe?"

His baby? "You're Goldie's father?"

"Son of a bitch," Cole muttered. "I underestimated you, Prescott. I thought you were nothing more than a scumbag traitor, but I was wrong. You're the big man himself. You're Baron."

Prescott wiped his bloody hand across his mouth, leaving a streak of crimson. "Not by choice."

Cole looked down at her. "Get the lock picks from my jacket pocket and put them in my hands. I need to get out of these cuffs."

Moments ago, she'd been complaining about the fact that he carried tools for a break-in. Now, she was glad. "Tell me how to do it. I can help."

"It's faster if I handle it myself. This isn't the first time I've been in this position."

When she reached inside his jacket, her physical connection with him was immediate and intimate. She couldn't deny their chemistry. Not that it mattered. Even if she forgave his deception and admitted how much she cared about him, they were going to be dead. "What's going to happen to us?"

Prescott answered, "They'll load us in a car, drive to the

mountains, kill us and bury our bodies. We won't be found until the spring thaw. By then, Jenna will be long gone."

She placed the picks in Cole's hands and turned toward Prescott. He seemed to be regaining strength. From experience, she knew that head wounds were unpredictable. He might have a surge of coherence, might even appear to be making a recovery. Or he might collapse into a coma.

"You're Baron," she said. "Why can't you stop them?"

"I don't call the shots. Jenna is in charge. She's always been the boss. Ever since I first met her."

"Was that when you came to the high school in Granby to lecture about the FBI?"

"Before that." He winced. "Jenna lived in Denver. We were engaged."

That explained the ring she still wore. "After you broke up, she moved to the mountains."

Rachel understood the need for a change of scenery. She'd done much the same thing when she joined Rocky Mountain Women's Clinic as a midwife. Like Jenna, she'd been searching for a place to start over.

Prescott said, "She invited me to Granby to talk to her class. That's when I met Penny. Poor, sweet Penny. I was attracted to her right away, but she was a high school kid. Too young. I wooed her. Gave her presents."

"A diamond tennis bracelet," Rachel said.

"I picked it up at a pawn shop, but she didn't know that. She thought I was her true love, her soulmate. All that lovey-dovey crap. And here's the funny part." He inhaled and straightened his shoulders. "I felt the same damn way. I waited until she was ready. I swear to God, I didn't make love to her until she was eighteen."

"Real decent of you," Cole muttered. "How did you get hooked up with Jenna again?"

"She pretended to be my friend. And Penny's. But she was scheming. Spinning her web. Like a spider. A black widow spider. A poisonous creature who…"

His words faded, and she could see him slipping toward unconsciousness. If he passed out, there was a good chance he wouldn't wake up. She went toward him, grabbed his arm and shook him. "Stay with me, Prescott. Tell me about Jenna."

"She's smart. Cunning. Has a master's degree in economics. She put together the whole robbery and money-laundering scheme."

"Interesting," Cole said. "Her logistics were complicated but kind of genius. How did she pull it off?"

"Untraceable email. Throwaway phones. She pretended to be a secretary and invented a boss nobody saw. Baron."

"How did you get involved?"

"She needed to hide behind a frontman. So she set me up with fake deposits to an account in my name. When we were engaged, she handled my bills, got my social security number, all my passwords. By the time she told me about it, there was enough evidence against me to destroy my career and my life."

"You should have turned her in," Cole said.

"I wanted to. But she had Penny on the hook. If I didn't do what Jenna said, Penny would pay the price."

The long confession seemed to invigorate him. Instead of growing weaker, his voice sounded determined. "When I found out that Penny was pregnant, I started making plans to run away with her. We could have had a decent life. Could have raised our baby. Could have—"

A burst of gunfire echoed from the other room.

Cole broke free. The cuffs dangled from his left wrist, but his hands were separated. "Let's get the hell out of here."

She didn't see an escape. The only window in the bathroom was glass bricks—the kind you can't break without a jackhammer.

"What's happening?" Prescott demanded. "Who's shooting?"

"We brought backup," Cole said. "But I don't trust them to be effective. We've got to get out of the bathroom. If those guys catch us in here, it'll be like shooting fish in a barrel."

He eased open the bathroom door. Over his shoulder, he whispered, "I don't see a guard."

If she'd had time to think, she would have been terrified, but everything was happening too fast. Cole grabbed her hand and pulled her behind him into Jenna's bedroom.

She scanned the room, looking for a place to hide. Under the king-size four-poster bed? In the closet? There was a lot of large, heavy furniture in dark wood. Floor-to-ceiling curtains hung beside two windows. Both had decorative security bars on the outside.

Shouts and more gunfire echoed from the front of the house. Cole peeked into the hallway and came back to her. "If we go that way, they'll see us."

He pulled her into the walk-in closet and closed the door. The closet was as big as a bedroom. A scent of cedar and cinnamon hung in the air.

Cole turned on the overhead light. The closet system combined hanging racks, drawers and shelving. Against the back wall were shoes, hats and a shelf with three wigs—black, blond and auburn. Jenna's disguises. Nothing was out of place. Everything was meticulously organized.

It seemed almost sacrilegious when Cole scooped the clothes off a low rack and took the pole where they had been hanging. He did the same with another pole and handed it to her.

"Weapons," he said.

Wooden dowels wouldn't be much use against bullets, but it was better than nothing. He pulled her to a position beside the door and whispered, "I need to explain about my wife."

"Not now. It's not important."

"This might be the last thing I ever say to you, and I want you to know that I'm not a liar or a cheat. The marriage was years ago. I was investigating the illegal gambling scene in California, and I had a female partner. There were problems with our undercover identities. Somehow, we ended up going through a wedding ceremony and signing papers that I suppose are still legal. But there was never anything romantic between us."

"Why should I believe you?"

"I never had to mention this phony marriage to you. But I'm trying to be honest. To tell you everything."

"So, what happened with this partner of yours?"

"She transferred back east. Neither of us bothered with a divorce. I didn't see a need. There wasn't anyone else in my life. Not until now. Not until you."

She heard more gunfire from the other room. There was no way out of this mess.

"That's a mighty strange story," she said.

"It's the truth."

A fake marriage to a partner? An unconsummated marriage? Not bothering with a divorce? If she hadn't gone through the past days with Cole and seen how many twists and turns his life involved, she would have dismissed his story. But she knew his life was complicated. Crazy. Wild.

"I believe you."

"I love you, Rachel."

Her arms closed around him. She wanted to be strong

and brave, didn't want to cry. But tears spilled down her cheeks. "I love you, too."

This might be the last time they embraced. She'd found love only to lose it.

"When we get out of this," he said, "I'll get a divorce and marry you."

"That's a hell of a way to propose." She scrubbed the moisture from her face. "What if I say no?"

"That's not an option."

The shooting stopped abruptly. She heard voices from the other room.

Cole turned off the overhead light in the closet and stepped in front of her. "Stay back," he said. "No matter what happens, stay in here."

The voices came closer. One was a woman. Jenna?

The closet door whipped open. Cole reacted. He swung hard with the dowel, striking the gun of the man who opened the door. He dropped his weapon. Cole dove, trying to reach the gun.

He was out of her line of sight. She heard shots being fired.

Then silence.

Panic roared through her. Without thinking, she charged through the open door with her dowel raised to strike.

The scene before her was a tableaux. Cole stood between Prescott and a mousy woman in a button-down shirt, striped vest and gray slacks. They both had their weapons aimed at him.

On the floor in front of Cole, another man lay bleeding.

"Drop your weapons," Prescott ordered. "Both of you."

Cole glanced at her and gave a nod as he dropped his dowel on the floor. "It's okay, Rachel."

"No." She refused to give up. "It's not okay."

"We can negotiate," Prescott said. "Nobody else has to die."

Rachel pointed her dowel at the woman. "I want to hear from her. Jenna Cambridge."

Jenna looked down her long nose. "Don't be stupid. I might decide to let you go after you've served your purpose as a hostage. I don't particularly want to kill you."

"Not like Penny?"

Jenna's dull brown eyes flicked nervously from left to right, but her gun hand remained steady. "That shouldn't have happened."

"Convenient for you that it did," Rachel said. "With Penny out of the way, your former fiancé can come back to you."

"I told you once not to be a fool," Jenna said in a teacherlike voice. "I won't tell you again."

"You won't get away with this."

"I'm a good planner." She glanced toward Prescott. "We're going away together. We'll have a new life with enough money that we won't ever have to work again. I've worked hard and I deserve that much, don't I, darling?"

Prescott crossed the room and stood before her. "You deserve something."

"There's only one thing I've ever wanted," she said with a simpering grin. "Your love."

"Sorry, Jenna. I already gave my heart."

He shoved his gun against her rib cage and pulled the trigger. She gasped. And fell.

She was dead before she hit the floor.

He tried to turn the gun on himself, but Cole was too fast. He wrenched the weapon from Prescott's hand. With surprising gentleness, he guided the wounded agent to the bed.

Prescott sat with his head drooped forward. "She would have killed you. Couldn't let that happen."

Cole patted his shoulder. "You came through when I needed you. I won't forget that."

"My life is over."

"Not yet," Cole said. "You have a baby."

"Goldie." He lifted his head. "Penny's baby."

"You need to see her and hold her. But first, you've got to get us out of this mess. The cops still think Rachel and I are fugitives."

"I'll take care of it." Prescott rose. He wavered for a moment before he straightened and walked toward the front of the house. "The police should be here any minute. As soon as I got out of the bathroom, I put in a call."

Eager to leave the carnage in the bedroom, Rachel followed him. She didn't get far. In the hallway, Cole caught hold of her hand and spun her around to face him. His hands rested at her waist.

He smiled down at her. "When you came charging out of the closet, you scared me."

"I think you have that backward. I was scared." She remembered how he'd told her that eventually the trauma would fade. "I guess our road trip to California is off."

"Hell, no. I'm not letting you out of my sight." He dropped a kiss on her forehead. "The world is a dangerous place. I need to protect my bride-to-be."

There were a million details to work out, but nothing seemed important. They were together. They were safe, and she wanted to keep it that way forever.

Epilogue

Nine months later, Rachel draped her wedding gown over her swollen belly. Turning sideways, she admired her profile in the full-length mirror in her bedroom. Pregnancy suited her well.

After a quick tap on the door, Cole slipped inside. She was too big for a normal embrace, but he managed to wrap his arms around her. "How's my bride?"

"Good." She'd felt a bit of cramping earlier. It might be a good idea to hurry. "And my groom?"

"Never better."

Given the fact that he was an uncompromising man, he'd been incredibly cooperative about making changes in his life. After the betrayal by his handler in California, Cole didn't want to return to the Los Angeles office of the FBI. He still loved the sun and the beach, but he decided that being a mountain man wasn't so bad.

Prescott's arrest had left an opening in the Denver office, and Cole stepped in to fill it. He still did undercover assignments, but much of his workload fell under the category of investigation. He was considered a rising star because he had not only put the Baron theft ring out of business but had also recovered the stolen cash.

She had also made concessions. Granby was too far

from his work, so she moved closer to Denver and opened a new branch for the Rocky Mountain Women's Clinic. When they bought their house in Idaho Springs, Cole had one stipulation. Twice a year, they would vacation on a beach.

Everything seemed to be working out neatly. Except for the wedding. She'd wanted a small ceremony, but things had gotten out of hand. All of her huge family was there as well as Cole's brother's family, his mother and his silver-haired gambler father, who was one of the most charming men she'd ever met. Cole's dad was making quite an impression on Pearl, who had full custody of Goldie the Miracle Baby.

As they made plans, the guest list multiplied. They couldn't leave out the people she'd worked with and the parents of the babies she'd delivered. Nor could they ignore Cole's coworkers. And then there were friends, including Xavier, who had gotten off with little more than a slap on the wrist for his involvement with Baron. She didn't resent the casino owner. How could she? He and his men had provided the gunfire and distraction that had saved their lives.

She kissed Cole on the cheek. In his black suit and white shirt, he was so handsome. Was she really getting married to this gorgeous man?

"How's the crowd?" she asked.

"Restless," he said. "Most of them have already left for the church. I should be going, too. But I wanted to see you one more time before we say our vows."

"Having second thoughts?"

"Hell, no. I just wanted to tell you how much you mean to me. I never imagined I could be so happy. And that's the truth."

"I love you, Cole."

When she reached up to stroke his cheek, the ache in her abdomen became more intense, more prolonged. Rachel knew the signs; she was going into labor.

"Something wrong?" he asked.

"Everything is right." She looked up at her husband-to-be and smiled. "It's time."

For the first time since the moment they met, she saw sheer panic in his eyes. He gaped. He gasped. He ran to the door. Then back to her. "Are you sure?"

She nodded. "This is what I do."

He placed one hand on her belly, leaned down and kissed her. "It's going to be all right."

And it was.

* * * * *

COMING NEXT MONTH FROM

H HARLEQUIN®

I N T R I G U E®

Available October 22, 2013

#1455 CHRISTMAS AT CARDWELL RANCH
by B.J. Daniels
Cardwell Ranch is a wonderland of winter beauty—until a body turns up in the snow. To find the killer, Tag Cardwell must work with Lily McCabe, a woman with a broken heart and a need for a cowboy just like Tag.

#1456 WOULD-BE CHRISTMAS WEDDING
Colby Agency: The Specialists • by Debra Webb
CIA agent Cecilia Manning has always chosen danger over playing it safe...in life *and* in love. And now Emmett Holt is her target.

#1457 RENEGADE GUARDIAN
The Marshals of Maverick County • by Delores Fossen
To save her child from a kidnapper, Maya Ellison must trust renegade marshal Slade Becker, even though he could cost her what she loves most—her son.

#1458 CATCH, RELEASE
Brothers in Arms: Fully Engaged • by Carol Ericson
When Deb Sinclair succumbed to the charms of a fellow spy for one night of passion, she never realized he would be both her nemesis and her salvation.

#1459 SPY IN THE SADDLE
HQ: Texas • by Dana Marton
FBI agent Lilly Tanner was once a thorn in his side. But Shep Lewis begins to rethink his stance when they're kidnapped together.

#1460 SCENE OF THE CRIME: RETURN TO BACHELOR MOON by Carla Cassidy
When FBI agent Gabriel Blakenship is dispatched to investigate a family's disappearance, the last thing he expects to find is a woman in danger and a desire he can't resist.

YOU CAN FIND MORE INFORMATION ON UPCOMING HARLEQUIN® TITLES, FREE EXCERPTS AND MORE AT WWW.HARLEQUIN.COM.

HICNM1013

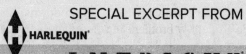
"Lily, I have a bad feeling that the reason Mia's condo was
ransacked and my father's, too, was that they were looking
for this thumb drive."

"Then you should take it to the marshal," she said, handing it to him. "I have a copy of the letters on my computer,
so I can keep working on the code."

He nodded, although he had no intention of taking it
to the marshal. Not until he knew which side of the fence
Hud Savage was on.

"Until we know what's really on this," he said, "I
wouldn't mention it to anyone, all right?"

She nodded.

"I need to get to the hospital and see my father, but I
don't like leaving you here snowed in alone."

She waved him off. "The plows should be along in the
next hour or so if you want to take my SUV."

He wasn't about to leave her here without a vehicle even
if he thought he could bust through the drifts. "Are those
your brother's cross-country skis and boots by the door?

If you don't mind me borrowing them, I'll ski down to the road and hitch a ride. My brothers and I used to do that all the time when we were kids."

"If you're sure…" She turned back to the papers on the table. "I'll keep working on the code and let you know when I get it finished."

She sounded as if she would be glad when he left her at it. He was reminded that she also had plans to talk to her former fiancé today. He felt a hard knot form in his stomach. Jealousy? Heck yes.

Except he had nothing to be jealous about, right? Last night hadn't happened. At least that was the way Lily wanted it. He fought the urge to touch her hair, remembering the feel of it between his fingers.

"I want you to have this." He held out the pistol he'd taken from his father's place. "I need to know that you are safe."

She shook her head and pulled back. "I don't like guns."

"All you have to do is point it and shoot."

Lily held up both hands. "I don't want it. I could never…" She shook her head again.

"Just in case," Tag said as he laid it on the table, telling himself that if someone broke into her house and tried to hurt her, she would get over her fear of guns quickly. At least he hoped that was true.

Start your holidays with a bang!
Be sure to check out
CHRISTMAS AT CARDWELL RANCH
by USA TODAY bestselling author B.J. Daniels

Available October 22, only from Harlequin® Intrigue®.
Available wherever books and ebooks are sold.

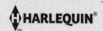

INTRIGUE